UNHOLY
GHOSTS

UNHOLY GHOSTS

STACIA KANE

BALLANTINE BOOKS • NEW YORK

Unholy Ghosts is a work of fiction. Names, characters, places, and incidents are the products of the author's imagination or are used fictiously. Any resemblance to actual events, locales, or persons, living or dead, is entirely coincidental.

A Del Rey Mass Market Original

Copyright © 2009 by Stacey Fackler

Published in the United States by Del Rey, an imprint of The Random House Publishing Group, a division of Random House, Inc., New York.

DEL REY is a registered trademark and the Del Rey colophon is a trademark of Random House, Inc.

ISBN 978-0-345-51557-5

Printed in the United States of America

www.delreybooks.com

9 8 7 6 5 4 3 2 1

To Cori. Not just my best friend, but my best reader. Her enthusiasm for this book in its earliest stages and beyond kept me going; her friendship kept me sane.

Chapter One

Had the man in front of her not already been dead, Chess probably would have tried to kill him. Damned ghosts. A year and a half she'd gone without having to deal with one—the best Debunking record in the Church.

Now when she needed her bonus more than ever, there he was. Mocking her. Floating a few feet off the parquet floor of the Sanfords' comfortable suburban split-level in the heart of Cross Town, with his arms folded and a bored look on his face.

"Too good to go where you're supposed to, Mr. Dunlop?"

Mr. Dunlop's ghost gave her the finger. Asshole. Why couldn't he just accept the inevitable?

He'd been an ass in life, too, according to her records. Hyram Dunlop, formerly of Westside, banker and father of two, all deceased. Mr. Dunlop should have been resting for the last fifty years, not turning up here to rattle pipes and throw china and generally make a nuisance of himself.

Right. She set the dog's skull in the center of the room, checking her compass to make sure she faced east, and lit the black candles on either side of it, her body moving automatically as she arranged her altar the way she'd done dozens, if not hundreds, of times before. Next came the tall forked stang in its silver base, garlanded with specially grown blue and black roses. She set the bag of dirt from Mr. Dunlop's grave in front of the skull for later use.

Her small cauldron in its holder took a few extra minutes to set up. Mr. Dunlop moved behind her, but she ignored him. Showing fear to the dead—or any sort of emotion at all—was asking for trouble. She filled the cauldron with water, lit the burner beneath it, and tossed in some wolfsbane.

With a stub of black chalk she marked the front door and started on the windows, stepping deliberately through Dunlop's spectral form despite the unpleasant chill. The set of his jaw lost some of its defiance as she pulled out the salt and started sprinkling it. "This is probably going to hurt," she said.

Her gaze wandered to the grandfather clock in the corner, just outside the sloppy salt ring. Almost eight o'clock. Fuck. She was starting to itch.

Not badly, of course. Nothing she couldn't handle. But it was there, making her mind wander and her toes wiggle in her shoes, when she needed to be sharp.

She'd just begun closing off the hallway when Mr. Dunlop bolted up the stairs.

The symbols on the doors and windows—she'd already done the bedrooms—would keep him from leaving the actual building, but . . . shit.

She'd forgotten the master bedroom fireplace. The chimney flue.

Pausing only long enough to snatch up the bag of grave dirt, she raced after him. The grave dirt wasn't supposed to come until later, when the psychopomp had already shown up to escort him, but it was the only way she could think of to stop him.

Mr. Dunlop's feet were only just visible when she

reached the bedroom, hanging in the fireplace. She grabbed a small handful of dirt and flung it at them.

Dunlop fell. His silent lips formed words that were probably not kind. She ignored him, ducking into the fireplace to mark the flue with chalk before he could try again. "There's no escaping. You know you shouldn't be here."

He shrugged.

From her pocket she pulled her Church-issued Ectoplasmarker—nobody ever said the Church was clever, just that they knew how to protect humanity from spirits—and uncapped it. Dunlop stared up at her, his face rippling in panic. She leaned toward him and he sank through the floor.

Before he managed to disappear completely she ran back downstairs and grabbed her salt, finishing the hallway while Dunlop floated through the ceiling—outside of the circle.

In the short time they'd been upstairs the atmosphere in the room had changed, her energy mingling with that of the herbs to fill the room with power. Chess glanced at her altar. The dog's skull rattled and clicked like a set of castanets, rising slightly from the floor. The psychopomp was coming.

Dunlop backed away when she started toward him, holding the Ectoplasmarker out in front of her. She'd already memorized his passport symbol. Now she just had to get him back into the circle and get the symbol on him before the dog came.

Only once had she heard of a Debunker who didn't manage it. He got lucky. The dog took the ghost. But that was luck, nothing else. Without the passport, the minute that dog finished materializing could be the last minute of her life.

Dunlop bumped into the wall and glanced back, surprised. Ghosts could choose to touch inanimate objects or slide through them . . . until the object was solidified on the metaphysical plane.

"I marked them." She used her foot to break the line of salt. "You can't get through them. You can't escape. This will be a lot easier if you just relax and let me do my job, you know. Why don't you come here and hold your hand out for me?"

He folded his arms and shook his head. She sighed.

"Okay. Have it your way." She crushed asafetida between her fingers and sprinkled it over the floor around him. "Hyram Dunlop, I command you to enter this circle to be marked and sent to rest. I command you to leave this plane of existence."

She jumped when the growl echoed through the room and the skull leapt into the air. The rest of the dog flowed into existence behind it, each bone sharp and clean in the wavering candlelight.

Shit! Shit, shit. She was still the only one in the circle.

Worse, they both smelled of asafetida. She hadn't rinsed her hands yet. The dog—magically created to sense the herb—wouldn't know the difference between them.

Chess screamed as the skeletal dog lunged at her, skin and fur growing over its bones. She fell into—fell *through*—Hyram Dunlop. The cold was worse this time, probably because she wasn't ready for it, or maybe because she was terrified by the sight of those sharp, shiny canine teeth snapping the air only inches from her arm. If they reached her—

The dog's mouth closed around her left calf, pulling. Eyes appeared in the formerly hollow sockets, glowing red, brighter as it firmed its grip and tugged.

Behind the dog the air rippled. Shadowy images superimposed themselves over the tasteful taupe walls of the Sanford house, silhouettes gray and black against lit torches.

Something inside Chess started to give. The dog—the

psychopomp—was doing its job, tugging its lost soul out of the Sanford house and into the city of the dead.

But her soul wasn't lost—at least, not in the way required.

Hyram's eyes widened as she reached for him again, her hand passing through his chest.

"Hyram Dunlop, I command you—"

The words ended in a strangled gurgle. It hurt, fuck, it really fucking hurt. It was *peeling,* as if someone was tearing away layers of her skin one by one, exposing every tender, raw nerve she possessed, and she possessed so many of them.

Her vision blurred. She could let go, if she wanted to. She could float away—the dog would be gentle once it knew it had her—and vanish, no more problems, no more pain, no more . . .

Only the boredom of the city, with nothing to take the edge off. And the knowledge that she'd died a stupid death and let this miserable jerk of a spirit beat her. No. No way.

She moved her hand, reaching again for Hyram. This time her fingers connected with something solid, something that felt warm and alive. Hyram. He wasn't alive. She was dying.

But in death she could grab hold of him and drag him into the broken circle. In death she could use the strength of her will to bring the Ectoplasmarker down on Hyram's suddenly solid flesh. In death she could mark him with his passport, the symbol to identify him to the psychopomp, and physically hold him in place.

Desperately she scrawled the figure on his arm, while her soul stretched between Hyram and the dog like a taut clothesline. She didn't dare look away to see what her physical body was doing.

She managed the last line as her vision went entirely black. Pain shot through her as she fell to the floor with a house-rattling thud, but it was physical pain this time, bone pain, not the agony of having her living soul ripped from her body as it had been moments before.

She opened her eyes just in time to see Hyram Dunlop disappear through the rippling patch of air.

Her fingers scrabbled at the clasp on her heavy silver pillbox, lifting the lid. She grabbed two of the large white pills inside and gobbled them up, biting down so the bitterness flooded her taste buds and made her nose wrinkle. It tasted awful. It tasted wonderful. The sweetest things were bitter on the outside, Bump had told her once, and oh, how right he'd been.

Her fingers closed around her water bottle and she twisted off the cap and took a gulp, swishing it around in her mouth so the crushed pills could enter her bloodstream under her tongue, so they could start dissolving before they slid down into her stomach and blossomed from there.

Her eyes closed. The relief wasn't everything it would be in twenty minutes, in half an hour as the Cepts were digested fully. But it was something. The shaking eased enough for her to control her hands again.

Cleaning up was the worst part of Banishings. Or rather, it was usually. This time the worst part had been feeling her soul pull from her flesh like a particularly sticky Band-Aid.

Carefully she put her altar pieces back in her bag, wrapping the dog skull in hemp paper before setting it on top of everything else. She'd have to buy a new one. This dog had tasted her. She couldn't use it again.

Her Cepts started to kick in as she swept. Her stomach lifted, that odd, delicious feeling of excitement—of anticipation—making her smile without really realizing it. Things weren't so terrible, after all. She was alive. Alive, and just high enough to feel good about it.

The Sanfords arrived home just as she knelt outside their front door with a hammer and an iron nail.

"Welcome home," she said, punctuating her words with sharp taps of the hammer. "You shouldn't have any more problems."

"He's . . . gone?" Mrs. Sanford's dark eyes widened. "Really gone?"

"Yep."

"We can't thank you enough." Mr. Sanford had a way of speaking, his voice booming out from his barrel chest, that made his voice echo off the stucco walls of the house.

"Part of my job." She couldn't even bring herself to be mad at the Sanfords right now. It wasn't their fault they were honest and haunted, instead of faking like ninety-nine percent of Debunking cases.

She finished driving in the nail and stood up. "Don't move that, whatever you do. We've found that homes where a genuine haunting occurred are more vulnerable to another one. The nail should prevent it."

"We won't."

Chess put the hammer back in her bag and waited, trying to keep a pleasant smile on her face. Mr. and Mrs. Sanford shuffled their feet and glanced at each other. What were they—

Oh.

"Why don't we go on inside, and we'll finish off your paperwork and get you your check, okay?"

The Sanford's anxious expressions eased. Chess couldn't really blame them. If she was about to be handed fifty thousand dollars from the Church just because she'd had an escaped ghost in her house, she'd be pretty relaxed, too. Just like she would have felt if she'd gotten her bonus. It would have been ten grand on this job, enough to pay Bump and have something left over until the next one.

Stupid ghosts always ruined everything, like loud babies in a nice restaurant.

They offered her coffee, which she declined, and water, which she accepted, while they signed various forms and affadavits. It was almost nine-thirty by the time she handed over their check, and she still had to stop by the graveyard before she could get to the Market. Damn Mr. Dunlop. She hoped he was being punished justly.

Chapter Two

The market was in full swing when she got there just
shy of eleven, with her body calm and her mind collected.
A quick shower and blow-dry of her black-dyed Bettie
Page haircut, a change into her off-work clothes, and the
sweet relief of another Cept working its way into her
beaten bloodstream were all she'd needed to feel normal
again.

Voices colored the air around her as she walked past
the crumbling stone plinth that had once been the entryway to a Christian church. The church, of course, had
been destroyed. It wasn't necessary anymore. Who wasted
their lives believing in a god when the Church had proof
of the afterlife on its side? When the Church knew how
to harness magic and energy?

But the plinth stayed, a useless remnant—like so many
other things. Including, she thought, herself.

Against the far wall, food vendors offered fruit and veg-
etables, gleaming with wax and water under the orange
light of the torches. Carcasses hung from beams, entire
cows and chickens and ducks, lambs and pigs, scenting
the cramped space with blood. It pooled on the dirt and
stained the shoes of those walking through it, past the
fire drums where they could cook their purchases.

Then came the clothes, nothing too professional or clean. The salesmen knew their clientele in Downside Market. Tattered black and gray fabric blew in the wind like ghosts. Bright skirts and black vinyl decorated the teetering temporary walls and erupted from dusty boxes on the ground. Jewelry made mostly of razor blades and spikes reflected the flames back at her as she wandered through the narrow aisles, paying little attention to the strangers darting out of her way. Those who knew her lifted their heads in acknowledgment or gave her a quick, distracted smile, but the ones who didn't . . . they saw her tattoos, saw *witch*, and moved. By strictly enforced law, only Church employees were allowed to have magical symbols and runes tattooed on themselves, and Church employees, no matter what branch, weren't exactly welcome everywhere. Especially not in places where people had reason to resent their government.

It used to bother her. Now she didn't care. Who wanted a bunch of people poking their noses into her business? Not her.

Chess liked the Market, especially when her vision started to blur a little, just enough that she didn't have to see the desperate thinness of some of the dealers, the children in their filthy rags darting between the booths, trying to pick up scraps or coins people dropped. She didn't have to watch them huddle by the fire drums even on a night as unseasonably warm as this one, as though they could store up enough heat to see them through the winter ahead. She didn't have to think about the contrast between the middle-class suburban neighborhood she'd just left and the heart of Downside. Her home.

Somewhere in the center she found Edsel lurking behind his booth like a corpse on display. The stillness of his body and his heavy-lidded eyes fooled people all the time; they thought he was sleeping, until they reached out to touch something—a ceremonial blade, a set of polished bones, a rat's-skull rattle—and his hand clamped around their wrist before they could even finish their motion.

Edsel was the closest thing she had to a friend.

"Chess," he drawled, his black-smoke voice caressing her bare arms. "Oughta get gone, baby. Word is Bump has the hammer down for you."

"He here tonight?" She glanced around as casually as she could.

"Ain't seen him. Seen Terrible, though. He's watching. Could be he's watching me, knowing you'll come here and say hiya. You need something?"

"We all have our needs," she replied, running her fingers over a set of shiny tiger's claws, marked with runes. Power slid from them up her arm, and she smiled. That was a rush, too; a Church-sanctioned one, even. "Actually, I could use a new Hand. You got any?"

He nodded, bending down so his golden hair slid off his silk-covered shoulders and hid his features. "Workin another case?"

"Hopefully will be soon."

Edsel held the Hand out to her. Its pale, wrinkled skin and gnarled fingers looked like a dead albino spider. She reached for it, stroking one of its fingertips with her own, and it twitched.

"That'll do. How much?"

"You probly don't wanna pay me now. Terrible sees you got money, it won't make him too happy."

"Does anything make Terrible happy?"

Edsel shrugged. "Hurting people."

They chatted for a few more minutes, but the crowds around her didn't feel as safe as they had when she arrived. All those people, and most of them had two eyes.

Not that it mattered. She had to see him before she left, she didn't have a choice. He could hunt her down or she could walk through that black door herself. She much preferred the second.

She put the Hand in her bag—its fingers tried to grasp hers as she did—thanked Edsel, and walked on. No point in doing any more shopping if Terrible was watching. Edsel was right. The sight of her spending what little money she had would only piss him off. So she headed straight for the lower office, figuring the element of surprise might swing things in her favor a little bit.

Too bad it was impossible to surprise someone lying in wait. Terrible grabbed her as she rounded the corner, his lips curved in what would have been a grin on a normal person, which he wasn't. On his scarred, shadowed face, the smile made him look like he was getting ready to bite.

"Bump looking for you, Chess," he said. His fingers dug into her upper arm. "He been looking awhile."

"I saw him two days ago."

"But he want you tonight. Like now. Come on, you gonna see him."

"I was already on my way to see him."

"Aye? That's good luck then."

She didn't bother trying to wiggle her arm from his iron grip as he led her, not to the black door, but around the corner to Bump's pad. A finger of fear slipped under her skin, penetrating the pleasant little fog in her brain. She'd never been to his place before.

Terrible knocked, a syncopated pattern that sounded like a Ramones song. She looked around them; a few people caught her gaze then turned away quickly, as if she could transmit her bad fortune through her hazel eyes. If only. There was an awful lot she'd like to get rid of.

"How're those big sideburns working for you, Terrible? You managed to find yourself a steady ladyfriend yet?" Hell, why not stick her hand in the cage? He wouldn't hurt her without Bump's say-so, and if Bump had already said so she wouldn't be standing here. She'd be in the filthy, urine-smelling alley behind the Market being beaten and puking up her guts. Sometimes her job had its advantages; roughing up a Church employee could lead to trouble.

"Never you mind."

"So you have! Is she human?"

To her surprise, Terrible's cheeks began to color a dull red. It almost made her feel sorry for him. Not quite, but almost. She hadn't known he had feelings.

The door opened before she could say anything else. One of Bump's ladies, she guessed, a petite blonde in a see-through gray top and a shiny, red miniskirt. The black makeup ringing her eyes made her look terrified, at least until she yawned as she inspected Chess and Terrible both from top to bottom.

Without looking away, she stepped back enough for them to slide past her and enter Bump's house.

If Chess hadn't known he was a drug dealer and pimp—among other things—this place would have told her in an instant. Everything was gilded or covered in fur, as though Bump had visited the Liberace Museum and decided to go it one better. Stylized paintings of guns and vaginas hung on the walls, turning the room from simply tacky to creepily Freudian in an instant.

Not that Bump would have heard of Freud. The Church kept a pretty tight grip on such things. But Chess had been allowed to study in the Archives, had spent months reading late into the night, every night. Gazing at Bump's ode to the id she wondered if Freud was as full of shit as she'd always thought.

The blonde led them down a glaringly bright red hallway—more id—and into a large red room. Everything was red, the carpet, the furniture, the walls. Different shades of red, like a nightmare. Chess's eyes dilated as the room shrieked at her. Being in this room straight would be bad enough. Being here while 400mg of narcotic simmered in her blood was like being trapped in the womb of a fiery spirit prison.

"Sit you down," Terrible said, urging her onto one of the velvet couches. "You wait for him."

"Don't think I'd be going anywhere, even if I tried."

"Naw, I'm guessin you wouldn't be." Those heavy sideburns moved as he showed her his teeth. "But we wait, just the same."

She leaned back and closed her eyes, shutting out the horrible red. It remained imprinted on the back of her eyelids, chasing her even into her own head. Her lips curved. Plenty of demons in there already.

Outside, the Market was slamming, full of bodies and radios and live music. In the office next door, people were fixing, lining up against the walls for their turn, heading downstairs to hit the pipes. She shifted in her seat. Pills were what kept her going, but the pipes were something else entirely. She'd been hoping to get down there herself before the night was over, to fill her lungs with thick honey smoke and float home to bed. That was looking less and less likely by the minute.

How much was she into Bump for? Three grand, four? The Sanford case turning out to be real had seriously hit her finances. Debunkers were paid shit, barely enough to cover her rent and bills. The bonuses were where the real money came from, paid for her supplies and . . . everything else she needed.

Three or four grand wasn't that much, though. She'd owed him more than that before and always paid.

Metal clinked and heat brushed her skin as Terrible lit a cigarette from a flame half a foot high. Chess sat up. "Can I have one?"

He made a "why not" face and held out the pack, then spun the wheel on his black lighter for her. She had to tilt her head to avoid burning her nose.

They smoked and waited for another few minutes, until

finally a door opened in the red wall and Bump slouched into the room.

He moved like he was riding a platform with oiled wheels, silently and smoothly, faster than he looked. Rings glinted on his fingers and diamond studs sparkled in his ears, but his clothes were surprisingly nondescript. Chess imagined it was his "at home" look, because the few times she'd seen him out on the streets he looked like a bedraggled medieval king. Tonight, though, he wore a plain burgundy silk shirt—another shade of red to add to the off-tune chorus—and black slacks. His feet were bare save a gold toe ring on his right foot.

He pulled a wilted sandwich bag out of his pocket and tossed it casually onto the table in front of her. Pills slept inside, each one whispering a promise. Pink Pandas snuggled against green Hoppers, blue Oozers and red Nips looked patriotic set against the pure, clean white of the Cepts. Every one was a different ride. Up, down, sweet, or sleazy. Two months' worth of good feelings, right there in front of her. Her mouth filled with saliva; she swallowed it, along with some of her pride for good measure.

"You into me, Chess." Bump's voice slurred low through the room, adding to the impression he gave of a man who thought slow, moved slow. It was a lie. Bump hadn't become lord of the streets west of Forty-third by being slow. "You into me fuckin good, baby."

With effort she tore her gaze away from the bag and focused on his scraggly beard.

"You know I'm good for it," she said, hating the faintly whining tone that crept into her voice. She cleared her throat and sat up straighter. "I've always paid before, and I'll pay again."

"Naw, naw. This ain't like before. You know what you owe? I give you the number, you see what you fuckin think. Fifteen, baby. Fifteen big ones you owe. How you pay that back?"

"Fift—I do not, there's no way—"

"You forgetting the interest. You owe Bump money, you pay interest."

"I never did before."

He shrugged. "New policy."

New policy, my ass. What the fuck game was he playing? She'd expected to be threatened, maybe. She hadn't expected this. "Even if that's your new policy, my actual debt can't be more than four grand. What interest rate are you charging, two hundred percent?"

"Don't matter what the rate is. I fuckin charge the interest I want to charge." He leaned back against the arm of the other couch and pulled a knife out of his pocket, then started cleaning his fingernails with it. "I says it's fifteen, so it's fifteen. When you pay me?"

"I can go somewhere else."

"Aw, sure, ladybird. You go anywhere you want. You head on over to Slobag on Thirtieth, see how them tattoos get 'preciated by the fuckin scum down there. But you still owe me."

Again she glanced at the bag. Bump smiled. "You want one? Go 'head. You have one. Whatever you like." He picked up the bag and held it out to her so it gapped open. "Go 'head."

She cocked an eyebrow at him. "What are you going to charge me for that?"

His laugh seemed to come from his feet and roll up his body. "I don't gotta charge you none for it, baby. You owes me enough already, ain't you?"

He folded his knife and tucked it into his pocket. "Course . . . now I'm thinking . . . could be I know a way you pay. A way you work off your owes."

"Forget it." She started to stand up. She'd never go that low, no matter what. Even she had a little self-respect, and the thought of letting a grease stain like Bump have his sleazy way with her . . . ugh.

"Aw, baby, I know what's in your head. Not that. Though if'n you wanted to I could take you on a real sweet ride. That's a promise from Bump. The ladies never had it so good as when I give it them."

He laughed, then shook the bag at her. "Go on. You take one. I know what you need, don't I? Don't Bump always know? Bump's your fuckin friend, yay? So you trust Bump. Take what you want, then we have a chatter. Maybe we help each other."

Warily she reached for the bag. Her impulse was to grab an Oozer, but she managed to refrain and took another Cept instead. She had a feeling she would need her brain for this one.

"Good, that's real nice. Now, why don't Bump tell you what? You hear my plan?"

She nodded, dry-swallowing the Cept.

Bump sat down next to her, close enough for her to smell the pipe room on his clothes. He smiled. "Maybe I got a problem. Maybe you help me with it."

Uh-oh. She was going to have to turn him down. The only people who ever asked witches for favors were those who wanted either unholy luck or unholy deeds done, and she didn't much feel like doing either. Especially considering Bump was already a pretty lucky guy, and she wasn't a killer.

"What's the favor? I'm not agreeing, I'm just asking."

"Oh, I think you agree, ladybird. I think when you hear, you say yay. Let me run this down. You know the airport?"

"Muni?" Even if the third Cept had kicked in—which it hadn't—she wouldn't have been more mystified. Triumph City Municipal Airport was a major hub, and one of the few areas that was heavily policed. Most Downside residents, especially drug dealers, stayed as far away from Muni and the surrounding factory district as they could.

"Naw, naw, what you fuckin say? Muni. Not Muni. Chester. You know Chester Airport."

"Chester's been shut down for years."

"Yay, it have. But maybe Bump open it back up. Maybe Bump expand his fuckin business, he open it up."

This was starting to make some kind of sense. "I don't have enough pull in the Church to lean on the city leaders for something like that, nowhere near enough."

"Bump got the pull. Bump already got that place wide up, see, wide up. But Bump gotta problem. Bump's planes—planes carrying them sweet pills you ladybirds like—Bump's planes crash. Something attacking planes, dig? Make they go all silent. Turns they off."

"I don't know anything about planes. I've never even been in a—"

"Not planes, ladybird. Ghosts. Say Chester haunted. Don't guess on that. Somebody sending signals, making planes silent. Electromagnetics and such, yay? You find sender. You find sender, you rid they."

He leaned back and lit a cigarette, letting smoke wreath around his head. "You catch me them fake ghosts, so my planes they fly. You catch, ladybird, and we even. No more debt to Bump."

Chapter Three

"Above all, to work for the Church is to be entrusted with the protection not only of yourself and your loved ones, but of the human race. You must never forget this responsibility."
—*Careers in the Church: A Guide for Teens,* by Praxis Turpin

Pleading exhaustion was not the best idea for getting out of doing something for a drug dealer. Or, to put it a different way, it was a very good idea. As Terrible drove them out toward the airport, Chess's entire body felt sparkly, light, as if someone was about to tell her the punch line of a very good joke at a fabulous party. At least that's how she imagined it would feel.

He'd even chopped up four more Nips nice and fine for her and bagged them, so she could snort them tomorrow if she wanted to. There had to be some advantage to having him grab her by the balls—figuratively—and squeeze, right? And this job wouldn't take long, probably only one night, so she should milk it for all it was worth. The kind of equipment that would down a plane couldn't be easy to conceal. She'd find it, she'd tell Bump, and four thousand dollars worth of debt that had magically grown to fifteen would go bye-bye. Not a bad deal, really.

She felt so damn confident and good in that moment she would have agreed to walk naked into a Church service.

Something cold and wet nudged her arm. "Oughta have you some," Terrible muttered, pushing the bottle of water up to her face now. "You don't realize the thirsty until morning. That speed, she make you dry."

"Got my own." She pulled hers from her bag and took a long swig. "Thanks for the reminder, though."

He shrugged.

They were out of Downside now, speeding along the highway. Chess couldn't see the stars through the city lights but she knew they were there, winking above them, forming patterns and shapes in the sky. She sighed and settled back in her seat, glancing at the speedometer.

"Are you really driving a hundred and twenty?"

Terrible shrugged again.

"Not real verbal, are you, Terrible?"

This time he glared at her, the greenish lights from the dash highlighting the astonishing ugliness of his profile. His crooked nose—it must have been broken several times—the way his brows jutted out like a cliff over the ocean, the set of his jaw. She held her hands up, palms out. "Okay. Just making conversation."

"Dames always wanna talk."

"Not like there's anything else they'd want to do with you."

Terrible reached forward and turned up the radio. The Misfits blared from the speakers, singing about skulls. It somehow suited the moment. Chess rested her head on the door, trying to see the stars.

She blinked, and they were at the airport. How in the world did Bump think he was going to smuggle drugs into an airport so close to town? Didn't he know people would hear the planes, see them?

Silly thought. Bump didn't care. Neither did she. In fact, the easier it was for him to get his drugs, the better for her.

Terrible rolled the car—a black 1969 Chevelle, built in the period known as Before Truth—to a stop just outside the remnants of the old airport building, now just boards impaling the sky. Chess had no trouble seeing with her pupils dilated like they were.

Grass grew on the runways in fitful patches like a rash. Nothing had landed here in decades, she guessed, since the Church made Triumph City its headquarters and the Muni was built. This whole area looked forgotten, *felt* forgotten. Neglect oozed from the ground into the sky.

Terrible came around and opened the door for her, a courtesy that surprised her so much she almost forgot to get out of the car. She did, though, grabbing her bag from the backseat.

He watched without comment as she pulled out her Church-issued Spectrometer and handed it to him, then grabbed a piece of black chalk and her knife, just in case. Some witches used salt to mark their skins, but Chess had better control over the chalk, found it worked for her and was easier to clean up. It was more efficient, and efficiency was its own reward.

"Come here, please."

Terrible obeyed, dipping his head as she reached up and marked it with the chalk, pressing her fingers to his jaw to help her balance. A protection sigil, crawling across his forehead like a scorpion. He closed his eyes for a second. Did he feel it? He didn't seem the type, but maybe she didn't either.

She was feeling something, too, wasn't she? Below the cheerful buzz of her body, or rather, inside it. The subtle, familiar creep of power, and the even more subtle slide of arousal.

She shook her head. She was standing in an abandoned, weedy parking lot with Terrible, for fuck's sake, and she was getting turned on. It was the Nips. Speed always had this effect on her. Too bad fucking on speed was so worthless. If it wasn't she might have Terrible drop her back at the Market, find a man who wouldn't ask questions and wouldn't ask for anything else either.

She shook her head to get her focus back and drew the sigil just above the bridge of her nose. Not necessary— most of her protection was in her tattoos—but something about this place gave her the creeps. It was probably Terrible. The idea that for even one tiny second she'd come remotely close to entertaining the thought of letting him touch her would give any sane woman the creeps.

"Okay," she said, stepping back from him. "You know this place or what?"

He nodded. His eyes glittered like dirty jewels in the shadows below his brow.

She took back her Spectrometer and turned it on. "Let's go then. Give me the tour."

He led her to a hole in the bowed, rusty chain-link fence and watched as she slipped through it, then followed.

Their footsteps crunched faintly in the bits of gravel still remaining by the fence, then went silent again as they crossed the cracked remains of the cement walkway. Weeds grew here, too, sliding over her boots, making her think with some discomfort of hands scrabbling for purchase on the scuffed thick leather.

The airport was larger than it had looked when they pulled up outside, the runways stretching back as far as she could see in the darkness.

A spot of light appeared on the destroyed wall in front of them. Chess jumped back, her heart pounding, and stumbled into Terrible's chest. He held a flashlight in one large hand.

"You scared the shit out of me! I thought that light was—damn it, please don't do that again."

"Sorry."

She had to be the stupidest woman on the planet. There was no other answer, because it had just occurred to her that she'd agreed to come to an abandoned airport in a slum neighborhood with the most feared drug enforcer in the city. If he left her body here, it would be months before it was found, years, if ever.

"Hey, Terrible. Um, you ever heard what happens to someone who kills a witch?"

He grunted. She decided to take that as a no.

"They're haunted for the rest of their lives. Especially when you kill a Church witch like me. The Church makes a special dispensation, did you know that? No compensation, no disposal. The killer's haunted every day and every night, no escape. Pretty awful fate, huh?"

"Nobody plan to kill you, Chess."

"But if you did you wouldn't tell me, right? I mean, you wouldn't just turn around now and say, 'By the way, Bump told me to kill you, so if you'd be kind enough to come closer I can wrap my hands around your throat,' right?"

He stared at her, then uttered a sound somewhere between a creaky door and the gurgle of an old furnace. It took her a moment to realize he was laughing.

"You one crazy dame," he said. "The speed crazy you up, don't it? Nobody's gonna kill you here. Bump need you. No other witches he got something on, aye? He needs you right."

It was probably the longest speech she'd ever heard from him, and she believed him. Not enough to tuck the knife back into her bag, but enough.

"Come now. What that box do, anyways? It supposed to beep or light up or something?"

"Something. Just show me around. We'll see what happens."

He took her arm again as he led her through the gaping darkness of the doorway to the building itself. Only part of the roof remained, rusted tin supported by rotten wooden pillars, but it was enough to blot out what little light the moon cast into the interior.

And it stunk, like woodlice and dead things and fuel, a cocktail of disgusting that made her sensitive, empty stomach twist.

They shuffled through layers of bones and garbage, while things scuttled away from them across the floor. The boards that had once been solid walls looked like zebra stripes, like camouflage as they picked their way through the bombed-out interior.

Still the Spectro remained silent. Of course, they hadn't explored very thoroughly yet. Who knew where the gadgets might be hiding? They could be anywhere, in the building, in the tall grass, under a rock . . .

She refused to believe the alternative, and more to the point, she didn't *feel* the alternative, the distinctive sensation of her tattoos warming, the hairs on the back of her neck moving. Something was off—an unusual energy was starting to wrap itself around her—but not ghosts, unless of course the Spectrometer wasn't working. Her body's reactions could be muddled by the speed, much as she hated to admit it, but the Spectro should work no matter what.

"Hand me that flashlight."

He slapped it into her palm with vigor.

She ran the light over the cracks by the roof. That was usually the place electronics could be found, especially something big enough to mess with airplane computers. Actually, she'd never seen anything big enough to do something like that, but old habits died hard.

People never looked up. They looked down, they looked from side to side, but almost never did they think to tilt their heads back and see what was above them. That little human idiosyncrasy left a lot of room for error, so Chess always checked above first, a task she could tick off her list.

Nothing appeared out of the ordinary up there, so she cast the light down. More difficult here, with all the debris. What she needed was a broom, but she somehow doubted Terrible would be carrying one with him. Instead she headed for the wall and shuffled along it, moving her feet in tiny increments. "Feel for anything solid," she said. "Anything heavy."

If they made a silly picture—the tattooed witch in her tank top and jeans and the hulking guard in his bowling shirt and trousers, black pompadour slipping down into his eyes, sliding their feet along the walls like they were trying to ice-skate over garbage—she didn't care. Nobody was there to see them, anyway.

Except the thing creeping silently along outside. Chess caught a glimpse of it through a gap in the boards, hunched and dark.

"What's in the eyes?" Terrible's voice rumbled across the empty space. "What you seeing?"

She smacked her hand down through the empty air, signaling him to be quiet. Blessedly he seemed to understand, and stood stock-still while she waited. They both waited.

She glimpsed it again, hovering just outside where Terrible stood, and pointed.

She knew he was fast, but didn't know how fast until his arm shot out through the gap and grabbed the apparition by the throat. It let out a distinctly unghostlike squawk as he pulled it through the boards. They crumbled like wet toast.

"Don't hurt me! Don't hurt me! I's just passing, I swear, I don't know nothing!"

Terrible didn't speak, but he didn't loosen his grip either. The flashlight's beam passed up and down the figure he held, little more than a child in ragged trousers and a stained poncho. The hood had slipped off when Terrible sucked the boy into the building.

"What business you got here?"

"I's just passing—"

"Nobody just passing here. You speak, boy, you tell me. What business?"

The boy glanced at Chess, his eyes wide and dark in his dirty face. "Lady, don't—"

The sound of Terrible's hard palm striking the boy's peaky face seemed impossibly loud. Chess stepped forward, her hand out, before she remembered. Lots of gangs used kids to do their dirty work. Just because the boy said he was innocent didn't mean he was.

"You tell me, or you get worse."

The boy rolled his eyes at Chess again, then looked down. "I heard there was ghosts. Wanted to see me one."

"Who told you?"

"Nobody."

Another slap. Chess refused to watch.

"Okay, okay. I tell you. It were Hunchback, you know him? From Eighty-third. Say he heard from somebody else, who was told by somebody else, that if you comes here some nights, you see them. The ghost planes, right? I came to see, that's all."

Terrible considered this for a minute. "What Hunchback look like?"

"Small guy, dig? With a limp. Crazy eyes and no hair. He call me Brain. Said I got one in my head."

"You don't, you come playing here," Terrible replied, but he let go of the boy. The marks made by his meaty palms were fading. "No place for kids here."

"I come here all—I sorry. I just wanted to see me some ghosts, is all."

"You here before? You see others here?"

"No, I never did. Just me. My friend Pat. We come, but we ain't seen planes yet. You gonna see them, you here for them?"

"Here on business." Terrible glanced up, saw Chess watching. She dug her notebook out of her bag and flipped to a fresh page. *Hunchback*. If he was spreading rumors about the ghost planes, he was as good a place as any to start asking questions.

Terrible must have thought the same thing. He folded his arms across his chest. "Go now. No ghosts tonight."

Brain had one leg over the edge of the hole Terrible had made in the wall when Chess's skin blazed with heat, her tattoos practically tearing themselves from her flesh. At the same time the Spectrometer made a long, solid yowling beep, every light on it turning bright red, casting an eerie glow against the damaged walls for a split second before the room lit up like day and the roar of an airplane directly overhead made Chess dive down to the filthy floor.

Chapter Four

It went on forever, the waiting to die, while her heart beat triple-time in her chest and Brain's thin, high scream hit her ears, barely audible over the noise. It was coming, it was coming to smash into them all and destroy them in a quick flash of rocket fuel and smoke. She tried to scramble out of the way but there was no way to get out of. The lights didn't dim or change direction, and she had somehow managed to fall against the only unbroken section of wall in the ramshackle place. She wrapped her arms around her head, knowing it wouldn't make one damn bit of difference.

Wood exploded next to her, splinters catching her cheek and bare arms. She tried to duck away from it but something grabbed her arm, something hard and hot, ripping her through the wall.

Terrible. He dragged her through the hole he'd punched in the rotted wood and out of the building, to her feet, and as she stood she realized the noise had stopped. There were no lights. There was nothing but Brain's panting sobs and the terrible rushing emptiness filling her ears.

Her body felt like rubber as she tried to stand but fell again. Terrible's arm wrapped around her chest, just below her breasts, and pressed her to his side.

"Nothing here, Chess, nothing here." She didn't know how many times he said it before it finally sank in, before the queasy vibrating stopped in her legs and she could raise her head and look at him.

"Thought you was good with the spook stuff," he said. "You look like some dead."

"And you look like Elvis vomited you up," she managed. "So?"

Hinges creaked in her ears again as he laughed. "So we both looking bad, guesses. But I do always, and you do never. You right now?"

"Yeah, yeah, I'm right. Come on. Show me around outside here."

"You little machine made the beeps, before the noise started."

"It's a Spectrometer. It measures disturbances in the metaphysical plane—ghosts exude metaenergy and leave trails of it behind."

His jutting brow furrowed. "So—"

"Woo-hoo!" Brain's cry split the darkness and made Chess jump back against Terrible. The Nips were making her too jumpy, with all the extra adrenaline. She needed to finish this up and take something to come down.

"I seen it! I seen a ghost! Wait'll I say! They all listen now, they all lis—" The words turned into a queer gurgle when Terrible's hand closed around his throat again.

"You say nothing, young one. You say to nobody, dig?"

Brain nodded.

Terrible let go. "Ain't no haunts here. We find who's pulling tricks, we kill them. You don't spread no stories, or I come get you and make sure you don't. Or worse." He turned and gestured toward Chess. "You know she, right?"

"I never seen—"

"You seen her *skin,* young one, you know she *is.* You

want her after you? She help me find you, but maybe I let her take care of your mouth."

Chess took a step forward, wanting to say something, but nothing came out. This wasn't her business, this was street business, Bump's business, and interference would be unhealthy.

Besides, the last thing any of them needed was for her involvement in the affair to become common knowledge. The Church might look the other way about a lot of things, but using their equipment and her abilities to aid drug traffickers probably wouldn't get her any commendations.

So she just watched while Brain nodded, his wide eyes gleaming white in the darkness, and Terrible dismissed him with a jerk of the head. The boy ran away in a tiny spray of gravel.

"Right," Terrible said, turning back to her. "Let's finish this up, go home."

The rest of the airport consisted mostly of scrub grass and broken cement. They wandered the perimeter, the breeze cool on her fevered body, but she didn't find anything. No transmitters, no interrupters, no projectors or even electromagnets. Nothing indicated the airport wasn't genuinely haunted.

And her skin, her own powers, clearly indicated it was, even without the Spectrometer's sudden violent awakening. But why had it hit her so hard and so suddenly, when the apparition was right on top of them? She should have felt something before that, shivers of warmth, goosebumps, anything.

Unless that speed was doing more than "crazying her up." Her Cepts didn't really interfere with her abilities, at least not in normal doses, but she didn't do speed very often, especially not while working.

It was odd that her Spectrometer hadn't so much as

beeped before redlining, but that was easier to explain. Someone could have sent a blast of magical energy to it at the same time as they switched on whatever powered the lights and transmitted the sound; there were lots of illegal gadgets that fucked with Spectrometers, which was why they were simply tools for detection used in addition to the Debunkers's personal powers.

Hell, if the gadget and the sound-and-light set was portable enough and whoever ran it was fast enough, they could have ducked through the fence and been gone before Terrible pulled her out of the building.

Either way, one of the first things she'd learned in her training was never to assume anything, and to keep investigating until an undeniable conclusion had been reached. Which meant, damn it, this was going to take a lot longer than she'd originally thought.

She was still ruminating on it when they reached the far end of the field. The remains of the building were little more than a shadow when viewed from here, and the grass brushed against her thighs.

Terrible plodded along ahead of her. His tall broad frame parting the weeds sounded like death whispers in the still night, like a predator sliding over the plains.

She took another step, and stopped short. Power shot up her leg, curled over her skin. Something had happened here, a ritual . . . a sacrifice, even. Something that cooled her blood and made her wish desperately that she was back home in bed.

"What's troubling, Chess? Why you so white?"

She shook her head. It was trying to talk to her, to tell her something . . . she just didn't know what. She couldn't hear it, it was trapped in the whispers, all the voices crowding together in her head.

Her skin crawled as dark energy skimmed over her tattoos. It took everything she had to step back, not to crouch down and listen, to put both feet inside the circle and let the darkness take her where it wanted to go.

"Somebody's been doing magic here," she whispered, then, feeling a little foolish, she said it again louder. "Forbidden magic."

"Like raising ghosts?"

"Maybe. I don't know."

She took a step to the right, placing her foot carefully, trying to feel the edge of the circle as best as she could. She did not want to walk into it again. At least, most of her didn't.

The breeze picked up, lifting her hair and cooling the back of her sweaty neck. It wasn't old, the spell. A month, six weeks at the most, but probably more recent. She couldn't imagine how much power there must have been here while it was being cast. The kind of power that required either a very experienced, very powerful sorcerer, or a very innocent victim. Or both.

Either way, it wasn't anything she wanted to be around anymore.

Three more careful steps gave her a good idea of how wide the circle was. Nine feet, big enough for several people.

Terrible started toward her, but she put her hand out. "Don't. You don't want to chance stepping into it. You still got that flashlight?"

He stopped and held it out to her, waiting patiently like a faithful dog while she examined the ground as much as she could from outside the perimeter. The prior week's rain, if not the general passage of time, had eliminated pretty much anything she'd have been able to see, but something glittered on the ground, very faintly, right near the center.

She adjusted the light, holding it high to try and get a better look. Small and gold, shiny as the edge of a razor blade and from what she could make out, almost as sharp. It nestled among several blades of grass, not revealing itself to her.

"Get me a stick or something." If it was part of a spell, she could conceivably break it simply by removing the thing. If it wasn't . . . she'd put it in the African Blackwood trunk where she kept any dodgy magical items she happened to come across. The energy of the wood was strong enough to block just about anything.

Terrible headed for the stand of trees just outside the fence. She watched him tear a new hole in the chain links and slip through it. Odd how such a big man managed to move so stealthily, but then in his line of work he'd need it. She wasn't the only person who'd ever been surprised to find him standing right in front of her, just the only one for whom the experience ended without broken bones.

Meanwhile she kept the light focused on the piece of gold, afraid that if she looked away it would change into something else or disappear. Some people might think such a thing impossible, but she knew better. With magic almost anything was possible; all objects had energy, and energy could be manipulated.

Funny how much cleaner the air tasted out here, only fifteen miles or so from Downside but away from the constant fires, the crowds, and the slaughterhouse. Even with the faint garbage odor wafting under her nose whenever the wind changed, it felt more like country than city, and she couldn't remember the last time she'd been out of the city on her free time. For that matter she couldn't remember the last time she'd been out of her apartment on her free time, save to buy food or score. What was the point?

The chain links jingled. Terrible headed back through the hole in the fence, his body a shadow that didn't appear to move but moved just the same.

Better tools existed to do the job, but the stick would

have to work. Her body ached from trying to keep still and balanced as she leaned out over the circle, using the tip of the broken branch to ease the medallion closer.

It wasn't working. Maybe if she put one foot in the circle, kept the other outside, she could get better leverage.

Probably not a good idea. Her heart, already beating rapid time from the speed, gave a sick little lurch at the idea. But she had to have that piece of metal. Had to. It wanted her to have it, and she wanted it.

She lifted her foot and planted it inside the circle, as far forward as she could.

Pain swallowed her leg, sinking in with teeth like thorns. She screamed and dropped to the ground, heedless of where she fell, tumbling headfirst into the remains of the circle.

Black. It was all black in there, and so cold, so cold her bones felt brittle, so cold she could barely remember what heat had felt like. Voices echoed around her like shouts down a wind tunnel, they were saying terrible things, they were laughing about death and horror and something in front of her had giant black eyes like hunks of obsidian set in its bony face and teeth dripping with reddish saliva . . .

Strength leeched from her body to pour into the dirt. She felt a hole opening beneath her, like the earth was becoming thinner somehow, and as it did the voice grew louder. Not taunting now. Cajoling, promising. For the second time in one night the dead called her, but this was seductive, not violent. If she let go she could have anything she wanted. If she gave up they would take care of her, they would erase all the bad memories and the pain and leave her light and free, filled with air.

She saw Terrible, his lips moving, but no sound reached her. All she heard were the whispers, words she didn't recognize but understood. She opened her mouth to scream, but instead of her voice what came out was shiny and red, a satin ribbon of air curling into the thick darkness around her. She could give in and it would all be over. All the pain, the misery, all of the memories, gone. What she'd been trying to achieve over the years with pills and powders and hard knobs of Dream, she could have it now, she could cease to exist and find the oblivion she couldn't find in life.

She reached for it. Her fingers closed around something cold and hard, something that cut into her palm with its sharp fierce edge.

Fire shot up her arm. Her blood had activated the metal, fed it, whatever it had done, but the cold blackness turned to heat, unbearable blue-white heat.

Through the haze of agony she felt hands circle her ankles and tug. She'd started to let go of the coin, but now she grabbed it again, squeezing harder, the pain a blessing that kept her conscious in the seconds before Terrible yanked her out of the circle.

Her vision returned in a rush, going from nothing to a confused series of images that failed to imprint themselves on her brain. Terrible hoisted her up over his shoulder and ran across the field while her hand burned and her stomach protested. A sharp piece of chain link scratched her cheek when he dove through the hole in the fence; she almost fell as he wrenched the car door open and practically threw her into it.

Music blared and gravel spewed behind them as he tore out of the parking lot. Chess looked down into her clenched fist. Blood dripped through her fingers onto her black jeans, soaking through them. In her hand was a copper amulet.

Chapter Five

"To violate law is to violate yourself, and thus be made unworthy. Facts tell us forgiveness is human, not divine; thus forgiveness must come from humanity; thus it must be earned by debasement and punishment."
—*The Book of Truth*, Rules, Article 30

Her skin crawled just touching the thing, but she wanted to try and see if she could make out anything of the complex pattern around the edge. Runes, maybe? They weren't supposed to memorize the runes—part of their power lay in the concentration it took to copy them—but it was impossible not to recall some of them, and a few of these symbols were familiar. The rest could have been invented, placeholders to confuse the curious or those unlucky enough to stumble across the copper piece, but somehow she didn't think so. The amulet was too powerful for that, and there were many magical alphabets Church employees were forbidden to learn.

Edsel might know, but she couldn't go to him until Sunday. Tomorrow was Saturday, Holy Day, and she'd need to be at Church for most of it.

She tucked the coin in her black box on the bookcase and said a few words of power, hoping it would be enough. Usually magic's edge of unpredictability fascinated her, but it didn't seem so much fun when it came to items like these. Who knew what energies might be manifesting in the amulet, how they might affect her and her home?

"Okay," she said, turning. "Has it stopped bleeding?"

"Aye, looks like it." Terrible peeled the thin towel away from the wound on his arm and inspected it. "I be right, Chess. Ain't you worry."

"Let me see." The bleeding had stopped, but the gouge in his skin from where the fence had caught him, too, looked deep and ugly. He'd saved her life. The least she owed him was some antiseptic.

An almost-full bottle of it rested in her bathroom cabinet. The sharp medicinal scent stung her nose as she soaked a clean cloth with it and pressed it against his wound. His arm twitched but did not move as she finished cleaning it and put a fresh pad over it, taping it into place.

"Sorry about the pain."

He shrugged. "Had much worse."

Which reminded her. She crossed back into her small, dingy kitchen and grabbed a fresh bottle of water from the fridge, then another for Terrible.

Awkward silence descended as they sat and sipped their water.

But what was she supposed to talk about with him? She barely knew him. Nobody really knew him. Nobody really wanted to. Better to run when they saw him coming.

He cleared his throat, gulped his water, cleared his throat. "Nice place."

"Thanks." It wasn't, really. It was bare, and plain, and dull, except for the enormous stained-glass window taking up one entire wall. But if she'd been forced to spend most of her time in the gynecological horror chamber that was Bump's place, she probably would have thought it was nice, too.

"So what you think, Chess? You think Chester haunted?"

She shook her head. "I don't know. I'd like to look at it during the day."

"On the morrow?"

"I have church. Saturday."

"Right. You not there they miss you, aye?"

"Yeah."

He nodded slowly and got up, taking his water with him. "I talk to Bump, give him what happened. Come to his place on the early. He'll front you."

"Thanks."

Sleep was out of the question when he left. Looked like she'd be pulling an all-nighter whether she wanted to or not. She shrugged and started chopping out another line. Might as well enjoy herself, watch some movies, dye her hair—her reddish roots were starting to show under the black—before Church in the morning.

Normally she arrived at church before the Reckonings started, in order to avoid having to watch. This morning she'd been busy organizing her CDs, so citizens with bags of ripe fruit and sticks greeted her when she finally stepped onto Church property at five to nine.

They weren't looking at her. They barely even noticed her, but she still felt exposed, as if they were all watching her from the corners of their eyes, waiting for her to turn her back so they could curse her and beat her. It was hard to remember sometimes that they wouldn't, that that part of her life had ended the day she entered the Church training program.

Two Minor Elders led the first Penitent into the square, a large man with a heavy beard. His bare, dusty feet shuffled across the pavement toward the stocks, but the look on his face belied his body's reluctance. He couldn't wait to be abused, couldn't wait to be cleansed by filth. Easy answers made everyone happy. Idly she wondered what he'd done. Broken an oath, told a lie? An information crime, perhaps? He didn't wear the gloves of a thief, so she guessed his infraction was a moral one; adultery, or lying, perhaps.

Chess didn't stop, crossing the square past the enormous stone 1997 Haunted Week memorial, remembering as always to dip her head in respect for the millions worldwide whose lives had been stolen.

She didn't remember Haunted Week herself, she'd been only an infant. She only knew the ghosts hadn't taken her own parents, whoever they were—or rather, that their death wasn't the reason she was in the system. They'd given her up already. But the story of Haunted Week she knew, of course she knew, as everyone did. She could only imagine what it must have been like, people huddled together in churches and homes and schools, praying and crying, while silent ghosts, risen from their graves, moved through the walls in search of them. Stealing their lives. Armed with knives and broken glass, armed with ropes and hatchets and razors, their blank faces impassive as they killed.

She wasn't the only one who saw the Church as her salvation, despite the few grumpy splinter groups who attempted to rebel in their small, largely useless ways. All of humanity—all that remained, a third of what the population had been before that fateful week—owed their lives to the only group, the only religion, that had been able to control and defeat the ghosts. Before Haunted Week—before the Church showed the world what Truth was—they'd been a tiny group, devoted to the theory and study of magic. Now they ran the world.

And she was part of it. It was the one thing in her life of which she was proud.

She pushed her way through the heavy iron doors so she stood in the cool blue entry hall of the Church of Real Truth.

It always felt a little like coming home, and why shouldn't it? The only constant thing in her entire life had been this building. A different set of parents every couple of months, a different house, different siblings. Take your choice between being beaten or fucked by a series of

Rent-a-daddies. But almost every Saturday she'd been brought here to listen to the Grand Elder, to learn the secrets of entering the city of the dead.

And of course, once they'd discovered she had some talent, it had become more than that. School, and the first place she'd ever been somewhat safe.

Her heels clicked across the tile floor. The sound followed her, a half beat behind her actual steps, rising up past the bare walls to the carvings around the ceiling. Skulls and shrieking faces on the west side, the beatific smiles of the rested dead on the east.

"Cesaria. Good morn to you."

Elder Griffin opened the door to his office and stepped out into the hall. His dark blue velvet suit glowed in the dim light, emphasizing the pure white of his stockings over well-defined calves. The broad brim of his matching hat cast his face into shadow, making his smile float like the Cheshire cat's.

He bowed over her hand. "You look tired, dear. Are you well?"

"Fine. Only . . ." She hesitated, but only for a moment. "I need a new case. I finished the Sanfords last night, I'll turn in the file before I go."

"But no bonus."

She shook her head.

"Any trouble at the Sanfords'?"

Um . . . "Actually, I need a new psychopomp, too. This one appeared early. It's not a problem, it's fine," she amended quickly, seeing the concern in his eyes. She did not want to be questioned on what had happened. "But I think the one I had would work better with a different Debunker from now on."

"Talk to Elder Richards before you leave. Did you bring the old one with you?"

She nodded. "And then I'm ready for a new case. Please."

"Is it your turn?"

"I think so. Please, Elder Griffin. I want to get started, I really . . . feel lucky."

He thought for a minute, narrowing his black-ringed eyes. "Actually, something came in late last night. Come with me. Elder Murray is doing the service today, I'm just leading the Credo, so I have time."

Light glinted off the silver buckles on his shoes as they clicked down the hall to the Reports Room, where Chess averted her eyes while he performed the necessary ritual to break the warding spell on the door. "I started the file this morning, haven't gotten the financial reports yet. The Mortons, out in Trebor Bay. They claim to have been having problems for several weeks, but they've only just called."

She raised her eyebrows. "Same old story."

"Exactly. Here we go."

Without the imposing figure of Goody Tremmell sitting behind it, the Reports Desk looked oddly empty, even with the jumble of loose papers and empty coffee cups scattered across it. The files stayed tucked in the long row of cabinets behind the desk; Goody Tremmell never allowed anyone but herself and the occasional Elder to go near them, much less touch them, and Holy Day was her day off. It felt like a violation simply to be in the room.

Griffin used an ornate silver key to open one of the drawers. Chess half-expected an alarm to sound, but the Elder simply selected a file and handed it to her, pushing the drawer closed behind him. "What happened to your hand?"

The wound she'd gotten from the amulet at the airport looked even worse this morning, jagged and red, so she'd wrapped her hand in a gauze bandage before heading in. She shook her head. "I cut myself opening a can of tuna, can you believe it?"

"You should have one of our doctors look at it."

"It'll be fine, thanks. It's not deep, I just want to keep it clean." Actually she suspected it was getting infected. Her entire hand throbbed.

"Well, if you change your mind let me know. You can probably get out there tonight."

"Get—oh, the case. On Holy Day?"

"Go after sundown. We've made a dispensation to get caught up after the Festival."

"Oh. Right." The Church was still trying to get caught up, and so was she. The Festival meant work, work and sleepless nights, and more work. One week a year of penance, mourning, and rituals, long daylight hours in Church and longer dark hours at home with blood and herbs on the doors and windows to protect the citizenry, and her skin crawling with ghostly energy. Six nights, during which the dead again walked the earth, separated from the people they wanted to kill only by the Church's knowledge and power.

It was scary, and difficult . . . but it certainly reminded people who was in charge. Not the Quantras with their useless protests, or the PRA with their attempts to use the Church's own government branch to undermine the Church's moral authority. Not the Marenzites with their threats or even the more sinister and effective Lamaru with their black magic and their complicated plots. All these groups wanted to be in control.

Only the Church *was*. And from the twenty-eighth of October to the third of November every year, they reminded the world very forcibly of that fact.

Elder Griffin smiled. "Take it, and see what you can do with it. Luck carry you."

She tucked the slim manila folder into her bag to examine later and followed him back down to the Temple, where Elder Murray was discussing the importance of respect. She'd heard this one before, but she slipped into a seat in the back, making sure he saw her. Making sure they all saw her. Living away from the church complex put her under scrutiny enough—especially lately—without being seen to miss services.

Which reminded her. She wanted to see if there were any records on Chester Airport before she left.

Elder Griffin stood at the podium and swept off his hat, so the blue light in the room shone off his blond hair and turned it silver. The whites of his eyes floated in the black makeup ringing them. Chess bowed her head.

"I have no need for faith." Hundreds of voices raised together, intoning the Credo; Chess imagined other Church buildings, other parts of the country, of the world, with everyone speaking in unison. "I do not need faith because I know the Truth. I do not need to believe. Belief is unnecessary when fact is Truth. I do not pray to a god. Prayer implies faith and gods do not exist. Only energy exists, and this is Truth. The Church shows me the Truth and protects me. If I hold to these Truths I will enter the City of Eternity, and there I will stay."

By the time they reached the last words, voices echoed and crashed off the walls, joyous, emphatic, trusting. The room's energy snaked over her skin and warmed her all the way through, as she knew it was doing for every Church employee. Sensitivity to such things was the first basic indicator of talent.

"Heard about the Sanfords," someone whispered. "Bad luck, huh?"

She turned, glaring right into Agnew Doyle's grinning face. He probably wouldn't be grinning so cheerily if she slapped him, but this wasn't the place. Doyle had caused her enough trouble already. She didn't need to start fighting with him in the middle of the hall.

"Hey, wait. I just wanted to say sorry, Chessie. I heard this morning how it was a real haunting, and I thought—"

"You thought you'd get the full story, some good gossip to pass on?" Bodies brushed hers as people left the hall.

Church services were very short, as a rule. They didn't
need to be long. What mattered most was the swiping of
identification cards to prove one had attended, to prove
one was faithful; coming to services wasn't mandatory,
but everyone knew those who did had a better chance at
getting good jobs, at getting their children into superior
schools. What benefits the Church provided always
went first to those who did their part.

No donations were solicited, no pleas for funding the
way the old religions used to do. The Church protected
the People, and the People paid their taxes to the Church.
No middleman, no quibbling about how tax money was
spent. It was spent the way the Church wanted to spend
it, and if the People didn't like it, there were hordes of
malicious ghosts waiting in the City of Eternity, eager to
rise again and murder the People should the Church decide to set them free.

Besides, the Reckonings were the real action. Nobody
wanted to miss those, and you had to attend services to
be admitted.

"That's not fair. Just because—"

"You know what's not fair, Doyle? That thanks to you
half the people I work with think I'm a whore, that's
what's not fair. Get out of my way." Just the thought of
being talked about, of having people *know* things about
her, made her squirm. Technically she and Doyle hadn't
violated any rules—they were unmarried and of age—
but being looked at, knowing her coworkers were pic-
turing it in their heads . . .

"I didn't tell anyone." He reached for her arm, then
pulled his hand back as if her skin burned. "Someone
found out, that's all I know."

"Right. Sure. All those spies hiding in your bedroom."

"Why would I tell? You're not the only one people
are looking at, you know. Somebody must have—" He

glanced around the empty room, lowered his voice. "Somebody must have heard us."

"So *somebody* is probably listening right now, too. I have to go. I have work to do."

"You can't have already gotten another case."

"I did, and unlike some people, I really need this one. We don't all get handed Gray Towers."

"That was luck."

"Luck and a besotted Goody, you mean."

Gray Towers was a mansion on the outskirts of town with a reputation for being haunted. Unfortunately, the owners had exploited that reputation, offering tours and going to the press with stories of various events—sounds, physical manifestations, even a psychic attack—making the case extremely high profile. Doyle had Debunked it. Rumor had it he'd earned close to a hundred thousand dollars, the biggest bonus ever given to a Debunker—ten times the basic single-ghost claim amount. Several others were fairly pissed about that one, not least Bree Bryan, who had been next in the case queue.

The corners of his lips turned down. "Why am I even discussing this with you? You don't believe me, fine. Whatever. Have a great day, Chessie. Good luck with your new case."

Watching him walk away was a mistake. The way his broad shoulders moved, the blue light bringing out highlights in his shoulder-length black hair . . . that hair was extremely soft, she remembered.

Following him was the fastest way to get to the Archives, but instead she took the longer route, heading out the door to the right past the elevator. This hall always made her skin prickle. She'd taken that elevator once—the long, slow journey below the earth's surface, and the silent twenty-minute train ride to the city itself—on her first evaluation visit, and she didn't have any real desire to do it again. That's why she chose Debunking instead of Liaising. The City of Eternity wasn't a fun place, at least not to her.

What everyone else saw as peaceful and happy, a long, well-earned rest, seemed cold and impersonal to Chess. Seemed like a lonely hell only slightly worse than the one she lived in every day. And no matter how hard she tried to understand what everyone else found so agreeable, she just . . . couldn't. Another missing stitch in the fabric of her soul, another feeling she could not share with everyone else. Another thing that made her different and alone.

Past the elevator on the left were the stairs, rising in a tight circle nestled against the wall. The old iron rattled under her feet. Nobody ever used these stairs, or this hall, for that matter. Only the Liaisers, and they didn't work on Holy Day.

Chess stopped about two thirds of the way up and dug for her pillbox. The extra Cepts she'd taken for the pain in her hand were making her drowsy, and this was probably the only place in the entire building where she could be certain no one would watch. There weren't even security cameras here, not after the Liaisers raised a stink about being observed as they prepared for their journeys. Chess didn't blame them. You had to go naked to the dead.

Her right hand didn't want to obey, so she was forced to set the pillbox on the stair next to her and use her left hand to open the clasp. It would have to be her right hand she'd injured.

Inside the box was the little bag Bump gave her the night before. She took a long barrette from the inside pocket of her jacket. Its slide was just the right width for doing bumps, and had a convenient dip in the center. She pinched it between her left thumb and forefinger and scooped out a little of the powder. Her right thumb closed her nostril as she lifted the barrette.

"I'm telling you, something isn't right."

"Bruce, Bruce. You're overreacting."

Chess peered down between the bars of the stairs. What was the Grand Elder doing here with Bruce Wickman? Bruce was a Liaiser. They never seemed to talk to anyone but one another or the dead. And why talk here, instead of the Grand Elder's office?

If they looked up they would see her. Good thing nobody ever did.

"I'm not, sir. The dead are . . . they're unsettled. I'm not the only one who noticed. If you'd loan me some materials, I could speak to one of the old Debunkers' spirits and see what they think."

"What do you mean, unsettled?"

"Restless. Like something's bothering them, scaring them. We've been having a hard time communicating with them."

"Their Festival just ended two weeks ago. They always get like this when their week of freedom ends. Don't you remember two years ago, Bruce, when they tried to escape three days after the gates closed? You were here then, weren't you?"

"Yes, but this isn't—"

The Grand Elder pressed his palm into the center of Bruce's back. It looked friendly, but Bruce jerked forward a little. "I'll look into it, Bruce. You tell the other Liaisers that I'm going to consider your request. But I'm sure things will go back to normal shortly."

Bruce nodded unhappily while Chess tried to ignore the tiny flecks of ground Nip falling from her hairpin. Her foot itched but she didn't dare move, not on these loud stairs.

So Bruce thought the City was unsettled? Hmm.

The Grand Elder did have a point. As the anniversary of Haunted Week drew near, the same astrological and atmospheric conditions that had allowed them to come back in the first place prevailed again; the planets aligned, the magical energy of the earth underwent its yearly shift, and in that space the power surged enough to give the ghosts what they needed to break through. The exact moment of alignment didn't last long, of course, but it took a little time for everything to go back to normal.

Despite her unqualified affection for and respect of the Church, Chess had always wondered if the Festival was more than just a chance to remind people of their debt and celebrate the Church, was in fact unavoidable: the dead had to be released from the City in a controlled way, under Church-and-psychopomp guard, or they would escape on their own—with dangerous results.

Not that it mattered. The Festival happened, end of story.

"Okay, Grand Elder. I'll tell them. But please . . . please consider it."

"I will. Go on, now, Bruce. Facts are Truth."

"Facts are Truth, sir."

The itch was starting to sting. The Grand Elder stayed where he was, staring at the elevator doors. Why didn't he just go already? He had places to be, and she had feet to scratch and uppers to snort.

"What frightens the dead?" he muttered, shaking his head. "What could scare the dead?"

Chapter Six

"So henceforth it shall be called Triumph City, because it is the seat of the triumph of Truth, and here we shall make our glorious home."

—The Grand Elder, dedication speech,
December 1, 1997 (After Truth)

The symbols on the amulet weren't in any of the standard books, which didn't surprise her. If they'd been there she would have recognized them. But it never hurt to look, so she did, going through every alphabet, finding only one match.

Etosh.

The word was only mentioned because it connected to another symbol in an example, though. No meaning was given. Dead end.

The Restricted Room would probably have more for her, but Goody Glass was manning the desk today, and Goody Glass hated her. The feeling was mutual. Chess didn't want to ask the nosy old Goody, with her pinched nose and hairy chin, to let her into the room. Too many questions would be asked.

So instead she headed for the cabinets on the far wall, doing a double take when the back of a familiar-looking head appeared. Not Doyle after all but Randall Duncan, another Debunker. If she'd been paying better attention she wouldn't have confused them; Doyle's hair was soft, shiny, and well taken care of, whereas Randy's straggled down his back, a sign that he simply couldn't be bothered to have it cut.

He stopped as if he felt her eyes on him, his face break-ing into a sunny smile.

"Hey, Chess! I looked for you earlier, but I didn't see you."

With anyone else she might have asked why, but with Randy she didn't need to. He'd tell her. Subtlety was not his strong suit.

"Everything good, Randy?"

He nodded. "Heard about the Sanfords. Tough luck."

"Yeah. Just got a new case, though. Looks like a good one. I could sure use it."

He nodded. "Couldn't we all? Or at least, most of us. Guess Doyle doesn't anymore."

She rolled her eyes to indicate agreement, and wished he'd go away. Paying attention to him was a waste of time. She wanted to check those files and couldn't with him standing there.

"Speaking of Doyle . . . I—I have to tell you something. Something I don't think you're going to like, about him. There's been a rumor about you two. You should know about that, what people are saying."

"Yeah, Randy, I know. Where'd you hear that?"

He shrugged. "I overheard one of the Goodys asking Doyle about it. He denied it, but, well, I just don't want to see you get hurt, you know? Doyle's kind of a user."

"Yeah. I know. I'm okay, Randy, don't worry."

He peered at her from under his thick eyebrows, then nodded. "Okay. Well, if you ever need anything, you know, even just to talk, you can always call me. Really."

She nodded, just as if that was something she would ever do. "Thanks, I might."

He patted her arm and left, throwing a little wave over his shoulder before disappearing into the stacks. So one of the Goodys—she bet it was freaking Goody Tremmell, thinking just because she handled case assignments she got to judge the Debunkers, too—thought she'd poke her sharp nose in, huh? No wonder everyone in the complex knew about it. Great.

She shook her head and slid the file drawer out.

C . . . *Ce* . . . *Ch*. Chester Airport did indeed have a file, a fairly thick one. She grabbed it and took it back to her table.

The airport had opened in 1941, and stayed open for fifty years, never expanding or becoming more than just a small local airfield. There were pictures in the file, surprising ones considering the wreckage she'd seen the night before. It had been a clean little building, sitting tidily in front of the runways like a kid on a church pew.

Old newspaper clippings crinkled against her fingers. Chester had had its share of accidents and fatalities, too. Twenty-three she could see, just in the last ten years it had been open. Of course, more of the small, private planes tended to crash than large commercial ones, but that still seemed excessive to Chess.

Had Bump's ghosts—if there were ghosts—been around for that long? If she operated on the Church-approved theory that ghosts caused death to feed on the living or out of jealousy, and no planes had flown into or out of Chester in almost thirty years . . . those would be some damned angry, hungry ghosts right about now. No wonder they went for Bump's planes like Downside children falling on scraps of meat.

But if someone was doing rituals on the grounds—not *if*, she knew they *were*—what might happen there? Had someone tried to Banish Chester's ghosts on their own, using some cheap piece of copper they'd picked up from one of the many magic charlatans the Church was always trying to prosecute?

She flipped open her notebook. *Ask Bump if he's made any attempts to Banish. Ask Edsel if he recognizes amulet.*

The thought of touching it again made her twitch. Magic was legal, of course; how could it not be? How did you make energy, the forces inherent in the earth and the air, illegal?

But not all magic was equal. The Church decided what was and was not permissible, and Chess was pretty sure that whatever was happening at Chester would not have been approved by any Elder in his right mind. She felt guilty just having it—but then, this whole situation made her feel guilty anyway.

Sniffling occasionally, she went through the rest of the file. No complaints of hauntings since it had closed, and nothing noted for the surrounding areas, either, which didn't mean much. Debunkers were supposed to mark files on all buildings in surrounding areas when a haunting was confirmed, but they almost never did. Chess herself forgot at least half the time.

So aside from the "neglected ghosts" theory, nothing indicated Chester was genuinely haunted.

Of course, nothing had initially indicated the Sanfords' was genuine, either, and it certainly was.

So much for initial indications.

The Mortons looked like any nice, normal semi-suburban family, struggling to make it all the way to that big cookie-cutter house with thirty feet of grass in every direction around it, but that meant nothing. In fact, it meant Chess needed to be more careful, more on her guard, because the Mortons clearly wanted that nice suburban home. It was all over their smooth, round little faces.

People who wanted things were dangerous. People who wanted things would lie and cheat and steal to get them.

She of all people should know that.

So she stretched her lips into a fake smile and dug out her notebook. "When did you say the manifestations started?"

Mrs. Morton paused for a minute, placing one dainty pink-tipped finger to one dainty pink-slicked lip. "I believe it was about five weeks ago, wasn't it, Bill, dear? While you were at the convention." Her gaze returned to Chess. "Bill's an optometrist."

"That's great."

What was she supposed to say? Bill could examine every eye in the District and she wouldn't give a shit.

But Mrs. Morton was obviously very proud of the fact that her husband had looked at enough eyeballs to become an expert on them, and the last thing Chess wanted to do at this point was alienate the family.

"I was in the laundry room," Mrs. Morton continued, "putting a load in the dryer, when I heard Albert here start yelling. It was odd, because Albert is such a brave, quiet boy. Just like his daddy."

If Mrs. Morton would stop verbally jacking off her husband and son, this would all be done so much more quickly, but then Chess figured it was just about the only sex the woman got. Mr. Morton, silent and pale in his sweater-vest, looked like the kind of man who ate ribs with a knife and fork. Not exactly a wild beast in the bedroom, she guessed, but then what did she know?

"Did you actually see the specter, Mrs. Morton? Or was it just Albert?"

"Well, I didn't see it that time, no. But he described it so well I felt like I did. Then later I did see it. In the bedroom. Just as I was drifting off to sleep."

"And what did it look like?"

"It was just horrible. Like a . . . a ghoul, or something. It made the room so cold, it felt so . . . evil."

She gave a delicate shudder. "Gray, and sort of wrinkly. Moldy, if you know what I mean. It wore just rags, might have been a dress once but I couldn't tell. I don't even know if it was a man or a woman, but it had been dead a long time. Did it escape from the City of Eternity? I thought they couldn't escape from there, but then if they really couldn't we wouldn't be haunted, right?"

"Some spirits never made it to the City. We're still cleaning up the old religions' messes."

Chess made another note on her pad. *Intensely interested in placing blame on the Church. Cannot describe entity with any degree of detail.* Then, below that, she added: *Vodka. Laundry soap. Toothpaste.*

Mrs. Morton must have seen something in Chess's blank expression, because she added, "Not that we blame the Church! Of course we don't. But this . . . this is pretty scary. Poor Albert is afraid to sleep in his own bedroom, and none of us are too comfortable being here by ourselves, and, well, this is our home. And we can't even sell it, not with some unnie hanging around!" Her hand flew to her mouth.

Chess ignored both the epithet and the exaggerated look of shock on Mrs. Morton's carefully painted face. When it came down to it, "unnie"—short for "undead"—was one of the less offensive terms she'd heard for them. Sure, it was worse than the Church-sanctioned "ghost," "spirit," "specter," or "entity." But as slang went it was pretty harmless.

"We hope you can help us." Mr. Morton spoke up for the first time, his voice surprisingly deep and pleasant for such a slight man.

"I'm sure I can. Perhaps you could show me all the places where the entity has appeared? I'd also like to see any locations where its presence was felt in some other way. Sounds, any symbols etched on the walls or maybe in the shower doors or mirror? They often try to communicate like that."

The Mortons stared at her, their eyes so wide they looked artificial.

"Has anything appeared on any other walls or windows? Any feelings of being watched? Movement seen out of the corner of your eye? Odd smells? Touches? Anything of that nature, now's the time to show me where it happened."

She pulled her tape recorder and Spectrometer out of her bag and switched them on.

The Mortons didn't move. Chess fought the urge to look down and see if something had spilled on her blouse when she wasn't paying attention.

"Is there a problem?"

"I'm sorry," Mrs. Morton said. "I just . . . you scared me. We haven't had anything as bad as some of that. Is that going to happen?"

"It might." Chess watched them carefully. Sometimes she could see the little wheels spinning in their heads as they planned how to stage a more potent manifestation. She'd caught someone out that way in her second year of work, when she'd finished her list and the client had blurted out "Messages in frost? I never even thought of doing that!"

"Oh, dear." Mrs. Morton clutched at her sweater. Her blue eyes examined the room, sweeping back and forth as though something was going to materialize and jump out at her any second. Either she was a great actress, or she was genuinely frightened. Was it possible the son— Albert—was doing it without his parents' knowledge? Or that Mr. Morton was behind it? That had happened once, too, a husband faking a spooking so his wife would be too afraid to ask for the house when he left her for another woman.

She scribbled on her pad: *Girlfriend Mr. M?*

"I'm sure we can take care of it before things start going really badly," Chess said. "Now, if you could please show me around the house . . . ?"

All three of the Mortons came along on the tour, much to Chess's chagrin. Extra bodies crowding around her in small spaces like the Morton's cramped hallway were not what she needed in the slightly nervous state the Nips had left her in. And if little Albert accidentally-on-purpose brushed against her breast again she was going to hit him. The quality and quantity of porn she imagined she'd find under his bed, when she got around to searching, would probably be staggering.

Mrs. Morton's pale fingers trailed over the picture frames in the hall. "We trace our family back over three hundred years," she said. "Roots are so important, don't you think?"

"Absolutely." She wondered what Mrs. Morton would say if Chess told her she had no idea who her parents had been, much less anyone further back.

Her tattoos didn't so much as tingle, nor did the Spectrometer beep, when they entered a small bedroom on the right, which looked as though some bizarrely pretentious child lived in it. Batman wallpaper warred with posters of mallard ducks and prints from the Tate gallery. A teddy bear slumped on the dresser next to a rack of silver cuff links. Books tilted on the scarred pine bookcase like crooked teeth, but when Chess stepped closer there were dust lines on the shelves. Someone had recently— probably very recently—removed quite a few titles.

Little Albert was into sci-fi and technology. All the big fantasy names were there—Tolkien, Card, Anthony, Weis—along with Sagan, Heinlein, Sturgeon, Straub . . . but no how-to tech books, not even a single Idiot's Guide, which was unusual because the more she looked around the room the more she noticed the bundle of cables peeking out from under the bed, the empty shelf under the flat-screen TV in the corner. Albert looked like an A/V Club boy, and A/V Club boys read books about hacking and splicing and F/X. They read about digital imagery and home theaters and how to rewire speakers so they went up to eleven.

When she came back later, or the next night, she'd have a more thorough look around.

She let the Mortons lead her through the spare bedroom and the bathroom, into the master bedroom. The signs of desperate upward mobility were strewn all over the house as if an L.L.Bean catalog had exploded; a beautiful dresser in a bedroom with mismatched bedside tables, expensive lotions on a cracked bathroom countertop. The copy of *The Book of Truth* next to the bed had been arranged so the light shone off the gold lettering and reflected back at her when she stepped through the doorway.

"This is where it was." Mrs. Morton waved a nervous hand at a spot on the floor to her left, about a foot from where she was standing. There was something vaguely familiar about the movement, about Mrs. Morton herself. Maybe the family really did attend Church sometimes and Chess had seen her there. "I was in bed, there, like I said, and it just . . . hovered here, and stared at me. It looked so angry, I just didn't know what to do . . ."

This was ridiculous, a waste of her time. She switched off the Spectrometer and tape recorder, shoved them both back into her bag.

"Well, I've seen enough for now. If we could go back to the living room and you could sign the complaint, we'll get started processing it."

"But . . . you didn't see the ghost, does that matter?"

Chess pulled the zipper on her purse shut, realizing as she did that her hand was shaking slightly. She glanced at the clock by the bed. Five to nine. This was taking forever, she needed to go.

"We're not done yet," she replied, trying to sound cheerful. "It'll take at least a week or two to really investigate. This was just to get the papers filled out, and so I could get a feel for what we're dealing with. You'll be seeing quite a bit of me, Mrs. Morton, don't you worry."

Mrs. Morton smiled weakly. The cheaters always hated it when she said she'd be around a lot. And the Mortons were faking it, she knew it. Not even a beep, not even a blip on the Spectro. Very unusual in an enclosed space with ghosts.

And the Mortons would certainly be learning about enclosed spaces if she was right, and they were faking. The Church didn't take kindly to attempts to steal from it; Mr. Morton would have a hard time examining eyeballs from a little blue cell.

"So let's just go sign those papers and I can leave you to your eveni—"

Something darted through the air behind Mr. Morton, so fast it took Chess a second to realize it wasn't just a hallucination. A black shape, man-size but crouched over. She had the impression of a hood hiding its face, of the light by the bed catching the sharp edge of a blade, before it disappeared into the closet.

It looked almost like a cartoon, like an image projected on the wall instead of moving in front of it, but it had been so long since she'd seen an actual cartoon, she could have been wrong about that.

She wasn't wrong about the sense of unease, though, more than simply the unease of her body starting to get serious with her about its needs—at least she thought it was. Fuck, she shouldn't have waited to take her pills, it was throwing her off. For the first time a ribbon of doubt slipped through her mind. Withdrawal, or ghost? No way to be sure.

The Mortons stood watching her, faintly perplexed, waiting for her to finish her sentence. They hadn't noticed anything—or perhaps they had, and they were watching her to see if she said anything.

Of course. The image had looked like a cartoon, like something being broadcast, because it was. When she came back later she'd look for the projector. It was probably behind the mirror over the dresser. The thought was comforting, but not enough to ease the cool sweat on her forehead and body. She felt sticky with it.

"To your evening," she finished. "I'm sorry I've kept you so late, my last interview ran long. And I'll be in touch."

Sooner than they knew.

Chapter Seven

"Debunking often looks like the most appealing of Church positions, but very few possess the skill, intelligence, and above all, *integrity* required."
—*Careers in the Church: A Guide for Teens,* by Praxis Turpin

All buzzed up and no place to go. At least, not until three, when she investigated the Morton house again.

The Market was closed. Bump's place would be open—Bump's place never closed—but she didn't particularly want to go there either. She had everything she needed.

But the walls of her small apartment were closing in, the faint colors from the stained-glass window sliding over surfaces like they were chasing her.

She could go get cigarettes. The Stop Shop on the corner had special dispensation to be open twenty-four hours. That might be nice. A little walk in the cool night air would clear some of the anxious cobwebs in her head.

What the hell had that thing been? She'd never seen anything like it. Projected image or not, it was menacing. She'd had the feeling that if it had turned and saw her, *looked* at her, she might have screamed.

Maybe she should eat. It wasn't like her to get so paranoid. Take a little of the edge off, fix the sourness in her stomach. The Stop Shop sold snacks, too.

She fished a twenty from her bag, then grabbed her knife and tucked it into her pocket. Walking alone and unarmed in Downside was never a good idea. She locked all three of the bolts on her door as she left.

Her building had once been a Catholic church, before the Church of Truth made every other religion redundant.

Many of the old places of worship had fallen into disrepair, but buildings with some sort of historical value or level of attractiveness were permitted to remain. Chess's was both, and she was glad, even if the extra floors built in ruined the effect a little bit.

It was still one of the prettiest buildings in Downside. And the air outside her apartment did seem clean, despite the odors of garbage and exhaust that never went away.

The heavy double doors at the end of the hall stood wide open, framing the empty street beyond. That was odd. The doors were normally closed and locked. Could be old Mrs. Radcliffe on the second floor left them open. They were difficult for her to move, and she always forgot what kind of neighborhood she lived in.

Or it could have been the four members of Slobag's gang from Thirtieth, lying in wait in the protective darkness between the huge slabs of wood and the walls. Chess reached for her knife but she knew it was useless. A hand closed over her mouth before she could open it to scream, and the sharp pinch of a needle was the last thing she felt before the world went black.

The itching woke her up. That, or the intense discomfort of lying on a cold cement floor. But she was pretty sure it was the itching. It burned a path from the palms of her hands and soles of her feet, up her arms and legs, and spread across her chest and throat as if she wore a cheap, terrible necklace she couldn't take off.

She had no idea what time it was, but if she was this bad off it had to be late Sunday morning, at least. Shit. She'd missed the Mortons' place. Not that they knew she'd missed, but still.

Her head pounded as she pushed herself to a sit. The worst possible thing she could do would be to scratch.

Scratching would only make the itching worse. Experience had taught her that. Once she started scratching those invisible itch-bugs wandering beneath the skin she might as well give up. It was like issuing them a challenge. Itch-bugs didn't like to lose.

Of course, her stomach was giving them a run for their money in the torture-and-discomfort department. It felt like she'd swallowed a big gulp of acid. The palm of her right hand screamed in pain.

Faint light entered the room through a window high up on the opposite wall. If she leaned her head back she could see a slice of gray sky. So it could be early morning, or simply a cloudy day. She bet on the latter. No way she'd be withdrawing like this if only a few hours had passed.

Slobag's minions had lain a quilt on the floor, but it hadn't made a difference. Now it did. She wrapped it around her shoulders to try and ease her shivering, and leaned back.

No point even trying the door. The heavy iron lock looked shiny new and very strong. There were no other doors. There wasn't even a convenient ring connected to a secret trapdoor in the floor.

There was a toilet, though. She wasn't about to use it, not when they could be watching, but at least it was there. Nothing like a considerate kidnapper.

Oh shit. What the hell did they want with her? It wasn't as though they could mistake her for someone else, or rather, something else. Not with her tattoos, not unless they were stupid, which Slobag's people weren't.

She didn't know much about Slobag—not her neighborhood, not her dealer. She didn't need to. Like Bump, Slobag ruled his part of town. Like Bump, he would be utterly ruthless. And unlike Bump, he would bear a grudge against her simply because of who she worked for, which was not good news for her. The Church's ascendance had been welcomed far more suspiciously in the Asian countries than it had in the West, and Slobag and his men were Cantonese.

She caught herself trying to scratch and folded her arms tightly around her chest under the quilt. Her body thrummed with need. She needed to get out of here. She *needed* her pills. Just the thought made her groan.

Metal scraped against metal as the lock unbolted and the door opened.

"So she's awake."

Chess didn't recognize the man standing in the doorway, his hair standing up in short black spikes. Everything about him was black except his skin, the silver chains he wore, and the chunky silver skull ring on his right hand. The black Chinese character tattooed on the back of his left hand would have identified him as one of Slobag's even if his features already hadn't. His people all carried the mark, something like the tattoos that granted her some protection against spirits and gave her additional power to fight them. She suspected there was some power in that ink, as well. Maybe not the kind of power hers carried, but who knew?

Through the gaps around his body in the doorway she saw a few others, their arms folded neatly in front of them. No chance at overpowering him and escaping, then. Of course, even if he'd been alone she probably couldn't have accomplished it, not in her state. Not in any state, if the rumors about this crew could be believed.

"Why the face, tulip girl? You look moanworthy indeed." His voice was deeper than she would have expected, and not accented like street no matter what the words were.

She bit her lip and turned her face away, hanging it forward so her dark hair could cover it. Not much choice except to look and act as docile as possible so they'd let her go. At least until she knew what they wanted.

From outside the doorway he produced a chair and sat down in it a few feet away from her, leaning forward to rest his elbows on his knees. "I'm Lex."

She glared at him.

"Don't feel like making the speech? Okay by me. Only maybe I got something might loosen your tongue." He reached into his jacket. Chess tensed. She didn't have her knife, didn't have any weapons at all, but if she had to, she could probably at least get him with her fingernails or a good solid kick in the balls.

He didn't pull out a weapon. Or rather, not a weapon that could hurt her. But nothing could have controlled her as effectively. Just as Bump had done, Lex produced a Baggie full of pills. Unlike Bump, he held it in his fingers, dangling it in front of his face. Her mouth watered.

"What you think, tulip girl? Maybe you want to talk, I let you have one?" He reached into the bag and pulled out a Cept, gleaming white between his burnished fingers. "Maybe two?"

The pill loomed in front of her, shining like a diamond. Her stomach was starting to cramp, her legs to feel weak. If she didn't manage to get something soon . . .

"I got all night. My guess is you don't." He leaned forward a little more, his voice dropping to a caressing whisper, an insinuating one. His black eyes never left her. "You feeling that pinch, hmm? Them itches? They get right in, don't they? Like you'll never stop itching. And the belly gets all fratchy there, those long legs turn rubber . . ."

She wanted to sink into the wall and disappear. She should have let the psychopomp take her. She knew it was a mistake to stay alive.

"Ain't gonna get better with time, tulip." He tossed the Cept into the air, caught it. Tossed it again, missed. It hit the stone floor with a small ticking noise.

Chess dove forward, but she was too late. His boot snapped down over the pill and ground it into powder.

That was okay. If he would just leave . . . It wouldn't be pretty, but the floor seemed reasonably clean, right? She didn't know if they'd taken her cash as well as her knife. She could roll that bill up just fine, even with her stiff and aching hand. If he would leave, if he would please just leave.

No such luck. He produced a bottle of water. "Jarkman."

The door opened, admitting another, smaller man. "Aye?"

"Fetch us some towels. I made a spill."

Lex uncapped the water bottle, lifted his foot, and slowly, deliberately, poured liquid over the crushed pill. Chess bit her lip so hard she drew blood.

Jarkman was back in a moment with a roll of paper towels. He wiped up the mess in silence and left.

"Want to try that one again? I got a whole bag here, it don't mind me if I crush them all. Jarkman needs the exercise."

He plucked another pill from the bag. "You know the worst part, aye? You been there? When the belly gets mad. Starts turning upside out. Methinks nothing in this world so bad as—"

"Stop." The word came out before she realized it. "Just stop, okay?"

He blinked. "And that's four words, ain't they nice. Here you go, tulip. You have that."

He tossed the pill to her like a bread crust to a duck. Not picking it up was the hardest thing she'd ever done.

"Aw, you think we give you poison?" She might have appreciated the smile he gave her if she hadn't been about to burst into tears. He wrapped his fingers around the top of the bag, shook it up, and plucked a pill out of it. She watched it disappear into his mouth, watched him wash it down. "No poison. True thing, tulip. Take it."

She wanted to be cool, but coolness was impossible in

the face of her screaming, throbbing body. The words were barely out of his mouth before she snatched the pill up from the folds of the quilt and gobbled it, grinding it between her teeth, turning it into a slick, bitter paste on her tongue.

Without a word he passed her the water, and she gulped it down. Some of the tightness in her chest eased.

"Ready to talk now?" He held out his hand, flat and open. Another Cept rested in the middle of his palm.

She took it, crunched it, washed it down. "Depends on what you want to talk about."

"What you suppose I want to talk about?"

"You think you have a ghost?"

His thin lips stretched into a smile. "Not bad, tulip, not bad. Tougher than you look."

"Why do you keep calling me tulip?"

"Ain't that the tattoo?"

"No, these are—you asshole."

She did have a tulip tattoo. Low on her stomach, just above the juncture of thigh and groin. Which her pants covered.

He shrugged. "Some dames hide weapons, aye?"

"So you had to strip-search me to make sure I wasn't?"

"I don't strip you, nay. Not me. Not the men. My sister Blue, she done the job."

Somehow she couldn't bring herself to thank him.

The knock at the door startled her. Lex turned. "Aye?"

"Seven."

"Right." He looked back at her. "Hungry?"

"What?" The shakes were only just starting to fade, how could she be hungry?

"I gotta be somewhere, have a talk to someone. Jarkman show you the bathroom, got a good strong waterfall. Then we talk."

"What the hell is going on? Those goons kidnapped me and threw me in here, then you show up and taunt me, now you want me to have a nice hot shower and some food? Are you insane? Seriously."

He shrugged. "Don't suppose so, nay. You stay here if you like it. But you don't leave this house until we talk. Your choice."

Chapter Eight

> "Crimes of morality are a betrayal of yourself, your family, and the Church. And because of this, betrayal itself is the most serious of moral crimes."
>
> —*The Book of Truth*, Laws, Article 75

The shower was good, she had to admit. By the time she got out she felt almost normal again.

Obviously they hadn't brought her here to kill her, unless this was part of some ritual she didn't understand. But why they would want to talk to her—what possible reason Slobag or any of his men would have for bringing her here—she had no idea.

The Asians hated the Church and anything or anyone who worked for it, as a rule. Since so much of their old religions were based on venerating the spirits of their ancestors—despite the fact that those same ancestors rose from the grave and killed them, just as they had everywhere else in the world—she couldn't really blame them, but it did mean that when she emerged from the bathroom and put her clothes back on, her hands shook a little. The clothes weren't clean, but it was better than not having showered at all.

The room adjoining the bathroom was undecorated, almost warehouselike in its barrenness. A small, hard bed hugged one wall, covered with a plain blue blanket. A cold TV sat on the floor opposite. Its blank screen watched her like an unblinking eye as she crossed to the window and looked out at the city. She'd never spent much time down here, so close to where Downside gave way to the Metro District. Farther beyond that the suburbs glinted like fool's gold as the hills rose to the misty darkening sky.

She assumed it was Sunday evening—Jarkman had said "Seven" through the door, and it clearly wasn't getting any lighter. Which meant she'd missed going out to Chester with Terrible that afternoon, which was not good. He'd be looking for her. All of Bump's men would be looking for her. Being found here would probably be the last thing she ever did.

Chess didn't have any specific loyalty to Bump aside from his dominance in her neighborhood, at least not when it came to buying her drugs. But given the investigations she'd just been extorted into doing for him, the inside information she now had about his plans—no, being found with Slobag's men could definitely be hazardous to her health.

Something clicked behind her. She turned to see Lex framed by the doorway.

"C'mon. I got food."

Not the most delightful invitation she'd ever received, but her stomach didn't care. Had she eaten the day before? Probably not, with all that speed. No wonder she'd slept for so long.

She followed him down a blank gray hallway, their feet echoing on the dark wood floor planks. As they moved farther down the hall the doors they passed grew more ornate, heavy red wood carved with dragons and pagodas. The contrast between them and the bare walls made Chess wonder what was hiding in those rooms.

Finally the hall ended in a large, wide room. Gold dragons and tigers fought in murals along the entire length of the walls, and the furniture was carved the same as the doors had been. It was like stepping into an elaborate set for a martial arts film, but at least it wasn't in quite as bad taste as Bump's place had been. Whatever genitalia the illustrated beasts possessed was mercifully hidden.

Lex gestured to a long polished table. "Sit you down, tulip. Got food for you. No poison there, neither."

"Why are you doing this?"

He shrugged. "I'm hungry. Not polite to eat in fronts of people, aye?"

"So why not just say what you need to say and then eat when I leave?"

"You gonna sit? Only I'm tired of standing here."

She sat. Up close she could see the fine grains in the table. It looked like real wood, a solid slab of it. She didn't think she'd ever seen a piece of wood so large.

They sat in silence while an elderly man brought in a tray and placed two white china bowls in front of them, along with accompanying silverware. Beggar soup—that favorite dish of the Downside—but an especially elegant version loaded with meatballs and chicken and herbs. She could never afford to have both meats. Of course, she spent most of her money on other things. Most Debunkers lived much better than Chess did. Life was all about trade-offs.

"So. Why don't we start talking now, aye?" he said, after she'd inhaled about half her bowlful. Hungrier than she'd thought, and free food was free food.

She stiffened in her seat. "Talk about what?"

"I guess you know what."

"Um . . . no."

"Hmm." He leaned back, lit a cigarette, handed it to her and lit another one for himself. "I been thinking we talk about airports, tulip. How you like that topic?"

"My name isn't tulip, you know."

"I know."

"So is there some reason you keep calling me that?"

"Maybe them tats interest me. Maybe one day you

show me." He cocked an eyebrow while smoke wreathed his spiky head.

"Maybe one day the Grand Elder will walk naked down the street."

"Maybe he will, no telling. Or maybe one day Bump gonna reopen Chester Airport, what you say?"

She sucked in a long drag of fragrant smoke. Not her usual brand, but nice. "I wouldn't know anything about that."

"Not what I hear."

"Maybe you heard wrong."

"Or maybe you lie to me, *Cesaria*. Only thing is, I can't figure out why anyone lie for a strut-speech like Bump. You got any ideas on that?"

"I don't lie for anybody." The filtered tip of the cigarette was tan, with little flecks of gold. They sparkled faintly when she turned it in her fingers.

"Seems to me you lie every day. Less you been telling them at your church what you do on your off-hours, right. They know you into Bump fifteen grand? They know why?"

When she didn't answer, he continued. "I know you lying to me now, and I know you was out at Chester Friday night. I even know why you lie, causin you don't want Terrible down on you like a load of steel. But you ain't hiding anything from me I don't know. And that's just fine. Got a deal for you, tulip. A deal you like right."

If Bump found out she'd discussed his airport plans with one of Slobag's men, he'd . . . he might even have her killed. Even the spiritual dispensation offered by the Church wouldn't protect her.

Then again, if she didn't hear Lex out and agree to his deal, he'd probably tell Bump she'd come here offering information. What did he care? One dead Debunker wouldn't exactly bother him.

"I'll listen," she said. "I'm not confirming anything about the airport, but I'll listen."

"Good. That's real good." He leaned forward and lit another cigarette. "So check the tale, tulip. Bump's got you down there, disproving them ghosts, aye? Only maybe we don't want them ghosts disproved. We sure don't want them banished or exiled or whatever it is you people do. I gotta tell you why?"

She shook her head. Bump being able to fly his drugs into his own private airport wouldn't be very good for Slobag.

"So that's where you come in. You tell Bump there's ghosts in that airport, real vicious ghosts ain't gonna go anywhere."

"He'll expect me to Banish—"

"But maybe you can't."

"But I can. I mean, it's what I do for a living."

He shrugged. "You figure something out. I got belief, me. But Bump don't open Chester. Big trouble for you if he does."

The smell of the stew started to cloy. She pushed the bowl away. "And if he doesn't?"

"Ah, good girl. If he don't, we got specials for you. How much you pay Bump? Them pills don't come cheap, aye? You visit the pipes, ain't cheap. You do what we wants, you pay less. Like, nothing. Bump wants his money, we pays it. Then you come to us for what you need. All taken care of, tulip. Just for you. Brought to your door."

Free drugs.

She could actually hold on to money for the first time in three years. Get a new car, maybe, with her next bonus, instead of using them to pay Bump her arrears. New clothes. Real hot food more than once or twice a week instead of snacks and junk.

Of course, Bump would notice if she stopped buying from him. Maybe she wouldn't stop, not entirely. Bump's pipes were a hell of a lot more convenient to her apartment. But making him think she was cutting back . . . Maybe that wasn't a bad idea at all.

She must be insane, to be even contemplating this. The thing to do was go to Bump, tell him what just happened here, and let him handle it.

How? By taking out Slobag's entire tribe? That wasn't going to happen anytime soon. And if she told, and Lex or any of Slobag's men found out about it . . . Her life would be even more worthless than it was now.

Shit.

Lex watched her expectantly, his rangy body splayed back in his chair. A ragged hole in his Stiff Little Fingers T-shirt exposed a slice of tawny skin on his chest.

"I'll think about it," she said.

"Aye, you do that, tulip. You think hard. And when you decide, you let me know." He dug a scrap of paper from his back pocket and produced a pen from his boot. "This my number. Private number, dig? Call me when you know what you wanna do. Or if you decide you wanna let me see that ink, aye?"

"That's not going to happen." She took the number, folded it, tucked it in her pocket.

"You'd be surprised, tulip, what happens when you not expecting it. Surprised, indeed."

"I'm not sure I want to go in there."

"Safest way home, tulip. Lessin you want me to walk you down the middle of the streets. Only it's hard to keep secrets, aye, when everybody seeing you."

"But it's a tunnel."

"I do know what it is."

Her skin crawled just looking at the narrow opening. Pale greenish light glowed from farther down the path, but whether it was safety bulbs or phosphorescent mold she didn't know, and didn't particularly care to find out.

"Didn't figure a Churchwitch to be a claustrophobe."

"I'm not!" Her voice squeaked. She cleared her throat. "I mean, I'm not. But being underground . . . It's, um, a respect thing. The City is underground." Wasn't the entire truth, but close enough.

He nodded. "Right. I get you. Still don't have no choice, but I see the origin." His warm hand circled her upper arm. "Them walls got iron bands, no worries. Let's us go."

She let him lead her through the slender mouth and down a long flight of cement stairs that gritted and scuffed under their feet. The temperature dropped as they got farther down, the air thickening with rot and smoke and something else, the pungent scent of cooking Dream.

They'd gone only half a block or so when the source of the odor presented itself. The needle lay on the dank pavement, its owner draped against the wall with his eyes half closed. By his bent leg rested the rubber catheter, the dented and oxidized spoon.

Lex nudged the crumpled form with the toe of his boot. "Ain't supposed to be down here, Big Shog. You know these tunnels ain't for shooting."

Big Shog mumbled something and shifted position. His mouth hung open, dried spittle caked white in the corners. Chess looked away.

"What are these tunnels, anyway? I've never heard about them."

Lex gave Big Shog one last glance, then started walking again. "They been here years. Since BT. The Church blocked them off, don't want nobody sneaking around. *You* know."

"When did you open them back up?"

He thought for a moment. They were farther down now, the ground sloping gently. Every thirty feet or so a weak fluorescent bulb in a metal frame fizzed at them from the ceiling. It made the whole experience even more unreal to Chess. She was actually walking underground on purpose, in a cold, dank cement tube that stunk of mold and offered no protection against anything. It was hard to remember the walls were banded with iron when it felt as if they were closing in on her, as if they could swallow her and turn her into another rust stain on their gritty faces.

"Three years past, four? Convenient. Nobody see where you heading, nobody know where you are."

"Do they go all the way under the city? I mean, everywhere?"

"Now you asking for secrets. Secrets you don't need."

Unless she wanted to find out how someone could have disappeared from Chester Airport so quickly the other night. "I just wondered. Curiosity. Maybe I'd need to come talk to you, sometime."

"You need to talk, you call." He paused. "Lessin you want to give me a secret, I tell you what I know." The gleam in his eye was definitely not related to the airport; in spite of herself, a little trickle of excitement worked its way up her spine. He was, after all, just her type: handsome, arrogant, and totally self-centered, as bad for her as her Cepts and just as appealing.

"Forget it."

"Your choice, tulip." He kept walking, forcing her to catch up. He may not have been the safest company in the world, but their footsteps echoed in the small space and she was overly conscious of how far underground they were.

The tunnel split into three separate shafts. Lex took the right-hand one, not breaking stride as he turned.

"How do you know where you're going?"

He started to whistle. Right.

They made another turn, a left this time. It was like a rabbit warren, but spookier. Her neck started to ache with tension. "How long are we going to be down here?"

"Until we get where we're going."

"That's not very helpful."

"I ain't a helpful guy."

She rolled her eyes. At least he'd stopped whistling.

Maybe that wasn't such a good thing. As the sound of their feet grew muffled by moss and slime covering the ground, Chess became aware of another noise. A low humming sound, burbling like distant laughter.

"What's that noise?"

He stopped. "You want to chat, or you want to get you home?"

"I want to go home. But . . . hold on." Her fingers closed around the hard muscle of his left arm as he started to turn away. "Is that a normal sound down here?"

"I don't hear nothing."

"That gurgling noise, like somebody talking."

It was louder now, as though whoever was making it was getting closer. Her skin prickled.

"Sorry. Not hearing it." He turned again, took a couple of steps. The next bulb they would pass under was burned out, casting that section into blackness.

"Damn it, will you stop a minute? Just listen. How do you not hear that?"

He shifted on his feet, his gaze in the dim light shifting up and down the tunnel.

"Well?"

"You said be quiet, so I'm being quiet."

"But do you hear anything?"

"I hear you."

"No, that's not—"

The rattle broke into her speech, the spine-crackling sound of dead vocal chords trying to live again.

Chess turned, her heart pounding an alarm in her chest, and saw the ghost staring right at her.

Chapter Nine

At first all she could see were his eyes, burning black holes in the pallor of his hard face. More details slid into view as she stood, frozen, unable to think of anything but the fact that her workbag was still in her apartment. She had no salt or bones, no herbs, no Ectoplasmarker, no way to protect herself or summon a psychopomp.

And the farther underground one went, the more powerful the ghosts became.

On top of his head sat a peaked cap of some kind, sepia tinged as though it had been brown in life. It matched his jacket and the suggestion of baggy trousers below his belt before his feet faded into nothing.

Lex, to his credit, stood rock still next to her. He barely seemed to be breathing.

"I thought you said the walls here were banded with iron," she muttered.

"I lied."

Great. Chess turned to the ghost, holding her hands palm up, hoping he would read innocence and helplessness from the gesture.

"We're just passing through," she said carefully. "We're not trying to disturb you."

It didn't work. The ghost shrunk, his features twisting

into a furious grimace, like a lion preparing to pounce. Chess spun away, grabbing Lex's arm.

"Get us out of here! Get us out of here now!"

The filth on the floor sucked at her feet as they ran into the darkness. Behind them she felt the ghost, felt the freezing cold of its spectral body almost touching her back. They couldn't get away, there was no way to escape it. Ghosts didn't get tired. They didn't give up.

The bulb ahead of them flashed, blinding her, before exploding in a shower of powdery glass. Chess ducked her head and yanked up the bottom of her T-shirt to cover her face.

Her left foot slipped sideways. She kept running, taking long, awkward steps in an attempt to keep her balance. Lex's fingers bit into her skin as he grabbed her, dragging her along like a reluctant toddler.

She didn't know what made her fall, if it was simply that she could not regain her stride or if the ghost somehow managed to hit her with something. Aboveground they couldn't attack humans without using a weapon. Below, all the rules changed.

Filthy water filled her nose and stung her eyes. It tasted like sewage and iron. She gagged, trying to raise herself back up, but something forced her head back down.

Her fingers curled into sludge as she tried to grab hold of something, anything, to help her. Filth oozed through the bandage on her palm and soaked her wound. In the chaos of the tunnel her heartbeat seemed unnaturally loud, only drowned out when the roar of a gunshot made the floor beneath her vibrate.

She thought her eardrums were going to explode. The sound didn't stop, reverberating through the confined steel-and-concrete space for what felt like hours, while she struggled beneath the weight on her back.

Gathering all of her remaining strength, she managed to shift her body sideways, lifting her face out of the foul wet slime. Air rasped into her throat to fill her lungs. A very dim light still shone, enough for her to see Lex backed against the wall, aiming for another shot.

"No! Put it away!" It was meant to be a scream. It came out more as a gurgle.

Metal glinted above her head as the ghost raised his hands. In them he clutched the end of a piece of pipe from the ceiling. If he touched her with it, she was dead. Even from her position on the floor she could see the wires sparking inside it.

Time froze. Chess watched the pipe start its descent, watched a single glint of light erupt from the end of it and die. Her fingers found a seam in the wall and gripped it, so hard she felt each individual piece of grit in the cement as she struggled to pull herself out from beneath the ghost's legs.

Lex stepped forward, his heavy industrial boot catching the pipe and trapping it between the wall and the rubber sole. The ghost turned to him, its face contorted in fury.

Chess scrambled out of the way as Lex fell backward. The ghost lifted the pipe again, aiming for him. He ducked. Metal rang against cement.

"Break the pipe!" she shouted, hoping Lex would understand as the ghost turned on her.

Lex did. Out of the corner of her eye she saw him leap up and hook the length still attached to the ceiling with his bent arm, using his leather jacket as insulation. For a moment he hung in the air, his legs spread like a professional basketball player making a slam dunk, before the brackets holding the pipe creaked and snapped and they were plunged into blackness.

"Get out the water," he gasped. Something scraped behind her as she braced her feet against the very edges of the floor.

It only took a second, but it felt like forever that she

stayed there, shivering and covered in filth, listening to Lex's heavy breathing in the dark.

Then light exploded through the tunnel as the live wires hit the sludgy mess covering the walkway.

Like a photo negative Chess saw Lex's tall, slim form outlined in blinding blue-white, saw the ghost contort and disappear. She squeezed her eyes shut as tightly as she could but still she saw it, still she heard the shrieking hiss as thousands of volts poured through the tunnel.

A final explosion, somewhere in the distance, and it was over. She didn't realize she was crying until she tasted salt on her lips.

"You right, tulip?"

He could have been anywhere. Right beside her, or fifteen feet away. She started to nod before she realized he couldn't see her, either.

"I'm fine."

His hand brushed her arm. "Didn't know electricals killed the kickers."

"They don't. I mean, it doesn't work that way. It was probably an energy overload. Shorts them out, same as the lights." It would also get her shoved into a cell for a few months if anyone from the Church ever found out about it. Spectral abuse was a pretty serious issue, ever since some descendants found out a Debunker purposely summoned a spirit wolf instead of a dog and it savaged the ghost. The descendants sued and won.

Metal clicked against metal, and the tunnel filled with a soft yellowish glow. Lex held the lighter up near his head. "More light a few turns away. Let's us move, aye?"

"Is the ground safe?"

"Safe enough. Transformer blew, I'm guessing." He stomped his feet in the sludge. "No volts here."

Not quite as brave as he, Chess stepped gingerly into the center of the path. "Okay, then. Can we get out of here now?"

He laughed softly. "Whatever you say, tulip, whatever you say."

Half an hour under the hot water in her own bathroom was just about enough to get the stink of sewer out of her nose. Funny how the tunnel itself hadn't smelled so bad, but that mess at the bottom . . . urgh. Her hand stung from the water and the gallon of disinfectant she'd soaked it in.

The only thing the shower didn't help was knowing what she had to do next. Terrible's note had not been eloquent, but it had been clear. He didn't appreciate being stood up when they were supposed to go back to Chester that afternoon, and she couldn't blame him.

She popped another Cept on her way out the door, preparing to be yelled at. He hadn't said on the note where he would be, but the Dusters were playing at Chuck's on Fiftieth, and she bet she'd find him there. The Mortons would have to wait. They wouldn't break down her door or cause her severe physical pain if she failed to break into their home tonight without their knowledge. Terrible might do one or both of those things if she didn't make an appearance immediately.

Donning clean jeans, a semisheer black top, and a pair of high-heeled boots, she tucked her knife—returned to her by Lex when he let her out of the tunnel six blocks from her house—a twenty, and her keys into her pocket and headed out.

Two steps down the hall she turned back and grabbed a small bag of asafetida, too. It had been stupid to go out without it the night before. She wouldn't make that mistake again.

Of course, it had been stupid to trust a word Lex said and go into the tunnel to begin with. It had been stupid to sort of agree to this. Hell, pretty much everything she'd done in the last few days had been stupid.

Nothing she could do to change it now. Surely some way to keep two drug dealers and their various minions in the dark about her activities, while pretending to one that she couldn't Banish Chester's ghosts, would come to her. Probably in the car. Most of her best ideas came to her in the car.

Her heels clicked pleasantly on the pavement as she rounded the corner of Fiftieth and Ace. The usual suspects dotted the street, shoulders hunched against the mild November chill—rockabilly punks like Terrible with their greased DA's and bowling shirts, a few old-school kids like Lex with spiked hair and padlocks around their necks, even some lounge boys in sharkskin jackets and creepers. Most of the girls dressed like Chess. Punks were like birds. The men got to decorate more than the women, as a rule.

The Dusters hadn't started playing yet, so everyone was outside drinking from paper bags. Chess bummed a smoke off a retro skater kid—complete with a ragged Lance Mountain T-shirt she imagined would fall apart if he tried to wash it—and crossed her arms, scanning the crowd for Terrible. Might as well get it over with.

He didn't seem to be there. Most of the faces were familiar, but his wasn't one of them. She circled the crowd, frowning. If he wasn't there she'd have to go to Bump's, and she'd rather see the show.

A couple made out against the gritty stucco wall on the side of the club. Chess watched them for a second, embarrassed to do so but unable to turn away, something quiet and small twisting in her chest.

The girl was a little thing, platinum blond, in a mini-skirt and a pair of platform heels that looked like they weighed more than her entire body. Her thin legs crossed at the ankle behind the guy's waist, while her tiny, pale hands dug into his back. Chess couldn't see her face; it was almost entirely hidden by the guy's hands, cupping her cheeks like he thought the bones might break. Chess didn't think she'd ever been touched like that. A pang of pure envy ran through her.

The girl caressed the back of his neck and lifted her hands to twine her fingers in his hair. His hips pressed forward, pinning her against the wall, and he dipped his head to kiss her throat. The light caught the prominent ridge of his brow and the crooked bump of his nose.

It was Terrible.

Heat rushed to her face. Yes, definitely Terrible. No wonder he'd blushed when she teased him about his side-burns. She'd never even thought of him as actually being interested in women. He seemed totally asexual to her, like instead of fucking he preferred beating people up. A silly assumption. He was a man, after all.

But then, she herself generally preferred drugs to fucking. In an ideal world she'd take both. So why expect he might not?

Taking a furious drag off her cigarette she turned away, intending to lose herself in the crowd until he was available for talking, but her heel caught a crack in the pavement and her slightly sore left ankle twisted. She didn't fall, but the scrape of her shoe on cement and the tiny yelp she couldn't keep inside was bad enough.

Heads turned. Including Terrible's. "Chess. Where you been, girl? I waited outside your place hours, you never show."

The little blonde gave Chess a look of smug venom. Bitch. If she pressed any closer to Terrible's side she'd start to sink into him like some sort of lusty Siamese twin.

"I got stuck at work," she managed. "Sorry. I didn't have your cell number or anything, so . . ."

"Aye, okay. Remind me, I give you the digits." He nodded toward the line forming at the door. The band must be getting ready to play. "You coming in?"

"Um, yeah. Thought I might, you know. Get a drink."

If she'd ever pictured herself feeling awkward around Terrible, it was because she imagined him getting ready to break one of her bones. Not because she'd just caught him practically having sex against a building. She didn't *care* that he'd been practically having sex up against a building, it wasn't as though *she* wanted to be the one against the building with him or anything. It was just . . . strange. Like imagining one of the Elders getting it on with a Goody in the chapel.

He introduced her to the girl—Amy—and they shuffled their feet for another minute or so before heading up to the doors. Terrible never paid to get into anywhere, by virtue of who he was. Chess never paid either, by virtue of her tattoos.

Inside the club sweaty bodies crushed together under the reddish glow of the neon Exit signs and the filters on the stagelights like a torch mob out for blood. Chess tried to make her way to the bar but gave up after having her toes stepped on three times. Great. Her hand still ached, her ankle was weak, her toes crushed.

Getting through a crowd wasn't a problem for Terrible. He shoved his way through like a plow through snow, and after the first few seconds people realized who he was and moved out of his way before he reached them. He parked both Chess and Amy in one of the booths at the far end and left to get drinks. He didn't ask what they wanted. Beer was the only option.

"Chess. Hey. I thought you might be here."

The words, practically shouted into her right ear, made her jump. Her discomfort did not ease when she realized who'd spoken them.

"What are you doing here, Doyle?"

"I like this band."

"I've never seen you at one of their shows before."

"That doesn't mean I've never been to one."

"They only play in Downside, as far as I know. Since when do you come here?"

She had to admit, he looked almost as if he belonged there. He was dressed in de rigueur black, from boots to jeans to thin car jacket. With his hair shining around his pale face his eyes seemed to leap out of their sockets at her.

"I come here sometimes. I thought maybe we could hang out."

"You thought wrong."

Terrible appeared, beer bottles dangling from his enormous hands. He didn't speak, just stood like a tree next to Chess, staring at Doyle with one eyebrow raised.

Doyle offered his hand. "Hi."

Terrible didn't move. Doyle stood for a minute with his hand out before sticking it back in his pocket. Even the red lights couldn't hide the color creeping up his face.

Terrible handed her a beer. "Cool, Chess?"

Was her body language that easy to read? "Yeah, fine."

"I need to talk to you," Doyle said. He smoothed his hair out of his face. "It's important."

He clearly didn't intend to leave until they'd spoken, so Chess sighed and stood up. "Five minutes."

Chapter Ten

[
"There is much humanity cannot comprehend. The Church comprehends for you."
—*The Book of Truth*, Veraxis, Article 2
]

Doyle pulled her uncomfortably close to the spot where she'd seen Terrible and Amy, hidden in the shadows of the building. "So, how's your new case going?"

"You dragged me out here for that?"

"You wouldn't talk to me in church. You wouldn't talk to me at the meeting. What else am I supposed to do?"

"Get the message that I don't want to talk?"

"Chess . . . you can't seriously be avoiding me because some people found out about us. So what? What difference does it make?"

She took a step back as he leaned closer. "There is no *us*, Doyle. One night doesn't make an *us*."

"It makes something."

"Yeah, it makes me a whore in the eyes of everyone I work with. What happens if the Elders find out? What do I do then?"

"You're not underage anymore, you haven't been for three years. They're not going to kick you out." His hands rested on her shoulders, warm and heavy. "I know you had it rougher than the rest of us did in training. I know how you were scrutinized because you were on charity. I was there, remember? But you're an employee now, not a ward. You even live off-complex. You can spend the night with whomever you choose."

"I wasn't on charity. I was on a scholarship."

"Sorry. Point is . . . I really like you. I think we could have something special, if you'd let us."

His fingers curled under her chin, lifting her face. Doyle was only five-ten or so; with her heels on they were almost of a height. She didn't have to move at all for his lips to find hers.

He was a good kisser. She'd liked kissing him before, and she still liked it, despite her doubts about him. But when his hands slid farther down to circle her waist, then down again to cup her bottom and pull her closer, she broke away.

"I don't think I'm ready for this." Her voice shook a little. Damn it.

Doyle bit his lip and looked down, then back up. "Okay."

"What do you mean, okay?"

"Just what I said. Okay. I can't pretend to understand it. It's not like we haven't already done a lot more than we just did. But I want to do this right, and if that means waiting, or giving you space or whatever, I'll do that."

He certainly looked sincere, with those big blue eyes focused right on her. Maybe this really was *her* problem. It didn't make logical sense to distrust Doyle. She'd known him for years. If she were honest with herself, she could admit she'd had a bit of a crush on him, off and on throughout those years. And the sex . . . it may not have been life-changing, but it definitely hadn't sucked.

He must have sensed her indecision. "Why don't we go back to your place and talk, okay? Have a drink, watch some TV or something and just . . . talk?"

No was on the tip of her tongue, but she caught herself. What else was she going to do? Sit in a booth and watch

Terrible and Amy practically having sex? Take another Cept and watch everyone else chatting with their friends, having a good time, from behind the glassy wall of narcotic peace?

Or go home, and wander around her apartment by herself until she finally fell asleep in front of the TV?

Doyle was decent company, if nothing else. They had plenty to talk about. They knew the same people.

"Come on, Chess. I promise I won't try anything. It'll be like having a eunuch over for the evening."

Chess laughed in spite of herself. "Okay. But no late night. I'm tired."

It was the wrong thing to do. She didn't want him here.

Chatting about Church politics and telling stories had been fine on the street, when the soft darkness wrapped around them and their feet moved along the pavement in unison. But in her apartment . . . he seemed too big for the space somehow. Like an invader. His restless gaze traveled over every item in the room, not picking out any one thing, but like he was trying to read her belongings and figure out the best angle to get her back into bed.

Chess pulled a couple of beers from the barren fridge and handed him one, glad for something to do with her hands. She perched on the edge of the couch with her feet on the cushion, her legs a barrier between them.

"What did you do to your hand?"

For Truth's sake, was everybody going to ask her that? "Cut it on a can."

"Did you go to the hospital?"

"No."

"Let me see." He held out his own hand, waiting for her to place hers in it. This she did, although she could certainly think of better topics of conversation than her injury.

He unwrapped the gauze. "Damn, Chess. That looks like it's getting infected."

Did it? She supposed so. The red line curving across her palm looked wider than it had the night before, the skin around it shiny and puffy. She tried to close her fingers over it. "It's fine."

"It probably needed stitches. Did you clean it?" He didn't let go, clasping her wrist tight in his warm fingers.

"Of course I cleaned it. I'm not an idiot."

"Why don't you let me try?"

She yanked her hand back. "I'm perfectly capable of cleaning myself, Doyle."

"You had it wrapped too tightly, and it looks like there's a few speckles of dirt or something on the edge. I'm serious, Chess. Let me do this for you. Go get all your supplies and stuff. Cotton balls and bandages and ointments. And get me a knife or something, too."

"Oh, no. No knives."

"It's healing over the infection."

"Why don't I just go to the hospital tomorrow?"

He folded his arms across his chest. "My dad is a doctor, and I watched him help my friends dozens of times. Go get the stuff."

Her palm felt stiff when she flipped the light switch in her bathroom. Maybe Doyle was right. Maybe it was even sort of nice, to have someone take care of her. No one ever had before. She should stop being so cranky and suspicious, and relax. Isn't this what normal people did, help one another?

She laid a towel over the toilet lid and started gathering all of her medical supplies. Debunkers often found themselves in attics and crawl spaces, or climbing through airshafts. Injuries were common. A few years ago Atticus Collins even got bit by a rat.

Odd, then, that this cut got infected, when she usually took such good care of her wounds. But then, being locked in a dungeon for almost twenty-four hours and being bathed in raw sewage wasn't exactly conducive to healing.

Her knives were in the kitchen, but she decided to grab a razor blade instead. The sharper the edge, the less it would hurt. She ran the flats of the blade over her tongue, just to make sure there wasn't any residue left on it. There was. The muscles in her cheeks tightened.

Finally she guessed she had everything. Antiseptic, cotton balls, gauze, antibiotic ointment, the razor blade, a straightpin. She chomped another Cept—this was probably going to hurt—and headed back out into the living room, carrying the little towel bundle in her left hand.

Doyle knelt on the floor in front of the bookcase, flipping through her copy of *On the Road*. "You have a lot of stuff from BT," he said. "I didn't know you were into that."

"I like history. I like to read."

"But this is, like, all BT."

"It just interests me. It's not a big deal or anything, they're not forbidden books. They're great literature."

"I know, I just . . . you seem so live-for-the-moment." He placed the book back in its slot on the shelf. "I always thought of you as someone who didn't have a past, so wasn't interested in the past."

"So because I'm an orphan and don't know my ancestry I'm not allowed to read?"

"No, no, I . . . It's cool, that's all. I think it's cool."

She thought about pressing the point, but decided against it. Someone who could trace his family back two hundred years wouldn't be able to understand how it felt when even your real name was a mystery, and she didn't particularly want to explain anyway. He'd already seen her naked. He didn't need to see her emotionally exposed as well.

So she held up the towel. "I have everything."

"Actually, I was thinking we probably should do this in the bathroom. Better light, right?"

Whatever. His show. They trooped back into the bathroom, where she sat on the toilet and held her hand over the sink.

He did know what he was doing. His fingers were quick and sure but gentle as he cleaned her palm with antiseptic and cotton balls, then picked up the razor blade and wiped it, too.

"Okay, get ready."

"I'm ready." Chess sat up straighter. She trusted him, sure, but if he was messing around with a razor blade on her skin, she wanted to supervise.

He slid the blade along the very edge of the wound, drawing a thin line of blood from her flushed palm. Halfway down the color paled as clear fluid oozed out.

"Yuck," she said.

"Yeah, it is kind of, isn't it?" He flashed her a quick smile. "But at least it's coming out, right? Imagine if it just built up under the skin and went nec . . ."

"Necrotic? Would that really happen?"

"Do you have tweezers?" He sounded strangled, like he'd just seen something that frightened him.

"On the shelf. What's wrong?"

"Nothing."

"No, clearly something is. What is it?"

His grip on her hand tightened as he grabbed the tweezers. "Don't move."

"What's—ow! Fuck! What are you . . ."

The words died in her throat as he lifted the tweezers from the wound. Caught between the sharp metal pincers was a small, fat worm.

Chess had to fight not to throw up as it wriggled and twisted like a fish out of water. Blood—her blood—dripped from its obscene tubular body. Even as she watched it shriveled, balling itself up like a creature in agony.

Doyle opened the tweezers. The worm fell into the sink, unmoving.

"Doyle, what is that? What the fuck is that?" Her voice rose to almost a squeal at the end, unnaturally high and loud in the small room.

"I . . . I don't know. Shit, Chess. Hold still."

"Is it a . . ." She swallowed. "A maggot?"

"I don't think so."

He pulled four more of them from the wound before they were done.

Chapter Eleven

"Chess, baby. Guess Terrible don't kill you after all." Edsel smiled and leaned back in his rickety chair. Weak sunlight glinted off the silver talismans and tokens dangling from a rack in the corner of his booth and cast bright spots on the tattered burgundy curtains behind him. The city clock hadn't even chimed noon yet, and Edsel's booth was still in disarray.

"You sound disappointed."

"Ain't never disappointed seeing you, you know that. What you need today? You try that Hand yet? I gots some new sleep potions, you interested."

"Sleep potions?"

He shrugged. "Lookin tired, baby."

Damn it. She should have bumped up before she left the house.

After Doyle finally left the night before, she'd tossed and turned for hours. She didn't imagine many people would be able to slide between the sheets with a blissful smile after watching bloody worms being yanked from their flesh.

That image—and several other ones even more unpleasant—chased her into her sleep, and she'd finally climbed out of bed just past dawn.

"I'm fine," she said. "I was actually hoping you might be able to help me with something else."

"Like what?"

She dug into her bag and pulled out the amulet, wrapped in a scrap of black velvet so she wouldn't have to touch the metal. Even holding it through the cloth made her skin crawl.

"You recognize any of these markings?" She set it down on the rickety countertop and unfolded the velvet.

"Where this came from?"

Chess shrugged. "Found it."

"Ah-huh." Edsel leaned closer to it, but made no move to pick it up. "Look to me like you best take it back you found it. Don't see no positive in that thing, baby. I feel it vibin at me from here."

"I can't take it back. It's . . . it's part of an investigation. None of the marks look familiar?"

"Can't say they does, but . . . on the minute. That there look like *Etosh*. And two down from that, could be *Tretso*."

"What do they mean?"

"*Tretso* a bastard rune, you get me? A combination of two. Intensifies other runes, adds power, but say nothing on its own. *Etosh* . . . it *feeds*. Directs *Tretso* to where the amulet maker want it to go."

"So I have two runes here calculated to add power to the others, but we don't know what any of the others are."

"Sorry I ain't better help." Edsel glanced at the amulet again, his lip twisted in distaste. "Don't guess nobody could help with that thing, if the Church can't."

They might be able to, if she could ask them. But she couldn't. What was she supposed to do, walk into the Grand Elder's office and tell him she'd found it on the street? Something like this?

She nodded. Her fingers moved slowly, sluggishly, as

she covered the amulet in velvet once again. "Thanks anyway, Edsel."

"Your hand right?"

She nodded. The cut on her palm did look less ugly this morning, but she didn't think she'd feel comfortable until it was healed completely. Worms . . . her nose wrinkled. "Just a scratch."

"Cool. You know . . . now I think on it, could be I know somebody help you with them runes. Name of Tyson, you know him?"

She shook her head. "Is he here?"

"Naw, not here. Don't live in Downside, not even in the city. Old-timer, aye? Got himself a place outside town, by the water. Don't know how to get in touch with him, though. He come by sometimes. Not stupid, Tyson. He come again, I give him your number?"

"You know if Tyson's his first or last name?"

"Only know Tyson. He never say nothing else."

Chess slipped the velvet-covered amulet back in her bag and zipped it up. "Yeah, give him my number if you see him, Edsel. Thanks."

"No problem. Keep it clean, baby." He turned away and started unpacking boxes, preparing for the day's customers, while Chess wandered off through the Market. Terrible was going to show up soon to take her back to Chester today, to hunt for electrical equipment she'd have to pretend not to see or ghosts she'd have to pretend not to be able to Banish.

She stopped and bought a bowl of noodles from a permanent booth not far from Bump's place, and slurped them with chopsticks as she loitered outside the doors. The couches downstairs would be full if she made her way down. They always were on Mondays, no matter what time the day or night. She had ten dollars in her pocket—enough for a long afternoon of soft dreams.

A long afternoon she couldn't have, and as if to confirm

that, heavy footsteps sounded behind her and she turned
to see Terrible advancing like a tank.

Chester Airport in the sunlight lost none of the feeling
of abandoned threat it held at night. The rickety old terminal huddled off to the left like a lonely widower, and
the rusty fences looked ready to blow away.

Chess tried and failed to keep from seeking out the
spot where she'd found the amulet. What ritual had
taken place here, in the dusty grass?

She didn't think she really wanted to know. She also
didn't think she would be able to avoid finding out.

"You wanna check the building again?" Terrible asked
as he held open the tear in the fence for her.

"I guess. Don't think we missed anything the other
night, though." Chess glanced over at the right perimeter
of the field. "Hold on, what's that?"

Terrible followed her gaze, but said nothing.

She wasn't sure how she'd managed to catch it, hidden
as it was by the tall grass as it was, but as she got closer
she saw she wasn't mistaken.

The stones formed a rough, loose rectangle, about fifty
feet long and thirty wide. Large sections had disappeared
entirely, so that only someone carefully looking would
have known they formed a shape at all and weren't just
piles of rocks. Without the specific angle of the sun she
doubted she would have noticed it at all.

"Another building," she said. "I wonder what it was."

"Supplies, could be. Even sleeping quarters. Barracks."

She glanced up at him. "Barracks?"

"Aye, you know. No hotels round here. Pilots they come
in, they ain't leaving till morning, needs to sleep."

She stood back up and looked at him. His impassive
face was turned away, studying the buildings just outside
the fence. Black sunglasses hid his eyes.

"That's a good idea, Terrible. You're probably right."

Again, no reaction. Chess paced along the remains of the walls, moving stones that looked light or loose enough for her to shift. Anywhere in this rubble would be an ideal place to hide the sort of equipment hoaxers would need, and with Terrible's attention elsewhere she could cover it back up—if she needed to, if it existed and the ghosts here weren't real.

If he caught her . . . She didn't even want to think about that. She hadn't heard from Lex since he'd dropped her off, and she wasn't sure she wanted to. It was so tempting to pretend she'd imagined the whole thing. Too bad she hadn't, and she knew it.

The stones yielded nothing, though, so she left a tiny motion-sensor video camera in the pile closest to the runway and they headed back toward the main terminal building. Chess glanced back, wondering what else hid in the jungle of stiff brownish grass, what nestled in the ground just outside the field. They'd have to search there, too.

Houses crouched close to the fence, as though they'd been shoved out of the way when it was put up. Duplexes, mostly. Over one door smears of blood remained from the Festival; the residents hadn't bothered to wipe it off when it was no longer needed. Probably figured the rain would get it eventually, and they were probably right. November was usually much rainier than it had been the last week or two.

Someone must have had a window open; the soft strains of a Willie Nelson song drifted toward them like a whisper.

Here and there pitted slides and rusty tricycles dotted the badly tended lawns. Chess could practically feel the cracked plastic of the aged toys beneath her. How many children in these homes were living lives like hers had been, right that moment? Being used as a source of income, and none of that money shared with them?

The buildings sat at odd angles to one another, adding to the air of something seedy and off about the street. One butted right up against the fence, with barely any yard. The next stood a good thirty feet off. "Do you know why the houses are crooked like that?"

Terrible shook his head. "Always been that way, my guess. It matter?"

"Just curious."

Sunlight shafted into the wreckage of the terminal building. "I guess we can try hunting through this mess again." She scanned the ceiling. It was clean, or rather, nothing but cobwebs lurked in the shadows.

They rustled through the garbage again, neither of them wanting to use their hands. This was a waste of time, and she knew it. Something very well could have been planted at Chester, but it wasn't in here.

"That dude last night, he yours?"

"Huh?"

"Mr. Clean you left the show with."

"Doyle? No. Just a guy I work with. How was the show, anyway?"

Terrible grinned. "Dusters always put on a good one."

"I wish I'd stayed."

He lifted his chin in a half-nod. "Missed out, you did."

She rounded the remains of the desk and crouched down. A few drawers remained intact, near the top. Chess steeled herself to open them. Mice liked to nest in places like this, mice and rats and spiders, none of which she enjoyed encountering.

"Amy seems nice," she lied, looking for something to say as she slid open the top drawer.

"She aright."

"Been seeing her long?"

He shrugged.

The drawer was empty. Chess opened the others, finding nothing but dust and dead bugs. Their dry carcasses reminded her horribly of the worms in her hand, and she shut the drawers harder than she'd planned. The last one cracked under the strain and her fist almost went through it.

"Okay, well, I don't see anything in here, so let's look outside, okay?"

"Your show."

The air outside seemed sweet after the dry rot of the terminal. Her nose itched as she handed him another little camera and told him how to attach it to the outside of the building, just under the roof. He didn't need a ladder to do it.

A few feet from the spot where he'd broken the wall to pull her out the other night was an old well and pump. *Shit.* "Um . . . you didn't happen to bring any rope, did you?"

"How much?"

"Enough to lower me down that well so I can see if there's anything down there."

"Like electrics and all?"

She nodded.

"Damn, Chess, you really wanna go down there?"

"Afraid you won't be strong enough to keep me from falling?"

His teeth showed in a grin. "Shit. You must joke."

"Of course I'm joking. Do you have rope or not?"

"Could be I do. Wait here."

He headed off back toward his car, while Chess poked around in the grass some more, always ready for that awful coldness to start creeping up her legs again. At night Chester was like a black hole in the city, devoid of life. Who's to say more rituals hadn't taken place out here? Anywhere you found empty spaces you found illegal witchcraft. People did their legitimate rituals at home— money charms, luck spells, easy things that didn't require power or talent. And the Church encouraged it, because when people saw the results of their insignificant spells, their tiny manipulations of energy, it reinforced the Church's Truth; gods did not exist. Magic did. And the Church was the gateway to magic.

Terrible returned in a few minutes, holding a thick roll of fibrous tan rope over his shoulder, which he uncoiled and laid on the ground.

"This long enough?"

"I guess we'll find out, won't we?"

Grateful that she'd worn long sleeves, she wrapped the rope under her armpits just above her breasts and tied it in a secure knot. The rope was flecked with brownish stains in spots. She didn't want to think about what it had been used for last, or, for that matter, why Terrible carried rope around in his trunk. His work was his business.

Finally she had the knot adjusted. From her bag she pulled her flashlight, and switched it on while Terrible wrapped the free end of the rope around his hands. The leads of her electric meter dangled from her pocket.

"Okay. If I get too heavy, pull me up—"

"You don't weigh nothing," he scoffed.

"Okay, I don't weigh nothing, but nothing can get a lot heavier when it's dangling at the end of a thin rope. Please, Terrible. I really don't want to fall, so if you think I'm getting too heavy, let me know and bring me back up, okay?"

He nodded.

"And please watch the rope, in case it starts to fray or something."

He raised an eyebrow.

"Just . . . please?" The mouth of the well gaped in the ground beside her like an entryway to Hell. Hell didn't technically exist, but the City did, and Chess did not want to be underground again. Not after what happened the day before, not ever. Panic rose in her chest and she focused her gaze on Terrible, taking what comfort she could from his steady gaze and bulging muscles, from the way the rope tangled around his big hard hands.

He nodded. "No worryin."

She sighed. "Okay, then. Thanks. Let's see what I find."

She crouched down at the lip of the well and let her legs slip down inside it. If praying were permitted, she'd certainly be doing it now.

Chapter Twelve

"That of all magics which can be done, the use of the human soul in magic is the most serious, and is thus forbidden save to those of the Church."

—*The Book of Truth*, Laws, Article 79

The ground swallowed her, leaving her dangling in the coppery-scented dimness until she grabbed her flashlight and tilted it so it illuminated the stones. The meter in her pocket remained still, no vibrations. No obvious holes jumped out at her, no hiding places seemed immediately apparent. She hadn't really expected there would be, but she had to look. Even if she would pretend she didn't see any equipment she found—at least, any equipment that wouldn't be easily visible. For all she knew, Bump had someone else checking her work. Not a pleasant thought.

"Lower," she said, and Terrible obliged, letting out more rope.

The well smelled of water, but when she turned the light down nothing reflected back up at her. It was dry . . . but very, very deep. There was no way she'd be able to investigate all the way down.

Her right hand slid over the stones, looking for loose ones, while her left aimed the light. The rope hurt and made it hard to breathe, adding to her growing sense of discomfort.

She stayed down for about twenty minutes, dropping as far as the rope allowed, before asking Terrible to bring her back up.

"Nothing," she said, untying the rope and resisting the urge to massage her aching chest. "Is that the only well here?"

"Naw, got another over there." He pointed to the far corner. Shit. She should have left the rope on.

They trudged across the empty brownish expanse of weeds and pavement, two figures in black like smears on a painting. Chess started to feel sticky and damp from the unseasonable heat, and vulnerable in the middle of the field.

"You do this many?"

"What?" She almost stumbled on a loose chunk of cement.

"This things. Down the wells, up in the attics . . . ?"

"Sometimes. Not usually underground, no."

"Right. Churchwitches ain't like the downs."

"Right."

"So best place for hiding, aye? Where nobody wanna go."

"Most people are nervous about going underground. Nobody likes to be too close to the City."

His head tilted. "They scared. Not you, though."

Nobody had ever called her brave before. Her face grew warmer than it was already. "I don't like doing it. It's disrespectful."

"Why do it?"

"I have to search everywhere."

"Naw, I mean, why do the job? You dig the ghosts?"

She shrugged. "Pays the bills."

"Lots of things pays the bills."

"So why do you work for Bump?"

She'd expected a flip answer like the one she'd given him. Instead he said, "Only thing I'm ever good at."

"What, beating people up?"

He nodded. "I got no school, you know. No family. Bump took me in, I just a kid. Getting in street fights for food, sleeping any flat wheres I could find. Now I don't have to fight. Nobody wanna dance with me." Faint pride colored his voice as he spoke the last sentence.

Most of this she knew, or at least suspected. It certainly wasn't an unusual story in Downside, where as many stray children roamed the streets as dogs and cats. There but for the grace of a god who never existed and a talent she never asked for . . .

"What happened to your family?"

"Don't know. Never knew them."

She nodded. She'd never known hers either.

"But why you do what you do? Work for the Church? Creepy in there, all them blue pilgrims with black eyes and buckle shoes."

"Same as you. I'm good at it."

"Sure hope so."

"Hey!"

They'd almost reached the far end by now. Terrible stopped. "Naw, don't mean no insult." His head moved back and forth as he scanned the field. "Hopin this gets solved, we fly them planes in. Make use out this place, aye? Watch em take off, come in low to land. Be cool."

"You like planes?"

But Terrible had apparently decided sharing time was over. He turned and crossed the last fifteen feet or so until he reached the lip of the well, sunken into the barren earth, and looked at her.

Chess couldn't figure out why they'd had the conversation to begin with, unless Bump had ordered it. He was almost garrulous for a few minutes there. She wiped her forehead with her sleeve and caught up with him.

"You tie back on," he said, bending down. A heavy disc of rust-crusted iron covered the mouth of the well. Terrible pulled a crowbar from his bag and fit the flat end into the barely visible gap between metal and cement. "Best clear out the way."

Chess took a few obedient steps back before he tilted the crowbar and grabbed the edge of the disc with his hand. One quick heave and the disc lay in the scorched grass.

"Oh, shit." He took a few steps back, covering his face with his palm, then grabbing the bottom of his shirt and using it instead. It only took a second for the smell to reach Chess, too. Her stomach heaved as she jumped to the side, trying to get upwind.

Decay and rot and putrefaction. She knew what the smell was without having to be told, without ever having smelled it before. Something had died down there, maybe animals or . . .

The well had been covered, though. How could an animal get down there? How could anything get down there, unless someone had deliberately put it there?

"Hand me over the light." Terrible held his hand out, palm up. His other hand still clutched the fabric over his nose and mouth. In the otherwise unrelieved black of his outfit the strip of white undershirt it exposed looked like a flag of surrender.

Chess fumbled for the flashlight and gave it to him, her face averted. If it was an animal down there . . . no matter what it was down there, she couldn't enter that well. Who knew what sorts of germs had multiplied in the cool, damp air? It was a perfect breeding ground. She pictured bacteria dancing on the breeze and tried again to move so it didn't hit her.

Terrible bent over, shining the light straight down the well. For a second only his hand moved, examining the bottom. Then he jerked back, coughing, and turned away from her, resting his hands on his bent knees and hanging his head as if he was about to throw up.

"Terrible, you okay?"

He waved his hand, whether to signal he was or that he wasn't she didn't know. Either way the safest thing to do was to stay away, so she did.

After a minute or so he got himself under control and turned to her. "Bad news, Chess. Bad news."

"Is it . . . is it an animal?" She knew it wasn't, knew what he was about to say before his mouth opened.

"Naw, no animal. Person. Dead body in there, all cut up."

The words hovered in their air between them, covered in their own sort of filth that had very little to do with whatever bacteria came from the well. Chess thought of the circle on the field, of the coin and the worms, and held out her left hand. "Give me the light."

"You ain't wanna see it, Chess."

"No, I don't, but I probably should. If it's related to all of this . . ."

He nodded and placed the light in her hand. The metal was warm from his skin.

Most of the well hid in shadow as the sun's angle sharpened. It was almost four o'clock, late enough that the homes on the other side of the fence started to come to life. Shift workers started returning home. Chess and Terrible themselves wouldn't attract much attention—everyone knew Terrible, knew who he was with—but if they tried to drag a dead body out of there? It wasn't even possible for them to do it, just the two of them. She certainly didn't want to go tie a rope around a dead body in the dark depths of the well, and she wasn't strong enough to lift Terrible if he did it. The man was at least six foot four or five and solid as the black '69 Chevelle he drove.

Standing as close to the edge as she dared, Chess tilted the light so it shone straight down. For a moment she thought Terrible must have made a mistake, that it was an animal after all. Then the beam slid across a pair of dead, whitish eyes, and she saw the open mouth, the pasty unreality of the face. The entire image came to focus just that fast, like a slide snapping into place.

Cut up, yes. But not the way she'd pictured. This wasn't

a dismembered body. It was a disemboweled one, the flesh on the abdomen and chest stripped away to reveal stained bones horribly naked in the light. As she watched, a rat skipped over the mess of dull dark red where the internal organs should have been.

Chess wasn't as strong as Terrible. She barely managed to stumble away from the gaping mouth in the ground before she collapsed, her almost-empty stomach twisting on itself and forcing out the remains of the noodles and Coke she'd had at the Market. Tears stung her eyes and her nose ran, but she couldn't move, couldn't do anything about it until the world stopped spinning beneath her.

Debunkers weren't investigators of murder. But they did investigate witchcraft-related crimes often, since so many times such things went hand in hand with ghosts. The sight of that body rang bells in the back of her head, bells that had nothing to do with her physical discomfort or her embarrassment at looking like a pussy. She was going to have to get a closer look at it, repugnant as the idea was.

Terrible nudged her shoulder, waving a semiclean rag by her face. She took it and a deep breath at the same time and wiped her heated skin. "Thanks."

He shrugged and bent down to hand her something else, a small black bottle. Funny, she'd never imagined him as someone who followed health trends.

"Bitter cardesca?"

He nodded.

"No thanks."

"Just take it, Chess. True thing."

She steeled herself for the taste and found it wasn't so bad, even if her eyes did start tearing up again. More to the point, he was right. Her stomach settled almost immediately and her head cleared. A lot of guys had taken to carrying cardesca when they went out drinking or drugging, the theory being it would prevent hangovers the next day. The fact that it cost over a hundred dollars for one tiny bottle didn't hurt when it came to showing flash, either, but maybe it wasn't just an affectation.

"Thanks," she said again, handing the bottle back.

He tucked it into his pack and pulled out his cell phone. Chess didn't ask. He was going to call Bump, and at some point tonight she was going to have to tell Bump the airport he wanted to take over was either truly haunted, or some seriously dark shit was going down there.

Sadly, she had to hope for the former. Battling black witches wasn't part of the deal.

The horizon glowed pink and orange before the grisly relic finally emerged from the well. Chess stood, smoking cigarette after cigarette, watching Bump's men milling around, trying to act like they were too tough to be bothered by the condition of the body, and debating the best way to remove it, none of which had a chance of working. Finally two unlucky souls had to be lowered in after it. It would have been funny if she hadn't been so chilled.

It—he, actually; a scraggly beard still clung to his weak chin—looked even worse once they laid him out on the ground. He was naked, his genitals gone, his midsection only visible ribs and a spine. Bare, fish-belly white arms and legs splayed out over the grass, almost glowing in the gathering darkness.

Chess swallowed hard and headed over, trying to keep her gaze focused on his skin and not the places where skin should be and wasn't.

"What you see, ladybird?" Bump somehow managed to lean even when there was nothing to lean against. "You think witchy?"

I think pukey. She put her hand over her nose and mouth and crouched down to get a closer look.

Finding cause of death wasn't part of a Debunker's

job. But a single glance was all she needed to know what had killed this man.

"Ritual sacrifice," she said. The words felt like lead in her mouth, heavy and hard to form, and crawled across her skin like insects. "They took his . . ." She flicked her gaze over his empty groin, saw the men's faces pale as if on cue. "Burned, probably. Seat of power, you know? And see the, ah, slashes on the wrists, the shapes? Those are runes."

"What say?"

She shook her head. "Black ones, I mean black magic. They're forbidden to us. But he couldn't have carved them himself, and—ah!"

They all jumped back, like the chorus line of an old Busby Berkeley musical, as the dead man's heart gave a slow, squelchy beat.

"Ain't dead! He ain't—" Bump started to shout, but Chess cut him off, waving a hand that felt stiff and clumsy with cold fear. Not just from what she was about to say, but from what she saw, the rune sliced into the dead man's heart, the rune that matched the amulet in her Blackwood box at home.

"He's dead. It—they—they're feeding off his soul. His soul is still trapped in there."

Chapter Thirteen

> "There is no proof, of course, that a clean, well-run home automatically equals a safe, ghost-free one, but why take chances?"
> —*Mrs. Increase's Advice for Ladies,* by Mrs. Increase

"Don't get how the soul and the heart got anything to do with each other." Terrible slid into the exit lane, heading off the highway to take her home. She couldn't wait to get there. The thought of that man—Bump had identified him as Slipknot, a cutpurse who worked the financial district—and the horror his last hours must have been, of the indignities his spirit was suffering even now and how she could do nothing to help him . . . She rubbed her forehead with her palm like she was trying to erase the unwanted vision.

"Technically they don't. But as long as there's life in the body, the soul can't leave."

"So he's not dead."

"No, he is dead. His soul is trapped. His body isn't sustaining life. The *spell* is sustaining his physical life so it can feed off his soul."

Terrible thought about this for a moment. "So they do the spell, use his blood and innards to power it. Then they trap his soul, aye, so's it can keep feeding the magic. And the magic keeping the body alive? Like a cycle?"

"Right," she said, surprised he'd caught on so quickly.

"And you can't help him? Ain't that what you do?"

"Normally we'd do a ritual to release the soul. Like a Banishing."

"Send him to the City, aye?"

"Right." She shifted uneasily in her seat. "But we can't in this case, because we don't know what the spell is."

"Don't it end the spell, you Banish the soul?"

"Don't know." She'd smoked so much that day the tip of her tongue burned, but that didn't stop her from lighting another. "If I can decode that amulet, find out what the spell is for, I should know how to end it. Probably. But as it is . . . detaching the soul might end the spell, or it might backfire. Somebody else could get sucked into it."

"Somebody like you."

"Yeah."

It almost had sucked her in. She'd never felt darkness like that, and greed. What was happening at Chester was far worse than a simple haunting. And thanks to her own stupid curiosity, she'd managed to get herself tangled further in the mess. The amulet hiding in her bag had tasted her blood. She'd fed it, in her small way, and she had no idea what that meant for her except chances were that if the spell needed another soul, hers would be the first one it came to. Whoever cast it hadn't been stupid or amateurish, that was for sure.

Fuck.

"We find the spell, we set Slipknot free?"

"I'll do my best."

He nodded. "Slip not a low one. He don't deserve it, being trapped."

"I don't think anybody deserves it."

"Aye?" he glanced at her, the dashboard lights coloring his face greenish as he turned onto her street. "Then you ain't had such a bad life at that, Chess."

* * *

Five hours later, after a restless nap that felt more like swimming through sleep than actually sleeping, she arrived at the Mortons' house. The street was soulless and blank, dark houses lined up like empty tombs while cars slept on their driveways. Only the trees spoke, whispering back to the breeze.

Chess set her bag on the stone walkway leading to the Morton's front door and unzipped it. The Hand's fingers tried to grip hers as she pulled it out and placed it next to the bag.

Lockpicks came out next, in their leather case, followed by a short, fat candle. The Hand twitched, then shriveled slightly as its muscles tightened around the candle's base. Her camera had fallen to the bottom, but she found it after a minute of searching and slipped the strap around her neck. Last was the steel syringe full of thick, oily lubricant for the lock.

This she squirted in, sliding the needle as far into the mechanism as she could get it. Some Debunkers used a spray can with a tube, but Chess found that too messy, especially after one of her books had managed to wedge against the nozzle of her old one and soak everything inside her bag. The syringe worked better, was quieter and more accurate.

After that sat for a minute she went to work with the picks as silently and quickly as she could, listening for the minute click that would tell her the catch had given.

It came. She grabbed her things, swung the door open, and stepped inside the house.

The Mortons did not believe in leaving a light on, it seemed, and they did believe in running the heater even on a night like this one, when autumn's chill barely touched the air. The heat didn't bother her but the lack of light did. People who were genuinely frightened of ghosts in their home tended to leave them on, often even sleeping under their glare.

"Algha canador metruan," she whispered, striking a match. Light flared from the tip, casting shadows on the tasteful ivory walls of the living room. Once again the Hand twitched as she lit the candle and shook out the match, placing it in her pocket.

She relaxed. The Mortons would sleep now under the Hand's magic, more heavily and sweetly than they had in a while, and she didn't have to worry so much about noise.

The living room held no secrets. In the faint glow from the flame Chess crawled along the perimeter, sliding her fingertips along the baseboards and joints, using her penlight to see behind the furniture. Not that it was too necessary. With the exception of Albert, the Mortons didn't appear to be readers. No bookcases gave hints as to the interests of the owners.

Instead the room was filled with what she thought of as spindly furniture: occasional tables with one single knickknack on top, or couches with tiny legs and space beneath. She slid the beam of the penlight beneath them and found only a thick coating of beggar's velvet. Mrs. Morton apparently didn't bother to clean under there.

Good thing, that. The dust made it clear nothing had been moved. No wire trails marked it, no scrapes indicated sound or film equipment had been hidden here. She hadn't expected there to be, but still good to know.

The kitchen was next. She set the Hand on the counter while she opened the fridge and peered inside, finding it stuffed with condiments and neatly labeled and stacked plastic containers, complete with dates. The freezer held numerous blocks of white paper, also labeled, that would become roasts and chickens when they were unwrapped. She made a note. If she found nothing else before she left, she'd have to come open them all, to see if they contained anything other than dead animals—or rather, the wrong kind of dead animals.

Probably not; the windowsill was lined with cook-books, their spines ridged and unreadable from heavy use. Chess picked them up one by one, flipped through them, glancing idly at the elaborate photos. *The Meat Lover's Cookbook* . . . *Cooking with Taste* . . . *Mrs. Increase's Family Recipes* . . . *Cuisine of the Bankhead Spa* . . . Wait. What?

The Bankhead Spa was the kind of resort where movie stars and extremely high Church officials went on vacation; incredibly expensive, incredibly dull, with a private ferry and hordes of asskissy staff. Not the sort of place she'd expect an optometrist—or was he an optician? She could never remember the difference—to visit. Not the sort of place she'd expect one to be able to afford, more important. But just the sort of place she could see Mrs. Morton insisting on being taken to. For people who gave a shit about such things, she supposed it would be quite a coup.

The spine on that book was not fuzzed with age. It cracked when she opened it, in fact. Brand-new. Definitely brand-new; the receipt was still inside. September. Only two months before.

No wonder they were still in this neighborhood. No wonder they needed money. With a faint smile, Chess snapped a quick picture of the receipt and the book, and replaced both. It might not be important, that was true. But it might be, and every little bit of evidence would help.

The only place she couldn't search was behind the fridge, so she pulled her electric meter from her bag and fed the wire around. A flip of the switch showed her nothing else back there used electricity. Next she tried the mirror on its long metal antenna. Clean—well, as clean as it could be behind a refrigerator.

This was a waste of time, but still she searched, following the Church-set routine so that if she needed to testify she could say she had. Cabinets stuffed with packaged food and sugary snacks—no wonder Albert looked like a small, squashy torpedo instead of a boy—and still more plastic tubs. Had Mrs. Morton once sold the stuff, or what? Chess couldn't imagine any reason why one small family of three needed the ability to store enough food to feed the entire Downside for a year.

Pots and pans clanked as she shifted them to look behind. The oven was clean and empty, the drawers practically overflowing with lids for all those tubs.

One last stop, the laundry room—actually a small alcove off the garage—where Mrs. Morton had been the day Albert supposedly first saw the apparition. Clean, as was the garage itself.

She climbed the stairs, listening to the heavy, regular breathing of the Mortons. Somebody snored so loudly that if it weren't for the Hand, Chess imagined it would have woken everyone up. The sound grated up her spine like a broken saw.

Ah. Pay dirt. Albert had replaced his books. Everything from electrical wiring for dummies to complicated texts on animation and film editing. She took several pictures of the shelf as a whole, then started removing books, shaking them by the spine in the hopes that something would fall out before photographing them.

His drawers were next. Chess grinned. Looked like Albert had been studying blueprints of the house itself. Interesting. She took more photos, and just out of spite decided to take pictures of his rather extensive collection of porn as well. Ha, she knew he'd have one.

Albert sighed and rolled under the covers as she bent down to search under the bed. The bag of wires she'd noted Saturday night was still there, along with an ancient DVD player and a few more books on film and wiring, suggesting Albert may indeed have been hiding his activities from his parents.

Wedged between the headboard and the wall was a small black velvet bag. Chess reached for it, then pulled her hand back, certain nothing electrical was inside it. It was a magic bag, a gris-gris, even, and she did not want to open it.

Most homes were full of such items, and none of them ever bothered her the way this one did. Perhaps it was simply tiredness, or the way her nerves still jangled when she thought of the dead man at the airport. But something told her this was not legal magic, not a basic protection bag or charm for safe dreams. This didn't even feel like magic Church employees were authorized to do.

She nudged the bag with the toe of her boot, trying to pull the thread holding it closed. No luck. It was knotted at the top and sealed with wax.

She slipped on a pair of surgical gloves—after the amulet, she wasn't taking any chances—and lit another match, slipping a small white china cup onto the carpet to catch the melting wax. Albert mumbled something in his sleep.

"What's that, Albert?" she said under her breath.

"Didn't mean to," he said.

Chess glanced up sharply. No, he was still asleep.

"I'm sure you didn't," she replied gently, shaking out the match. Most of the black wax had melted into the cup. "Why don't you tell me what happened?"

He sighed. "I was hungry and I didn't have any money, and I like chocolate . . ."

Whatever. So he stole a candy bar from a convenience store or something. Big deal.

He kept droning on while she untied the bag and held it upside down over another dish, then snapped a few hasty pictures of the contents. Black salt, a crow's talon, some pink thread tied in knots . . . nothing particularly unusual here. It might be unorthodox for a dream safe, but within legal limits certainly—it was personal, and it didn't affect anyone else. So why did her skin crawl, why did she feel as if something large and black and sharp were about to swoop down on her?

Her hands shook as she snapped a quick photo then poured everything into the bag, resealed it, and stuffed it back behind the headboard. She wanted to leave. Wanted to get out of this house that was suddenly suffocatingly warm and filled with eyes.

Eyes like the ones of the hooded figure watching her from the doorway.

Chess jumped up so fast she stumbled against the rickety bedside table, banging her knee hard on the edge. The lamp fell over and crashed to the floor while she tried to stuff herself into the corner, to get a better look at the shape.

He was made of darkness, it seemed, the complete absence of light behind him making the outlines of his robe—or whatever it was—squirm and ripple. Her gaze couldn't seem to catch on anything, to find the definition of his form outside that narrow, pale face and the terrible black depths of his eyes.

He smiled, revealing sharp, dingy teeth, too many teeth. His nose hooked down, thin and crooked like a stalactite in the center of his face.

He should have been another flat image, a film projected from a hole somewhere in the wall, as she'd thought the first time she saw him. But he wasn't, and she knew it. She felt him, felt the absence of humanity and conscience crawl over her skin and try to invade her body.

His hand materialized in front of him, stretching toward her. Not a gesture of supplication, but of threat. He was coming for her, and she could not escape.

It felt like hours Chess stood there, with his eyes burning into her and his presence staining her soul, but it could not have been more than a few seconds before he moved, so fast she couldn't track it. He seemed to disappear only to reappear again a foot closer to her, inside the doorway, as though a strobe light was flashing in the room.

Her legs refused to move. She tried and tried, but they would not budge, as if her feet had sprouted roots and dug themselves into the thinly carpeted floor.

Closer again, standing at the edge of Albert's bed while the boy muttered in his sleep and shifted under the blanket. Now the creature's other hand was visible, also held out to her, fingers curled in preparation to close around her throat. Her skin there burned already. Her lungs fought to inflate. He was going to kill her, this was it, there was no way she could escape him. Especially if she couldn't get her fucking feet to obey.

Another movement. He stood in Albert's bed, mired to the thigh by it as though sinking into quicksand. Another. He stood in the corner. Another. He hung in the air by the ceiling, playing with her, disorienting her, forcing her to look wildly around the room to find him.

The knife in her back pocket dug into her. She reached around to grab it, closing her fingers over it, and her palm shrieked in pain. Only then did she realize it had been throbbing for several minutes.

As a weapon the knife would be useless, but it made her feel better, stronger, to hold something as she crept out of the corner holding it in front of her.

He appeared again, right at her side, so close she could see a droplet of red fall from the sharp edge of one canine tooth. Chess screamed and waved the knife at him, but he disappeared again in a breath of icy cold.

Her chest ached as she spun toward the door and started running, banging her shoulder hard on the doorframe and hurtling herself down the stairs. He could have been on those stairs, he could have been anywhere. The darkness was so complete, she couldn't see where she was going, couldn't see anything at all, and she could feel his hands on her neck as she fell the last few steps and landed in a heap on the polished wood floor at the bottom.

He was across the room. He was in the doorway to the kitchen. He was everywhere in the house, in her head. Her palm hurt so bad, she thought it was going to explode. Her shoulder ached, and both her knees where she'd landed on them. No matter. She had to get out, out into the cool fresh air, back into the world she knew existed outside this house of horror.

It wasn't until she was there, crumpled on the street, brushing tears off her face, that she realized she'd left the Hand inside, along with her bag and everything else.

Chapter Fourteen

> "Now the lack of gods is fact, which is Truth and need not be believed or doubted. The Church offers protection, and so the Church makes law."
>
> —*The Book of Truth*, Origins, Article 1641

Lex shoved his hands into his pockets and stared up at the Morton house. "I gotta touch what?"

"A hand. A dead hand. It's on the floor of the bedroom on the right, at the top of the stairs. Just grab it, and my bag, and bring them down here, okay?"

"Don't know I want to touch some dead witch hand, tulip. No offense."

"It's not a witch's hand, it's a convicted murderer's, and it's harmle—never mind. Are you going to do it for me, or should I call someone else? There's not a lot of time left until sunrise."

Chess waited for him to call her bluff. There was no one else she could call. Her only options had been Doyle or Lex, since she didn't have Terrible's number. Lex had won easily. At least he wouldn't spread news of her ridiculous flight all over the Church in the morning. Maybe that wasn't fair to Doyle, but she didn't care, not when the thought of going back into that house made her feel like she was going to wet her pants.

"Aye, I'll do it." His dark eyes scanned her up and down, in her black jeans and snug black top. "But I get something in return."

"Fine. Just go get my stuff, okay?"

She watched him slouch his way up the walk and disappear into the house, half-convinced he wouldn't come out. And now he wanted something in return, and if she were honest with herself, she'd known he would when she called him.

And maybe that, more than anything else, had been why she called him. The thought didn't make her comfortable, but then most of her thoughts these days didn't. Her mind seemed to be endlessly turning over pieces of a broken vase she couldn't put back together. Airports and ghost planes and runes and bodies and *eyes*, those black eyes that seemed to sear right into her flesh when they focused on her . . . Why hadn't he killed her?

Cold seeped through her jeans as she leaned back against the side panel of her car and crossed her arms. A window brightened in a house down the street, some early riser starting their day. She'd gotten here around three. It couldn't possibly be later than five now, but blue light streaked the horizon and turned the chimneys into blackened teeth against it.

What the hell was taking him so long in there? It wasn't a mansion, for fuck's sake, it was a damned two-story Colonial.

Maybe the ghost . . . no. Lex hadn't been frightened in the tunnel, not even a little bit, and although the thing in the house was worse, much worse, she still somehow doubted it would bother him.

Come to think of it, it didn't seem to have bothered any of the Mortons either. What she'd seen in Albert's bedroom didn't resemble the description Mrs. Morton had given in the slightest. No gray rags decorated his shapeless form, and he had definitely been male. Did more than one ghost haunt the place? But then why was she the only one who'd seen the figure in black?

And why hadn't he killed her? He couldn't be real. That was the only possible answer, the only thing that made sense. He wasn't real, and she was on so many drugs, her body didn't even know what it felt anymore. She rubbed her forehead, the bridge of her nose. She was losing it, oh shit she needed sleep, needed to give the speed a rest and let herself kick back down to normal.

Lex appeared, holding her bag in one fist and the Hand in the other. The look of disgust on his face would have been comical anywhere else.

"Don't fancy carrying this thing for work," he said, handing everything back to her. "Don't know how you do it."

"You get used to it." She tossed the bag into her car and set the Hand on the passenger seat. Normally she would blow out the candle as soon as she left a house, but given how late it was, she thought it would be better to get away first. People tended to wake up immediately from enchanted sleep, and she didn't want to take a chance that she'd be still visible when they did.

Lex stood for a minute, watching her. "So you head home now?"

"That's the plan."

"Ain't you gonna ask what your owes is?"

"I assume you'll tell me." She didn't particularly want to unzip her jeans and show him her tattoo here on this empty morning street, but she would. She did owe him. And all things considered, it was a pretty harmless request.

"Aye." He nodded his head, but his gaze didn't leave her face. "Thinking I got an idea."

She swallowed. "What?"

"Touching that Hand, you know, weren't pleasant. Kind of a big favor, aye?" He'd stepped closer to her, close enough for her to see each individual eyelash and to smell cigarettes on his breath. Her heart rate sped up.

One hand caught her neck, gently, with his thumb under her chin. The other slipped around to the small of her back. His body trapped her against her car, but there was no threat—or rather, no malice.

"Think I kiss you, tulip," he murmured. "How's that for an owes?"

Chess opened her mouth, unable to think of a reply but feeling certain she should make one. She didn't have a chance. His lips took hers with the utter confidence of a man who knows his kiss is welcome, and fear blossomed in her chest as she realized he was right.

Heat snaked through her body, into her arms and legs, into the fingers she gripped his shoulders with and slid along the back of his neck. His tongue insinuated itself into her mouth, finding hers, greeting it and leaving again as he pulled away from her.

"Guess like we all even now," he said. His car door opened with a faint snick, and he got in. "You call me, keep me on the update, aye?"

She hadn't quite gotten her mouth to form words again when he sped away up the brightening street.

Smoke curled into the sky as she turned the car off the highway onto her exit. Nothing surprising in that. Once a month or so someone's firecan turned over, or a junkie passed out with a lit cigarette in whatever squat they inhabited at the time, and a deserted building became a destroyed one. The craggy, black-stained walls interspersed with whole buildings mutely testified to the poverty of Downside. No one would pay to have the wreckage removed. No one would pay to build new. And no one really mourned the dead.

Of course, they weren't supposed to, not in the way mourning had been done Before Truth. Bodies were incinerated, souls transported to the City and kept there. For a prohibitively large fee those left behind could still, with the aid of a Church Liaiser, communicate with them. All neat and tidy, all controlled in the same careful and precise way the Church had controlled everything since Haunted Week twenty-three years before. Almost exactly twenty-three years, in fact. The anniversary was just a few weeks past.

But Chess didn't have time to think of how busy she had been during the Festival, or of anything else. Her bones ached with tiredness. Her head felt like it was stuffed with cotton balls. Her hand—among other parts—still throbbed faintly, and she craved sleep almost as much as another Cept.

Her ramshackle little car—on its last legs, but how was she supposed to afford a new one?—crawled through the deserted streets, past boarded windows and graffiti, finally sliding into a parking space half a block from her building. Chess grabbed her bag and her knife and headed for home.

She crossed the entry hall that had once been the nave and headed up the stairs, only to stop halfway up the first flight. It wasn't unusual to find people in here trying to escape either rain or cold or people with weapons, but the boy sprawled across the landing was neither.

"Chess," he said, and that slightly high, nervous voice placed him in a way his narrow face had not. "I talk to you?"

"What are you doing here, Brain?"

"I talk to you?" he asked again, glancing around the stairwell as if he expected someone to leap out of the solid wall and attack him. His nervousness bothered her. If someone was after him she didn't want to be involved.

But neither could she tell him no and send him back out on the street. He was just a kid. Damn it.

"All right," she said, pushing past him up the steps. "Come on."

It felt like she hadn't been home in weeks. She half expected to see a shroud of dust covering all the furniture. Or rather, more dust than there was already.

Brain closed the door behind him and stood, shifting his weight from foot to foot. In his small face his eyes looked huge, shiny as marbles.

"So what's up, Brain? What's the tale?"

"Hunchback. He . . . He heared about t'other night. Guessing Terrible gave him the speech. He mad at me, Chess. Say he don't want me around no more . . ." He blinked rapidly, his thin mouth twisting.

Shit. "What did Terrible say to him?"

"Angry, methinks. Of cause Hunchback saying the tales about Chester being haunted and all. Hunchback blame me now. Say I not so brainy after all." His too-big black coat bunched up around his shoulders as he crossed his thin arms over his chest.

"Ain't got no other place, not now. Maybe I sleep here? Just a few hours, aye? Then I find a new place. I knows other people out there, somebody help me. Only none of them awake now."

Something about the way his eyes shifted as he spoke made Chess suspect this wasn't the entire truth. He'd had no reason to believe she'd be awake either, but he'd come here, and if what he'd said about Hunchback on Friday night was true, his squat was a good twenty blocks away. A long walk in the chilly, dangerous Downside predawn.

"You can stay for now," she said, setting her bag on the kitchen counter. "But just for now. You're not moving in, got it?"

"Aye, oh my thanks, Chess, my thanks, you ain't gonna even know I's—"

"No, I won't, because you're not going to be here long enough for me to notice. You can sleep on the couch. Don't touch anything, got it? Nothing."

He nodded.

"And don't tell anyone either. How did you get into the building?"

"Back door lock's loose."

"What do you mean, loose?"

"I only had to play with it a minute afore it gave. Loose."

"You broke in?"

"Was I ain't supposed to?"

She sighed. As if her money situation wasn't bad enough, now she'd have to pay to get the lock fixed and new keys made for everyone in the building. Leaving the back door unprotected was out of the question.

In fact . . . she always carried spare nails, good strong iron ones so they had the additional benefit of warding spirits. That would at least put a temporary stick on it. It wasn't a fire-safe stick, but the chances of someone breaking into the building were a lot better than those of it catching fire. She didn't particularly rate the odds against either.

"No. You weren't supposed to, but it's done now. You can fix it before you go to sleep. I'll get you some nails and a hammer, you can close the door and jam the lock."

"Ain't suppose you got some eats? Only my belly getting tight. Can't remember last food I put in."

Chess ignored him and set a couple of nails on the counter. Their pointed tips reminded her she'd need to refill her lube syringe, so she grabbed the bottle of oil from under the sink, too.

"Chess? Got me a few dollars, I could help for some food . . ."

"Take a look in the fridge. I don't think there's much."

There wasn't. Brain stared into the empty depths as though a four-course meal would magically appear. When one didn't his shoulders sagged. "I have a beer?"

She shrugged. "If you want one. Get me one, too." Hey, he wasn't her kid, and chances were he'd already done a lot more than have a beer or two. Kids younger than him OD'd every day.

He handed her one. "I ask you something?"

"Sure."

She filled the syringe and a spare and set them on the counter. Her bag was a jumble of magic items and mundane; she really ought to clean it out. No time like the present. For some reason she didn't feel like going into the living room and sitting down. Perhaps it was the unexpected presence of a child in her apartment, or maybe she was just afraid that if she did she'd fall asleep.

"You gonna try to clear them ghosts at Chester?"

"Why?"

Brain leaned against the opposite wall and studied the floor. "I just curious. About what you do. Good thing, right? Good magic clears the ghosts."

"In general, yes. The Church doesn't do black magic."

"But do you?"

"What is that supposed . . . Brain? Do you know something about that airport?"

His eyes widened. "Don't know what you're meaning. I just curious, is all."

No. He'd started to say he'd been there before, hadn't he? Friday night with Terrible. He'd almost said he went there all the time.

"Did you see something out there, Brain? Did you see something happen?"

"No! No, I never been there cepting when you met me. I see nothing there." His fingers wrapped around his beer bottle were white.

"You can tell me, you know. If you saw something, it might be important. Really important, okay?" She paused. "I bet Bump would be grateful if you saw something that helped him open that airport. Might even give you a job."

"Terrible hate me."

"Terrible doesn't hate you. And even if he did . . . he'd like you if you helped. Wouldn't you like that? Working for Bump? Having Terrible as a friend? You could tell

Hunchback to fuck off right to his face and he wouldn't be able to touch you."

Some of the fear drained from Brain's face. "Thinking so?"

"I do. If you know something, Brain, you should tell me. It might be important. And I'll . . . I'll keep you safe. You can stay here, as long as you need to."

"With you?" The hopeful expression on his face was like an arrow straight into her heart. How many times in her childhood had she dreamed of safety, of being somewhere no one would hurt her or of being so powerful no one could?

Now she was. Practically untouchable, thanks to her position with the Church and her new alliance with Bump. No wonder he'd come to her.

"Yes, with me."

"True thing?"

"True thing, Brain."

He sighed, a long, shaky sigh that seemed to come from his toes and work its way up, and nodded.

Chess picked her beer up off the counter. "Okay, great. So let's go in the living room and sit down, and you can tell me all about it, okay? Everything you saw."

The knock at the door startled them both. Months went by and not a single person came to visit her. Now she had two, at the crack of freaking dawn. Great.

Doyle held up a white paper bag. "Thought you might like some breakfast."

Chapter Fifteen

He took her silence for assent, and brushed past her to come in. "I was up, and I figured you'd be up—you went to the Morton place last night, right?—so I figured, why not. Wanted to find out how that hand is doing, too. Have you been cleaning it?"

He set the bag on her kitchen counter and started unpacking it. Sodium fumes filled the air, along with the scent of damp sausage. It didn't make her remotely hungry.

Chess's first instinct was to send him away, but Brain had wanted something to eat. If Doyle was so eager to feed someone he could feed him. They'd get some food into the boy, then Doyle could go away and she could hear what Brain had to say. And if Doyle didn't like it, too bad. It was awfully presumptive of him to just show up here like that.

"How did you get in the building?"

"Somebody was leaving." He glanced at her. "It's okay, isn't it?"

"Well, yeah, but I just wish——"

"Chess?"

Brain stood in the middle of her living room, his cheeks

paler than usual. "I gots to go, Chess, sorry, I forgot something I's supposed to do, aye?"

"But there's plenty of food, we can talk after—"

"No! I meaning, no, it's cool. I catch you another time."

"Brain, don't—" Too late. The boy moved fast when he wanted to. He was down the stairs before she could get into the hall and stop him. "Shit."

"Who's that?"

She shrugged. Now she was going to have to be alone with Doyle. And mountains of food. "Just a kid. He said . . . never mind."

"He looked pretty upset."

"His boss kicked him out."

"And he wanted to talk about it? Why'd he come to you?" He opened cabinet doors, finally finding her mismatched plates and grabbing two of the three she owned.

"I guess he knew I'd be up."

"Just like me." He gave her one of his killer smiles and headed past her into the living room, holding the plates piled high.

"Yeah, um, about that . . ."

"You're going to tell me you don't want me to just come over unannounced, right?" He plunked himself down on the couch, right in the center so if she wanted to sit she'd have to be practically touching him.

"Something like that."

"I'm sorry. I just . . . I wanted to talk to you, and not over the phone or on Church grounds."

"Why?" She perched on the arm of the couch, curious in spite of herself. She never got to hear gossip.

"You know Bruce Wickman, right?"

"I know who he is." Damn. This was probably going to be the same thing she'd overheard between Bruce and the Grand Elder the other morning.

"He says the City's going crazy. Like, more than usual

after the Festival. He thinks something might be going on."

"Has he talked to the Grand Elder?"

Doyle nodded. "Says he doesn't believe him, though. Bruce is scared. He said in ten years of Liaising he's never seen them like this. He said he's been having trouble sleeping, that he's been seeing things. In his dreams."

Chess cocked an eyebrow. This was sort of interesting, but she didn't want to let him know that. "And?"

"So I think he's right. I've been having a hard time sleeping lately, too. So have Dana Wright and a couple of other people."

Dana was a Debunker, like herself and Doyle. It wasn't unusual for Liaisers to have issues with spirits—if they weren't careful they could be tailed or even possessed when a spirit refused to leave them after a Liaising, another reason their pay was higher—but Debunkers . . .

"Randy's, like, panicking. He actually wanted to sleep at my place last night, he said he'd had some horrible nightmare. Typical, huh?"

Chess laughed, but not unkindly. "Randy's just having a hard time, I think. Maybe the job is getting to him. He's been off for a while."

"Have you been? Having trouble sleeping, I mean?" Doyle leaned closer. "You look kind of tired."

"I never sleep well."

"But you don't usually look tired like this."

She scooted herself back along the arm of the couch so she wasn't quite so close to him. "Thanks."

"I don't mean it that way. I just . . . Bruce thinks something is going on. We thought if we could get a few of us together, try and figure out what, we might have enough evidence then to force the Grand Elder to listen."

"And you want my help."

He nodded.

Telling him she never slept well wasn't a lie. She didn't. Which made it impossible to say if her recent troubled rest was a normal reaction to a fairly stressful few days or something else.

"There's more, too," he said, lowering his voice and glancing around like he thought Church spies might be hiding behind her television. "I've had nightmares. Like, real ones. And I thought I saw—no. You'll think I'm crazy."

"I already think you're crazy."

"Bruce has seen him, too, though. In his kitchen."

"Seen him? Who?"

Another glance. "The man in the robe," he said. "The nightmare man."

Damn it, damn it, damn it!

After a fat line of crushed Nip she didn't feel like sleep was something she'd need for another couple of days, but that didn't change the fact that she hadn't been able to. Whether it was because of Doyle's information or . . . something else . . . she didn't know, but sleep had done nothing but taunt her while she lay in her bed with the covers piled high, shivering although the room wasn't cold, watching the hours tick by on her clock until the early afternoon sun streamed through her narrow bedroom window.

Where was Terrible, anyway? She checked the slip of paper Bump had given her along with another package of chemical cheer, and glanced at the faded numbers on the empty storefront. Number seventeen. Her destination was a couple of blocks away yet.

This was stupid, a stupid sidetrip on a stupid job she couldn't even do thanks to stupid Lex.

Or not just thanks to stupid Lex. Whatever she'd seen at the Morton house, whatever it was that Doyle claimed was stalking Church employees . . . she was beginning to think she wouldn't be able to handle it anyway. Not if the night before was any indication. Some tough Church-witch, calling someone else to retrieve her stuff from the spooky haunted house.

A small gang of teenage goons edged down the street toward her in their black bandannas and latex-tight trousers, fanning out like they were about to run an offensive play. Which they probably were. Without making eye contact Chess shrugged her tattered gray cardigan off her shoulders, letting them see her ink. Their formation tightened up. They might not be afraid of the Church, but they'd be stupid not to know Bump had the only Churchwitch in Downside working for him, and everyone was afraid of Bump.

Their fear didn't keep them from hissing at her and making lewd comments, but those she could ignore. Too bad she couldn't ignore everything else, and just stay home today listening to records and getting high. Or even doing her actual job. She should be interviewing the Mortons today, not wandering the streets hunting for a tattoo parlor so she could then go find an adolescent boy.

The parlor was easy enough to find, at least. Just walk until the scent of Murray's hair pomade drifted to her nose, then turn left.

"Looking for Terrible," she said to one of the greasers guarding the door. Inside the building she heard the unmistakable sounds of hurried movement, not quite drowned out by the Sonics record playing at high volume.

He barely looked up from the hangnail he was trimming with his butterfly knife. "Aye? Business you got witim?"

"Business."

"Aw, chickie, you don't gotta keep no secrets from me, I ain't—"

Terrible's voice rumbled from the back room. "Quit playin, Rego, an let she in."

Rego glanced over in that direction, then up at her,

really looking for the first time. She hadn't slipped her sweater back over her chest and upper arms, and when he saw her skin his blue eyes widened.

"Shit. You that—"

Chess didn't bother to reply. She brushed past him and walked inside, pausing for a moment so her eyes could adjust to the comparative gloom inside. She'd lost her sunglasses again.

The place smelled of antiseptic and smoke, of male bodies and the curious sharp odor of ink and oil. Frames filled with bright flash covered the walls, save one suspiciously clean spot at the left. That explained those frantic scraping movements. The shop dealt in illegal ink, magical symbols only the Church was allowed to use—symbols like the ones covering her own arms and chest, making her easily identifiable. Other people might get the tats, but not where they could be seen; to do so was like asking for a prison sentence and a date with a white-hot iron slab to remove them. She gave a mental shrug. None of her business. Enforcement of nonmoral law was a totally different department, government rather than religion.

It was a very different room from the one where she'd been given her tattoos, in the ceremony that had officially made her a Debunker. That room was a pure, pale blue, bare save the table and the artist's equipment, and her fellow initiates and the few older Debunkers attending had knelt, chanting, increasing the energy in the room until she'd felt ready to pass out and hadn't noticed the pain of the needle anymore, or the power searing itself into her.

"What say, Chess?" Terrible interrupted her reverie, glancing up from where he sat with his bare chest pressed against the slanted back of a chair. She hadn't realized how many tattoos he had, aside from the almost-full sleeve on his left arm and the small script circling the base of his throat. His shoulders were covered, too, and something decorated his left side from underarm to waist and into his pants. If he hadn't been so wide, dwarfing the chair, she wouldn't have seen it.

"I want to—" Her mouth snapped shut.

"What?"

"I . . . What are you having done?" She watched, fascinated and a little disgusted, as the tattoo artist peeled a long, thin strip of bloody flesh from Terrible's back.

"One more," the artist said, and Terrible glanced back at him and nodded.

"Terrible . . . what the fuck?"

"Scar, Chess. You wait. Ain't had the fun part yet."

"Um . . . there's a fun part?"

The artist came back with a scalpel, shining silver, and bent over. Terrible's eyebrows twitched, but he stayed silent—they all stayed silent—while the artist cut and peeled off another strip. He blotted the blood with gauze.

"So what happen? You right?"

"Yeah . . . um . . ." The artist had a bowl of something now that looked like ashes. As Chess watched, he started rubbing handfuls of it over the wound he'd created—at least she assumed it was over the wound, she couldn't see it. "Have you seen that kid Brain?"

"Naw, can't say so. Why?"

"I want to find him. He came by my place this morning, said Hunchback kicked him out, but I—"

"Fuck." Anger poured over Terrible's face like molasses. "That squidgepopper. I fuckin told him, ain't the kid's fault. We see him, too? I'd sure do with paying him a visit now."

"Ready, T?" The artist stood behind Terrible, rocking slightly on his feet like he wasn't sure if he should run or pretend everything was fine. Chess didn't blame him.

She was half ready to run herself, her legs twitching and
her heart pounding. She was jumpy enough, she didn't
need two hundred and seventy pounds or so of furious
man in front of her.

"Do it."

Terrible clenched the opposite sides of the chair back,
his biceps popping, as the artist drew closer. In his hand
he clutched what looked like a small disposable cigarette
lighter. What the . . . ?

He flicked his thumb. Terrible's fingers tightened, his
eyes shut, as the gunpowder packed into his open wound
flared in a sharp, cauterizing burst of flame. Chess gave a
high-pitched squeal that embarrassed her before it even
left her mouth, but it was either lost in the smattering of
applause or the men tactfully ignored it. Or they were
afraid of what she might do if they made fun of her, which
was the more likely. Most people had a highly inflated
idea of what kinds of powers she had—unless they were
dead, she couldn't do much to them. Of course, there was
no point in clarifying. Why take away that protection?

She watched as the artist brought a couple of mirrors
and angled them so Terrible could take a look, managing
to catch a glimpse herself while he adjusted them. Lines,
an impression of wings? The mirror moved too quickly
for her to tell, but Terrible was apparently pleased. At
least he didn't look any angrier than usual as the artist
began smearing antibiotic cream on the wound and ap-
plying gauze pads with tape.

It was strange to see him without a shirt on, though.
Chess tended to think of his bowling shirts as armor,
and stripped of them he . . . well, he still looked like a
tank.

A surprisingly attractive tank. Tattoos and scars decorated his bare skin and a patch of thick dark hair spread
over his chest and dipped down in a thin line to his
waist, but underneath them was solid, sculpted muscle,

exquisitely delineated, obviously created from real work and not trips to a gym.

He glanced at her, then looked again with an eyebrow cocked, and she realized she was frankly staring. Heat rushed to her face as her fingernails suddenly became fascinating to her. It wasn't until she heard him saying goodbye that she looked up again.

Together they passed Rego, back out onto the bright street. Terrible had sunglasses, sleek black ones he snapped on the moment they left the doorway.

"So who? Hunchback? Where Brain go, he still at yours?"

"No, he took off." She sketched out the conversations she'd had with him, and how he'd left before he could tell her whatever it was he seemed to be hinting at. "I think he might have seen the people who killed Slipknot. Maybe not the actual murder, but the same people."

Terrible leaned against his car and rubbed his chin, sunlight glinting off the spikes of his armband and the thick silver chain he wore on his wrist. "Aye, sound like it to me. I ain't know where Brain rest. Got any clues?"

She shook her head.

"Look like we go see Hunchback after all." His grin sent a shiver of fear through her body.

Chapter Sixteen

"And they crowded into the cities, seeking with their numbers to overwhelm the dead, and found it futile."
—*The Book of Truth*, Origins, Article 120

The Chevelle's tires squealed in protest as Terrible yanked the wheel to the right, sliding up in front of a warehouse building by the docks in a cloud of dust and the Devil Dogs' "354." The car shook when he slammed the door.

"You seem really worried," she said, quickly adding "About Brain, I mean," when he glared at her.

"I ain't."

"Then why are you so mad?" She rushed to catch up with him as he strode into an alley on the left of the building.

"Hunchback been told," he said. "Watch the young one. Get it, Chess? He seen us. We ain't want nobody else hearing that, aye?"

"He said he wouldn't . . ."

Terrible wasn't listening. A small door, covered in cracked paint faded to the dusky color of unripe blueberries, hung slightly open halfway down the wall. Terrible yanked it open and thrust himself inside, with Chess hurrying behind him.

Again it took her eyes a moment to adjust. By the time she could see again, Terrible was already in action, one meaty hand clasped around the throat of a smaller man who could only be Hunchback, holding him up against a pitted steel pillar in the center of the cavernous room. Chess wrinkled her nose; the warehouse smelled like a gymnasium drain.

"Where Brain?"

"I . . . I ain't . . ." Hunchback's eyes, mismatched and huge with fear, rolled in her direction, then back. "Ain't knowing."

Terrible lifted him higher. "What I fucking say to you, Hunchback? Ain't I say, keep the boy close? Ain't I say watch him?"

"Aye . . . b-but, you ain't say I can't punish him, he going out to the—" The sentence ended in a stifled gurgle as Terrible's fist tightened around his neck.

"Punishing ain't sending him out on the street. You ain't watching, you ain't doing what you fucking told. You need reminding?"

His fist connected with Hunchback's face before the man could open his mouth to answer, snapping Hunchback's head sideways. Chess willed herself not to move, not to gasp, not to do anything at all as Terrible started methodically beating the shit out of Hunchback.

She'd seen the results of his anger—of his attention to duty—before, once or twice when someone crossed Bump or owed him money. She'd never seen him in action, the dispassionate way he moved, as though he were crunching numbers at a desk or watching a not particularly interesting film on television. It terrified her. It took her breath away.

She wasn't the sole onlooker. Several painfully thin young teenagers of indeterminate sex stood near her, their mouths hanging open as Hunchback's shaved head moved with the impact of every blow. Blood arced from his mouth and spattered the cement floor, turning black in the layer of dust. Hunchback's fingers scrabbled feebly at Terrible's shirt, trying to grab hold as if he was afraid he would fall off the earth if he couldn't get that fabric in his grip.

It only lasted a minute or so, but it felt like much longer to Chess—though not, she imagined, as long as it must have felt to Hunchback.

"What say, Hunchback? You gonna listen next time you're told?"

Hunchback gurgled. His head bobbed up and down like a fishing float.

"So where Brain rest when he ain't here? Where he hang out?"

Hunchback shook his head. "Ainno." The words sounded strained through wet linen. "Ainnever tell me."

One of the teenagers stepped forward, twisting the hem of its T-shirt enough that Chess could barely tell she was a girl. "Um . . . Terrible? Sir?"

"Aye?"

"Sometime Brain go up Duck place. You knowing it? Sir?"

"Behind Fifty-third?"

The girl nodded. Her wide eyes and spiky fire-engine red hair made her look like a junkie Raggedy Ann doll.

"Aye, I know it." Terrible dropped Hunchback with an unceremonious thud and straightened up. "Think he there now?"

She took a hasty step back, as if she thought he might hit her too if she was wrong. "Can't say for sure, but he go there a lot. Say it safe for him most times."

Terrible nodded. "Thanks, chickie. You gotta name?"

The girl stepped back again and shook her head, sending her ropes of hair flying, but one of the others poked her.

"Tellim, Loose!"

The girl glared, then spoke. Her voice squeaked. "Lucy, sir."

"Aye, Lucy. Here." Terrible dug into his pocket and

pulled out a crumpled ten-dollar bill. "Get yourself some eats, girl."

Lucy hesitated.

"Goan, take it. I ain't hurt you. Lookin all starved. Hunchback, you start feeding yon kids, hear me?"

The bill disappeared from his hand as if by magic as Lucy snatched it away and leapt back, tucking it into her pocket. "Thankee, sir."

Terrible nodded. "He ain't feeding you, you find me. True thing, Lucy girl. Aye?"

Lucy nodded.

"Cool." Terrible gave Hunchback one last nudge with his toe, and turned to Chess. "Let's get us moving."

His bad mood wreathed his face like smoke as he drove through the bright streets without speaking. Chess glanced at him, glanced again, but his eyes stared straight ahead.

"That was a nice thing you did," she said finally. "Telling that girl to come to you."

He shrugged. "Hunchback ask Bump for work, sayin he gotta take care of them kids. So Bump lets Hunch operate, and Hunch letting them kids starve. Ain't right. They need food if they working."

"I didn't know Bump was such a philanthropist."

He glared at her. Oops.

"That's a person who runs charities and—"

"I know the meaning."

"Oh. Sorry."

He turned another corner, heading farther into a part of the city Chess wasn't familiar with. Like most Downside residents she tended to stay in her neighborhood as much as possible. You never knew what you might find on an unfamiliar street.

Here it was apparently a street fair, like the Market but less organized. The Chevelle rumbled past booths selling scarves and silver, clothing and cell phones, past firecans with spits propped over them. The scent of roasting meat floated in through the window, and Chess realized she was a little hungry.

She grew even hungrier at the end of the street, as Terrible pulled up in front of a barbeque stand. It was nothing more than a large black barrel grill and a folding table, but she couldn't remember the last time she'd smelled anything so tempting. The wizened man behind the makeshift counter nodded as Terrible stepped out of the car.

"Aye, T-man," he said, his voice high but smooth as the motion of his arms as he flipped the long row of meat with a rusty metal spatula. "You eating from me today? What you need?"

"Maybe later." Terrible opened Chess's door—another courtesy she didn't expect, she'd simply been so busy watching the barbeque man's sweat-shiny arms move like pistons, she hadn't thought to get out of the car. "You know Brain? One of Hunchback's kids?"

"Aye, I knows him. Seed him earlier, that's what you askin. He powerful scared. Ain't in no trouble with you, hoping?"

"Naw, not with me. Trying to find him though."

The barbeque man shrugged. "Headed down the aisle, guess to Duck." His gaze skittered over Chess's body, then back to her face, but he said nothing.

"Thanks."

For the second time that day Chess followed him down an alley, but where the first one had been wide and sun-drenched, this was so dark it felt more like nighttime. She slipped her sweater back on and checked her watch, surprised to see it was almost six. No wonder she was hungry and restless. She dug in her bag for her pillbox.

Terrible waited while she swallowed a Cept and washed

it down with a slug of water, then started moving again as soon as she screwed the cap back on the bottle.

"Gonna be dark soon," he said. "Best be back in the car afore then."

"Where are we?"

"Near Chester, but the other side. Docks that way. Ain't nothing good come out of them docks at night."

She shivered. The alley grew darker as they walked down it, like the sun didn't dare shine there. Terrible turned left at the end, into a space even more narrow. The walls were lined with chicken wire and damp, moldy rocks, and it smelled like a burned-out urinal.

She couldn't see to the end of it, either. It curved away to the right, giving her the bizarre impression that it pinched shut at the end. Her stomach was empty enough that the sweet peace of her pill started seeping through her blood quickly, but it didn't entirely eliminate her nerves. Nor did having Terrible's huge body right in front of her. Brain came here? That skinny, pale child made his way through this foul-smelling darkness alone?

When she was young she'd often thought kids like Brain had it better than she had. She didn't anymore— two different kinds of misery were still both misery—but when she saw places like this it made her wonder. She seriously doubted Brain had made it to whatever age he was without having his body violated, his bones broken, his spirit crushed. Just like her, but at least she'd known where the threat came from most of the time.

She wished he hadn't left her place.

They took another turn, right this time. Chess started to wonder how long they would be in here, if they would ever get out. If they at least could get out before dark. She had her knife, and she knew Terrible was armed to the teeth, but somehow that didn't reassure her.

Finally they reached a makeshift door, a scrap of warped

and broken plywood hung in a ragged hole in the wall by straps of leather. Terrible opened it and they stepped inside.

A single flame gave the only illumination save the fading sun's rays trying desperately to cut through the grime on the windows. Here and there a panel was broken, and light forced its way in, but was defeated by gloom before it could have an effect.

Bodies crowded the space, hunched together along the walls and slumped across the floor. Some young, some old, all covered in rags and stiff blankets.

"What business you got here?" demanded a voice, and Chess turned to face a small man, holding a candle of his own. The light made him look bigger somehow, making his dark skin gleam as if he'd been carved from mahogany. "Ain't no need for Bump to bring people into my place."

"You know Brain?"

The man—Duck?—didn't even blink. "Can't say I do."

Terrible didn't blink either, but he held his hands out, palm up. "Ain't looking to hurt nobody. Young one might be in trouble, me and the lady just wants to help him out. She got a home for him up her place."

"Since when does Bump take an interest?"

"Ain't Bump's interest. The lady's interest. You wanna keep Brain safe, you tell me where I find him. True thing, Duck."

Chess felt like she ought to speak, but the mental pissing contest between the men was too fascinating to interrupt.

"Gonna need your word on that, Terrible. And who she is."

Terrible opened his mouth, but Chess was faster. She liked this man, Duck, and she revised her earlier thought as she took in both him and her surroundings. Brain was definitely luckier than she'd been. It might be a scary place to come to, but it was safe once you arrived. "Cesaria Putnam. I'm a Debunker for the Church."

Recognition flared in Duck's eyes. "You Bump's Churchwitch."

"No, I'm Cesaria, and this has nothing to do with Bump." Which was kind of a lie, but not enough to keep her from meeting his eyes clean. Whether Bump had gotten her involved or not, Brain still would have seen what happened at the airport and would still be in danger because of it.

"Brain over there," Duck said after staring at her for a long moment. "In the corner, in the back."

At his words a tiny gasp sounded; a flurry of movement caught her eye, and she saw the back of Brain's head disappear through a dingy flap in the far wall.

Chapter Seventeen

"From the cemeteries they came, from the battlefields long overgrown, from the forests and the lakes . . . the forgotten dead walked again and sought vengeance."
—*The Book of Truth*, Origins, Article 18

Her heart threatened to pound out of her chest and her legs felt like someone had tied lead weights to them by the time they stopped running. It was impossible. Brain had disappeared into the twisted warren of alleys and buildings, and as darkness set in Chess almost started not to care. It was late, she hadn't slept, the line of Nip had long since worn off, and she was starving and cold. Surely Brain would be safe for one more day.

Terrible shook his head when his breathing slowed. "We keep looking, you want."

"I don't know how we'd find him."

"Neither me, but we keep looking if you want."

"Shit, if you don't know where to find him, how would I?"

He smiled. "Ain't you got them witchy skills?"

"Oh, of course. Let me just send some magic dust into the air to find him."

His laugh didn't sound as creaky as it had before. "Aye, you do that one. Like to see it myself."

They stood for another minute, letting their blood cool. Chess had no idea where they actually were. None of the buildings looked familiar and there were no street signs anywhere.

"Do with some eats, Chess? We ain't as away from my car as it seem."

Dinner with Terrible? Well, why not. They'd probably get faster service than she could get on her own, and she didn't feel like being alone again quite yet.

"Okay, sure."

He turned to his left and took a couple of steps, but Chess froze in place. Her skin crawled.

Only one thing could make her feel that way.

"Stop," she murmured, reaching into her bag. After the other night with Lex she'd thrown some spare asafetida into her bag, along with generic graveyard dirt. It wouldn't be as effective as the personalized stuff, but it would do. Where were all these ghosts coming from? Aside from Mr. Dunlop this was her second in three days, and that did not feel right at all.

What was stirring up the ghosts of Downside?

At first she couldn't see it, only feel it, but as she strained her eyes into the shadows at the end of the alley it started to take shape. A hat first, perched jauntily on top of the head. Then features, indistinct but all present and accounted for, and finally shoulders, a torso, and legs.

The ghost wore what looked like a double-breasted jacket, but the cut was tighter than Chess had seen before and flared slightly over the hips. A tiny patch of lighter, more iridescent space sat just above the chest on the left side, and as she watched a belt formed at the waist.

Lips parted in a grimace and the ghost started toward her, moving slowly and precisely. Another followed him, dressed similarly and with the same solemn expression. Not anger, necessarily, but . . . need. It—they—wanted something, and she had no doubt that that something would be her head on a plate if she didn't act fast.

Beside her Terrible moved. She flung her hand out toward him. "Don't!"

But he moved again, and Chess couldn't spare a

moment to glance at him because her fingers fumbled with the bag of graveyard dirt as she tried to gather a handful. It slipped over her skin, cool and full of power, but even as she pulled her hand out of the bag the ghosts stopped moving, stopped looking at her.

They looked at Terrible. Their right hands raised in unison. And they disappeared.

"What the fuck—how did you do that?"

Terrible cleared his throat, and lowered his own hand. He'd been saluting.

He opened his menu and shrugged, but the color on his cheeks hadn't faded. "Just a guess," he said again. "Thought maybe if they seen we was holding respect they'd back off."

"I don't even know how you guessed."

"They was wearing uniforms."

"Was that what they were—" She paused. The ghost she and Lex had encountered in the tunnel was dressed similarly. "I didn't know."

"Ain't you guys supposed to learn that stuff?"

"Not military. Armed forces are a special branch, they have their own Debunkers."

"It matter? I mean, can you Banish soldier ghosts?"

She lit a cigarette. "Oh, I imagine I could. It's the same thing, I just wouldn't be allowed to try it. Once they'd identified the ghost as military the case would be taken away. Because of the POW problems during Haunted Week, they figured . . . well, they wanted people with special training."

The waitress interrupted them to take their orders—burgers and fries for both—and left them again. Outside the diner the street came to life, hookers cruising up and down in their teetery shoes and spandex, Bump's minions hovering on corners with their pockets bulging, gangs of teenagers wandering around looking for trouble. Downside woke up around nine every night and kept going until the horizon turned pale again, even though most stores closed by eleven.

"How long you been doing the job?"

"Three years, almost four. Well, I started training nine years ago—they start at fifteen—and then when you turn twenty-one you're hired. Or not. One kid from my class didn't make it."

"What the training like?"

"Um . . ." Was he really interested? He certainly looked interested, and it was easier to talk to him than she'd ever imagined it would be, but something still held her back. "Like regular school, I guess, but with more magic studies and lore. You know, which herbs serve which purpose, how to direct energy and control it, Banishing rituals, summoning—although we're not supposed to do that. They do refresher courses, too, and regular energy raisings and cleansings on grounds."

"You ain't live there why? I thought all you had to live in them cottages there."

"I didn't want to."

"Just like that?"

"Yeah, just like that." She blew out a stream of smoke, and relented. "I . . . I had some problems living on grounds and applied for leave. I'm not good with living in a group situation, is all."

"You lose family in Haunted Week?"

"Didn't you?"

"Dunno. Guessing I'd remember if I had, but . . . don't recall no family."

"How old are you, anyway?"

He shrugged. "Older'n you, but ain't sure the number. I recall Haunted Week, aye, maybe a year or two before. So twenty-seven, twenty-eight? Somewhere there."

Chess was glad the waitress came back with their food. It gave her something else to look at. She'd never guessed he was so young, although she didn't know why. It wasn't as though he looked old and grizzled, he was just . . . so big. It made her uncomfortable to know he wasn't so far off her in age, as if he was somehow more real. She cleared her throat and picked up her burger.

"So how's Amy? Where's she tonight?"

"She right. Off doing whatever she do, guessing."

"You don't know?"

"Ain't tied to her."

Ouch. She had to swallow the enormous bite she'd taken—it was delicious—before she could answer, which kind of took the edge of her reply. "I was just asking."

"She ain't mine, dig. Just a dame I know."

"Well, sorry I assumed, okay?"

He looked for a minute like he wanted to say something else, but started eating instead. So much for that conversation. She ate, too, shifting her gaze upward, looking around the room. She'd never been to this place before, even though it wasn't far from her apartment. They didn't do much of a take-out business here, and she rarely had the urge to eat by herself in public—rarely meaning never—so it wasn't on her personal radar. She'd definitely come again, though, if the burger was an indication of their regular food and not part of a separate stock they brought out for Terrible.

It was even clean, which was saying something. No wonder it had filled so rapidly. She didn't recognize a lot of the faces, but some she did, people who ran stalls in the Market, a guy who lived in the building across the street from her, a shadowy face with coals instead of eyes half-covered by a black hood . . .

Her hamburger fell from her hand.

"Chess? You cool? Chess?"

She barely heard him over the roaring in her ears. Her legs wobbled as she tried to stand, her stiff fingers fumbling for her bag even though she knew it would be no use. Whatever he—it—was, it would take more than a few herbs and some dirt to send him away. She'd have to go in with Doyle and the others, take their case to the Grand Elder . . .

But just as Terrible had appeased the alley ghosts earlier, so she hoped she could make him disappear, just for now, just until . . .

"Chess! What you seeing?"

She thrust herself out of the booth, smacking right into a waitress carrying a heavy tray. The edge of it caught her in the ribs; the waitress fell sideways with a squeal that seemed to go on forever.

The man was gone.

Chess scanned the restaurant, her heart pounding, unable to believe it. He'd shown up and then just . . . disappeared again? Was he following her? Hovering invisible over her while she wandered the city all day?

No, he couldn't have, right? She'd have felt him.

You didn't feel him just now, did you?

Her legs gave; she gripped the edge of the table to keep from falling. Only then did she realize Terrible and the waitress were talking, that she'd knocked the woman over, and that a vanilla milkshake had flown from the tray and poured all over Terrible's shirt.

The sketch on the folded piece of paper made her heart give a funny leap in her chest. No words, but the artful rendering of a tulip in black ink could only have been left by one person.

Terrible was apparently too discreet to ask—she imagined he had a lot of practice at ignoring things, working for Bump—but his heavy eyebrows rose. She folded the note and tucked it into her back pocket.

"Right. Get that shirt off and give it to me."

"I just wash it home, Chess, no worries on it."

"I don't want it to stain. Come on, it's the least I can do."

He stared at her for a minute. She stared back. The white patch on his black shirt taunted her, reminded her how she'd lost her cool, how she'd been losing it ever since she saw that thing in Albert Morton's bedroom. She couldn't erase the memories or the shame of them—although she'd be able to blot them out awfully well when she opened her pillbox again—but she could erase that stain from Terrible's shirt.

Finally he shrugged and lifted his hands to the buttons. "You so determined, you have yourself a time, then."

The wet fabric slid across her fingers as she carried it into the bathroom, followed by Terrible in his white T-shirt. The room seemed to shrink around him, and when he sat on the edge of the tub his feet almost touched the opposite wall. Splotches of white stood out on his jeans like he'd been playing with bleach.

"Maybe you should give me your . . . um."

He glanced down. "Keep em on all the same, aye?"

"Sure. Of course." She busied herself at the sink with the liquid laundry soap she used on the few good items of clothing she owned. Her right palm stung; she'd almost forgotten about the wound, it had been healing so nicely.

"You not bad at that washing," Terrible said. "Maybe I start bringing all my clothes here, aye?"

Surprise tore the smart reply right out of her mouth. Terrible made a *joke*?

"You do mending? I tore on the fence the other day, you recall."

"Ha ha." The white stain had come out. She rinsed it and started soaping again just to be sure. "Don't think I'd be too good at that. It's not really my thing, you know?"

"Not dangerous enough?"

"I'm not into danger, either."

"Aw, Chess. You so into it you ain't climb out with a rope. Why else you do your job, live down here, buy from Bump?"

"It's just—I mean—I just do, is all." Her cheeks burned. She shouldn't have let him come in here. She should have just sent him home and let him wash his stupid shirt himself.

"No shame in it. Some of us needs an edge on things make us feel right, else we ain't like feeling at all, aye?"

"Your shirt's done." She handed him the sopping bundle, suddenly eager for him to leave. "You can wring it out, if you don't mind. My hand's still a little stiff."

He accepted the change of subject and turned around. Water splattered into the tub, again and again, until the shirt was almost dry and looked as though it had been pushed through the eye of a needle.

"Thanks again for your help earlier," she said, hoping he would take the hint and go. She had a kesh all rolled and ready to smoke, and she had a pillow calling her name. "With those army ghosts."

"Ain't army."

"What?"

Terrible strode back into the kitchen and put his hand on the doorknob to leave. "Ain't army, them ghosts," he said. "Air force. Them pilots we saw."

Chapter Eighteen

"Those who seek to undermine the Church's authority through their own communion shall be punished; and their sentence shall be death."
—*The Book of Truth,* Laws, Article 40

The image of the man in the hood—whom Doyle had called "the nightmare man"—hovered in front of her as she tried to sleep. He wasn't present, physically, in her apartment, but all the same he was there. Haunting her. Taunting her. Every time she started to drift off he appeared, chasing her into her dream, startling her awake. Refusing to go away and give her peace, even with the soft light and sounds of the TV on low.

Bed hadn't seemed very inviting. Not with the small pale walls of her bedroom closing in on her. The living room felt safer, as if the colored light from the stained-glass window somehow sanctified it, even though she knew there was no such thing.

Being on the couch didn't help her sleep. But it did mean when the picks scratched faintly in the front door deadbolt she heard them immediately.

Her knife was— Shit! Where was her knife? Had she set it down in the bathroom when she washed Terrible's shirt?

The lock clicked. Oh, fuck.

She slipped forward off the couch and scrambled across the floor, pushing herself to her feet as she went. She had razor blades in the bathroom, at least, if her knife wasn't there. She had—

They burst into the room, throwing the door open so hard she heard plaster crack as the knob hit the wall. Only a muddled impression of shapes, big black shapes in hoods, made its way through her mind before they were on her, arms like steel around her waist, a hand painfully tight over her mouth and jaw while another hooded figure knelt and hugged her legs so she could not kick. She tried to anyway.

"Where is it?" The voice in her ear was an accentless hiss. "Where is it?"

Her head was pressed back against the figure's shoulder. She could not move, could not bring her face forward, could not elbow him. Her skin burned from the friction of struggling against them both, her muscles ached from the hard pressure of their hands.

She had no idea what they wanted from her.

"Where is it?" he said again, loosening the pressure of his hand enough for her to open her mouth.

Chess didn't hesitate. She threw her head forward and back again. Pain exploded in the back of her skull as it connected with her attacker's teeth.

He grunted and stumbled back, letting go of her. Unfortunately the man kneeling in front of her pushed her legs back, so she fell with him. They hit the ground hard, shaking the floor.

She brought her right leg up and kicked out with it, catching the kneeling man in the throat with a glancing blow. His head tipped back, but she hadn't hit him hard enough to really hurt, and there wasn't time to try again. She didn't need to escape, she just needed to get her weapon, to give herself some advantage. They didn't seem to be armed; if they were she would have known it by now.

He reached for her again as she slammed her elbow back into the other man's gut and threw herself to the side. The kitchen. She'd left her knife in the kitchen.

The edge of the counter scraped painfully on her side through her thin T-shirt as she launched herself past it, bouncing off like a pinball but managing to keep her footing. They were right behind her, their hands brushing the ends of her hair.

They caught her in front of the sink. Her fingertips brushed the handle of her knife but couldn't grasp it. She stretched her arm, scratching at the countertop, but just as she thought she had it the first attacker caught her by the throat, pushing her back so her head hit the faucet.

She slapped at him, tried to kick, but he positioned his hips between her legs and pressed forward, immobilizing her lower body. Her hand flailed out to the side and knocked the knife back into the shadows by the microwave. She didn't think he'd seen it.

"Just tell us where it is," he whispered. Out of the corner of her eye she could see the other start lifting couch cushions, pulling books off the shelves. "Just tell us and we'll go."

"I don't know what you're talking about." She couldn't see his eyes well enough to know what color they were; beneath the hood he wore a black stocking pulled over his face, which turned him into a featureless ghoul, a lump of flesh like a human earthworm.

His fingers tightened around her throat. "Don't lie to me!"

Her left hand slipped along the edge of the sink, and farther outward, looking for something she could use as a weapon. Something cold and hard hit her fingers, something slim and round.

Her syringe. Filled with lubricant. Thick, oily lubricant. Two choices. She could ask him what he wanted, try and figure out what was going on here, but that might only make him angrier and wouldn't distract him. Or she could lie and hope he might loosen his grip long enough for her to hurt him.

The man in her living room gave a shout, a wordless cry of triumph. Her captor turned his head to look, and Chess made her move. One second to gird herself, to tense her body ready to attack . . . her fingers closed around the steel tube.

He turned his face back to her just as she brought her hand up, but he was too late. She slammed the needle into his neck, angling it back, hoping if she didn't hit a vein she could at least hurt him badly enough to immobilize him. Her fingers did not shake as she pushed the plunger in, giving him the full load. At the same time she used the heel of her right hand to smack him in the nose, barely noticing the pain the action caused. His head jerked back and he stumbled, his face turning back to her.

His mouth opened, but before the scream could materialize, his body collapsed, crashing like a bag of loose rocks to the tile floor.

The rattling thud interrupted the other one as he ransacked her living room and brought him running across the floor. Chess spun sideways, her legs steady now, a curious elation replacing her fear. The handle of her knife in her palm felt almost better than anything ever had. She braced herself with her legs slightly bent, holding the blade in front of her, and waited for him.

Lex got there first.

How or why he'd come to see her she didn't know, but he certainly moved as if he knew exactly what was going on, drawing a long, thin knife from an inner pocket of his jacket with his right hand while his left reached out and tangled in her attacker's hair.

The man started to turn, drew his fist back, but stopped

short when the blade penetrated his throat. His mouth opened, his fingers scrabbled madly at his neck for a moment as though to scratch an itch.

Then he fell. Blood poured from the wound and spread across her floor as Lex withdrew the knife.

"Damn, tulip," he said, wiping the blade clean on the dead man's robe. "You sure know how to make a man feel welcome, aye?"

The air left her chest in a long, harsh gasp. "What are you doing here?"

"Ain't you get my note? Coming by to get my update, but this better. Ain't every day I gets to kill people for a good reason."

"I'm so glad I could help." There were two dead bodies on her floor. In her apartment. Two men had broken in and tried to kill her—or if not kill her, to steal from her, to scare her, to do whatever it was they planned to do.

Two dead men. In her home. She'd killed one of them. Her knees went weak.

"Whoa, hey now. Thought you was a tough dame. Sure looked tough I walked in. Remind me never get you mad."

Chess lifted a shaking hand to her head and pushed her bangs out of her eyes. "Yeah, well, lucky for you I'm in a good mood."

He smiled in acknowledgment and dipped his head toward the corpse on the floor. "What they want, anyroad? Just robbing, or trying to hurt you?"

"Robbing. They . . . they wanted something. They asked me where it was . . ."

"What? They find it?"

"I don't know." She shook her head, trying to clear it. Lex's victim had shouted something, hadn't he? She glanced into her living room. Her Blackwood box lay open, its contents spilling out onto the floor.

The box where she'd put the amulet.

Grabbing a tattered dish towel to guard her bare hands, she crossed the floor and knelt beside the body while Lex did the same, slicing the nylon over the men's faces to reveal their features. Unfamiliar, both of them. Too bad, but not a surprise. Why should something go right?

The voluminous robe was soaked in blood, but the symbol on the front was still visible. A crooked line like a lightning bolt rose above a more traditional-looking set of entwined runes, she couldn't tell which ones. It looked vaguely familiar, but then, most magical sigils and symbols did, didn't they?

She found the pockets after a minute of searching. The amulet hid in one of them, tucked in the bottom, as shiny and bright as ever.

"They wanted this," she said.

Across the room her phone buzzed like a hornet caught in a jar, audible even over the Pagans album playing in the background. It had been going off for an hour or so, while she sat on the couch at Lex's place trying to summon the strength to move.

"Oughta pick it up," he said, chopping out some fat lines on a mirrored tray. No sleep, again, and her eyes burned. "Ain't you got no people be worried?"

"No. I don't have any people."

"Sounds like maybe you wrong." He finished his work and slid the tray a few inches toward her, holding out a silver straw.

She took it, leaned over, vacuumed up the line. Blessed numbness hit her nose, worked its way into the back of her throat along with that bitter battery-acid flavor that always made her teeth tingle. She dipped her index finger in the glass of water he'd set out and snorted a few drops to chase the powder back. Damn. Every time was as good as the first time, wasn't it?

Or at least close.

She sniffed again, sucking air through her sinuses to drag more powder into her throat and lungs, and reached for the phone. She didn't want to talk to anyone but Lex, didn't want to be anywhere but here. Drugged inertia set in, and would last until she suddenly started itching to be elsewhere, but at the moment there was no place on earth cozier than this bedroom where she'd spent a chaste and sleepless night alone in the bed while he took the couch. Quite a surprise, that, but then she'd been so tanked on the Oozers he'd given her she probably wouldn't have felt a thing if he had tried it on.

The phone buzzed again in her hand. Might as well get it over with. "Hello?"

"Chess? Damn, baby, where you at? Terrible ripping this town *apart* looking for you, said something about your door open and your place all scraped? You alive?"

Shit! "Um . . . I answered the phone, so . . . Yes?"

Edsel gave a short laugh. "Right. Coursen you are. What happened your place?"

"I had a break-in. I'm fine. Tell Terrible I'm fine and I'll call him in a few minutes, okay?"

"Got it. Hey, saw someone you need last couple hours ago. Recall I tell you my customer Tyson? Came by here, left his directions. Say he think he can help if you still need, come by his place later."

"Oh, awesome. Thanks, Ed, thank you so much." She mimed writing at Lex, who stared at her for a moment as if she'd gone insane, then twigged and handed her a pen and a slip of paper. Chinese characters covered one side of it, so she used the other.

"Just you watch your back, Chess. Tyson okay far as I know, but I ain't *know,* dig me?"

"Got it. Thanks again."

This was the best news she'd had in days, despite Edsel's warning; the prospect of meeting someone he obviously mistrusted didn't please her, but she needed the information more than she worried about the source. If she could decipher that fucking amulet she could figure out what the soul-powered spell was doing, and if she knew what it was doing she could figure out the best way to stop it and set Slipknot's soul free. Not to mention hopefully ending the possibility of more hooded thugs showing up at her place.

Next were her messages. Terrible. Edsel. Doyle, then Terrible twice, then Elder Griffin wanting to know if she'd made any progress on the Morton case yet, then Terrible again. She'd have to stop by the Church at some point today and drop off the photos of Albert Morton's books for Goody Tremmell to add to the file. She also needed to interview the Mortons. Maybe she could do that later, if there was time after going to see Edsel's acquaintance.

Finally she called Terrible. "Hey, it's Chess."

"Chess?" Pause. "Shit, where you at? You cool? Somebody got you?"

"No, no, I'm fine, I—I had a break-in, and I got scared and—"

"You ain't called me, let me know. Went your place on the morn, dig, got blood on your floor and you not there. Whose blood? They get away?"

She blinked. Lex had called some people to take care of the bodies. Apparently they hadn't bothered to tidy up, which she guessed was only to be expected. "Yeah, they got away. Ran away. It wasn't my blood, though. I managed to get one of them with my knife."

"Good job, aye. You see who was it? Thinking got something about Chester?"

"Yeah. They were wearing robes, they . . . I think they wanted the amulet. So yeah, I think it was. What time is it?" *Let it go, let it go* . . . She did not want to talk about the implications of the break-in and how exactly the invaders had gotten away. Didn't trust herself to talk about it, not just yet.

"Just past midday."

Damn, midday already? The windows in Lex's place were covered by such thick blinds it was impossible to know how bright it was outside, like being in a secret cave somewhere. A safe, secret cave. Just the thought of the noonday sun made her eyes hurt. "I'm fine, Terrible. I came to stay with—um, with a friend on Church grounds."

"Aye, safe there. Good idea." She could hear his breath through the line. "You heading back now? Only Edsel said he might have someplace I ought to take you."

"Yeah. Look, I'll meet you at Edsel's booth in an hour or so, okay?"

Lex laid another line for her while she called Elder Griffin and let him know she'd be by, then bagged up some powder for her before walking her to the door.

"You coming back here this night?" His index finger lifted her chin, a brief touch that sent an unwelcome shiver through her body.

"I don't know. I'll call you if I need to, okay?"

"You do that."

She expected the kiss, even felt confident it wouldn't affect her the way it had before. But it did. Her knees went weak as his fingers twined in her hair, as he pulled her close to him with a strong hand on her hip. "You do that, tulip. I'll be waiting."

Chapter Nineteen

> "Do not attempt to form a connection with one of the dead, no matter how it may seem profitable. It is not."
> —*The Book of Truth*, Rules, Article 35

She'd never been this far out of the city. Had the day been as bright and sunny as she'd pictured, it would have been a pretty drive. As it was she could barely see. The Chevelle's wipers slapped a quick beat across the windshield and fog obscured any view there might have been. It felt as though they were hurtling through space, she and Terrible, talking occasionally while Chuck Berry came softly from the speakers and she made notes for her interviews with the Mortons later. Elder Griffin hadn't been upset by her lack of progress, but she was, and seeing Randy Duncan hovering around again hadn't made her feel better. He'd lost his edge, what little edge he'd had. She didn't want to do the same.

"Do you know where we are?"

"How many times you gonna ask that?"

"Until we get there. We've been driving forever."

"Not even an hour. You always this impatient?"

"I'm bored. I feel cooped up. It's too foggy outside, I can't see anything."

"Ain't much to see."

"How do you know?"

"You the only one in this car never been out the city."

"I've been out of it. Just . . . not in a long time."

"Not much purpose in it. Not much out here, not anymore."

As if to illustrate this, he slowed down to make a turn. Through the mist loomed a blackened, craggy shape; the remnants of what had once been a church, one of the many destroyed by furious citizens when Haunted Week finally ended. The country was littered with these brick and granite corpses, silent testaments to a system of belief that had served mankind for centuries but ultimately proved as worthless and obsolete as a black-and-white television.

"Roll down yon window some," he said.

"But it's raining."

He raised an eyebrow and glanced at her. "Ain't say open it wide."

They seemed to be rolling through a neighborhood now. She could barely make out the shadows of buildings at regular intervals, and he'd slowed to about forty. Maybe he wanted to throw things out of the car? Whatever. She grabbed the crank and gave it a half turn.

"What is that smell?"

"The ocean."

"Doesn't smell like the ocean."

"Naw, don't smell like the *bay*, what you used to. That's the for real ocean, Chess. Ain't it sweet?"

It was. She'd never smelled anything like it. Tangy and salty, with an undercurrent of sour fish that should have been nauseating but somehow made her feel clean instead.

"Are we going to see it?"

"Guessing, aye. Look like your friend live down on it."

"He's not my friend."

"Let's hope he ain't an enemy. This don't have the right feel to me."

"What do you mean?"

"Just we don't know the man. You don't know him,

and I don't know him, and he maybe knows too much himself about some shit nobody want to be involved in if they got their sanity working right." He made another turn, then swung left onto a road Chess imagined would have been almost invisible even on a clear day. It couldn't even be properly called a road, really, more like a track, two shallow ditches winding through tall brown grass. The Chevelle rattled and bumped over it like a lumbering insect, finally coming to a halt by the edge of a cliff.

"We here," Terrible said, and he did not sound happy about it. She knew he was right. She wasn't really sure why she was in such a good mood, unless it was Lex's excellent speed. Certainly there wasn't much for her to be so cheery about. Edsel's warning that he didn't know much about Tyson came back to her, a warning she should heed. Edsel was her friend; if he said she should be careful, she should.

Just the same, she was cheery. Or at least she wasn't depressed, which was a victory in itself. Drugs or not, she hadn't felt this good in a long time. Which meant it was time to make sure she didn't come down unexpectedly.

"Hold on a minute." She closed her window and brought out Lex's Baggie and her hairpin. "You want some?"

"Naw, thanks. Jerky enough out here. Ain't the city, feels empty."

She shrugged and bumped up, then tucked everything back in her purse as he came around to open her door. The fresh-smelling wind caught her full in the face, and she sniffed it and her drugs down in one long deep inhalation that sent sparkles all the way to her toes.

And there was the ocean, in front of her, stretching out into the fog like a piece of napped gray velvet. Her hair whipped around her face and stole the view. She pushed it back with an impatient hand and closed her eyes, lifting her chin, letting the wind wash her clean.

"Can we touch the water when we're done? Before we go, I mean?" Smiling, she turned to him, but he looked down before she could catch his eye and started digging in his shirt pocket for a cigarette.

"Aye, if you're wanting," he mumbled, turning away from her to light up. "C'mon, let's get this done."

The cliffs hunched over Tyson's little house, sheltering it from some of the rain and giving it the appearance of a troll crouching under a heath. Chess almost expected it to leap out at her, and her mood went from unusually good to cautious and tense in the space of an eyeblink. Edsel's warning reverberated through her head, and this time it caught her. She wondered what exactly Tyson purchased from him. She decided she was very, very glad she had Terrible with her.

That thankful feeling grew as they walked across the flat stones laid in a path to the front door. Each one was carved with runes, most of which she knew but a few she didn't. One in particular sent a shivery tingle up her leg when she stepped on it, like someone had rung a bell in her veins.

In the doorframe were more runes and symbols carved deep into the wood. Totem images and swirls, letters in some of the ancient alphabets, pentacles . . . too many for her to take in before the door swung open and Tyson stood framed before them.

Something slithered behind his eyes, clouding them smoky gray like an overcast sky for a second before they normalized again. But Chess had seen it, and the hair on her nape stood on end. Tyson was not human, not entirely. Whether he'd been born that way or whether he'd made himself what he was through dealing with the Underworld she did not know, and she hoped she wouldn't find out.

He rubbed the palm of one surprisingly large hand

over his short white hair. Now that she'd had a second to adjust she realized he wasn't old, as she'd first imagined. He might have ten years on her, possibly twenty, but not more. His small, stooped frame had been bent by something other than age.

"Thou must be Cesaria," he said, his voice pouring over her like whiskey. "And thou has brought an escort. A guard?"

"Just a friend," she said.

"Awfully big friend, is he not?" Tyson looked Terrible up and down, a shifty half-smile playing on his lips, then shrugged. "Aye, welcome in. Edsel sayest thou needs information? About some runes?"

"Yes."

He bowed and stepped back, sweeping his right arm wide to usher them in. "I have information, indeed."

For a moment the size of the place made her dizzy. Had he somehow subverted the rules of physics, made his little hut bigger on the inside? Then she realized why the room smelled of dusty rock, dry and powdery in her nose. With the exception of the weathered wood front wall, the rest of the house was made of stone. He'd tunneled back into the cliffs. She made a mental note not to walk farther back if she could help it. The thought of all that heavy rock—and one BT muscle car—with absolutely nothing to keep it from falling . . .

Focusing on the house itself did nothing to put her at ease. Shelves lined every wall, stuffed full with jars and bottles, with bones and feathers and fur. Why did this man shop at Edsel's, when he had virtually everything a spellcaster could ever want right here? Skulls from at least fifteen different animals on one wall, rows of various other parts on another. Jars of herbs stacked one on top of the other, three deep, intruded into the room from the back, framing a small black door that she imagined led to Tyson's bedroom.

She turned around to see Terrible brushing cautiously at the objects hanging from the ceiling as he entered. Amulets and charms, all tied to colored ribbons and strings. They would have hit him in the face if he didn't push them aside, but she could feel his reluctance to touch them and couldn't blame him for it.

"I have made refreshments," Tyson said. "Would thou care for some? A drink? A cookie?"

It should have been amusing, the offer of a cookie from a man whose eyes kept sliding into and out of gray and lived in a museum of sorcery. But his smile was a little too wide, a little too full of teeth. She couldn't help but wonder what sort of cookie he might have made.

According to Church law, world-bound souls were not permitted to exist. The human host could be sent to prison, one of the special prisons where souls were tortured and escape was impossible. Chess wondered why Tyson did not seem afraid she might report him. Most tried to hide their binding. He did not.

"No, thank you," she said, realizing he and Terrible were both watching her. "Can we just get down to business? I'm afraid I'm in kind of a hurry today."

"Of course. The formalities are only that—formalities. Having dispensed with them we may conclude our transaction at any pace thou desires."

"Um. Great." She pulled out the amulet, wrapped in its tea towel. "I was hoping you would be able to decipher some of the runes on this, they—what?"

Tyson collected himself with some effort. His eyes smoothed back to gray as he forced the smile to leave his face, but Chess could still feel his amusement, could still hear his light laugh in the air. "I am sorry, Cesaria. Tell me, where did thou find this thing?"

"I can't say."

He nodded and held out one large hand, his too-slim

fingers curving gently like seaweed in the tide. "May I hold it, please?"

She set it and the cloth in the center of his palm, hoping he didn't notice her reluctance to touch his skin. He whipped the towel away, closing his fingers around the amulet and holding it up.

"Oh, aye," he said. "It does its little job, does it not? Hmmm." He brought it to his nose, stuck out his tongue for a taste. His eyes rolled back in his head. "Thou has given it blood, Cesaria."

"It was an accident."

He chuckled, like a clogged engine coughing its way into life. "Accidents do happen." His hand snapped shut. "I can tell much of it. What shall I get in return? The book needs its sacrifice if it is to open."

"What book? Can't you just tell me?"

"The words cannot be spoken unless cast. Thou must read them, but not say out loud."

Nothing good could possibly come of this. She saw herself at the door, saw Terrible behind her as they left and climbed back up the hill to his car, saw them hauling ass away from here and back to the city.

Then she saw Slipknot, with his body rotting more every minute and his soul trapped inside the maggoty, desiccated ruin, and she knew she could not go.

"What's the price?" She picked up her bag, ready to dig into her wallet. For that matter, she was ready to make Terrible dig into his. Bump would be paying both of them back. This was his project, he could use his own damn money.

"Oh. Thou offers money." Those extra teeth of Tyson's glowed in the dim light. "The book does not require such cold sacrifice, dear. It asks for something more . . . Perhaps thou had better see. Wait here."

Chess and Terrible exchanged glances as he got up and

disappeared through that black door, the shiny gold and red fabric of his robe floating behind him.

"You ain't get this learning any elsewhere?"

She shook her head.

He sighed. "Ain't liking this, not one bit."

She was about to reply when Tyson swept back into the room, holding a book flat in front of him. At first Chess thought Tyson had cut himself on something in the other room, that he either hadn't noticed or didn't care. Then she realized the blood spattering onto his robe and absorbing into the dirt floor wasn't his.

It was coming from the book.

It dripped dark and clotted from the covers and oozed out from the pages. Chess's skin crawled. She did not want to read that thing, didn't want to touch it, didn't want to go near it. Her palm burned and itched, the tattoos on her arms warmed as the book was brought closer to her.

Tyson nudged a small table with his foot and looked at Terrible. "Will thou bring it over?"

Terrible's face did not move as he lifted the table and set it in front of Chess, but when his eyes met hers she read the message in them. He felt it, too, didn't like this any more than she did.

It couldn't be helped. She tried not to cringe away when Tyson set the bloody book on the table, forcing herself instead to reach for it. Tyson's hand stopped her.

"Thou is sure? Thou is ready to touch the book?" His eyes gleamed.

"I don't have a choice, do I?"

Terrible stepped forward. "Give it me."

"No. This isn't your—"

"Ain't having you do it, Chess. It's why I come along, aye?"

Droplets of blood plunked onto the dirt, loud in the silence while she and Terrible looked at each other.

"One of thee decide, if it pleases," Tyson said. "Charming as this little moment is, I haven't got all day to watch."

Chess reached out, but Terrible was faster. The tips of the fingers on his left hand brushed the cover, and the book flew open, scattering drops of blood everywhere, onto him, onto Chess, onto the walls and furniture.

She barely noticed. She could not tear her eyes away as the pages shifted, fluttered, brushing against Terrible's hand, then finally falling open, clean and white. The blood was gone.

For a moment, anyway. Then it started again, spreading across the pages in a crimson flood, forming words and symbols that seemed to float above the parchment.

Terrible grunted softly, an uncomfortable sound, one she did not like. His hand, which had been resting on top of the book, seemed to shrink, to flatten, and she realized it was actually sinking in. The blood on the page now was his.

He sank to his knees, his face flushing, his eyes closed.

"Terrible? Terrible?"

He shook his head. "Ain't . . . no . . ."

"Terrible!" She reached for him, meaning to pull his arm away, but Tyson's voice stopped her.

"Thou had best get the knowledge," he said. "Quickly, lest the book kill thy guard before thou do."

Chapter Twenty

"Often we find ourselves as parents unsure how to guide our children. In those cases we should simply look for the Truth, and we will be correct. Protecting our children is the highest way of serving humanity and Truth."
—*Families and Truth*, a Church pamphlet by Elder Barrett

Terrible moaned, a sound so low and frightened it felt like someone rubbing tinfoil against her brain.

"Stop this!"

Tyson shrugged. "His time shortens while thou speaks."

Fuck! Fuck, shit fuck. Where was her notepad? And her pen? The words in the book had almost finished forming, stretching across the pages like the footprints of bleeding ravens. An image started to form in the center, the amulet, the runes around the edge growing and shrinking.

"No . . . not me . . . not me . . ." Terrible's body convulsed, folded over on itself, his head bowed. His entire body trembled and shook as he sank farther to the floor, shrinking into a semifetal position. Red symbols scrolled up his arm, swirling around his elbow and creeping over the slice of bare skin showing at the back of his neck, then back down to spread over the page.

Finally her fingers closed over the pen and pad. She started writing, hardly paying attention, just trying to copy the pages and stop this. If it would stop, if she hadn't just sacrificed a man's life just to decipher that stupid amulet. Slipknot could rot forever for all she cared, who cared, just please let this end . . .

Tretso, yes. To power. And the other one, *Etosh,* to direct it. More. *Vedak,* to trap the soul. *Arged,* to feed from it. Who the fuck had done this, had concocted something so foul? The lettering flowed faster across the parchment now, almost too fast for her to follow.

"That's good," she heard Tyson say softly. "So much pain . . . and strength . . . the book is pleased . . ."

"Fuck you," she managed, but it was drowned out by Terrible's roar, like a tiger in pain, setting every hair on her body on end.

The last rune formed now, pulsing bigger and thicker, the red marks forming a rune, then a face, then a rune again, the words stretching out even as Chess's heart thudded and skipped. That face was that of the nightmare man, and his name was Ereshdiran, the stealer of dreams.

"Done!" she shouted. "I'm done! I'm finished, stop this now, stop it please . . ."

Red ink covered Terrible's face, fiery bright under his skin, under the tears squeezing out from beneath his closed eyelids.

"No more, no more, no more, not me, please, please don't." Over and over, a litany she could not bear to hear any longer.

Terrible's eyes flew open. Chess screamed. His irises were red, bright glowing red, his pupils nothing but black pinpoints against it. It was *in* him, oh fuck, whatever it was was inside him, eating him . . .

Tyson laughed softly as she reached out without thinking and grabbed the book, trying to yank it away.

Tyson's house disappeared. Instead she was back in a bedroom, a familiar one, though she had not seen it in years, while heavy footsteps clumped across a wooden floor as she pulled the covers tighter over her head. She was only ten, she didn't want him in here, didn't want him to make her do those things again . . .

A different room, a different father, his beefy fist swinging backward to catch her across the face . . .

Another hit. A heavy, sweaty female figure climbing into her bed. Her clothes torn. Every image Chess ever wanted to forget flashing before her eyes, and over it all the despair, the pain, the misery and loneliness of never being touched except in anger or lust, of being outside, not belonging to anyone or with anyone, of hating herself so much it made her choke. She couldn't even feel her body anymore, couldn't see or hear anything but the voice in her head that reminded her every minute of every day how worthless she was, the voice she tried to dull with drugs and work but never really went away, it never would go away, not until she finally died and went to the silent and cold City beneath the ground, a place she'd always thought bad enough to make life just a tiny bit preferable to it. There was no solace there for her, no peace, just endless days and nights of drifting . . .

"Noooo," she sobbed, and just like that it ended. Her knees hurt from hitting the floor. Every muscle in her body ached, but it was done, the book was closed, and Terrible was halfway across the room before she stopped feeling the imprint of his hands on her arms.

He grabbed Tyson by the throat and lifted him, flinging the smaller man against the rough-hewn stone like a ball at the end of a tether. Tyson made a small choked sound that could have been a cry or a laugh, his eyes slithering back to solid gray.

"Lemme hit him, Chess," Terrible moaned, his voice breaking. His right hand fisted and flexed, fisted and flexed, the muscles on his arm bulging as his whole body trembled. "Just let me . . . you . . . you fucking . . ."

"Thou saw things thou did not want to see again." Tyson smiled like a zipper sliding open. "Bad memories, guard? Was it worth it?"

"Chess . . ."

"No! No, Terrible, don't, don't—wait." Her leg bumped the table as she got up and crossed the room, leaving a smear of blood soaking into her jeans. "Wait. Who else saw this, Tyson? Who came here before, and made that amulet?"

"I know not—"

"No, you do. You do, that's why you laughed when you saw it, isn't it? Who was it? Tell me, or I'll let him beat you. I'll let him kill you if he wants to, and I think he does." She glanced at Terrible, but his eyes were still focused on Tyson with the intensity of a hungry wolf watching a housecat. "Do you want to, Terrible?"

"Aye."

"Thou cannot kill me. I am more powerful than thou knows."

Terrible growled.

"You know what I have in my bag, Tyson? Melidia weed. Melidia, and my psychopomp. I can send you and whatever that thing is you're hosting into one of the spirit prisons so fast you won't even have time to beg for mercy, and I can let Terrible break every fucking bone in your body first. Now tell me, and we'll go. Fair evens."

Terrible tightened his grip on Tyson's throat. Tyson's eyes bulged slightly, rolling back into his head. "Like thou," he gasped. "A dark man, inked like thou . . . ahhh . . ."

His arms stretched out at his side, his fingers spreading as his eyes went pure silver. Shit.

"Terrible, let him go!" She grabbed his arm, trying to pull him away from Tyson. "Let him go, now!"

Terrible obeyed just as the thing inside Tyson freed itself, flying from the man's open mouth and into the air over their heads like pale, misty vomit. Chess ducked, pulling Terrible with her. They fell to the dirt in a jumble of arms and legs as the thing formed itself into a face, vaguely human, with huge empty eyes and a mouth that opened as if on hinges.

It spread across the ceiling, growing larger and larger. A long finger of tattered ectoplasm brushed Chess's cheek, leaving a trail of freezing slime across her skin.

Terrible's fingers were warm and hard in hers, painfully tight, as he yanked her up and pulled her across the room, throwing his body against the door to break it open. The thing screamed behind them as they ran, but nothing emerged from the ramshackle hut, and after a moment silence fell.

"My bag," she gasped. "I left my bag in there."

"Shit. You joking me?"

She shook her head. The wind blew so hard she couldn't seem to catch her breath, or maybe her lungs were simply frozen in terror. *Inked like thou,* he'd said. A Church employee? "I have to have it, I have to go back for it."

"Oh, naw. You stay."

She couldn't argue. All she could do was watch as he ran back into the house and emerged a few moments later dangling her bag from one bloody-knuckled hand.

"What did you do to it?"

He looked down. "Ain't my blood. Couldn't just let him get off free, aye?" He was breathing too hard, the knuckles of his other hand white.

"Sit down, okay? Just sit here with me for a minute."

"We oughta go, he cold out now but—"

"Please? Just . . . just sit with me."

He sank to the ground beside her, with his legs bent and his arms resting on his knees, while the ocean shifted and whispered before them. The sound soothed her, but she did not think the harsh fire in her stomach would be appeased so easily. Those images, those memories . . . it all felt again as if it had just happened.

"Thanks. I mean, thanks for doing that for me, I didn't think, well, I didn't know it would be—"

"Nothing, Chess." His shoulders moved in a casual shrug, but he didn't take his gaze from the water before them. "Why I here."

"No, it's not. That was—I don't even want to think about what that was, and you couldn't have—"

"Forget it. It's over now, aye?" Now he glanced at her. She caught a glimpse of his eyes red-rimmed in his pale face before he turned away again. "Over."

What had he seen? She would never ask. It was private, just as hers had been private. But at the same time she was aware of her curiosity, irritating and unwelcome like a splinter in her finger. She felt she owed him something now, in a way she hadn't when he'd helped her at the airport . . . when, she realized, he'd helped her several times over the last few days. And she'd assumed, when they'd come here, that he would do it again. Shit, when had that happened? When had she started trusting him? She should know better than that.

But it was there, nonetheless, mixed with her curiosity. She trusted him, and she owed him.

"You know," she said, scooping up some sand and letting it fall between her shaking fingers, "ancient people used to think the ocean had healing qualities. They said if you left offerings to it, if you sat before it long enough, all of your problems would wash away in the tide."

"You think there's truth in it?"

"No." Her voice cracked. She owed him something, but she couldn't carry through the lie. "No, I don't."

He nodded. "Me either."

Waves broke and crashed against the shore as they got up and started trudging back up the hill, taking their time, until Chess's hair clung to her head and she could not tell anymore if her face was wet with tears or spray.

* * *

A silent drive, two Cepts, and a line later, she sat in the Mortons' tidy living room and frowned. Nothing. Either these people were particularly good, or the lack of food in her stomach combined with speed and pills was putting her more off-kilter than she should be. Their faces were so distorted by fear it was like looking into a funhouse mirror. Would she see the same bizarre warping of her own features?

Shit, this wasn't right. She'd never had problems with what she took before, not like this. A little memory fuzz once in a while, sure—it was one reason why she took copious notes—or sometimes asking people to repeat things because she couldn't get their words to process in her head, but . . . sitting with them now was like sitting in a wind tunnel.

Something else was different, as well. All the lights were on, though the sun was just setting.

"I don't know why you're asking all these questions," Mrs. Morton said, for the third or fourth time. "I haven't slept in days. Please, when will you be able to get rid of it?"

"We're working on it. Have you thought of staying somewhere else for a while? A friend's house, perhaps, or a hotel?"

"We can't afford a hotel," Mrs. Morton snapped. Her eyes widened. "I mean, a hotel for weeks would be very expensive."

Chess didn't react, or make a note. She didn't need to—this part was set hard into her brain. "According to the records you gave us, you have approximately ten thousand dollars available on your credit cards. Surely you can stay at a hotel for a while? You would of course be reimbursed by the Church after the Banishment."

She said it with such confidence, she really did. Just as

if she hadn't found out earlier that one of her fellow Church employees was doing illegal magic to call forth something whose name she'd never heard before. Something that reeked of evil like a dead dog in the street reeked of decay.

And speaking of decay . . . The image of Slipknot's rotting flesh, sliced open, marked up like a demented child's tortured dolly, refused to leave her. What his soul must be suffering as he lay trapped in the stinking wreckage that was once a living, breathing body, was unimaginable. And she was responsible for it, because she hadn't yet figured out how to release him.

It was hard enough not to think of herself as someone who barely deserved to live, without that kind of shit smeared all over her conscience.

How could one of her coworkers do such a thing? For what felt like the millionth time since leaving the beach she tried to think of illegal ink, forbidden tattoos, the possibility that the culprit might simply be someone who looked like a Church employee.

But no. Tyson knew who he'd seen, would know the difference between genuine Church tattoos and illegal ones. *Inked like thou*, he'd said, and it couldn't have meant anything but Church ink.

She hoped he'd been lying. She couldn't deny the possibility that he hadn't.

"Yes, well, we'd rather stay in our home and have everything taken care of quickly, instead of being inconvenienced by living in a hotel," said Mr. Morton. It took Chess a second to remember what they were talking about.

"Has the haunting escalated? You said last time that it was just a gray sexless shape, Mrs. Morton. Has it taken form? Started moving objects, anything like that?"

"It's not gray anymore." Mrs. Morton pulled at the

string of pearls around her neck as if they were choking her. "It's black. A man, in a black hood. He . . . he
watches us while we try to sleep, he sneaks into our
dreams . . . he scares me."

She dissolved into sobs, sobs Chess could not hear over
the pounding of her own heart.

Chapter Twenty-one

"So they found the open spaces beneath the surface of the
earth, and found the power there stronger than even that
of the spirits, and they sent their guardians and messen-
gers to the surface and brought the spirits to their new
home, and imprisoned them there."

—*The Book of Truth*, Origins, Article 400

She didn't want to go home. Not after the break-in—
had that really only been the night before? It had, and she
couldn't bear the thought of spending a night there alone.
Not now, when she knew the person after her knew her,
knew everything about her, had worked with her for
years.

Tyson could have been lying, but Chess knew he hadn't.
Knew it the way she knew what the Truth was, the way
she knew . . . the way she knew the only safe place
now, even in the midst of all her doubts, was the Church.
This late at night the building would be deserted, no one
would be in the great library, and she had a key. She could
do some research, try to decide what everything meant.
She could just sit and breathe. The locks in her home
could be picked, but the locks of the Church buildings
were impregnable.

Of course, whoever had murdered Slipknot had a key,
too. But they wouldn't know where she was. It was still
the safest place she could think of.

She spread her notes on the table before her, scanning
them to make sure she hadn't forgotten anything, looking
for things she might have missed, before starting.

Neither Ereshdiran nor the symbol on her assailants'

robes appeared in any of the standard texts. She hadn't expected them to, but wanted to be thorough.

Why would someone want to summon a Dreamthief? This wasn't the first time illegal entities had been summoned, of course. When Chess was still a student someone had tried to call an elemental hate spirit, to show off at a party. Those who'd survived the carnage had failed to be impressed.

But a Dreamthief . . . ? She kept thinking if she could remember where she'd seen that damned symbol she might have some idea what was going on, but her memory of it seemed too fuzzy. She couldn't be sure in her mind it actually looked like she remembered, or if she'd embellished it somehow, made it up.

Sighing, she closed the last book and glanced at the clock. Almost ten. She'd have to leave soon if she wanted to replenish her supplies, and she definitely wanted. Only a desire to get to the bottom of this had kept her from running straight for the pipes after Terrible dropped her off. After the book . . . after the memories, carving themselves fresh into her head and leaving bloody tracks running down her neck . . . if she hadn't been determined to make that hellish experience worth the price of admission she would have done it.

She gave herself half an hour more. Enough time to check a couple of the restricted books. Then she'd go. Straight to Bump's.

The door to the Restricted Room locked, but Chess knew where a spare key was kept, tucked on the ledge at the top of the center desk drawer. She'd never needed to steal it before, but then she'd never done research like this after hours before—the library Goodys had always been there to let her in. Feeling a little like a criminal, she felt around the ledge with her fingertips until the key dropped into the drawer, then crossed the room and slipped it into the lock.

It gave an audible click as the catch released, a click that seemed to echo in the big, empty room. Chess froze. Had that just been the lock, or had another click followed it, so closely she just mistook it for an echo?

She whipped around, her gaze skittering from shelf to shelf, across the empty expanse of shining wood floor and up the walls to the fans hanging like bizarre spiders from the ceiling. Always look up. Nobody ever looks up.

Nothing was there, and gradually her heart rate— already fast from all the speed—calmed down. She gave a soft, snorting laugh at herself, like a child bravely declaring themselves unafraid of the dark, and turned the knob.

She'd always loved the Restricted Room. Here were the banned books, the esoteric books, the relics of past forms of religion. Ornate gold crosses and a diamond-encrusted Star of David in glass cases lined the walls and glittered in the dim light, welcoming her into their presence like they'd been waiting for her. Bibles and Korans rested silently on pillars, their wisdom no longer needed, and in one corner sat an enormous gold Buddha, his benign smile blessing them all—if blessing had been permissible, anyway.

To own such items without proof of historical worth outside the Church meant heresy. Here she could look at them all she wanted, read the archaic words, piece together what life must have been like even thirty years before, much less centuries in the past.

She padded across the thick carpet to the Esoteric shelf at the far end, flicking the light switch as she went. The main library room disappeared as the light hit the long, tall windows separating the sections. Funny how she'd never really noticed that before, but then she'd never been in the Restricted section this late at night, when the great library was a cavern of silent secrets between thick dusty covers.

Her skin prickled as she grabbed the largest book, one

of her favorites. If it couldn't be found in *Tobin's Spirit Guide* it probably couldn't be found anywhere. The heft of the book comforted her as it always had, but even it could not hide the fact that she'd thought she heard another sound.

A rustle, like breeze blowing a sheaf of paper or, she thought with a vague sense of nausea, the sound made by the pages of Tyson's horrible book when Terrible's fingers brushed against it.

She stopped and stood rock-still, with the weight of the *Spirit Guide* starting to make her wrist ache. Looking toward the windows did nothing to help. That damned glass may as well have been a mirror; all she saw was her own pale face staring back at her.

Her muscles creaked as she stood there, letting the seconds stretch into minutes, her ears straining for another sound, but the silence continued for so long she started to doubt herself. She hadn't slept in days, not really. She was so wired she imagined her pupils were the size of pinpricks and her fingers felt grimy no matter how many times she washed her hands. Of course she was hearing things. It was probably Brownian Motion, or her own brain sizzling as the speed burned away at the cells.

Had she heard a noise, really?

She was being ridiculous. No, not in being cautious. Caution was the only way to stay alive. But in thinking she'd somehow been followed here by the unknown Church employees who'd imprisoned Slipknot's soul. Tyson didn't even own a phone. The idea that he'd somehow managed to get himself back together and notify whomever it was, that they'd managed to track her down here when she'd told no one where she was going, was stretching things a bit.

Thus convinced, she sat down, grabbed her notepad, and started checking the *Guide's* index. Eraduac,

Eramuel, Erbereous, Eredmiam . . . Ereshdiran. Page one hundred fifty-three.

She pulled off the cap of her pen with her teeth as she used her left hand to flip through the pages. Ugh. The line drawing was crude, but it captured the thin, cruel face and the hooked nose. It even managed to suggest the bloody teeth.

Her pen scratched across the paper as she made notes, her skin growing colder with every word. She was going to have to call Doyle, to agree to go with him to see the Grand Elder. This wasn't something she could handle on her own—or rather, it wasn't something she wanted to handle on her own.

Who the fuck had summoned him, and why? What possible reason could there be to invade dreams, to invest that much power into something as banal as sleeping patterns? If they wanted to put homeowners to sleep so they could break in, they could get a Hand of Glory like hers, or perform some other sort of spell. How many homes could they invade in one night? And the damned thing simply wasn't safe, there was no real way to—

This time the noise was definite. A click, like the step of a hard-bottom shoe on the wood floor. She might not have heard it if she hadn't paused in her writing, but she had, and so she did. Someone was in the library, and whoever it was had not come simply to do some research. No one called her name, no one noticed the lights on in the Restricted Room and asked who was there. Instead there was only silence, clogging her ears, pressing in around her until she felt her body would collapse under the weight of it.

Sweat beaded on her brow as she casually flipped a few pages in the book, her muscles aching from the strain of keeping her movements slow and even, as though she hadn't heard anything. Two exits led from the library: the main one she'd used earlier, and the second one she'd used the other day when she overheard the Grand Elder and Bruce talking by the elevators.

Talking about the fear infecting the ghosts, about their unusual behavior. Looked like she had an answer for that, at least. Ereshdiran. The presence of an entity like him would drive normal ghosts crazy.

She'd take the amulet to the Grand Elder, tell him what was happening— No. She couldn't, not without admitting she'd been out at Chester Airport, that a body had been found and not reported. The amulet explained clearly to anyone who could read it exactly what powered the spell.

So would setting Slipknot's soul free end it and send Ereshdiran back where he belonged? Or would he start feeding on her, as she'd worried originally? Her blood had fed the amulet . . . and it had left its little calling cards burrowing into her skin, hadn't it, in exchange?

Her fingers ached. She looked over and realized her knuckles were white around her pen, and that perhaps this was not the best time to start pondering the ins and outs of ritual but, instead, would be a good time to get the fuck out of the library before whoever was out there decided to make his or her presence known.

The side exit would probably be best. She couldn't be sure, but she thought the sounds came from the direction of the main entrance.

Okay. Smoothly she grabbed her bag and set it on the table, slipping her pen and pad back into it while pretending she was simply looking for something. She wouldn't be able to turn the lights in the Restricted Room off without advertising the fact that she was leaving and losing the element of surprise. The Element of Surprise had always struck her as a really good name for a band. This probably wasn't the time for thoughts like that either, but her mind seemed to be working triple-time and she couldn't quite catch her breath.

So. Casual, busy, unaware. She set her bag on the floor next to her, wrapping the strap around her wrist under the table. With her left hand she flipped forward in the *Guide*, hoping to disguise what she'd been looking at.

Another footstep sounded, closer this time. Her entire body ached, her muscles so tense she was surprised blood still flowed through them. They were coming—he, she, it, whatever was coming, and she couldn't see them but she might as well have had a neon arrow over her head, and she needed to move. She'd been so stupid. So careless, and so stupid.

Her legs shook. *Go! What the fuck are you waiting for, get up and go! Go!*

Carefully she slid her chair back, keeping her gaze focused on the book in front of her, as if she was just trying to get more comfortable. They were watching, she knew, she couldn't see them but all the same she *saw* them, big shapes in black with no faces, their heavy boots moving across the floor toward her, their arms outstretched to grab her, to choke her, to slide a blade into her throat—

Go!

This time she obeyed, ducking down and slipping off the chair. If luck was with her—what a joke, luck was never with her—they might think she was looking for something, scratching an itch.

Of course, they might also think the perfect time to attack her was when she wasn't looking. Crablike she scuttled across the floor, keeping her head down. The fifteen feet or so to the door had never seemed like such a great distance; now she felt like an insect running across a hockey rink in full view of a crowd.

She reached the door and stood, not breaking her stride but speeding up, and knew immediately that her gamble had not paid off. The other feet, the other person, was running, too, their heels making loud clicking thumps across the floor as they headed for her.

Chess yanked her knife out of her pocket as she ran, but she didn't think she'd have a chance to use it. It just made her feel better, sharper somehow, as if she herself could become steel. She ran as fast as she could, not seeing anything but the vague outline of the side door in front of her.

She burst through it and almost fell. The rickety stairs clanged and rattled beneath her as she raced down them, her bag thumping against her legs and threatening to trip her with every step.

Halfway down she heard the door above her open with enough force to make the staircase shake. She didn't dare look up. She had to keep going, once she got around the next curve she could probably jump the rest of the way . . .

This she did. The impact sent pain shooting up her legs and she knew her pursuer would unfortunately follow her lead, but she had no choice. The only choices she had right now were to try and go through the chapel, or get into the elevator, plunge into the earth to the platform for the ghost train, and head for the City. Neither appealed. If she went through the chapel she might be caught, and she'd still have to run through the hall and out the front doors to the parking lot.

On the other hand, aside from her general discomfort and dislike of the City, there was no escape from there at all. The only way out was the way back up, and she didn't particularly want to spend the entire night there while silent ghosts stared at her and her skin went pink then white with cold. Underground . . . underground was never safe.

Unless . . . Hadn't Lex said something about those tunnels? How they went everywhere under Triumph City itself? That probably extended to the Church grounds, right, since before Haunted Week this had been a business district?

At the foot of the elevator was a platform where the train waited.

Hadn't she seen a couple of doors down there, when she went? One of them might lead into the tunnels. And if she could get into the tunnels, despite the confusing twists and turns, she could find an exit. She knew she could. She had her compass with her, tucked into its little pocket in her bag.

It wasn't a great idea, but it was the only one she thought might work. She slammed her palm against the elevator button. The second or two it took for the door to open stretched out like hours while the footsteps on the staircase grew louder, and she threw herself into the car as the railing rattled and she knew her pursuer had jumped over the side.

Just before the doors closed she saw him, a hooded figure all in black, the symbol on his chest iridescent in the glow of the safety lights, and memory clicked into place like a bullet into a chamber.

Oh, *fuck*.

Chapter Twenty-two

> "... they were not aware of the earth's power, and so pumped their garbage through it, and dug into it for all manner of things."
> —*A History of the Old Government, Volume III: 1800–1900*

Six minutes down, six minutes up. Then six minutes back down, if he decided to follow her, which she was sure he would—why wouldn't he, when as far as anyone knew there were no exits? Alone with one of the Lamaru—the Lamaru with their fucking precious symbol and their bloodthirsty black magic. And they'd infiltrated the Church itself, actually gotten in the building, recruited another employee like her.

If they had one, did they have more?

If they were in the Church now . . . no one was safe. Not the Elders, not the Goodys, not the regular employees. And definitely not the People, who counted on the Church to keep them safe. The Lamaru didn't want to keep anyone safe. They just wanted power. Wanted control, wanted adulation. And would do anything to get it.

So what were they doing now?

Unfortunately there was no way to hold the elevator, no emergency brake or lever to flip. So she had twelve minutes to get as far away from here as she could, into the tunnels, if she was even right, and those doors were tunnels and not simply a couple of supply closets or utility rooms full of wires tangled like snakes.

Chess shivered. It was always so cold down here, and

silent. The train with its dim, blue interior and flat opaque headlights watched her with the incurious gaze of a predator as the elevator started returning to the surface. Six minutes up, six minutes back.

Two doors cut into the damp cement walls, one on each side of the train. She'd lost her syringe full of lubricant, of course, but sound didn't matter so much when there were none to hear it. Luckily the lock was easy to pick, a basic tumbler with a rolling catch that she lifted in about thirty seconds. How much time had passed now? One minute, two? Shit, she could almost feel that Lamaru in the room, his black-gloved hands reaching for her, his eyes burning dark from blood sacrifice or who-the-fuck-knew what kind of spells he'd been working . . . She spun around, ready, but saw only the train's empty eye staring back at her.

Wasting time. Back to work.

It was just a closet, as she'd feared. A mop and bucket— she couldn't imagine why they were there, unless it was simply that closets of this nature grew cleaning implements like fungus. Some wires. A fuse box—oh, fuck yeah.

She jimmied it open with her thinnest pick. How much time had passed now? Three minutes? All of the fuses were lit, they gave no indication of whether or not the elements they controlled were in use, and the elevator shaft was tall enough that she wouldn't hear the car itself until it got closer. No labels decorated the shiny black metal of the box, either. There was nothing to do but to flip them all, one by one, and if flipping one of them gave her no result at all, she could assume it powered the elevator and leave it off.

Unless one powered more than just the elevator. Shit! All right, she'd leave them all off then, and get out of here as quickly as possible. Assuming she could. If that other door didn't lead to a tunnel, but instead held another mop and bucket, she'd be down here all night, alone. In the dark.

Still probably better than whatever her pursuer had in mind. And with any luck, he'd spend the night trapped in the elevator, suspended three or four hundred feet below the surface of the earth.

She gave it another minute to be sure. If nothing else, freezing the elevator would stop him—the fuse box in the Church building was unreachable without several keys and a ladder—but if she could trap him he'd be caught in the morning, which would be nice. A Church member, involved with a secret magical organization. A secret *anti-Church* magical organization, one who'd been trying to overthrow the Church practically since it had come into existence. Was it wrong that for a moment she was glad the penalty was death?

Did she care if it was wrong or not?

The fuse switches were stiff, stiff and cold against her palm. Her right hand burned as she shoved with all her might against the switches. Fire shot up her arm as the first row finally gave. She'd torn the wound back open.

The lights on the platform still burned dully. Chess stared across the cement for a few seconds, trying to estimate the distance between the doorway of the closet and the ditch where the tracks were, and shoved against the other switches.

The platform disappeared. The closet disappeared. No light came from the train, from the silent fluorescents, from anywhere. She was seven hundred feet underground, in the darkness.

Cursing herself for not having grabbed her matches before she cut the lights, she dug them out of her bag. While she was at it, she cursed herself for not buying a fucking lighter. One like Terrible's, with an eight-inch inferno exploding from the wick.

Shuffling her feet, she left the closet and made her way

onto the platform to light the first match. The glow, almost lost in the blackness of the cavern around her, showed she was still a good fifteen feet from the edge of the ditch. She walked as quickly as she dared across to it, and sat on the cold rim just as the match burned down to her fingers.

She had five matches left. Five matches, and who knew how many miles of long dark tunnel ahead of her. This sucked.

The train loomed dark and silent beside her. She couldn't see it but she knew it was there, could feel its presence the way she would have been able to feel a ghost had one shown up. So far none had. She didn't know how much longer she would be able to say that.

With the power to the train out she should be able to walk straight across the tracks without worrying about the electric rail, but taking chances didn't exactly appeal. So, using her left hand, she fumbled around until she found her electric meter, then fed the wire across the ditch—at least she hoped it was across the ditch. No reading. Still . . .

Holding her pen like a wand, she slung the bag onto her back and bent over. The pen didn't make a great cane, but it worked. She pushed herself off the ledge and dropped into the ditch on both feet. The gritty thump of her landing echoed through the platform.

Wave the pen, take a step. Wave the pen, take a step. A trickle of sweat ran down her cheek despite the cold. Anything could be behind her, icy hands reaching out to close around her neck, to shove her down . . .

She jerked upright, her neck craning despite the fact she could see nothing. Her breath left her chest in a whoosh.

"Okay, Chess, you need to get it together," she said aloud, then regretted it when her voice danced in the stillness around her and made it seem even darker, lonelier. Hostile.

Stop being such a wimp! She forced herself to bend back over, to wave the pen and take another step, and to ignore the prickling on the back of her neck. It was behind her again, she knew it was—

The pen clicked against the metal of the first rail. Good. She stepped carefully over it and continued. Maybe the thing waited at the other side, waited for her to blunder into it like a bee into a spiderweb. Then its cold, spindly arms would close around her, crushing the life from her body . . .

Damn it! She would be down here all night if she didn't grow a pair of fucking balls and get to that door on the other side. Why was she such a wimp, why couldn't she—

Terrible thought she was brave. She remembered it now, heard his voice in her head as if he stood next to her. "They scared. Not you, though." Terrible thought she was brave, and if he—a man whose name was *Terrible,* a man whose path people scrambled to get out of—thought so, it must be true. She could do this, she *would* do this.

Inch by inch she shuffled across the ditch, waving the pen in front of her. Two rails, then three, then she was dragging herself out of the ditch and trotting toward the wall with her hands out in front of her, feeling her way until she found the metal door, sliding her fingertips over the smooth painted surface until she found the lock, then pulling her picks out of her pocket.

She'd never picked a lock in total darkness before, but she'd never picked one in total silence before either. Every click made by steel against steel amplified itself, helping her visualize the tumbler. Got it, got it . . . shit. The pick slid, dropping the latch.

And something whispered in the tunnel.

Ghosts weren't supposed to be able to leave the City and head up here; the doors were made of iron, and should have been locked tight. Apparently this one had snuck out before they were shut, or it had never entered the City to begin with.

A third possibility, that her pursuer had been down here, messing with the doors—that more of them might still be down here—occurred to her, and she shoved it from her mind as quickly as she could. Ghosts were bad enough. If she started thinking about ghosts and Lamaru hanging around, hiding in the darkness, she'd never move. The hair on the back of her neck prickled and tingled and she felt goose bumps raise on her arms.

Deep breath. *Try again. Slide the pick in, ignore the whisper getting louder. That thing is going to follow you into the tunnel, a human murderer might follow you into the tunnel, if this door even does reach into the tunnel. Don't think about that. Just get the lock, and you'll figure out what to do next.* Get it, get it—the whispers getting closer, a cold breeze on her back that couldn't possibly have come from anywhere—got it!

She flung the door open and hurled herself through it, slamming it behind her. This was not a closet, she could hear the faint trickle of water and feel the space around her just as she'd felt that ghost just a moment ago. Nothing else to do but run. So she did.

For as long as she could she kept running, her feet splashing along the floor, trailing her fingertips along the rough pitted walls on either side of her so she could feel when there was a turn, and she made the turns by pure instinct. Left, then right, then left twice, trying to move herself in the direction of Downside and Lex. The tunnels he used had been lit. If she could find a lit space, she wouldn't need to use another precious match.

This was starting to not look like the best plan after all. Her heart felt like it was going to explode, she wanted her pills, she was thirsty and cold, and she just wanted to go home. At least to take a shower and change the clothes she felt like she'd been wearing forever. She could prop a chair in front of the door and take her knife with her.

The smell hit her before she even realized it. There had been no advance warning, no faint odor growing stronger. It was as though she'd passed through some sort of membrane and into a room filled with dead, rotting things. Her feet slid, almost going out from under her, and she braced herself against the wall and reached for a match, fighting to keep her empty stomach from turning in on itself.

It was a losing battle. In the weak illumination from the match—light that nonetheless hurt her eyes after spending so long in the utter darkness—she saw bodies, rotting, molding, half-eaten by rats and other small beasts. Sightless eyes stared at the ceiling. Empty sockets mocked her. Open mouths tried to tell the story of lives long since ended, stories told anyway by the bullet holes and slashed throats. Bits of scabrous flesh dangled from bloody bones. Chess threw up, angry at herself for doing so, knowing she would have to light another match to get out of this and angry about that, too.

When the world stopped spinning she straightened up, taking shallow breaths, and lit the next match. Three left after this. The tunnel of bodies went on for another ten or fifteen feet, ending in a door. Dead end. So to speak.

Unless she could pick that lock as well. She checked her compass. If she was right about the way she'd been going, she wasn't far from Downside. If she could just get out, she could walk or get a cab. Walking might not be safe, but at this point she didn't care.

Her feet slipped and squished in the deliquescent foulness covering the floor but she ignored it. There was a lock, slightly more complex than the others but still pickable. The match went out as she worked but she'd had enough. No more turning around, no more panic attacks. She didn't give a shit anymore.

Light dazzled her eyes as she swept through the door, but something caught her eye before she could close it. A wallet. Resting on a corpse's chest.

She shouldn't touch it, shouldn't even think about it. But these dead men were people once, people with names. She used the picks to flip it open.

No ID. No credit cards, no cash. Apparently someone had taken them all, left nothing but—she slid a pick inside—nothing but a few scraps of paper, receipts, and . . . ooh.

A wrinkled bit of plastic caught on the end of the pick and poked from the mouth of the wallet, inviting her to pick it up and take a look.

The Baggie was dusty and limp in her fingers. It looked like it had been there for several years, and she knew it had when she saw the dull purple color of the pills inside. Valtruin. Almost impossible to get. They'd been outlawed a couple of years ago—not even for pharmaceutical use anymore. Even Bump couldn't get them. She doubted Lex could get them.

And here were two of them. She dropped the wallet.

"Sorry, guys," she muttered, tucking the Baggie into her pocket and slipping through the doorway. "I guess you won't be needing them anyway, right?"

She'd made it. For a long moment she just stood, breathing in air tinged with mold, ammonia, and damp but still unbelievably sweet after the chamber of horrors she'd just left.

So these would be Lex's tunnels, then. She wouldn't know how to find her way to a specific spot but there were doors to the street dotted along every so often. She could find one.

Holding the compass in front of her like an oracle, she

started walking. Another left turn. A right. Someone breathing.

This time it was simply that junkie she'd met before—what was his name? Big Shog? Yes, Big Shog. He crouched against the wall, his attention so focused on fixing he didn't notice her until she was almost on top of him.

"How do I get out of here?" she asked. Her voice sounded odd. "Where's the door?"

"Aono." He tugged the rubber catheter on his arm, dropped the needle. "Ainnoin, goddet? Ainno nothn."

"No, seriously, just tell me, how do I . . ."

He was asleep, his mouth hanging open to show off a row of fuzzy, broken teeth. But he'd gotten in. Last time she'd seen him they'd been not far from a door. There had to be one nearby.

"You shouldn't be down here," she said, without really knowing why, and left him there in search of a way out. If she could retrace his steps, she should be able to find it, but which way had he come?

"Ai! T'other way, t'other . . ."

Big Shog was already passing out again, but before his hand fell to his side she saw the way he was pointing. Great. Chess fished a five-dollar bill out of her bag and tucked it into his pocket. "Thanks."

The door was only a few minutes down the tunnel, tucked at the top of a short flight of stairs, and she walked through it with the air of someone about to start a new life. She'd survived. The moon was full overhead—it must be at least eleven o'clock—but she'd made it out of the library, out of the church, out of the tunnels, and here she was, on a dingy street in an unfamiliar part of town that smelled of smoke and filth. Sometimes things worked out, after all.

Chapter Twenty-three

"All Church employees are expected to comport themselves in a manner befitting their stations at all times. You represent everything that is right and holy in the world. You must never forget it."
—*The Example Is You*, the guidebook for Church employees

After two Cepts, a hot shower, and one purple Valtruin, it was as though the entire day had never happened. Chess strolled into Trickster's Bar just before one with her face set in a permasmile and her body feeling as though it existed on another planet where nothing bad ever happened. Not like this world. Not like the stuff she had to tell Terrible about before she could head off to Lex's place for the night. Lex . . . Lex and that slice of bare skin she'd seen, Lex and that kiss . . . Him she *didn't* trust, not at all. Not that it mattered; trust and sex had nothing to do with each other, at least not for her.

She had to tell Terrible what happened first, though. Because they needed to set up a time and place where she could perform the ritual to set free Slipknot's soul. Because she was supposed to keep reporting in, and Bump was nowhere to be found. But mostly . . . mostly because she owed him the knowledge, as fast as she could get it to him. He'd involved himself when he didn't have to, he'd touched the book for her, and he deserved to know exactly what they were dealing with. And who might be coming after him.

It took a moment for her wildly dilated eyes to adjust to the light, and another minute to find him. The interior of Trickster's was like a dive bar in a hell dimension, scented with smoke and stale beer and lit with blue lights and red gels so everything white glowed fluorescent red.

Terrible stood in the back, talking to some men whose faces she couldn't identify but who looked vaguely familiar. From the tattoo parlor, perhaps, or just guys she'd seen around. Downside was a small, small world. Chances were the person you robbed on Tuesday would be dating your neighbor on Thursday.

She floated across the room to him, aware from about halfway that he was watching her.

"Hey, Chess. You right?"

"Right up. Can we talk somewhere?"

He gave her a slow nod. She followed him back into the hall where the bathrooms were. The music was quieter here, by just enough that they didn't have to shout, but the hall was narrow, forcing her to stand a little closer to him than she'd intended, close enough to smell soap and beer.

"So I found out about him," she said. "About . . . the name, on the amulet. What he's doing here. I mean, I found out what he does, I don't know what he's doing here, why they wanted him specifically." She felt she was babbling suddenly and stopped short. Was he looking at her oddly?

"Aye."

"He's a Dreamthief. That's how he gets people—he sneaks into their heads while they sleep and feeds on the energy of their dreams. He's like a demon, but not a demon, just a very nasty spirit with a lot of extra power. Like a huge entity made of junk from other ghosts."

"Thought demons wasn't real."

"They're not, it was just the only thing I could come up with. He's powerful like they were supposed to be, is what I meant."

"He that powerful to start? Or causin he feeds up on a lot of sleepers?"

She thought about it for a minute, which was harder than it should have been. "Probably a bit of both. The book didn't really say exactly how he came into being, or when, but . . . Sometimes spirits disintegrate, or meld—sometimes one part of them feeds on the rest, absorbs it, and then combines with other bits from other souls. So he was already pretty jacked up. What he gets from humans only adds to it."

This still didn't explain why he hadn't killed her when he had the chance. Some ghosts needed to work hard to be able to kill people or do damage, but he should have been strong enough right from the beginning, especially with the power of Slipknot's soul keeping him earthbound.

"Why somebody wanna call a thing like that?"

Oh yeah. He didn't know what had happened to her at the Church. "Not just somebody. The Lamaru."

His eyebrows raised. Right. Why would he know?

"They're a . . . they're an illegal coven. Not one we want to get involved with. You remember a couple of years ago, when they found that—that kid, on Belden Hill?"

Terrible nodded, his eyes darkening. Not a surprise, that. Almost three years on nobody liked to think of what that child's last hours must have been like.

"That was the Lamaru. We're still not sure what they were doing, it looked like they were trying to force his soul into slavery or something, but the point is, they're involved in this, and they're not people anyone wants to mess with. They summoned the thief. And they have an ally in the Church, somebody I work with. They tried to attack me tonight at the Church library."

Quickly she sketched out the story for him, eliminating

her terror in the dark and making it sound as though she'd heard about the tunnels from one of the Elders. She was inordinately proud of herself for remembering to do so, especially as looking back at what happened only a couple of hours before felt like trying to remember a story she'd been told once in childhood. "Only an employee could have gotten in."

"How'd they know you there? They following you? Shit, Chess, you call me, aye? Don't go off alone."

She was going off alone, all right. Her head felt stuffed with cotton, her skin electric and so sensitive, the hair on her arm stood up when it brushed the wall beside her. She giggled, then tried to turn it into a cough, which failed when she actually choked. This struck her as even more amusing. It was several minutes and a sip of Terrible's beer before she was able to speak.

"I didn't see anyone following me, and I paid attention."

"They waiting for you. At the library, aye? Knew you'd figure it out, so they just waited."

"Someone would have noticed them there, I'm sure of it. Nobody's supposed to be in there after dark, it's—"

"Aye, but you there, and someone else, too." He shook his head. "You ain't count on no rules to save you, Chess. You oughta know that. Don't know where your head was."

Her head was floating off somewhere in the distance, bobbing along to the heavy beat of The Stooges' "I Wanna Be Your Dog." Her entire body pounded along with it, so it was hard to concentrate, and she knew she'd been stupid and he was right, but the Church was *safe,* it was the only place in the whole world that had ever been entirely *safe,* didn't he know that?

"So's a lot of people in this one, them tonight and last night, too. Any guesses what they after?"

"No," she admitted. "Well, yes, but no. The Lamaru . . .

they're an anti-Church organization. You know, like some of those groups who run protests sometimes?"

He nodded. "Hear on em, aye."

"Right. But the Lamaru isn't in it to get money or publicity or whatever reason. They want to overthrow the Church, they've been trying for years to take over, but I have no idea why they would want to call a Dreamthief. He's deadly, you know. Eventually you just . . . you just stop sleeping out of fear, and you can't dream anyway when you do sleep, and you get so tired he sucks you into permanent sleep and feeds off you until you die. No dreams . . ."

"Your brain ain't recharge itself." He peered at her a little more closely. "How long since you slept right?"

"I never sleep."

"You look like you ain't been sleeping at all, not like usual."

"I'm fine." How long had it been, really? Only a few days. And she'd been doing so much speed, a lot more than normal. "I'm fine," she said again.

He raised an eyebrow, but didn't respond. "So this thing, he attached to that book? He what Slipknot's soul powering?"

She nodded.

"Bump wanting an update. He—he's getting on the impatient side, dig. Wanting me to bring you in to him, find out when you plan on clearing all up."

"Impatient?" She was so high she actually smiled a little. "Did he tell you to lean on me?"

Terrible shrugged, but wouldn't look at her. There was her answer. "Getting impatient, is all."

"Yeah, okay. I can see him tomorrow, no problem."

"Hey, I think I gotta line on somebody maybe tell us something about the ghosts at Chester. You know Old-timer Earl?" When she shook her head he continued. "Been living here since before Chester opened, way back in the when. Word is he might know what's up. Tomorrow we find him, aye? After seeing Bump? Maybe he know how this connects to yon Dreamthief, maybe he downing them planes?"

"There might not be a connection at all. Could be they just decided it was a good place to do their ritual."

"Possible he's brought them ghosts with him, making them stronger or aught like that?"

"It didn't say anything in *Tobin's Spirit Guide* about him being able to control other spirits, but he'd sure upset them, stir them up. You raise a ghost somewhere, you're going to cause problems with other ghosts that might be around—especially if you do a ritual like that. That life force sitting at the bottom of a well, but connected to him so they can't get at it . . ."

"Piss em off right, aye?"

"Yeah. But as for making them stronger, I don't know. I guess it's possible. It's more likely he would . . . He might be feeding off them. Or— No, that doesn't make any sense."

She shook her head. "I don't know. I don't know. I keep feeling like if I had one piece of information, it would lead me to find the other pieces, but I don't even know what that piece could be or where to look." She pictured pieces bobbing in the air in front of her, and had to fight not to reach out and try to grab them. That would look weird. She didn't want him to think she was behaving strangely. What happened to them earlier didn't seem to be affecting him at all.

Someone brushed past them on their way to the bathroom, breaking her concentration. "What?"

"Where you think we might find that? You got any ideas in the people you work with? Maybe some of them shady? We can check them out."

"We? Did Bump tell you to shadow me or something? Why are you so into this?"

He shrugged, but his gaze skittered away from her to the floor and his hands burrowed deep into his pockets. "Something different, aye? Solving a mystery."

"Scary, though," she said, and the words hurt. "Scarier than anything I've ever done."

"Naw. We keep our heads, we stay safe. No reason for that."

Chess didn't know how it happened. It didn't even make any sense that it would have happened. She lifted her hand to his chest, hard and hot beneath the black fabric of his shirt. She opened her mouth and looked up at him, ready to say something—to thank him, or to ask what time he'd pick her up in the morning, or just to make some sort of joke.

But nothing came out. Nothing came out, because her eyes met his and it felt like he'd looked all the way through her. Nothing came out because her back was slammed against the wall and her arms were wrapped around his neck and his lips were on hers, ruthless and tender and demanding all at once, and now she really was flying, up toward the ceiling, out of the building.

Lust exploded through her body, as if he'd somehow flipped a switch when his hands found the small of her back. Nothing existed in her head but Terrible, his tongue now sliding into her mouth with a skill she never would have expected, his fists gripping the back of her shirt and pulling her even closer to the monolithic wall of his body, as if they could fuse together from the heat and pressure between them.

Her fingers slipped through his hair, down across the nape of his neck, under the collar of his shirt to feel the scarred flesh of his back. With a gasp he lifted her, curving his palms under her thighs, then shifted so one hand supported her behind and the other raised to tangle in her hair. She wrapped her legs around his narrow waist and held on, pressing his pelvis against hers. Damn. Six feet four and everything in proportion, the quote went. It was true in this case. She couldn't seem to get enough air. She didn't think she needed air, not when he was holding her, possessing her, making her feel safer than she'd ever felt.

"Chess," he mumbled. His lips traveled away, down the side of her throat, eliciting buzzing tingles that made her entire body vibrate, and back up to steal her mouth again. "Chessie. Never thought . . . so pretty . . ."

The low rumble of his voice made her vibrate more, and she clung to him tighter, certain that if she let go, she would fall, and keep falling all the way through the floor.

This couldn't be right, this had to be the drugs, or maybe he was making it worse, she didn't know, but she had some vague idea in her head that if he didn't agree to take her back to his place in the next minute, she might actually die. His hips rolled against her in a slow, easy rhythm, turning the flames in her body even higher.

He was still mumbling, kissing her collarbones, nibbling at her throat with surprising delicacy, when she summoned the courage to remove one of her hands from his shoulder. His arms bulged beneath her palm as she slid it down, finally wedging it into the miniscule space between them so she could feel the ridge of his erection hot through his jeans.

"Terrible," she managed. "You know how to use this thing?"

He pulled away to meet her gaze, and for a minute he was transformed. Still the same features, the lumpy nose and the jutting brow and the hard, dark eyes, but not ugly anymore. Full of character. Full of strength. She looked at his face but she didn't see it, not the way she had before. The smile spreading across his features was intimate, sexy. The darkness of his eyes concealed so much more than she'd ever imagined.

"Oh, aye," he said. "You gonna let me show you?"

She giggled, a single gasping little laugh, as every internal organ she had flipped. "You know, I think I am. Can't get any crazier, right?"

His smile faltered, just a stutter, then came back. "Guessing not. Come on, let us get outta here."

He pulled away, setting her back on her unsteady legs. She almost fell.

"Oops." Her giggle lasted longer this time. "Oops, my legs are kind of weak. D'you think you can give me a minute?"

She looked up, expecting to see him laughing, too, but his eyes narrowed instead. She imagined for a second that they narrowed because all of his extra skin was needed for that incredible bulge in his jeans, and that made her laugh even harder, until she had to stretch out a hand and grab his to keep from tumbling to the floor in a heap.

"Chess."

"Just a minute, Chess will be back in a minute, okay?" What on earth was so funny? Why couldn't she stop laughing? It was getting hard to breathe.

"You fucked up, Chess?"

"Who, me? Noooo . . ." She shook her head, trying to look solemn and honest but unable to wipe the grin off her face.

"What'd you take? What you on?"

The look on his face stopped the giggles, anyway. Had she imagined that glimpse she'd caught of that other Terrible? Because he looked as forbidding now as if he'd been an Elder catching her wasted in a bar trying desperately not to pee herself laughing.

"Nothing, nothing, really. Just, um, a couple of Cepts, and a Valtruin I found, have you ever had one of those? It's really . . . wow. I mean . . . What?"

His hand covered his face, wiping from forehead to

chin. "I ain't believe I'm doing this," he said, and stepped
back. "I'm gonna call somebody, dame I know. You can
crash her place, aye?"

"What? Oh, no. Wait. This isn't why, okay?" Laughter
burbled up her throat again, embarrassed and slightly
hysterical. She fought it back down. "It's not that. You
just . . . No, don't look at me like that. Look like you did
before. When you didn't look like you."

His head jerked back as if she'd slapped him. Oh, shit.

"No, Terrible, I didn't mean it like that. I just meant
you look different now, I mean . . . listen."

She stood up and leaned toward him, putting her hand
out to touch his chest, but she knew before her fingers
brushed the fabric of his shirt that it was too late.

Terrible stared at her for a long moment, as impassive as
a stone effigy, and pulled his cell phone from his pocket.

"Forget it. Just forget it, okay?" Escape was the only
decent option at this point. If a hole had opened in the
floor, she would have leapt into it headfirst just to avoid
his gaze. He didn't want her, he pitied her and she disgusted him, and now she'd made him mad, too. She tried
to push past him but he caught her with one hand on her
arm.

"Hold it. Lemme call, aye? You ain't just leave like
this."

"I'm not. I have people I can call, too."

"You ain't go back to that Church tonight. Not
after—"

"I am fully aware of what happened earlier." The
words felt forced out through a wad of cloth. Her face
burned with shame. "I am not going back there. Let go
of me."

"Naw, look, I—"

She jerked her arm away, almost falling into the opposite wall. "Get your fucking hand off me!"

That did it. Whatever hint of sympathy he still had for

her—amazing he had any at all, and it made her feel even worse—disappeared. He shrugged and turned away. "Whatany you want."

"Yeah, this is what I want!"

But he'd already disappeared back into the bar, leaving her in the hallway with a bunch of strangers and her own fierce regret.

Chapter Twenty-four

> "There is no sin, as the misguided and incorrect old religions would have people believe. There is crime, and there is punishment. There is right and wrong. But these are based on fact, and not belief."
> —*The Book of Truth*, Veraxis, Article 56

"Turn here."

Doyle obeyed, easing the car around the corner. "Where are you going, anyway?"

"Just a friend's."

"Is there some reason why you don't want to tell me? Don't you think you kind of owe it to me, after you dragged my ass out of bed and all the way down here?"

His voice was like the buzzing of a gnat in her ear. Why had she called him, again? She should have just walked. "You didn't want to give me a ride, you should have said no."

"And left you stranded alone in a bad part of town. I couldn't do that."

"Then don't bitch about it." Chess folded her arms tighter around herself and stared out the window. Rain blurred the red spots of traffic lights, oddly festive against the blackness of the empty street. She could almost imagine she was in a spaceship, or a boat, gliding smoothly across a calm glassy sea. All alone. Just the way she wanted to be.

She could *almost* imagine it, because Doyle wouldn't stop talking. "I'm not some errand boy, you know. I don't appreciate being treated like one."

"What the hell is your problem?"

"No, what is your problem, Chessie? You practically leapt on me and dragged me into bed with you, then you treated me like a leper. You don't return my calls, then you wake me up in the middle of the night and beg me to come down here."

"You didn't have to—"

"Don't give me that, you sounded like you were about to burst into tears on the phone, what was I supposed to do? And you look like damn, seriously. Like you haven't slept in— Wait a minute." The car, already crawling along at a speed that would have made a sober Chess nervous about being carjacked, slowed down even more. "Have you seen him? The nightmare man?"

"I don't know what you're talking about. I told you before."

"You have to come with me to talk to the Grand Elder. We have to tell him what's going on."

"I'm not talking to anyone about anything." Shit. How many people had he gone around discussing this with? If the Lamaru were after her because of what she knew, how much danger was Doyle in, Doyle who could not keep his mouth shut to save his life? Unless—

No. No, that wasn't possible. He couldn't have done it.

"You never talk to anyone about anything. I've been trying for weeks to get you to and you won't. You won't talk to me, you don't talk to anyone else, you just hang around here in your precious ghetto with all these fucking crazy people who talk like they've never heard a proper word spoken in their lives, like that big guy who looks like somebody hit him with a brick full of stupid, and—"

"You're such a fucking snob, Doyle, you know that?" The words tumbled from her mouth too fast, almost hurling themselves across the space between them. Doyle was a snob, an insufferable snob, and she couldn't figure out why she hadn't seen it before. That damn Valtruin was showing her a new side to everyone, wasn't it? "You don't know anything about him, he's not stupid, and just because you can trace your ancestors and your—"

"Hey, at least I don't make a habit of inviting diseased-looking homeless kids back to my place or spend all my time at that creepy market."

Brain. Holy fuck, she'd forgotten about Brain, hadn't she? She hadn't even thought to look for him today, hadn't even asked Terrible if he'd seen him.

Brain had left when Doyle showed up. Brain had been about to tell her something—to tell her what he'd seen at the airport—when Doyle arrived, at the spur of the moment, with breakfast. And he'd looked scared, hadn't he? Trying to picture it in her mind now, she thought Brain's eyes had been wide, his upper lip damp with sweat.

He'd seen Doyle at the airport. It had to be. Doyle had tattoos like hers. Doyle knew where she lived, knew she'd been in contact with the amulet—he'd picked the fucking worms out of her palm.

Doyle would have known she was investigating Ereshdiran, that she would visit the library after hours to do that research. No, he wasn't trapped in the elevator, but she didn't know that she'd trapped the man following her.

Had it been so airless in the car a minute ago, so hot?

Doyle? Doyle in the Lamaru? Doyle had performed a ritual murder?

Doyle had touched her, kissed her, taken her to his bed. For a moment the shadows inside the car looked like blood trails smeared over her skin. She hadn't even suspected, hadn't known. She'd called him to drive her thinking he was at least a friend, a decent person regardless of their issues, and she'd been so wrong. So wrong it made her throat close up and her stomach hurt.

"Okay, here it is," she said, trying to keep her voice smooth. "You can just drop me off here."

He hit the brakes so hard Chess lurched forward and almost hit the dash, her strained nerves twanging with fear. "What, that's it? Just drop you off, never mind that I'm trying to talk to you, never mind that you owe me something after this, I'm just a fucking chauffeur to you. Is that it? Do you have any idea how many girls would kill to have me bring them breakfast? How many of the girls we work with still call me?"

"No, no, I just, I only needed a ride, and this is where I need to get out, okay?" The rainswept street outside was empty of everything but shadows. Not the most appealing place to be outside alone, but if she was right about Doyle, she'd happily take her chances. She wanted to get out, to get away, she had to.

"No, it's not okay. You use people, did you know that? That's all you do, and it's all you are. And why you think you can treat me like this I have no idea, but it's not going to work."

Her heart pounded so hard in her chest she thought for sure he'd be able to hear it. "I'm—I'm sorry," she said. "I'm just . . . I have a lot going on right now. I'll call you tomorrow, okay? And maybe we can do something. But I really have to go, my friend's waiting for me."

"Friend? Or some other quick fuck?"

If she'd had time to think, she would have stopped herself before it happened. If she hadn't been out of her mind with fear and misery about what happened with Terrible, and barely rational from narcotics she would have sat on her hands to make sure she didn't do what she did. But she was all of those things, and furious and desperate to get away, and her hand swung out and slapped him soundly across one ruddy cheek.

Pain shot up her arm. She'd used her right hand, and

the wound on her palm had hit his jawbone with a re-sounding smack.

There was a second of gasping, horrible silence, and then he hit her back.

She saw his lips twisting in rage, his hand moving in slow motion, and ducked, but he still got her right in the nose, and her entire head burst into agony. Her vision blurred, her breath caught in her chest. Something trick-led down the back of her throat and she had a horrible suspicion it was her own blood.

"Chess," she heard him gasp. "Oh, shit, Chess, I'm sorry, I haven't slept, I didn't mean to—"

He reached for her, but she shoved her door open be-fore he could touch her again. The pitted asphalt of the road stung her hands and water seeped through her jeans when she hit the ground, but it didn't matter. Without turning back she ran, with his voice calling her name, echoing on the barren street behind her. But he did not follow.

Her nose hurt. Her entire face hurt, as if someone had slammed a shovel into it. Her eyes felt heavy and some-how full, like they would explode if she prodded them. Oh, shit.

"Morning, tulip," Lex drawled from across the room. "How you feel?"

She groaned and rolled over, turning away. Images from the night before pounded their way into her poor bludgeoned head. Doyle, Doyle's fist. Her certainty that he was involved. Terrible . . . oh fuck, Terrible. What had she done? How the hell was she ever going to be able to face him again, after that?

At least she'd slept, she thought. It may have been more of a drug-induced coma than restful sleep, but her thoughts were clearer than they'd been in a few days and she didn't feel too bad physically, aside from the heavy profundo thumping of her nose.

"Aye. Figured on that. That boy gave you quite a slam, didn't he. What'd you do, insult his mama?"

It took her a minute to rasp the words out through her dry-as-dust throat. "Slapped him. Didn't I tell you last night?"

"You ain't said hardly a word making sense last night. Something about a guy named Boil, and a bar, and a quick fuck. I thought maybe you was hinting, but you weren't in any shape with all the blood and all. Looked like something death threw back."

"Thanks." She forced one eye open and saw him standing by the bed, his weight shifted on one leg, holding a tall glass of water.

He shrugged. "Weren't your best moment, is all. Can't say as I blame you."

The soft sheets slid across her bare skin—where were her jeans?—as she pushed herself up to a close approximation of a sit and held out her hand. He put two pills into her palm, then nodded for her other hand to take the water.

It was cool and crisp, and the first sip started to bring her slowly back to life. She shoved the Cepts into her mouth and washed them down with the rest of it, gasping after every swallow like a child. Her nose was too blocked to breathe through.

"Not Boil," she said. "Doyle. A guy I work with. He's . . . I think he's one of them. One of the guys who did the ritual at Chester, who made the amulet. And I found out what it's for, too. It's . . . they've summoned a Dreamthief. A really powerful ghost—he's like a ghost made of parts of other ghosts, if you know what I mean. Not a basic entity, a complex one. Very strong. Very unpleasant."

"He the reason you in my tunnels last night?"

Her mouth fell open. "I . . ."

"Ain't no fears, just askin. Big Shog tell me he saw you, trying to get out. So how you get in, if you ain't know how to find the out?"

Shit. He didn't look mad, but then how the hell would she know how he looked when he was mad? She couldn't trust the bland curiosity on his face any more than she could trust anything else about him, which—although his behavior so far had at least eased her fears—wasn't much. "What happened to my clothes?"

"My sister take them off, put you in bed. What you doing in the tunnels, when you say you ain't like the underground?" He still looked curious, nothing more than that, but he would have been stupid not to be concerned and Chess knew it. She was working for Bump. As far as Lex knew, she was planning to double-cross him over the airport. She wasn't stupid enough to try it—he could obviously reach her just about anywhere, although not while people were out and about—but he'd be an idiot if he hadn't considered the possibility.

That he hadn't shown any interest at all in the thief didn't surprise her. That was her problem, not his. The tunnels . . . those were his problem, and she needed to be careful.

"I got chased," she admitted finally. "I was at the Church doing research and somebody came after me. Do you know who the Lamaru are?"

"Heard of em, aye. They in this?"

"Yeah. I think they're behind it all. I mean, I don't think, I know. They chased me down to the platform—the train to the City—and I escaped through a tunnel there."

He nodded, his gaze appraising. Did he know those bodies were down there? Did he know she'd walked past them to get into "his" tunnels?

"Mighty resourceful, aye." His weight barely shifted

the mattress. "You know, some of them tunnels ain't been explored in years. You could have gotten yourself mighty lost. Lost enough to never be found."

She swallowed. Her throat still felt gummy.

"Fact is, they say some folks have. Got lost, meaning. Saying they go down for some explorations, finally end up killing theyselves rather than starve. Maybe them bodies still down there, what you say?"

"I didn't see any." It came out as a creaky whisper. She licked her lips and tried again. "Just rats and mold."

"Aye? Benefit. Seeing something like dead bodies down there be mighty freaked, I imagine." He reached out and brushed her hair back from her face with warm fingers. "Whyn't you shower up, tulip, get feeling better."

The hot water stung her face and her palm, but it felt great. Too bad it couldn't do anything to help the turmoil in her head.

Terrible. Oh, shit. She was going to have to face him today, to go see Bump and Old-timer Ed—or was it Old-timer Earl?—with him. For a minute she entertained the glorious notion that he might not want anything more to do with her, but she couldn't be so lucky. Bump wanted this done, no matter how much of an ass she'd made of herself the night before, and Terrible worked for Bump.

Should she apologize to him? But how? Did she even want to?

Apologizing would mean having to explain to him that it had been the drugs talking when she said she wanted to go home with him, wanted to share his bed. Just a side effect, and that was all. In the cold light of morning the inferno that had raged in her blood the night before seemed . . . precipitous. She squirmed uncomfortably under the heavy spray.

He was Terrible, for fuck's sake. Scary and ugly and

cold. She couldn't want him. She couldn't even think about wanting him, it was crazy.

Maybe it would be better just to let it go. It had happened, it had not gone further. What was the point of going further? He didn't really want her, either. His reaction to her, the stony expression on his face, told her that.

There was a reason she preferred one-night stands, and this illustrated it perfectly.

But how could she apologize without admitting any of that? No. Best to pretend she didn't remember it, any of it. Spare them both an embarrassing scene.

And as for Lex . . . were his questions about what she'd seen in the tunnels a threat? Or was it genuine concern, or even a way of removing himself from responsibility for the dead men she'd seen. A subtle message that she shouldn't think he was a murderer, which was rather amusing because of course he was, and she'd have known that even if she hadn't watched him stab a man through the throat in her kitchen. So was Terrible, so was Bump, so was Lex's boss Slobag—although come to think of it, she still didn't know exactly what Lex did for Slobag. Given that Slobag was reputedly at least as bloodthirsty as Bump, if not more, though . . .

In the entire Downside she'd probably have a hard time finding more than a handful of people who'd never sent another soul to the City before its time. It was certainly a group to which she no longer belonged, not after the break-in and the syringe full of lubricant.

She switched off the water and dried herself. The only clothes she had were her panties and the Dead Kennedys shirt she'd been put to bed in, which she assumed belonged to Lex and slipped back over her head now with the feeling that she was acquiescing to something by doing so.

Her face in the mirror almost made her scream. Her nose and left eye looked mottled and swollen, like someone else's features superimposed on her face. The pain had lessened some with the pills and the shower, but it was still there, a constant reminder of her confrontation with Doyle. As if she needed one.

She brushed her teeth, applied deodorant and moisturizer, and opened the bathroom door. "Hey, Lex, where are my clothes, anyway?"

He was sitting on the end of the bed, leaning back on his hands so his long, wiry torso curved beneath his shirt. "Having them washed. Might be ready soon."

"So . . . what, I'm stuck here until they're ready?"

"Methinks my jeans may be some big on you, aye?"

"How long?"

"Half an hour, hour maybe. How you think we fill that time?" His eyebrows raised, his gaze focused on her bare thighs beneath the hem of his T-shirt. Chess looked back at him, her expression just as frank.

He wasn't really a nice person, but again, neither was anyone else she knew. He'd kidnapped and taunted her. But he'd also helped, the night he killed that Lamaru in her apartment and, somehow more important, the night he'd driven out to the Morton house to retrieve her Hand for her.

She didn't care much about him, but she liked him well enough and he was certainly sexy and appealing. He wasn't—well, he wasn't anyone she imagined she could ever be serious about, and that was a good thing. If she'd felt anything real for him, any real trust or affection, if she'd had any sense they could have an actual future together, she wouldn't even be able to consider letting him have what he so obviously wanted. But what connection there was between them was based on nothing more than mutual attraction and mutual semitrust, and she wouldn't have any regrets if she never saw him again after everything was finished. Which made him pretty close to perfect for the time being.

And in the last couple of days she'd almost been killed too many times to count, and there was a very good chance she would actually die in the days to come. So why not?

"I don't know," she said. "Got anything in mind?"

"Aye." He sat up and leaned forward, resting his elbows on his knees. "Whyn't you show me that ink?"

Chapter Twenty-five

"Once a person has begun to break the laws, they will continue unless punishment is received so their souls may be cleansed. For this reason it is important to watch your neighbors and your friends as well as your family, in order to protect them from damning themselves . . ."
—*Families and Truth*, a Church pamphlet by Elder Barrett

Her breath caught in her chest as she stepped forward, her feet cool on the smooth floor. About a foot away she stopped and lifted the edge of the shirt to her waist.

"Aw, I ain't see it that well. Awful small, aye? Come closer."

She took another step.

"Closer."

Now she was close enough that his face was hidden. All she could see were the thick black spikes of his hair.

His fingers slipped under the top edge of her panties and pulled them down far enough to reveal the whole tattoo, the black-and-red tulip she'd gotten when she turned eighteen and entered the Debunker training program.

"Mighty pretty, tulip," he said. His breath caressed her skin. "Why's it for?"

She shrugged. "Just for fun."

She'd had a foster mother once—one of the few who were nice to her—who'd grown tulips, dozens of them, before she died unexpectedly and Chess was sent somewhere else. She'd been only a little girl then, but she'd never forgotten those bright, steady flowers in a place that had almost been her home.

Goose bumps rose on her skin when he pressed his lips

to it, his fingers curling and dragging her panties farther out of the way. He followed them with his mouth, scraping his teeth along her hip bone. His other hand slid around her waist, dipping down to caress her bottom, then back up to grab her opposite hip. One quick movement of his hands spun her around. Another pulled her back so she landed on the bed beside him. She lost track after that.

Somehow she was on her back, and he kissed and nibbled a line from her hip up over her ribs to her breasts, pushing the shirt out of his way then impatiently tugging it off her altogether. Somehow his lips were on hers, gentle so she could still breathe but sending shivers through her entire body just the same. Somehow her hands were fumbling with the button fly of his jeans, tugging them apart, hooking into the waist of his boxers and pushing them down so his erection bobbed against her thigh.

The scent of cigarettes and spice made their way through her clogged nose as he kissed her neck and shoulders, as he palmed her small breasts and took them into his mouth, and she lost herself in it. She didn't have to think about anything, her embarrassment about the night before, her fear about facing Terrible again later, her worries about what lay in store when she tried to free Slipknot's soul. All she had to do was feel his bare chest against hers when he took off his shirt, so warm and solid and male save the cool metal of the chain he wore around his neck. All she had to do was arch her back eagerly when he slipped his fingers between her legs to toy with the wet, swollen flesh there. All she had to do was gasp and bite back a scream when her body clenched and released so hard she even forgot her own name, which was the best part of all.

Somewhere in the hazy fog she felt him pull away from her and heard the sound of tearing foil, then he was back, kissing her, tugging her panties all the way off. She waited for that awkward moment she was used to, when it seemed most men forgot basic anatomical fact and attempted to insert themselves into her thigh, but it didn't come. Instead he slid into her, straight and smooth, while she dug her fingers into his back and wrapped her legs around his.

He was bigger than she'd expected, but not painfully so. Just enough, filling her without making her uncomfortable, and he rolled his pelvis against hers, slowly exploring every inch of her until she thought she might explode. She raised her hips to meet his steady thrusts, begging him to go faster, harder.

"Aye, tulip," he whispered. "Sweet... damn sweet..."

Chess mumbled some sort of assent and forced his lips back to hers. Breathing didn't matter. Nothing mattered, because he was speeding up, slamming into her with a single-minded force she understood and shared. His left hand shifted; he slipped his thumb down to caress her most sensitive spot, and she rocked toward him, matching his rhythm, driving herself and letting herself be driven to another mind-shattering climax.

This time he followed her, their voices mingling in the still air of the room, until he finally collapsed on top of her.

"Tulip," he said, kissing her neck, "You is one dangerous girl."

"Only if you cross me. I am a witch, you know."

"Thought y'all weren't allowed to put the hurt on nobody." He slipped away, reaching down and pulling the cool sheet over their bodies, then taking two cigarettes from the pack by the bed and lighting them. The movement emphasized the sinewy muscles of his chest and back. Not bad at all, she thought, reaching up to take the smoke.

"I'm just making a point."

"Aye? I gotta point to make with one of your witches too, dig. You tell me how to find him."

"What? Who?"

"Mr. Friendly Fist, there. Boil or Doyle or whatever the fuck. Got a few things to say to him."

"Forget it. He's in enough trouble. I'm going to have to tell the Elders what he did. The ritual, I mean, not the . . . other thing."

"Ain't no such thing as enough trouble for a guy like that."

"I did hit him first."

"Fuck that, tulip. No excuse. Tonight you gonna take me over there, show me him, aye?"

"Lex, really, I appreciate it but it's not necessary."

"Is for me. C'mon, tulip. I got me a sister, aye?" He looked up as the doorknob rattled, then leaned in to kiss her throat. "Look like your clothes here now. You want em, or you want me tell her come back in an hour?"

Almost two hours later she trudged up the stairs of her building, her clothes and body clean again but the pleasant sense of relaxation fading with every step.

There would probably be a note. Worse, he might actually be waiting for her. And she had a huge black eye and a swollen—but apparently not broken, thankfully—nose. How in the world was she going to pretend she didn't remember anything that happened at Trickster's, but that she did remember who hit her? Because saying she didn't remember being beaten . . . that was too much.

Would he believe that she'd fallen down? Probably. That's what she'd say, then, when she saw him. Meanwhile . . . she had to call Elder Griffin, tell him she needed to see him and the Grand Elder and find out if anyone had been trapped in the elevator. She needed to figure out how this related to the Mortons. Her initial thought was that Ereshdiran had followed her there, but that didn't make sense. The first time she'd seen him had been there, and he'd appeared there most strongly. So he had to be somehow connected to the place. Maybe she should stop by there first, or ask Elder Griffin to meet her there. Especially now, with the Lamaru involved. Someone should know about it, someone higher up than herself.

As for Chester . . . she had no idea what to do. Hopefully Old-timer Earl would give her something she could use, assuming the place truly was haunted, which it seemed to be. Later she would retrieve the cameras she'd set up and confirm it.

Then . . . she didn't know. She couldn't just pretend to be incapable of handling the ghosts. Bump would wonder how she managed to keep her job. Neither could she handle the ghosts, considering the deal she'd made with Lex. Sometimes her addictions were more trouble than they were worth.

Her key ring jingled in the silent hall as she slotted the key into the lock and twisted it. The bolt slipped without a sound. Was that right? Possibly it was still lubed from the break-in. All the same she pulled her knife out of her pocket. The amulet was hidden in her bag, but whoever had come looking for it—be it Doyle or one of the people he was working with—didn't know that.

She threw the door open, holding the knife in front of her with her free hand, but the kitchen was empty. For a minute she waited, standing in the doorway, until finally she had to take a breath. No one was here. She was being paranoid—not too hard, all things considered.

But the thought failed to calm her. Something wasn't right. She didn't remember the lock giving so easily the night before, and she was just as strongly on her guard then as she was now. And that smell, wasn't there an odd kind of smell in the air? A high, musty, sweaty kind of odor?

She'd tidied up a little before she went out. Now she was grateful she'd taken the time, because she could see the searchers had been back. The stack of books she'd placed on the arm of the couch had been turned so their spines faced the wall instead of the seat. Her papers had been shuffled. The little piece of malachite she kept on the bookshelf had fallen back to the floor. She knelt and pulled out the Blackwood box, then popped the lid.

Everything seemed to be there, though it had definitely been rooted through. Ha. It wasn't great news, because they would know the amulet had to be on her person, but she still couldn't help but feel some pleasure at having thwarted them again. Although she'd certainly paid for it. Even smiling made her eye and nose ache.

Everywhere she looked turned up tiny evidences of strangers' hands, pawing through her belongings. Her skin crawled. They might as well have touched her, stroking their hard, dirty hands over her body. Her amusement at having won a small victory faded as reality set back in. Her home was all she had. The only place that was hers, even if it was rented. It was private. It was where she could be alone. And now someone had invaded that privacy, stolen it from her, as everything else had always been taken from her her whole life.

She didn't want to look anymore. She didn't want to do any of this anymore. She just wanted to go to bed.

Someone waited for her there.

He lay on top of the covers, his eyes wide and staring at the ceiling, his hands folded on his stomach. Chess stared, her breath stuck in her chest, her mouth desert dry, almost unable to take in the gaping wound at his throat, the tiny runes carved into the exposed skin of his scrawny chest. The symbol of the Lamaru on his forehead, lurid and bold like a rash.

Brain was dead.

Chapter Twenty-six

"It's tempting to view faking a haunting as an easy way to earn money. After all, the Church has promised to protect us, and to make amends when it fails. But be warned! You will be caught. Debunkers are among the most highly trained, intelligent, and skilled employees in the Church, and they are not easily fooled."

—*Families and Truth*, a Church pamphlet by Elder Barrett

She flew to the door and flung it open, interrupting Terrible mid-knock. The sight of him hit her almost as hard as seeing Brain's poor skinny body on her bed.

"Where—what?" He started into the apartment then stopped dead, his face paling. "They get you, Chess? They waiting for you?"

"What? No, no, nobody's here, I—"

"Who then? Who hit you?"

"I—" What was she going to tell him? She'd thought of something, but it faded under the blazing fury in his eyes. "No, I fell down, that's all."

"It were Mr. Clean, aye? What the fuck, Doyle, you left with last night. Him."

"No, I— How did you know?"

"Watched you. Watched, damn it, thinking you'd be safe." He shook his head. "Knew I shouldn't just let you go, fuck, why'd I just—" The flat of his hand slammed into the wall with enough force to make the whole thing shake, once, twice. He braced his palms on it and leaned forward, staring at the floor.

"He hurt you?"

"What?"

"Did he—did he hurt you. Dig?" He glanced at her, his face mottled with rage, his eyes black holes.

"Oh. No."

He nodded, then nodded again as if he was trying to convince himself of something. "Right. Right."

"I'm fine."

Well, at least her worries about how she would face him again were gone. Tension broken. Maybe she should thank Doyle.

"Right." He shoved one hand through his hair, resting it for a minute on the back of his neck. "Where Brain, then?"

She led the way, guilt slowing her footsteps. There was no way to look at Brain's death as not being her fault, no way at all, even if she hadn't been aware of it at the time. She'd let Doyle in, she'd even given him the kid's name. She hadn't searched hard enough for him, had forgotten about him. Yes, she had a lot of other things going on, but still . . . he was just a boy, and now he was dead, and she could have saved him.

Terrible stopped by the bed. "Them runes, do they trap he soul, too?"

"No. They're just random. They're not even from the same set. I think they're a calling card, you know? As if I need one."

"Damn. Poor kid." He shook his head. "You got any ideas who done it? Who in the Church, meaning?"

"Yeah, actually. Um. I think it was Doyle."

His nostrils flared.

"See, I was thinking about it la—this morning. Brain was here the other day, but he took off right after Doyle arrived. I didn't think anything of it, I thought he was just nervous to have anyone here, but now . . . Doyle was snooping around in my apartment, too, one night when I left the room. And he was the one who first told me about the Dreamthief. He said a few of us had seen him and wanted to ask me about it. He wanted me to go to the Grand Elder with him and a couple of other people, to tell them what was going on."

"Figure he playing you on that? Trying to sniff out your knowledge?"

"Basically."

Terrible reached over and closed Brain's eyes. "Poor kid," he said again, then looked up. "Aye. So here's the day I got. Bump waits for us out in the chiller, dig, where he got the body resting. Old-timer Earl visit the pipes on Forty-fifth round three most days, we stop there after. Then let's us head to that Church, see who we can talk to. That fucker give you names? Other people seen the thief?"

She nodded.

"Good. We talk with them. Maybe you check with them Elders, give them the know. Cool?"

The clock next to her bed told it was just past two. "What about Brain?"

"Bump got people take care of it. Might want to buy you some new bedding, though."

"Yeah. I already figured I would." Tears sprung to her eyes, stinging the tender flesh, and she turned away lest he see them. Why her home, of all places? She didn't know if she would ever feel safe there again. Even the wards she'd put on the doors hadn't kept them out—of course not, Lamaru or Church employees would know how to undo them with ease.

Her small, spartan bedroom with its plain gray walls and watermarked ceiling had never looked so cold. New bedding, hell. She'd have to buy a new bed. She couldn't imagine ever putting her own body where Brain's had been.

She cleared her throat, aware he was watching her but unwilling to acknowledge it. The tension she'd thought had disappeared curled around her, around both of them. What was he thinking?

"I guess we should go, then," she said finally. "Just let me, um, let me change, okay?"

He nodded. "Whyn't you use a different room. I'll stay here with him."

"Thanks." She opened her closet, gathering a dark red top and jeans, then crossed to her dresser. Feeling a little stupid, she turned her body so he wouldn't see her adding clean panties and a bra to the pile in her arms, then folded the jeans over them.

"Where'd you stay last night, anyways? Not here, aye, and not with Doyle, guessing."

"Um. No. I got a hotel room." She glanced back, but he wasn't looking at her. Instead his gaze was fixed out the narrow window.

"Good idea. Hey. You know them people, live there?"

"What people?"

"Cross yon street. I see right in their place. This window awful small, so they probably ain't see in here, but . . . how's the other windows? The living room, say? You think anyone see in?"

"Oh. I don't know."

He edged to the side when she stepped near, letting her take over the window. Or maybe he just didn't want to be so close to her.

He was right about the view. She could see in the window across the street, if the curtains were open. She'd never really wondered if they could see into her room for the very reason he'd mentioned. The window was narrow, the wall thick, and she hardly spent time in here anyway except to sleep or dress. She never brought people here. Never men. Sometimes to the apartment itself, but in her bedroom . . . no.

"I think I left the curtains open in the living room last night. They're closed now."

"How about that big stained-glass window? Anybody see through that?"

"I don't think so."

"We ask anyway, cool? Been thinking about the blood on yon floor. When they break in? Only ain't no blood in the hall or nothing. Only your place. Seems kinda odd, aye, no blood dripping. So I figure maybe they got a place near here they stay, send somebody over to clean up the hall, but ain't bother with your place whatever reason? Maybe the blood some kind of magic, something like that? A warning?"

Fuck. Why couldn't he just be stupid, just once? Lex's men must have wrapped the bodies in plastic or something.

"It didn't feel like a spell," she said, choosing her words carefully. "Maybe someone interrupted them cleaning up."

"All the more reason to ask up, aye?"

She nodded and glanced at him. He stood by the wall, almost pressed against it. "Listen, Chess . . ."

Shit. "Hey, I should, um, apologize," she said before he could continue. "I think I was pretty fucked up last night, I don't really remember much of anything. Did I . . . did I act strange, when I saw you? I did see you, didn't I?"

His face didn't move for a long moment. Then he looked down, shaking his head. "Naw. Naw, you was fine. Don't worry none, aye?"

"Thanks."

Silence stretched uncomfortably between them. Chess felt sticky, as if her deceit had turned into a thin layer of grime and covered her whole body. "I should get dressed," she said.

She pulled her shirt over her head, arranged it over her hips, and grabbed the phone. Time to call Elder Griffin, she guessed, waiting while the phone rang, hoping he would pick up his line himself.

He didn't. Randy Duncan did.

"Chessie, how are you?"

Her brow wrinkled. Why was he answering in Griffin's office? "Fine, Randy, what's up."

"I've been talking to Elder Griffin. About . . . about some of the strange stuff going on lately."

"Strange?"

Pause. "You haven't heard?"

"No."

"Somebody broke into the building last night. Well, they didn't break in, but they managed to get down to the platform and pull the fuses. The elevator, the train, everything was shut down. It even looked like they'd worked the City doors, tried to get in there. And I thought I . . . never mind."

"No, what? You thought you what?"

"Have you seen anything odd lately? I mean . . . like a ghost, but a strong one?"

She bit her lip. "No, why?"

"I just, I heard about it, then I . . . Look, have you seen Doyle lately?"

"Why?" It wasn't original, but it would do.

"I think something's going on. With Doyle. I thought I saw him last night, around ten, running across the lawn. I think maybe somebody's after him, Chessie. Somebody who wants to hurt him, maybe hurt all of us. I'm worried about him, you know? He seems really nervous lately. And I thought you might know why."

"Sorry, Randy. I don't really talk to Doyle very much, you know."

She heard him breathing over the line for a second before he spoke. "Right. Okay, well, listen. If you do, or if you see him, could you tell him I'm looking for him? But don't tell him why. I just want to help him, I mean, if we would all just be a little closer to one another, really band together, we could accomplish so much more. And I told Elder Griffin everything I know and he agrees."

Typical Randy. Next he'd be telling her love made the world go round. What a fucking sap he was.

She rung off and sat down on the couch. So Randy had seen the thief, too. He hadn't said so in as many words but that had to be what he meant. And he'd seen Doyle right around the time of her attack. Awfully damning.

It should have been difficult to believe Doyle would do such a thing. It wasn't. Doyle thought he was above everyone else, smarter and better-looking and more skilled. It was that arrogance that had attracted her to begin with, wasn't it? The unconscious knowledge that he didn't really give a shit about anyone but himself, wouldn't put any pressure on her? Was it so strange to think someone so aggressively self-centered might get involved with Lamaru?

If her life had taught her anything, it was that you never really knew what people had going on beneath the surface. People were shit. The only difference between them and animals was people felt the need to hide it.

That was why she hadn't quite bought it when Doyle showed up trying to sweet-talk her. It was one thing to fall into bed with someone because you wanted to. It was another thing to be duped into it with bullshit.

Oh, Doyle . . . She shook her head. It was so much better to know you were nothing of importance. She might have done a lot of things she was ashamed of but at least she hadn't ever gotten confused about that.

Chapter Twenty-seven

> "That no god exists is Fact, which is Truth. That the soul exists is also Fact and Truth. That the soul must be protected, that it can be used by the unscrupulous, is a most terrible Fact, and the Church condemns those who would seek to do this."
>
> —*The Book of Truth*, Rules, Article 154

Not quite an hour later, she followed Terrible across the flat, brown scrub grass at the edge of a long row of dilapidated storage units and down the block. The steady beat of a drum came from the far end of the row; a lot of bands rented places like these to practice, especially in Downside where neighbors with noise complaints used fists and knives rather than phones to make sure things quieted down.

Terrible's broad shoulders blocked her view of the inside of the storage space, but the chilly air flowed around him and blasted her before she reached the doorway.

Cold indeed. Bump had apparently had this place modified. Dull steel lined the walls, broken only by the industrial mesh faces of heavy freezing units. Terrible had said "chiller" but she hadn't thought he meant this. Her thin cardigan was no match for it. Might have been nice if he'd warned her, but then he looked completely undisturbed by it himself. His bare arms didn't even roughen with goose bumps as he staked himself a spot off to the left.

Bump stood in the middle of the room, wrapped in a heavy fur coat, with a black silk top hat covering his fuzzy head and unnecessary sunglasses hiding his pale face. He looked like the Abominable Snowpimp.

"Well, well. Miss Chess gave up to come here after it all. Why ain't my fuckin airport runnin, ladybird? Thought we had ourselves a fuckin deal, yay?"

The words made her head hurt. Or maybe it was the cold. All she knew was by the time Bump finished speaking he sounded like he was talking through a tin can and her temples throbbed.

"Takes time, Bump," she managed.

"Bump ain't got time. Got shipments. Got them pills waitin, got lashers need goin in my fuckin pockets. I ain't get my fuckin pills, *you* ain't get yon pills. You dig?"

Without waiting for an answer he stepped to the side, sweeping his arm to the right with the air of a man showing off his new car.

Slipknot's body lay on a metal table, covered to the chest with a nubbly brown blanket that looked like it had been wrapped around car parts then wrung out in swamp water before being placed on his ruined skin.

"Bump thinkin maybe you take another fuckin lookie here, maybe you see all what you needs to see. What you say? Maybe you miss you a clue, it bein dark last time you fuckin see. Leastaways you give Bump some knowledge what thing we after, yay?"

"He's a—like a hybrid ghost," she managed to say. Wanted to say, because her feet felt stuck to the floor and if she talked she could delay the moment when she had to look at the body.

"What you meaning, hybrid? Bits of other fuckin spooks and all? How the fuck that happen?"

Chess glanced back, saw Terrible open his mouth. Fine. Let him explain it; she didn't want to. Felt like trying to would make her even sicker than she already was.

Slipknot's heart gave another horrid squelching beat when she stepped closer. The condition of his body had deteriorated further since she last saw him, or perhaps it was simply that without the blazing sunset gilding his body she saw him as he truly was.

Ghastly white skin like candle wax, covered with a fine sheen of what looked like oil but was probably some sort of secretion she didn't even want to think about. The cold had slowed the process of decay, but hadn't stopped it the way it would if he hadn't been powering a spell; the magic keeping his soul trapped warmed his corpse enough to keep him from freezing.

Tears stung her eyes. She wanted to say something, do something to soothe him, but nothing came to mind. There *was* nothing. His soul was still there, but it was beyond communication, beyond any help she could give, at least until she managed to set him free. Guilt made her chest ache, a dim, faraway pain she couldn't quite feel. She'd only taken a couple of pills, no more than usual, why did she feel so disconnected . . . ?

Her vision wavered. She lifted a shaky hand to rub her eyes, but before she reached them, Slipknot's heart beat again. Droplets of blood flew up from it. She saw each one, deep crimson against the wreckage of his body and the silvery walls, hanging in the air for what seemed like hours before they fell again, landing in tiny explosions on his raw flesh.

"Chess?" Terrible sounded like he was speaking from another room entirely. "You right?"

"Fuckin strange," Bump remarked. "That heart of his ain't beat but once every half hour or so, yay? So why's it up now?"

The hand that hadn't reached her eyes covered her mouth instead, pressing her lips against her teeth so hard it hurt, trying to hold back the scream. This was what she'd been afraid of, this was what she'd been half-certain had happened from the minute she found that fucking amulet and was stupid enough to touch it.

It had fed from her. She was connected to it. She was

connected to the Dreamthief, and she was connected to Slipknot.

At least now she knew why Ereshdiran hadn't killed her the other night at the Morton place. Why do that when he could feed off her so easily, keep her as a second power supply should Slipknot's body fall apart so much it could no longer hold his soul?

She stumbled back, trying to keep cool but not quite making it.

"Chess," Terrible said again. "Chess, you need a seat?"

"Why you all white, ladybird? You ain't sicking up on Bump, is you? Aw, fuck, this ain't—"

"I'm fine." She forced her hand down, clenched it in a fist at her side. Bump and Terrible were both watching her, Terrible concerned, Bump unreadable.

This thing was attached to her. Connected to her blood, to her soul. Was this why her reactions at the Morton house had been so slow?

"Tonight." She drew a hard breath through her nose and let it out slow. Fuck the airport. She'd either find out if there were other ghosts there or she wouldn't, but there was no fucking way she was letting an entity attach itself to her like a fucking metaphysical tapeworm. "We do the ritual tonight."

Terrible slid his Chevelle into a spot on Thirty-fifth as neatly as a puzzle piece. Chess got out before he'd made it around to open her door for her. It didn't feel right to let him do it, not anymore. If it bothered him he didn't say anything.

She'd never visited the pipes here, but the man guarding the door looked familiar. He barely looked at her as he nodded at Terrible and stepped out of the way.

"Hey, Bone," Terrible said. "Old-timer Earl in there?"

"Aye. Five minutes ago, maybe. Sent him down, but I ain't tell him you coming."

"Good. C'mon, Chess."

She followed him through the heavy wooden door into the hall covered with faded green paper and carpeted with thick brown shag. The faint odor of Dream filled it, Dream and bodies and whiskey from the saloon at the end. She would have known she was in one of Bump's rooms even if she hadn't known, just from the color on the walls and the jazzy lounge music piped in. He thought it helped keep fights from breaking out while people waited. Probably not true, as it drove everyone she knew nuts, but Bump insisted.

On busy nights and first thing in the morning the line to use the pipe room would stretch all the way down the hall, even into the street on a weekend, but afternoon traffic was light. They headed into the saloon, where another guard waited to open the door for them.

"Want a drink first?" Terrible asked, but she shook her head. Who could think of drinking anything, of doing anything, when they were so close? And it had been so long. She needed her pills, but Dream . . . Dream was like a dozen pills all at once, Dream was like falling asleep on a cloud. Dream was forgetting the world even existed, much less her own self.

And she couldn't have any. Not now. But she could smell it, she could watch. She could live vicariously through the lucky few lounging with their pipes. When this was all over . . .

The room she usually visited, the one off the Market, was blue. This one was red, a rich crimson that glowed in the light from the candles and the dim oil lamps under the pipes. Red glass chandeliers floated in the space between the high, arched ceiling, once white but now dirty ivory from smoke, and the vast room below. Red couches, curved like seashells, rested in groups around the gleaming hookahs in the back and trays of single pipes near the front.

Most of the couches were empty, but some held people, their bodies stretched on the wide seats as they smoked or stared at the ceiling or dozed off.

And even in the middle of the day the attendants wandered ceaselessly between the couches like characters in a well-choreographed ballet, spearing small lumps of sticky Dream on long, silver needles and shaping them expertly over silver dishes, ready to pop into the pipes to be dissolved into smoke. They handed out fresh pipes and took the used ones back to be cleaned, wiped out Dream bowls with tools like tiny hockey sticks and collected the ashes. They trimmed the lamp wicks and refilled the pots of oil. All of these tasks they performed silently, with only the scraping of metal against metal and the snick of their trimming scissors announcing their presence.

With no windows it could easily have been nighttime down here in the cellar, but the feeling of daylight still clung to Chess's skin and clothing. The cavernous room was less like an escape than it was a cafeteria before the lunch rush, a stage set for a party no one was attending. Even the smell of smoke, so heavily ingrained into the furniture and walls she doubted it would ever come out, didn't manage to change that impression.

"That's he, there." Terrible nodded to one of the occupied couches and headed down the stairs. Chess followed, trying to pick out which one he'd indicated while at the same time watching her step.

They reached the bottom and turned, weaving their way between the couches and the attendants, until they reached a low, straight, padded platform against the wall. On it lounged a man who could only be Old-timer Earl.

Old-timer wasn't quite right. Ancient worked better. No other word fit the wizened creature on the cushions, his bony legs drawn up almost to his chest, the knobs of his wrists huge against his scrawny forearms and arthritic hands. An attendant rolled his bowl for him, manipulating the Dream ball with her needle, moving off to the side when Terrible jerked his head at her.

"Lady gotta word with you, Earl," he said. "Bump wants you tell her some things."

Earl pulled his mouth away from the pipe and glared at Terrible with dozy eyes. "Ayegahnotrubblooump," he rasped. It took Chess a minute to translate that in her head to *I got no trouble with Bump*. Great.

"Ain't say you got trouble with him. Only might be, you don't answer the lady. Aye?"

Earl frowned. Terrible nodded at the attendant, who pulled her needle away, leaving Earl with an empty pipe.

"Ey!"

Terrible shrugged. "Answer the questions, she bring it back."

"Fy, fy. Brinback, aye? Esswastin."

Once she got used to his slurred speech, it wasn't so bad. A good thing, because when she asked him about Chester the floodgates opened.

"Always bad, there. Bad luck. Don't know why they built that damn thing there. Back in forty-one, y'know, things was booming. Then the war started, got booming even more. And so many people! This city sure something to see back then. Even here. Never a rich part of town, get it, but we had style then. Not like today."

Chess and Terrible exchanged glances. He was describing a time over eighty years before, how did he know what the city was like then? He looked old, sure, but . . .

"I see what you're thinking." He gave a short, sharp cackle that made Chess jump. "You don't know how old I am, neither do I. But I was there, oh yes, maybe a little older than Mr. Terrible here, and I remember it all. Lots of us grumbled when they built that airport. Wasn't right, using that land again, no ma'am it wasn't."

Wan'tight, usinatlanagin, nomamiwan't. The cadences of his speech drew her in, made her lean forward. "What do you mean, using it again?"

He took another long drag from his pipe and blew out a thick steam of dirty tan smoke. "I'm getting there, missy, don't you rush me."

"Ain't got all day, Earl."

"Don't you start with me either, boy. I tell it my own time, my own way. You wanted me to talk, you're getting talk. Just you relax."

Terrible raised an eyebrow, but did not reply. Earl nodded.

"Some of us tried to tell them no, when they talked about it. Building there, I means. Those days there was more land than you could shake a stick at. Guess it was kind of like it is now, only half the population hadn't died. Or hadn't died yet. Those damn Nazis and their Jap and Dago buddies sure killed enough in the years to come, oh yes. Near enough killed me, at least, one of them traitorous slimebag Vichy did. Wanna see my scar?"

His leer should have disgusted her, but the smoke was going to her head and she was finding his offensive patter oddly amusing. She'd never heard such words actually used in conversation before. It fascinated her.

At least, it did until she thought about Lex, about what those bygone words actually meant. Earl probably wouldn't have been so eager to show her a scar on what she thought must be someplace normally hidden by layers of cloth if he knew who'd been seeing her bare skin— and exploring it fairly thoroughly—only a few hours before. Twice. Lex wasn't Japanese, but she doubted Earl would care about the distinction.

"No, thanks."

"Got some scars of your own, I see. And bruises. Did Terrible here do that to your face?"

"What?" She'd actually almost forgotten. "Oh, no! No. I fell."

Earl made a face. "Sure you did. My momma used to say that, too." He sucked in another chestful of smoke, his eyelids fluttering.

"But like I said, there was plenty of places for them to build their airport, instead of on those grounds. Wouldn't have been so bad if they built homes or stores, but to bring planes there again just seemed wrong."

"What do you mean, planes? Nothing was on that land before—what was there before?" The documents at the Church hadn't said anything about the way the land was used before Chester was built.

Earl shook his head. "Such a terrible tragedy. I was just a boy then but even I remember when it happened, the night bright like I'd never seen before and didn't see again until I got shipped overseas. Them flames rose so high looked like they were trying to burn down heaven—that was when we thought such a thing existed, you know, I ain't saying it now."

"Of course. Go on, please. What burned?"

"The base. The air base. Thought the Hun had crossed the ocean to get us."

"The Hun? Wasn't Germany the Nazis then?"

He glared at her. "What you think, missy, you think I don't know the difference betwixt Hitler and Wilhelm? I say the Huns I mean the Huns. That fire happened when the air base stood, the *base,* not that damned Chester Airport. Not World War Two. The Great War. That base—Greenwood, they called it—burned down in 1917."

Chapter Twenty-eight

"Shoulda known," Terrible said, nosing back into traffic. "Heard about Greenwood, aye, but nobody ever agree whereabouts it was. Only a story. Ain't even can find it in most books."

"What do you mean?"

"Books on the war. Even them old ones don't but mention Greenwood. One of the first bases for airmen. Knew they closed it, but none say why. Never even guessed it was around here."

Chess glanced back over her shoulder as the Dream den disappeared in the mist. Old-timer Earl hadn't been much use after telling them when Greenwood AFB burned down. Two more hits from his pipe and he'd started dozing, interrupting only to make a feeble pass that she suspected was more about his ego than anything else.

"No, I mean how would you—you have a lot of books about World War One?"

He hesitated. "Aye, well, it's interesting, innit? Different world, first real air battles, aye? They called them aces, you know. Flying aces. Just ain't figure out why I never connected it. Them ghosts we saw in that alley—bet that land used to be part of the base."

The same knowledge that excited him made Chess feel

even more lost. What difference did it make, except that she was now dealing with military ghosts, an entire battalion or whatever of them.

"Why would they hide that, though? It was a fire, what was so bad about that?"

"Aye, but not just a fire. All sorts of rumors about it, Chess. You heard about the study the Old Government done back in the when, in Tuskegee? With syphilis, aye? Or when they spray germs in the air, or in World War Two they studied tear gas and shit. Used people for them experiments, most of em ain't even know."

"Yeah . . . they were doing the same at Chester, at Greenwood I mean?"

"Nobody agree what they doing. Some say mustard gas, but I ain't buy it. Others say more brain shit, dig. Holding them from sleeping, no food, no air, like that. They—"

"Sleep deprivation?"

He glanced at her. "Aye."

"The Dreamthief."

"Ain't knowing for sure. But some say that fire was no accident. I got a book I found long time back, little book like a pamphlet. Says one of them pilots escaped, said by the time they place burned they all crazy from no sleep. Said maybe somebody set that fire. Ain't believe I don't think of it, but everybody guess Greenwood down South somewheres, way down, aye? If it even true."

"I can't believe—I mean, wow. You know a lot about all this." Of course he did. Memories clicked into place. He'd known the ghosts they'd seen were pilots. She remembered the rapt look on his face at the airport, when he talked about having planes there again. She thought of the flash of wings she'd seen in the scar on his back. It made sense, didn't it, that he would see himself as a soldier—after all, he basically *was*—and that this sort of thing would interest him? She wouldn't have been surprised to discover the entire Chester thing was his idea.

"Passes the time." He turned left, heading for the highway onramp to take them out of Downside. "Ain't knowing Earl got so much knowledge on it. Knew he were old, aye, but not that old. Ain't figure anything could be. You ever heard ought like it?"

She shrugged. "There's spells you can do, but I don't think he did. That's really dark magic, the kind that leaves a mark, you know?"

"Figure he just forget to die, aye? Or too mean. Too high, maybe. He at them pipes every day long as I recall."

Silence fell. Chess felt his discomfort, wondering if he'd said the wrong thing. Thinking of her own habits, hoping he hadn't offended her.

"Terrible?"

"Aye?"

"Who taught you how to read?"

He shrugged like he wasn't going to reply, then glanced at her. "Her name Lisa. Bump's woman. *Was* Bump's woman. This back when he took me in, dig. She liked me. Said I needed to know. Used to sit right next to me, wearin some low-cut slippy thing, making me sound out letters and write sentences."

"Must have been quite encouraging."

He grinned. "When I did right, she'd lean over and clap her hands, her top would fall open. I learned fast."

"I bet you did."

They sat in companionable silence for another minute while he merged into traffic, with the stereo on quiet and the windshield wipers keeping slow time across the glass.

"So there no news in the Church about Greenwood? No way anybody there mighta found out?"

"Not unless they took it from the file. Which I guess is possible, but it would be awfully hard to do it with the library Goodys watching."

"Like Goody Smith, Goody Jones, them type of Goody?"

"Yeah. One always sits in the library and watches. You'd have to wait until they left for something or turned their backs on the desk—they have security cameras, too."

"Cameras?"

Chess shook her head. "They don't record. They send a signal directly to the screens behind the desk, and that's all."

"So which Goody's in the library?"

"There's . . ." She shook her head.

"What?"

"Nothing, I . . . For a minute I thought I remembered something. It's gone now, though."

Her phone buzzed against her thigh as a call came in. She tilted it just enough to see the little name display on the window. TNL. The code she'd programmed in for Lex, a play on "Tunnel" she figured was subtle enough to keep secret but obvious enough that she'd remember it even if she was so high she could barely think. Damn, why couldn't he have called earlier? Whatever he wanted would have to wait. She couldn't talk to him with Terrible sitting right next to her.

They were here, anyway. Terrible pulled into a spot and cut the engine, glancing around as he did so. "What you wanna do first? You wanna ask them people if they know anything, or you wanna go talk to the Elder?"

"I should probably go inside and see Elder Griffin first. He'll listen to me. You'll wait here?"

Pause. "How long you'll be gone?"

"I don't know. Half hour, maybe? Hour? If you want to go somewhere, I'll call you when I'm done."

"Naw. Think I'll stick here, aye? Wait up, keep an eye out."

She waited until she'd gone through the heavy double doors to call Lex back.

"Hey, tulip, where you hiding?"

"I'm at the Church. What's up?"

"Thought you was gonna wait and I go with you. Stay there, aye? Lemme come talk." He said something else, but static drowned it out.

"What? No, Lex, you can't come here, Terrible's here, he can't see you—"

"Ain't no fear." Followed by a series of gulped syllables as the signal cut out intermittently.

"Yes, but, please, don't do this. Not now— Damn it!" The phone went dead. Hands shaking, she tried to redial, but the signal was gone. Stupid rain. Stupid thick iron in the walls and ceiling. It was necessary, of course, but it made satellite signals difficult to get, and she didn't want to step back outside. Terrible might not ask who she was calling—of course he wouldn't ask—but the thought made her uncomfortable just the same. She'd just have to try and hurry things up and get out of here before he arrived.

The empty hall enveloped her, but the sense of security she'd always felt on entering the building had disappeared in the terrified haze of the night before. Sadness sunk through her chest into the pit of her stomach. This building and her home had always been safe. Been sanctuaries. Now neither of them felt that way and might never again.

She tapped on Elder Griffin's door, but he was either not in or not answering, and it was locked when she tried the knob. He might be up with the Grand Elder, or maybe back in one of the other offices. Worth a try. She might as well check with Goody Tremmell, too, and see if anything new had come in on the Mortons. Sometimes the advanced computer background checks took a few days.

Voices murmured somewhere in the warren of rooms, but Goody Tremmell's chair sat empty. Shit. Chess wasn't in the mood for more dirty looks, but she had to see that file—had to see it now. Her life quite literally depended on it.

Most files started with a call sheet, on which Goody Tremmell took the initial complaint and ran the name through the computer. Financial, police, and employment records all came up within a few minutes, and were printed and added to the file. Then it was copied, the copies handed to whichever Debunker was next in the rota to start casework, and any information they gathered was added to the master file. All the Debunkers kept were the initial reports. It all worked very smoothly, at least in theory. In practice . . . not so much. Goody Tremmell famously played favorites—hence Doyle getting the Gray Towers job when it was supposed to be Bree Bryan's turn.

Of course, that was partly how she'd ended up with the Morton file, wasn't it? Elder Griffin had given it to her without checking whether or not it was her turn.

Chess licked her lips and pulled her thinnest lockpicks from her bag, glancing around one more time as she did. This was serious, more than stealing the key to the Restricted Room or even snorting speed on the stairs. This was a crime. A big one.

Her shoulders tense, she slid the picks into the lock. Those few seconds were the worst; expecting a heavy hand to fall on her shoulder, expecting an alarm to sound or the lights to dim or—something, anything. Expecting to get busted.

But nothing happened. The lock clicked, the drawer opened, and Chess pulled the Morton master file and started thumbing through it. She hadn't even had a chance to analyze the photos she'd taken the other night, either before or after she dropped off the copies here.

The thick stack threatened to slip out of the file altogether, so she cleared a space on Goody's desk and set the stack down. Her hands shook a little as she flipped through them. The living room, the kitchen . . . all that plasticware.

The stairs, family pictures and genealogy. Chess picked the photo up and held it under the light. Was a picture missing? A pale space showed between one of a chubby toddling Albert and Mr. and Mrs. Morton at some sort of party. A short space, as though a smaller picture had been taken down and the other two moved to hide the empty patch where it had hung.

She set that photo aside and kept going. Albert's room, now. His porn. Horny little bastard. His science books, his film books, his camera equipment and projecter, the walls, the odd Dream safe behind his bed . . .

It was an odd bag, wasn't it? Might be strange for a regular sleep charm, but if it was made to ward off something in particular, a Dreamthief, for example, an entity more powerful than a regular ghost . . . and thus worth more money . . .

She pulled her notepad out and flipped through the pages. Black salt, a crow's talon, pink knotted thread. But in the photo it looked as if something else had been in the bag as well. Two things. A single black hair. And a tiny, almost invisible flake of copper.

It had caught the flash, which was why she noticed it now. As for why she hadn't when she was there, she didn't even need to think. By the time she'd photographed the Dream safe she'd been antsy, ready to leave. Only one picture followed it, a confused shot of Albert Morton's bedside table and the space behind it.

But that piece of copper, copper like the amulet, and that black hair that didn't match anyone in the Morton family, those were important. Just as important as the realization that the black hair in the Dream safe could have come from Doyle.

Chess tucked the Dream safe photo and the one of the empty space between pictures in the staircase into her bag and closed the file. Just the safe alone might be enough to implicate Doyle, at least enough to make the Grand Elder take her seriously when coupled with the amulet.

She turned to replace the file in the cabinet and almost tripped. Her toe caught on something heavy, something that made an odd chinking noise. Goody Tremmell's purse, now lying on its side with its contents scattered.

"Damn it." Chess glanced around. Still no sign of anyone, but it seemed the voices were getting louder. Bad enough to be caught digging around in the file cabinet, but to be caught with items from the Goody's purse in her hands, whether or not she was trying to put them back in, probably wouldn't help her case.

She barely looked at the items as she stuffed them into the gaping leatherette bag. Tubes of lipstick, pens, wadded tissues, the general detritus of any woman's purse. Chess shoved it all back in, heedless of order, because the voices were getting louder and any minute Goody Tremmell and Elder Griffin would be on top of her.

Keys, the ring a block of Lucite inside which was an amusing picture of a cat. Ha, ha, ha. A little golden disk, emblazoned with "The Bankhead Spa" in pale blue enamel—

Wait. The Mortons had been to the Bankhead Spa. Hadn't they? Quickly she flipped through the photos again.

Yes. The cookbook. The Bankhead Spa. A little chill ran down her spine, a shiver like the first rush of speed.

She shook her head. Goody Tremmell and the Mortons? No, it wasn't possible . . . No. It was. The Goody had been away in September, supposedly to have "a minor surgical procedure"; Chess remembered it well, because Elder Waxman had taken over the allocation of cases and had complained loudly about it the whole time.

How the hell would Goody Tremmell have been able to

afford the place? Goodys were paid shit, almost as badly as the base rate for Debunkers but without the bonuses. Yes, the spa catered to a lot of high Church officials, but those were people like the Grand Elder and the head of the Black Squad. Not Goodys. Not even regular Elders.

A bead of sweat crawled down the side of her cheek, tingling and itching. She took a deep breath, dropped the keys back in the bag. A key ring was not evidence. Even a key ring and—Doyle made a lot of money from the Gray Towers case. Money he could have shared with the woman who jumped him up in line and gave him the case.

Okay, look for something more. Even with her suspicions of Doyle, even with the key ring, she'd be laughed out of the Grand Elder's office if she tried to present a conspiracy. That wasn't evidence, it was a guess.

But there might be evidence. Evidence she could use. Chess ran her fingertips over the carpet beneath the printer tray and pulled out fifty cents and an earring back, then tried again for good measure and caught something else. Paper, it felt like, a paper ball.

This was stupid. Glancing up over the printer to make sure no one had neared the room yet, she shoved the little wastepaper basket aside and pulled the tray out from the wall. This probably wasn't something from the Goody's purse, but the way it was uncrumpling in her palm and the fact it hadn't collected any dust made her curious enough to pull it open.

An invoice for a storage space. Not just any storage space, a storage space in the name of Albert Morton.

This belonged to her case.

Belonged to her case, but had not been in the file, which meant two things. One, that the Mortons had a storage space somewhere in a warehouse district that they hadn't told her about, and two, that Goody Tremmell had for some reason kept the information out of Chess's hands.

It had to be Goody Tremmell. No one else had access

to those files once they were assigned; items were handed
to the Goody and she placed them in the appropriate file
herself. Yes, the Elders had access, but all the information from the background checks went straight to the
Goody as well; she opened the sealed envelopes and filed
the contents herself.

She never allowed anyone behind her desk. She hovered over the Debunkers and glowered when they asked
to double-check their cases.

And the Records Room was locked when she left for
the day, locked and magically sealed by the Elders—even
Goody Tremmell herself couldn't get in without an Elder's help.

And Goody Tremmell had been to the Bankhead Spa.

There was no other explanation for it; Goody Tremmell had tossed out the invoice.

Oh, shit.

Chapter Twenty-nine

She stuffed the invoice into her bag and flung herself at the file cabinet, jamming the Morton file back in just as Elder Griffin, Goody Tremmell, and Doyle rounded the corner.

"Cesaria! Are you all right? What happened to your face?"

Doyle went bright red, his mouth hanging slightly open, but she barely looked at him. She barely looked at any of them. Was Elder Griffin involved in this? Elder Griffin, her favorite? He'd been the one who gave her the Morton file to begin with, hadn't he? And he'd been the one Randy talked to. So he knew something was happening.

Hard to believe. She didn't want to believe it. But she couldn't exactly ask him about it, not with Doyle and Goody Tremmell standing right there, not when Elder Griffin's hand rested casually on the Goody's shoulder like they were friends. Especially not when Goody Tremmell's eyebrows drew down and she studied Chess as if she knew what Chess had found. Her stout arms stretched the seams of her plain black dress as she folded them, and the ties of her cap had come undone. She looked like a woman unraveling, piece by piece, like the tension inside her was shaking all the outward trimmings loose. Chess took a step back.

"Cesaria?"

"I fell," she said. "Last night, in the rain. The stairs in my apartment building were wet, and I had my hands full, so . . ." With effort she stopped herself from continuing.

Elder Griffin, can I talk to you for a minute?

Just say it! You have to tell him, you have to tell somebody!

Elder Griffin, can I talk to you?

"Why are you behind my desk?"

"I apologize, Goody Tremmell. I was . . . I was on my way to the Mortons' and I remembered I wanted to check something in the file, so I was waiting for you. But then I remembered what it was, and I—I dropped my pen." Sweat trickled down her side. *Elder Griffin, can I . . . Fuck it.* "So I'm going to go now, and, um, good morrow, and Facts are Truth."

"Facts are Truth," Elder Griffin repeated, but Goody Tremmell didn't speak. Chess turned and headed for the hall, trying to keep her gait calm and unconcerned while expecting fingers to close on her shoulder at any second.

"Chessie, wait a minute." Doyle caught up to her as she passed through the office doorway. Just the sound of his voice made her jump. Did he have a knife or would he kill her with his bare hands? "Can I talk to you? Please? I'm—I'm so sorry, and thanks for covering for me, I don't deserve it—"

"No, you don't. Get away from me." If he was talking about hitting her, he might not know what she knew. She might be able to fudge it, pretend she hadn't discovered what he was, at least until she got outside. Terrible was outside. She quickened her pace.

Doyle matched it. "Listen, I didn't mean it. I tried to tell you last night, but you ran away too fast. It was just because I haven't slept, and you surprised me, it was just a reflex. You know I would never—"

"No. I know you *did*."

"Don't I at least get a chance to apologize?"

"No." She pushed open the front door and walked out into the mist, increasing her pace as much as she could without running. Terrible's car was about fifty feet away, off to the side in an effort to be less conspicuous.

"Will you just hold on a minute?" His fingers closed around her arm.

She yanked it away. Her heart kicked in her chest; her skin where he'd touched it felt slimy, as though he'd left a trail of blood on her. Blood from his hands, Brain's blood. It was hard to speak clearly. "Fuck *off*, will you? I don't want to talk to you, I don't want anything to do with you, how do you not get this? You fucking hit me, Doyle, and you're involved in whatever— What?"

Doyle stared over her shoulder, eyes widening. A strangled sort of gasp left his throat.

Terrible was coming, his gait easy and steady, but the way his gaze fixed on Doyle and the tire iron dangling loosely from his hand were more eloquent than anything else could have been.

Doyle spun away from her, his feet slapping the wet cement as he started to run. Terrible's pace didn't change. The tire iron flew from his hand, spinning sideways like a Frisbee. Chess barely had time to gasp before it caught Doyle in the legs, knocking him to the ground.

His scream was muffled in the mist and drowned out by the clank of the tire iron skipping across the cement, but Chess felt it reverberate through her entire body just the same. The hair on the back of her neck stood on end. Still Terrible did not speed up, did not even glance at her as he passed, moving as purposefully and inexorably as a river cutting through mud.

Doyle had made it halfway to a stand when Terrible

reached him, knocking him back to the pavement with a swift, neat kick to the jaw.

They were at the edge of the lot. Five feet away it ended in soft grass, and Doyle, flat on his back like a turtle, flipped over and tried to crawl toward it. He barely advanced an inch before Terrible picked him up and threw him—*threw* him—onto the grass.

"Wait, wait," Doyle said, scrambling to his feet and holding up his muddy hands. "I'll file a complaint, I'll swear a warrant, I'll—"

He doubled over as Terrible's fist slammed into his stomach. Next came an uppercut, flinging him back to the wet grass.

Terrible yanked him up by the hair. Doyle made a feeble attempt to hit back, his arm swinging wide and short.

Another punch, and another. Blood flew everywhere, pouring from Doyle's nose and mouth, spattering his shirt and the grass. He fell to his knees, his shoulders slumped, almost unrecognizable save the thick, shiny hair on his head. Even that didn't identify him, she thought, not when from behind he and Randy Duncan could practically have been twins.

Speaking of Randy . . . Chess glanced in the direction of his cottage. That was all she needed, was for him to be watching. By morning everyone in the Church would know that Chess and some guy had come along and beaten Doyle up; Randy was incapable of keeping a secret.

But then, most people who wanted to be liked as badly as he did were.

Terrible let go of Doyle, who dropped like a corpse. Only the weak moan pouring from his mouth told Chess he was still alive.

The faint snick of Terrible's switchblade finally galvanized her into speech. "Terrible, no!"

He didn't even look at her. Instead he knelt beside

Doyle, turned him over, and pressed the blade to his throat.

"You thinking on touching her again?" he asked, low and impersonal, as if he were asking what Doyle thought of the weather or if he could direct him to the nearest gas station.

Doyle shook his head. Chess, unable to look at his fear-white eyes, glanced away and saw he'd wet himself.

"That's good. You touch her again, I kill you. Dig?"

Doyle managed to nod.

"Chess? You got any asks for him?"

"I-Is Elder Griffin in on it, Doyle?" It wasn't the question she meant to ask, but it was the first one that came out. Probably the most important, too. She had better sense than she should, staring at Doyle's ruined face.

"What?" His voice sounded thick.

"Is Elder Griffin in on it? Is he with you?" When Doyle still stared dumbly at her, she crossed her arms over her chest impatiently. "The Lamaru. The Dreamthief. Goody Tremmell. Is Elder Griffin one of you? Did he do the ritual with you?"

"What—the Lamaru? What ritual?"

Terrible pressed the knife harder. A drop of blood appeared at the point. "Ain't got time for games. Give her the answer."

"I can't! I don't know what you mean!"

Terrible lifted his fist, ready to slam it into Doyle's face again, but Chess reached out and grabbed it. "Doyle . . . when did you see the Dreamthief?"

"I told you. I didn't know what I was seeing until Bruce told me about it. I saw him in my bedroom once, and in a couple of Dreams. Why are you asking me this again? Why are you talking about the Lamaru?"

Chess and Terrible exchanged looks. Doyle could have been lying. He wasn't bad at it. But would he really be willing to die to protect Goody Tremmell—and Mrs. Morton?

"Please, I swear I don't know what you're talking about. I don't know anything about the Lamaru or rituals or anything." Tears rolled down the sides of Doyle's face. "Please, Chess, I'm sorry, I'll never come near you again, but I don't know! Please don't let him hit me again."

"How well do you know Goody Tremmell?"

"What?"

"You talk to her a lot. How well do you know her?"

Doyle coughed. A little blood ran out of the corner of his mouth. "I don't, I mean, not well. We don't *talk* talk. We just . . . chat. I'm nice to her, that's all."

"Have you ever seen her with any other Debunkers?"

"Well, we all talk to her, don't we? When she assigns cases and stuff." Doyle's brows wrinkled. He winced and touched his forehead with his fingertips. "What are you getting at?"

"But does she seem to have a particular friendship with anyone else?"

Both he and Terrible looked up at her. She shrugged, knowing her face was coloring. "I don't live on grounds, remember?"

"I can't think of anyone. She doesn't seem to . . . Wait a minute. Is this something to do with the nightmare man?"

"Never mind, Doyle."

"You don't suspect Goody Tremmell's behind that, do you? Goody Tremmell mixed up with the Lamaru? Shit, Chessie, you're even crazier than I thought if you really think—"

She opened her mouth to say something snotty back, but Terrible got there first. He grabbed Doyle's left hand and, with one quick savage twist, snapped Doyle's pinky finger. Doyle screamed. Terrible didn't even blink.

"You need ought else, Chess? Or we done here?"

They needed to get out of there. Lex was on his way, and she wasn't eager to have him face-to-face with Terrible. She needed to get a few more things from Edsel so she could do the ritual to free Slipknot's soul that night—Slipknot's and her own, she remembered with an ugly twist in her gut—and figure out then what to do about Chester's ghosts. Chances were good the Mortons were home, too, and she wanted to have another chat with them. Get this over with. She wanted this case closed like she wanted her Cepts.

Speaking of which. Her palms were starting to sweat.

"Yes, we're done," she said. "At least here."

A smile broke over Edsel's thin face when he saw her coming. "Hi, baby. What you needing? Hey, Terrible."

"Ed, you know any other uses for copper? Anything aside from the usual stuff? I've got something else to show you."

"Hope it ain't like that amulet. Gave me the creeps, that thing did."

"Yeah, well, your buddy Tyson gave me more than that, so we're even."

"Ain't my buddy, just a customer." Edsel took a contemplative drag off his long pipe and leaned back. "He ain't scared you too much, hoping?"

"No, I'm fine. Take a look at this." She pulled the photo of the Dream safe out of her bag and handed it to him. "You ever seen anything like that before?"

If he wondered why she didn't simply look it up in the Church library, he didn't show it. Instead he examined the photo, lifting his dark glasses to get a better look. "Look like a Dream safe, but an odd one. Least with that copper and the hair. Like it made to ward a specific entity, aye?"

"That's what I thought. Not just a Dream safe, but a protection."

"Awfully small piece, though. Don't know as it's even big enough to work."

Chess thought for a minute, chewing her lip. "Could it be sympathetic? I mean, if it's related to that amulet I showed you, have you ever heard of that, using the same thing that called a spirit to ward it?"

"Remind it of what's holding it, meaning?"

She nodded.

"Aye, could be, could be. Gang I knew once, back in the when, used to do experiments with metals. Like alchemy, only not trying to turn things into gold, just trying to see what vibes everything had. Some metals ain't magnetic, but they can *work* magnetic—sending energy away, like a shock."

"And copper is electrically conductive. Which makes it magically conductive."

Edsel nodded. "Somebody build a thing like this, they know what they doing."

"That's what I thought." She pulled out her notepad. "There's a few things I need, okay?"

Chapter Thirty

"The Debunker protects, first and foremost. He or she protects the Church from fraud and falsehood, yes; but above
all the Debunker protects humanity. From spirits, from
their own natures, and from others who seek to do them
harm."
—*Careers in the Church: A Guide for Teens,* by Praxis Turpin

Cool wind blew across her face as she knelt before the
lock. Pretty basic, really. Shouldn't take her more than a
minute or so to pick.

What was going to be more difficult were the wards
and spells. An itch that had nothing to do with drugs
crawled across her skin, made her jaw clench like she'd
just chewed a couple of Cepts.

She slipped one of the smallest lockpicks from its case
and stuck it into the ridged slot in the bottom of the
lock. The mere fact that it was a key lock and not a combination one worried her. Someone from the Church
would know how easily those locks could be picked.
They must have a lot of confidence in their spells.

"Okay," she said, glancing back over her shoulder while
her gloved fingers worked the pick. Terrible stood with his
back to her, watching the empty parking lot. At the sound
of her voice he turned his head just enough to acknowledge her.

The lock clicked. Chess snaked the shackle out of the
metal hasp in the door. "I'm not sure what they've got
protecting this place, so . . . just give me a minute."

Another short nod.

If the last few days had taught her anything, it was to be

prepared, and the trip to Edsel's had certainly helped. From her bag she pulled sandalwood, benzoin, and two glass jars wrapped in bubble wrap. The larger jar contained an infusion of herbs; the other a mixture of inert salt and her own menstrual blood, which all women in the Church were required to save and share with the men.

Chess would have saved it anyway; the blood was too powerful—potent for both positive and negative spells—to simply discard. She saved her hair, too, the tangles from her brush or the ends after a trim, and burned it to keep anyone else from using it in magic against her. Hair wasn't like blood; it couldn't be depersonalized and used as a generic spell ingredient. If someone was doing magic with her hair, they were doing it with her as a specific target, and although it was possible they had positive results in mind, it was far more likely they were trying to harm her. She'd learned early in life to make "cautious" her default setting.

All the same she hoped Terrible wouldn't ask what it was. It wasn't simply the personal nature of the blood powder; it was magic itself, the complex system of energy and meaning, the way her own magic differed subtly from that of the next Church employee, and theirs from the next after. One of the most important parts of training was developing one's own style, finding what energies worked best. It became as personal as a fingerprint in time, identifiable if one knew how to read it; too bad the group nature of the Lamaru magic made it impossible to trace to any one person.

Last she grabbed a half-full bottle of water, in which rested three iron rings, and three stubby black candles.

The late-afternoon sun felt good on her back, but had warmed the pavement a little too much. She sat anyway, wincing slightly as her tender skin scorched through her jeans, and pulled off her boots. "Terrible, I need you to switch your shoes."

"What?"

"Put your shoes on the wrong feet."

His broken, scarred face didn't do "nonplussed" very well, but she caught definite hints of it.

"Footprints are powerful. Magically powerful, I mean, the left one is. If someone's going to hex you, it's one of the first things they'll go for. So if you switch your shoes—"

"Confuses em, aye?" He nodded. "Okay."

Even just the short moment of shared laughter when they both looked at each other's feet, now in the wrong shoes as if they were toddlers who'd insisted on dressing themselves, eased a little of the tension in her chest. Her sense that she'd been correct to come out here, correct to connect this place to the Lamaru—of course, what other explanation could there be, for the way Goody Tremmell had tried to bury that invoice—grew with every passing moment. Unfortunately so did her sense of foreboding.

"You wouldn't happen to have a little broom or something in your car, would you? A brush of some kind? I remembered all this other stuff . . . Do you have one?"

"Lemme see." He popped the trunk. Chess wiggled her toes in her now-uncomfortable boots and watched his head disappear into the blackness of the Chevelle's trunk.

He popped up a minute or two later with a small paintbrush, only an inch and a half wide or so, but good enough, and watched as she used it to thoroughly dust the rough cement lip at the bottom of the door. Her legs ached by the time she was done; she was crouched as far away as she could be, holding her breath so as not to accidentally inhale any dust, if it was there.

"Basic warding," she said, seeing his expression. "Sprinkle goofer dust or any kind of hexing powder, and people pick it up on their shoes."

"Damn."

"Yeah, I know. Give me your hands."

Wearing gloves helped; she didn't have to feel his bare flesh against hers. All the same, the memory of those hands elsewhere on her body, holding her up, buried in her hair . . . She swallowed and focused on moving the black chalk over his palms and the back of his hands, made herself casually avoid meeting his eyes when she reached up to draw another sigil on his forehead. He didn't move during this process, didn't even blink, focusing his stare somewhere over her shoulder.

Businesslike, she sketched the same patterns on her own hands and forehead, and bent to light the candles. *"Saratah saratah . . . beshikoth beshikoth . . ."* She dumped the herbs and the blood powder in her little firedish and set them alight. "Power to power, these powers bind. Let this power, my power, become pure."

Energy, invisible but tangible, swirled around her; the energy of the earth and air, the inherent energy of all living things, which the Church taught her to channel. She waved her hand through the smoke, making sure to cover the entire door and Terrible in the fumes. Her skin warmed, but not from whatever hexes had been placed on the door. Her spell was working.

One last thing, a Church-designed anti-hex. Goody Tremmell would surely have used a Church ward to protect her space.

Chess spun counterclockwise, closing her eyes, feeling the energy vortex rising from her toes up into the sky. Her mouth opened; it would be so easy now, not to say the words, to keep letting the power take her, to ride it like any other high. To keep spinning, and spinning, until she didn't even exist anymore, until she exploded.

But the words came anyway. *"Hrentata vasdaru belarium!"*

Her spell flew forward at the words. She felt it invade the space behind the door, felt it unlock the hex ward inside the unit. Dizzy, she stumbled sideways, her feet in the wrong shoes unable to find purchase. Terrible caught her then jerked his hands away. She didn't blame him, wouldn't have even if it weren't for what had happened the night before. She could only imagine what it felt like to touch her just then, while her hair still stood on end. A shock for a normal person, but for someone she suspected carried a bit of power himself, not enough to work for the Church but enough to convey some sensitivity . . . it must have been like trying to grab the business end of a stun gun.

Without waiting for the dizziness to pass, she nodded at him and grabbed the handle jutting from low on the right side of the door. Terrible grabbed the one on the left, and together they rolled the door up.

A blast of malevolence hit her in the face, like the foul breath of an evil giant. Her eyes stung, her throat locked up, her legs shook. It only lasted a few seconds, but when it was done Chess was gasping, hanging on to the brick dividing wall between the storage unit and the one beside it.

No sooner had her breath returned than it left again. Not because of power or magic, but because she saw what waited inside the unit.

Stacks and stacks of junk, boxes full of magic implements and ragged parchments. Against the back wall stood a rack covered with jars and bottles of blood like carbuncles on the rusty shelves. There were herbs, and bones, and rough sketches of every kind of magic symbol she'd ever seen, and some she hadn't.

She handed Terrible a pair of gloves and together they started sifting through the boxes, working quickly. Chess's heart refused to slow its pounding; she may have rendered the hexes inactive, but they had not disappeared. She could feel them waiting in the air. One wrong move, one wrong word, would be all it would take to set them again, and they could strike before she knew what happened.

She couldn't help the sound that burst from her throat when she unrolled a particularly large scroll, though. Tucked in the corner with the air of something temporary, it gave off no energy at all. A Church scroll, specifically rendered inert.

A map of the City of Eternity. Why would they . . . Pieces clicked into place in her mind.

"Fuck." Her hands shook as she looked up, finding Terrible across the small room, letting him see the newly found panic in her eyes. "The Festival. That's what this is about. The Festival. They want to free the ghosts again."

They stared at each other for a beat, perhaps a moment longer. Terrible opened his mouth, started to move, but at that moment Chess's ears exploded with sound, a deep loud ringing like she'd plunged headfirst into an impossibly deep pool of water.

She'd said "Festival." She'd set off the spell.

Tendrils of blackness snaked across her vision, obscuring her view of Terrible's face going from concerned to confused. Shit. Her tattoos offered her more protection, she could probably fight her way out of even a spell as powerful as this one. But he couldn't. All he had was what little she'd been able to give him with her chalk, with the smoke she'd smudged him with.

Like swimming, like wading through oil, she moved toward him, her hands outstretched. She opened her mouth to speak but all that came out was a high-pitched squeal. Her lips refused to form words. She saw him reaching for her, his eyes clouding over.

Gloved hand met gloved hand. She touched him, felt the heat of him through the layers of latex, and grabbed hold.

She couldn't speak but she could think, words of power echoing in her head as she tugged him toward the wide open door. The clear air she saw through it seemed miles away but she fought anyway, dragging his reluctant weight, only daring to glance back once to see him stumble and almost fall under the weight of stinking evil.

Her tongue felt thick and heavy in her mouth, rigid as the soles of her boots. When she tried to speak, it fought her, refusing to become pliable enough to form words.

She screamed instead, calling on every bit of power she possessed, turning her panic and horror at the full scope of the Lamaru's plan into energy, letting it sing from her throat.

It worked. Her feet moved faster, yanking Terrible toward that open door, until finally they reached it. She tumbled out into the bright empty road; Terrible practically fell on top of her, and the storage unit door slammed down behind them.

She shoved some french fries into her mouth and waved the box under his nose, hoping their sodium fragrance would cut through the herbal scent inside the car. They'd rinsed their bare skin thoroughly with her tincture and shared swigs from the iron-ring water; she'd sprinkled pinches of the red salt in their shoes. It was the best she could do to cleanse them and keep them safe at the moment. "You have to eat. I'm not hungry either but really, you have to."

Finally he consented to take one, eyeing his own burger with distaste. "No wonder you so tiny, if yon magic shit feel like this all the time. First Tyson, now this . . . Damn, Chess."

"It doesn't though. That was particularly nasty. A trap—it would have held us there, fed off of us, if we hadn't gotten out. You'll get over it, trust me. You just need to get some food in your stomach."

That was apparently good enough. Out of the corner of her eye she watched him eat, gaining enthusiasm about halfway through. Good. Sometimes people suffered long-term problems from spells like that. Apparently he was strong enough to overcome them. She was relieved, but not surprised; he'd gotten over what happened at Tyson's place quickly enough, though that hadn't been the same type of spell.

"So they after the City? Them Lamaru, meaning."

Her food turned into a horrid lump in her throat, hot and solid as rage. She forced it down and nodded. "I don't know why I didn't figure it out before. I guess I was so focused on the Mortons, you know? But Bruce—he's a Liaiser, you know, he travels to the City and talks to the dead—I heard him the other day saying the spirits were all stirred up, like they were scared or upset or something. And the Grand Elder even mentioned how it takes them a while to calm down after the Festival, but I didn't even think someone would be going down there, trying to break in. . . ." She had, almost. In the bar, when he'd asked her if the Dreamthief would control the other spirits. If she hadn't been so fucked up then she might have caught it.

"That's why they're using the thief. Some of the other Debunkers have dreamed about him already, see? He can get into dreams, almost anyone's. He'd eventually become powerful enough to possibly invade even the Elders' dreams, to draw from them and force them into sleep. Then, once the Lamaru had figured out how to get the City doors open . . . I think they were down there, last night. Investigating. That's why there were ghosts on the platform."

"The spooks wander free, aye, and no Church to do nothing because they all sleeping?"

She nodded. Genius, really. Certainly the most ambitious Lamaru plan she'd heard of—and the most deadly. Thousands of people could die if the spirits were set free like that, all of them swarming out of the earth in silent, bloodthirsty waves, while the Church slept.

Even if none of the Church management were asleep, Banishing the entire City back would be difficult. There was a reason why the Festival was so controlled, why only a set number of ghosts were freed each night. It was too dangerous to have them all out at once. Not to mention how terrifying it would be, how people would lose all faith in the Church if there was a mass breakout in the City just as they'd lost all faith in the old religions during Haunted Week. People were fickle. "And the Lamaru can take over."

"Shit. Ain't figure on that as a good thing. Figure they really can? Ain't people notice, say aught?"

"That's the problem, though. Nobody would know. It would just look like a mass breakout in the City that the Church couldn't control. So the Lamaru steps in and handles it, and there you go. No more Church." She shivered. Those bastards. The Church was her home, the only one she'd ever had. Those utter and complete shithead bastards.

"You want me take you back to the Church? Tell them?"

"I can't. I still don't know who's involved in it, you know? If the plot goes as high as Goody Tremmell, it could be anyone."

"So we handle it, aye? Send the thief back where he come from, an it all ends?"

"Yeah. I hope so, anyway."

"Still think we got time to check all out, your place? Like to ask your neighbors there. Oughta not take the chance we miss ought, dig, something snap back at us later. If them Lamaru's the ones break in, could be they nearby watching."

"We can't do the ritual until it's full dark at least, anyway. We might as well."

The evening stretched before her like an obstacle course. So many things still to do, so much to prepare . . .

And later still the ritual. The ritual that would either kill her or save her, would either defeat the Dreamthief or defeat her.

For a moment she considered Terrible's suggestion again. It would be easy to head back to the Church. It might even be easy to bypass Goody Tremmell and head straight for the Grand Elder.

But even if she did, and he listened, what would happen? He hadn't taken Bruce's concerns very seriously, and she'd heard his thoughts on the Lamaru before, his utter confidence that they were little more than a band of amateurish thugs.

He might be willing to help, eventually. She might even be able to think of a good reason why she'd been out at Chester Airport to begin with, why she'd found Slipknot's body.

But in the meantime . . . while she waited for him to come around, while she waited for help, her soul would still be food. She had enough monkeys on her back, didn't she? Enough memories to suck all the joy out of her life and crush her under their weight.

Her addiction she shouldered willingly, even eagerly. She refused to do the same with the Dreamthief.

Chapter Thirty-one

> "Remember, you're not a Church employee—some spells will simply be beyond your reach. That's okay! There are still lots of fun rituals to do in the privacy of your own home, and the results will amaze you."
>
> —*You Can Do This! A Guide for Beginners,*
> by Molly Brooks-Cahill

Chess followed Terrible up the rickety stairs of the building across the street from hers. Perhaps it was a wasted trip at this point, but if there was a chance someone had seen something, they might as well get the information.

Lex had called again, twice, but she let the voice mail get it. Hadn't he understood when she said she was with Terrible? Didn't he understand how important all this was?

They reached the dingy landing, lit by one weak naked bulb hanging on a wire. A rat huddled in a corner, its bare skinny tail whipping the air. Chess shuddered as Terrible knocked on the door of number five.

They waited, then he knocked again, and again, until finally the locks clicked and the door opened a crack.

"Ain't got no dealings with Bump," said a husky voice. Chess couldn't see the speaker's face.

"Ain't about Bump," Terrible replied. "About the apartment across the street. The old church, aye? Your windows look in there?"

"That Churchwitch? I see her sometime. She wander around in there like a ghost, all by herself. Ain't right for a woman to be alone like that. She in trouble?"

"You see anything there this morning, before sunup? Last night, maybe?"

"Seen some dude in there t'other night. With her. Looking like he trying to make some moves."

Chess's face felt hot. Must have been Doyle, when he'd come back and taken care of her hand.

"Last night, I'm saying. You see anything last night, this morning?"

Pause. "Could be I do. What's it to you?"

Terrible reached in his pocket and pulled out a folded bill. "You see, or not?"

"Aye. Aye, I see. Two guys, dig? Didn't see no faces, not good. Pale guys. Dark hair. One snuck back into her bedroom, carrying something I don't know. T'other poking around her main room there. Look like he take something, but left something else. From he pocket."

"How long they in there?"

A hand slipped through the crack, palm up, and waited. Terrible slapped the bill into it.

"Half hour, maybe. Could be longer. I ain't watching. I got my own shit, aye? But I see them."

"Where he leave the thing? You see where he put it?"

"She mighty sweet, Terrible. Sometime she hang around in just little underwears."

Chess made a mental note never to open her curtains again. She'd thought with the smudgy filth covering every window in Downside she wouldn't have to worry during the day. She also never attempted to look in her neighbors' windows. Obviously they had none of the same disinterest.

"Just answer. Where he put it?"

"On the shelf somewheres. Near the top."

Terrible nodded. "Aye."

"Cool, then." The door started to close. Terrible put one hand out and stopped it.

"What? You need more? Ain't know more, that's all I see."

"You see too much, dig? Keep them eyes away from her windows. I find out you peeping in her windows, I come back."

"Shit. Stealing all a man's fun." The door closed.

Chess bit her lip as she followed Terrible back down the stairs and across the street. Something left in her apartment. A charm, maybe? Some sort of curse? Or something worse than that, a camera or recording device to keep tabs on her.

It was both.

Precious minutes disappeared while they hunted for it, flipping through books and dropping them on the floor. Chess was starting to wonder if she shouldn't just leave them there. The top shelf yielded nothing, not even when she slid her fingers over the bottom of it and probed the space between it and the wall. She was thinking of giving up when Terrible picked up the small silver wolf she'd bought a few years back.

"No, that's mine," she said.

"Aye? What's the little mouth hole for?"

She took it from his hand. "Shit. This one isn't mine."

The drill hole was so minute she couldn't imagine how anyone had even managed to find a bit that small. Further inspection revealed they hadn't. The wolf was molded around the camera. Masterful. Masterful, and almost certainly created by a Church supplier. Several companies did special contract work creating just this sort of thing, useful in especially difficult cases.

"These things can take weeks to make," she said. "Unless someone pays extra to put a rush, or has some real juice."

"Figure that—" He grabbed the wolf from her and strode into the kitchen with it, then tossed it into the fridge, closing the door on it with a thud. "That Goody you mention got some right, ain't she?"

"Yeah, but they would have made this in, like, two days. I don't think any of our contractors can work that fast."

"Why two days?"

"The first break-in was only two days ago."

Terrible shrugged. "Who said that was the first?"

Suddenly she was very tired. Terrible watched as she slumped down onto the couch and dug a battered pack of cigarettes from between the cushions. Empty. He lit one of his and handed it to her.

"Bump only asked me to investigate the airport on, what, Friday? Yeah, Friday. And I got the Morton case the next day. That's not even a week."

"But your friend across the street there says something planted here this morning. So they left the camera first, aye, then come back today, drop off Brain and leave something else."

"I don't see anything on the shelves, though, and he said they put something on the shelf."

"Maybe he only checking the camera. Don't mean nothing else got left, today or before. What's the last time you gave the place a lookover?"

She would have felt it, wouldn't she have, if something magical had been left in here? Like she'd felt the power sneak up her legs when she walked over that spot by the runways.

She hadn't felt anything different here, or rather, she hadn't felt anything she didn't attribute simply to the general creepiness of having strangers in her home. But if it had only been planted in the last couple of days, and she'd spent hardly any time here at all . . .

Terrible's dark gaze followed her as she stood up and started pacing the room, keeping her eyes half-closed. It wouldn't be by the bookcases. She'd stood there and felt nothing. But the rest of the room, the rest of the apartment, she'd barely touched.

They wouldn't have put it under the bed, which was the most obvious place to put a curse bag or anything of that nature. They wouldn't put it there because it would be too easily discovered when she changed the mattress. It wasn't under the couch, because she would have felt it when she sat down. So where else did she go all the time, where else would she be in close proximity but not close enough to immediately sense it?

She got her answer when she stepped close to the old armchair. The minute her foot brushed the heavy brown corduroy valance, her stomach did a flip.

"Terrible. Grab me my bag, okay?"

She heard him moving but didn't turn her head. The warped lines of the chair merged and spread as she stared at it, an optical illusion she couldn't seem to look away from. Whatever they'd hid, it was powerful. Powerful enough that her heart rate sped up and she had to force herself to stay still or she would run away.

Terrible placed the bag in her hand and she fumbled in it, finding by feel her gloves and slipping the left one on. Her knees creaked as she crouched beside the chair and lifted the cushion with her right hand so she could poke around beneath it with her left. That was a mistake.

The ache in her palm, a constant low presence since the day she'd cut herself on the amulet, turned into a screaming, searing burn. With a cry she dropped the cushion, and rocked back so hard she almost fell over. Her hand throbbed, the stinging pain shooting up her arm to her shoulder and down her side.

"Chess? Maybe you ought not—"

"I'm fine." She grabbed her other glove and forced her hand into it, trying not to touch her palm but failing. Sweat beaded on her brow.

"Whyn't you let me—"

"I'm *fine*."

He didn't speak again. She felt him close to her, the warmth of his body on her bare arms, and after a minute she took a deep breath and tried again.

The ache in her hand strengthened when she touched the cushion, but it did not slice through her with razor-sharp blades as it had a moment ago. Her left hand slid along the fabric covering the seat base, into the crack down the left side, along the back . . . and brushed against something with the semisolid consistency of rotting fruit. An itch like thousands of tiny demons holding pokers inside her skin started in her hand, worked its way up her arm, across her body. Chess gritted her teeth to keep her stomach from revolting and yanked the curse from its hiding place.

Instantly the itching worsened. Her right palm caught fire again and went damp inside her glove, whether from sweat or blood she did not know, and she was afraid to look. That fear pissed her off and she did look, turning her hand to see through the whitish latex of her glove.

It took her horrified brain a minute to realize exactly what image it was receiving. The glove, pinkish now with blood but still white in the center, a dirty white like curdled milk . . . squirming movement . . . that maddening itch, deep in her bones . . .

Something fell from the top edge of the glove onto the floor, writhing feebly. A worm. The worms were back. Oh shit the worms were back, and she was screaming, trying to tear the glove off as worms poured from the wound in her hand and made the glove bulge out, as they crawled out of the glove and pattered to the floor like obscene, bloody pearls from a broken antique necklace.

The glove finally left her hand with a snap. The curse bag lay on the floor, surrounded by worms, with her blood slowly seeping toward it. Instinctively she reached for it with her right hand, pushing it away, but when her skin touched the bag, agony tore her apart. A new gush of filthy life vomited from her skin, from the gaping red wound that looked like a vicious mouth.

Hard hands grabbed her and lifted her, just enough so Terrible could slide his arm under her legs and scoop her up like a child. Into the kitchen he carried her, heedless of the worms falling from her hand onto his bare skin. He set her on the countertop next to her cracked sink and turned on the water, holding her hand beneath it while he flipped on the disposal switch.

"Cool, Chess . . . Don't look at it, just look at the wall across, aye? Stare at it real hard. Keep starin."

His footsteps sped across the room, then back to her. Her head started to clear as the pain receded, but her stomach almost lost the battle when she looked down into the sink and saw it filled with nasty brownish-red water, saw whitish bits of flesh still wriggling as they drifted into the whirlpool at the drain and were sucked down. Her drain never had worked very well. She swallowed and stared back at the wall, trying to erase the image of those hundreds of horrible little bodies, squirming their blind way out of her skin as if her own soul had become filth.

Or rather, as if the filth in her soul had become flesh.

Terrible returned a moment later. "Looks to be about finished," he said, grabbing her hand and turning it, prodding it with one big gentle finger before sticking it under the faucet. "I moved yon bag away from the blood, aye?"

She nodded. "Th-thanks."

"Cool." His eyes met hers for a second, barely the amount of time needed for her to acknowledge it had happened at all, before he turned away and grabbed some paper towels to dry her hand.

"What you figure? This need bandaging, or leave it open in case they comes back?"

"Clean it and close it, for good. Those things . . . the wound created them, the wound and the curse. At least I assume, because the wound's been clean."

He rubbed his chin. "Close it, though . . . close it good's gonna hurt, Chess. Leave a fuck of a scar."

She nodded.

"Right." He disappeared for a minute, coming back with her bag. "I'd fetch you some pills, were I you, and give me them lockpicks you use. They steel, aye?"

She told him they were and watched as he lit the burner on her stove. Her hand itched as she clumsily dug out the picks and her pillbox, and crunched three Cepts between her teeth. She'd taken two only a couple of hours before. Nothing was going to make this painless, but hopefully it might make a difference, even if taking pills for actual physical pain felt like such a waste.

Terrible examined the lockpicks with a practiced eye, then selected the largest one, which she hardly ever used. Her ears started ringing when he held it over the blue gas flames of her stove.

"Maybe you oughta sit on the floor. Ain't want you falling off."

She slid onto the cracked linoleum and waited, watching him heat the pick until it glowed.

"You sure you wanna do this?"

She nodded and held out her hand, bracing her elbow on her knees to keep it steady. She could still back out, she could tell him she'd changed her mind, he wouldn't think any worse of her if she did . . .

Too late. His left hand grabbed her fingers, squeezing them together with bruising strength, and he pressed the bright red steel into the wound on her palm.

Chapter Thirty-two

"Do not be fooled into thinking penitence is possible through any means but those designated and performed by the Church. Pain itself does not cleanse."
—*The Book of Truth*, Laws, Article 82

Her entire body convulsed. Her arm tried to jerk away—she didn't move it, it was pure reflex—but Terrible held it fast. Tears poured from her eyes. She lunged forward, hoping to surprise him into releasing his grip, but he simply twisted his upper body, capturing her arm between his biceps and chest with enough force to cut off her circulation.

Her throat was raw from screaming. Her head ached. With her free hand she hit him, beating his broad back, and when that didn't work she leaned over and bit him like an animal caught in a trap. She shook, she forgot her name, forgot where she was. All she knew was pain, unlike anything she'd ever felt, pain which lessened for a few seconds at a time while he reached up to reheat the pick, then exploded again when he applied it to her skin.

Nothing had ever sounded sweeter than the clattering of the pick as he dropped it onto the floor. Chess rested her head against him, breathing in the comforting scents of smoke and pomade and soap, wretched sobs erupting from her throat. She didn't think she'd have the strength to lift her head. She knew she wouldn't have the strength to stand.

Terrible did. Disentangling himself gently from her

grasping arms, he got up and opened her freezer. She watched through blurry eyes as he wrapped ice cubes in some paper towels and came back, pressing them into her hand. It felt wonderful. Adrenaline rushed through her body in a tidal wave, leaving her with the inexplicable desire to laugh. She did laugh, weakly, a hysterical giggle that sounded nothing like her, and tasted blood on her lips. Not her blood; her lips felt fine. His.

"I'm sorry," she began. "I didn't mean to hurt—"

"No problem."

"But . . ."

"Just keep that ice on for a minute. An tell me how to break yon curse."

"Shit." She gave another shaky laugh. "I actually forgot about it, can you believe?"

"Aye."

"Okay." Deep breath. Deep breath. "Bring it here."

He looked doubtful, but did, setting it a safe distance away from her. The burning cold of her palm made it impossible to tell if the bag affected her or not, but she didn't think so.

Following her directions, he used the picks to ease the bag open and empty it. Her eyes bulged. "That's not just a curse. That's . . . that's a death curse."

He nodded. "Figured it were some heavy shit. What do I do?"

For a minute she just sat, clenching the wad of soggy paper and ice in her hand. A dead insect. Black powder. Broken pins and a coffin nail. A ball of black wax that proved, when carefully scraped at, to contain a slip of paper with her name on it, and a long strand of hair, crinkled from the wax.

Her hair. How the fuck did—right. Someone from the Church. Someone got hold of a piece of her hair. Harvested it. Plucked it from her shoulder, from her bathroom floor or her bed. Taken from Doyle's pillow, perhaps, the morning after? The worst thing she'd ever done was let that slimeball put his sticky little hands on her.

Well, obviously not the *worst*. That was a long fucking list. But it had been a stupid mistake, one she wouldn't make again.

Terrible's lips twisted as the last items fell out. A fleck of copper that made her shudder and press her lips together, but didn't surprise her. A smaller ball of tight, curly hair, and a wad of fabric stiff and brown with dried blood.

"Hair from a corpse. Menstrual blood," she said, answering his unspoken question. The blood could be hers, too, for all she knew, taken from the Church's supply. At least Doyle hadn't gotten hold of *that* during their night together.

He shook his head. "Some nasty. What happen iffen we ain't find this?"

"I probably would have died. Eventually. Death curses take time to work. Weeks, maybe. If I spent a lot of time at home it'd be faster—it would have had more time to affect me—but I haven't been around much lately."

He nodded. "So who done this, then? Any clues?"

"Lots of clues. No answers. Something like that requires a lot of fucking power, more than I would think— whoever it was probably performed another sacrifice for it, but that body would have been discarded somewhere." She moved her legs and tried to get up. That seemed to work, so she stood. The room spun onto its side for a second, but righted itself quickly enough.

"Shit. Ain't even know you can do that shit with magic, for real an all."

"It's just energy," she said. "Everything has energy, you know? It's just a matter of how you use it, whether you have the ability to use it. The more powerful you are the more you can do."

"So them made this, they powerful."

She nodded. Fear slid down her raw throat; fear not

just at what they were facing, but at the reminder that some of that power was *her* power, thanks to the stupid blood connection. A mishmash hybrid ghost comprised of sick and evil, made stronger by her own blood. And nothing to do but fight it.

Speaking of which . . . "Want to wash that all down the sink and come lurk menacingly in front of a dull suburban family?"

His face broke into a grin. "Lead the way."

They were too late. The Morton house was silent as death, the harsh light from the overhead bulbs leaching the color from the Mortons' faces until they looked ethereal, the babes in the suburban wood forever sleeping.

They *were* sleeping, the deep, untroubled sleep of the just, no matter that they were guilty. Their still bodies curled like newborn kittens on the couch and floor. Either they hadn't made it to their beds or they'd become too afraid to sleep in them.

From outside the house came only the sounds of crickets chirping, of wind rustling through young trees. Every house on the street was dark, revealing nothing as they'd walked past; was everyone asleep? Had the thief already begun stockpiling power?

Chess raised a nervous hand to her forehead, careful not to smudge the sigil there but wanting to reassure herself. Terrible's eyes rolled up as if he could check his that way, but outwardly he seemed completely unconcerned. She tried to tell herself that was because Terrible hadn't endured having red-hot steel thrust into an open wound, but that wasn't the case. Terrible also hadn't dealt with the Dreamthief before. She didn't think either of those facts truly accounted for his calm.

Still his presence reassured her, loath as she was to admit it, and she made her way up the stairs with more purpose than she felt. About halfway up she stopped to examine the blank space she'd seen in the picture. It wasn't as clear in the eye-crackingly glaring light, but it was still visible.

The Morton bedroom hadn't changed much either. Still just as tidy, but *The Book of Truth* was nowhere to be seen. They probably stuffed it under the bed.

"What we hunting for?"

"Anything. Pictures, especially. Spellbooks or books on entities. Charm bags. Letters."

He nodded. "Any worries on keeping this hidden?"

"No. Let's just be quick."

They worked without speaking for a while, with the sounds of drawers opening and hangers rattling the only sounds. Terrible was handier than she'd thought he would be; he could see on top of furniture and along the top shelf of the closet, and he could move furniture with ease.

The charm bag hid between the headboard and the wall, just as Albert's had done, and when she opened it she found the contents identical.

"But they sleeping," Terrible said. "Because they away from the charm, or because the charm ain't work?"

"I don't think it works," she said slowly. Shit, those extra Cepts might have helped her hand, but they sure weren't helping her head. "Whoever put it together didn't activate it, or they didn't use enough power to do it properly. Amateurs."

"Like them."

"Yeah, like them. I wonder if . . . hmm. I wonder if they were given the ingredients and told what to do? Maybe someone wrote it down for them."

Terrible started hunting again, dumping drawers out onto the pale carpet and sifting through the contents, while Chess stared at the objects on the bed.

It was possible someone was trying to kill the Mortons. Screw *someone*, she might as well say Goody Tremmell, using the Lamaru as her instrument. It was possible

Goody Tremmell was trying to kill the Mortons, and she'd deliberately given them inadequate Dream safes to make them think they were protected. Possible she'd hatched this little plot at the Bankhead Spa with the Mortons, then figured she'd double-cross them.

Goody Tremmell issued the payout checks. Goody Tremmell could easily make the check out to herself, or funnel the funds into a separate account, or whatever other scam she could think of.

But why give them these safes at all, then? With materials that Chess's reading had indicated would certainly hold some sway? She almost could have believed they were powering Ereshdiran in some way, except the amulet that powered him was still in her bag and the soul that powered him—aside from hers—was due to be moved back to the airport later so she could break the spell.

The Lamaru wouldn't summon the thief from here, but if her theory was right—and it had to be, it just had to be—there had to be something here. Something to direct the entity, something to ward it, something to control it, something.

Black salt was common enough. Most Banishing spells or controlling spells used it. The claw was more unusual, but as she'd noted when she found the safe in Albert's room, it wasn't completely out of place. Lots of magic systems used bird parts to signify dreams or sleep, and the pink witch's ladder would bring good dreams, too, provided such intentions were tied into the knots. The fleck of copper and the single black hair. That had to be it, it had to be.

The hair could be anyone's. Not any of the Mortons', but anyone else, any one of the Lamaru. Whoever had committed the murder that summoned Ereshdiran could in theory control him with that hair, at least to some degree.

"Cool, Chess?"

She jumped. "Shit! Sorry. I forgot you were here."

"Look like you a million miles away. Been starin at that stuff for five minutes, like you listening to it."

"No, I just—what?"

"Look like you trying to make it talk."

Her knees went weak. "Trying to—of course. Of course! They're trying to talk. They're trying to keep tabs. Remember what Edsel said about copper conducting electricity, so it conducts magic, too?" Shit, she should have thought of it herself, would have if her head hadn't been so fuzzy.

"The amulet is copper. These bags have flecks of copper in them. They conduct together. There's probably more bags, too, I bet everyone involved has one, so they can sense if the Dreamthief is active and gaining power, keep tabs on him, you know? The . . . the power sends out a signal, like a shiver, and if you're sensitive to it you'll feel it."

"So sayin I got a bag on me, and the Dreamthief is moving around by one of the other bags. I might know it?"

"Exactly. And it . . . even that little bit of charged copper would draw him. Keep him under control, by limiting his movements—fuck, so would the damned bird claw, birds are psychopomps too, they conduct spirits to and from the City. So he can't be brought here and then just disappear somewhere else in the country. He's forced to stay in the area, it's like one of those electric fence things."

One of those bits of copper had been in the death curse at her place. A calling card, or a summons?

"Stay in the area, or stay nearby the copper bits? Ain't they summoned him partly so he could haunt here? So they build their safe thing, to keep him from killing the Mortons, aye, but they put yon copper in to make sure he stays here and haunts em."

She could have kissed him. Might even have done it, if he hadn't been all the way across the room and . . . well.

He was right. It wasn't so much a fence as a magnet. They'd bound him to certain places, certain spots. At least they'd made some attempt to minimize the risk, although only the truly arrogant could have thought it would actually work for long. But then they didn't need it for long, did they? She had no idea when they planned to stage their breakout.

So in leaving that piece of copper at her apartment, they'd tried to bind him there as well. To kill her. Maybe they thought she no longer had the amulet? Or maybe it was simply to strengthen the effect. Either way, she'd had enough.

She thought of the Church, of all the employee cottages and the larger buildings where the Elders lived. Dozens of hiding places there. Hundreds. Had the Lamaru and Goody Tremmell already planted them, or were they hoping to get the Morton payout first?

Her hand still throbbed as she started going through one of the file boxes Terrible had dragged out of the closet. All she wanted to do was get to Chester and get this done, but she needed to find out if she was right about Goody Tremmel or not, if money really was the only motive. The key ring and the tossed-out invoice were good, but she needed something better. Something she could give someone in authority, anything to prove to them and to herself that she hadn't climbed quite as high on the crazy tree as she felt she had.

It was so tiring, all of it. She was sick of this case, sick of these people, sick of it all, and her back ached under the strain. Bump, Terrible, Lex, the Mortons, the Lamaru, Doyle, Goody Tremmell . . . it was enough, it was too much. If her life and the Church's very existence hadn't been in danger she would have abandoned all of it and holed up in a Dream den for the next week.

She kept digging through the files like an automaton, her body working independently of her mind. Bills, bills,

bills. Receipts. She discarded them one by one. None of them contained anything that might possibly relate to Ereshdiran or Goody Tremmell or anything else.

But then, Goody Tremmell would know where she would search, and when. Which made possible hiding places in the house few and far between. Chess hadn't yet gotten authorization to go into the Mortons' safe-deposit box.

But then, Goody Tremmell wasn't the most imaginative woman as a rule, right? It had been pretty careless—or arrogant—to just throw out that bill or toss it into her purse instead of shredding it, hadn't it, even if the Goody usually took her trash to the incinerator herself? So perhaps the Mortons were just as dull.

"Help me lift the mattress," she said, turning around.

Chapter Thirty-three

> "It is always wise to have a fireproof safe, or perhaps a
> safe-deposit box located elsewhere, in which to store fam-
> ily photos and documents, particularly those of a genealog-
> ical nature. You never know when disaster might strike."
> —*Mrs. Increase's Advice for Ladies*, by Mrs. Increase

The envelope wasn't under the mattress, not quite. It
sat inside the box spring, tucked into a clumsily mended
slice in the flowered fabric, but Chess's breath caught just
the same. She hadn't expected it would be there. Most
people destroyed incriminating documents, or at least
stored them elsewhere. In the normal run of a case Chess
might interview dozens of friends and acquaintances,
would break into their homes later to hunt for anything
they might have been given and told to hide. So for this
to be here, still in the house . . . inside the box spring
was a safe hiding spot, but not the safest.

Unless they'd known it was all going wrong, had felt
their energy being sucked away as the thief gained power,
and had put it there in hopes it would be found by someone who could help them. Someone who would need to
know who'd done this to them, so the culprit could be
punished. Also possible.

She shrugged. Wasn't up to her why they'd chosen to
incriminate themselves, only that they had. She picked up
the envelope and straightened the pins on the flap.

The contents were light. Only a few sheets of paper and
two faded photographs. One of a woman—barely more
than a girl, really—with a tired, mournful expression,

holding a baby. The other was of a young man at a graduation—a Church graduation, wearing a blue brimmed hat and sash. Chess had a hat just like that in her apartment, still in its clear plastic box shoved to the back of her closet shelf.

Oh, fuck. She'd been wrong, wrong and stupid. The awkward smile on the face staring back at her—how many times had she seen that smile, dismissed it? Dismissed him? Not a good Debunker, boring, not very smart . . .

Looked like Randy Duncan was a lot smarter than she'd thought.

Randy Duncan who, according to the birth certificate in the envelope, was Mrs. Morton's illegitimate son. Now that Chess was looking at it she saw the resemblance, the very thing that had bothered her the first time she met Mrs. Morton.

Randy never told her he'd found his birth mother, or anything about his life at all. Chess knew he was adopted, but all of this—the birth certificate, the bill from a private investigations firm showing how much money the Mortons had invested in finding him—he'd never mentioned. Not once. Of course . . . He wouldn't have. Not when he figured he could use the Church to recoup their money for them and finally get them that bigger house.

The Mortons would report a haunting. Randy would investigate and claim it was a real one. The Church would pay, and everyone would be happy.

Until she stepped in and took the case. Now at least she knew whose name had been next in the case queue.

Was this really what all of this was about? Why the fuck had he brought the Lamaru in on this, what the hell was he thinking? Was he really such a failure he'd needed to turn to them to summon a ghost, instead of doing it himself? They learned basic Summoning in their second year, for fuck's sake. She could have summoned a ghost right there, if she needed to—it would have been illegal, but she could do it—so why couldn't Randy? Why had he needed to go to the Lamaru, why summon an entity like Ereshdiran instead of a basic ghost?

That just didn't make sense, didn't fit, even as the rest of her questions were answered. Her instinct at her first visit, that the Mortons were faking, had been right on. They had been—before. But somehow during that visit, they'd managed to get Ereshdiran here—Ereshdiran, jacked high on her own power—and all hell had broken loose, with her in the center of it. And all because Randy wanted to help his family. Poor, stupid, naïve Randy—Randy who'd gotten mixed up somehow with the Lamaru.

No wonder Mrs. Morton hadn't destroyed these, hadn't even been able to bear storing them elsewhere. It must have been awful, giving up a baby, searching for years . . . Chess couldn't imagine it, any more than she could imagine what it would be like to have someone spend that much money and time just to be a part of her life.

She cleared her throat. "Okay. I think this is all we—"

"Not so fast."

Oh, shit. She spun around on legs that felt ready to collapse beneath her to see Randy in the doorway, barely three feet from her, with a dull, black hunting knife clutched in one shiny, pale hand. His normally messy hair stuck to his forehead in crooked, sweaty stripes; his teeth gnawed at his dry lips, leaving red spots where they tore the fragile skin.

How stupid was she? Of course Randy was going to show up here. Of course he would have a knife. Had she actually thought a locked front door would keep him out?

She'd thought she was being so clever, having Terrible park one block over so their presence in the house wasn't advertised, bringing him up here with her to help her search so it would go more quickly. It hadn't even occurred to her to set any magical traps of any kind.

Now she would pay for that with her life.

Terrible was on the other side of the bed. There was no way he could reach Randy before Randy reached her, and she wasn't a bad fighter, but she didn't think she could take Randy down before he hurt her badly. She caught Terrible's eye, gave her head a tiny shake.

"I think you have something that belongs to me," Randy said. "Quite a few things, in fact, starting with my birth certificate and ending with my amulet. Drop the papers and tell me where the amulet is, please."

The papers fell back to the bed with a quiet rippling sound. "It's in my bag. Over there by the closet."

"Oh, no. You go get it. I'm not taking my eyes away from you and whoever this thug you're hanging out with is. Not after what he did to Doyle."

"So you ran into Doyle, huh."

"Get the bag. Move slow."

She slid her foot to her left, inching sideways across the carpet. Terrible stared at her, his face immobile but his eyes a little wider than usual, a little more intense. What?

Randy's hand slid over her shoulder to grip the back of her neck. "I don't think I want you too far away from me," he said. "And yeah, I ran into Doyle. He told me you were asking about Goody Tremmell—like *she'd* have anything to do with this, please—and about the Lamaru. Why don't you mind your own fucking business? Didn't you learn anything from what happened to that kid you were hanging around with?"

Brain had seen the ritual . . . From the back Randy and Doyle could almost pass for each other, especially in the dark. Especially when the witness was a terrified young boy. No wonder Brain had run, and run again when he saw her coming for him. He'd thought she was involved. He'd died thinking she'd given him up.

She felt sick, tried not to show it. There'd be time for that later. And Goody Tremmell—Randy must have broken into the filing cabinet, taken that invoice, and tossed it away, while he was hanging out in the Church earlier, intercepting phone calls and such. Not the Goody at all. He must have given her the keyring, too; a bribe to make sure she didn't skip his place in the queue? She thought of offering a silent apology to Goody Tremmell, but remembered the snotty look on her face when she'd seen Chess behind her desk and decided not to. What she didn't know wouldn't hurt her. "What I don't understand is how you got mixed up with them in the first place."

"Yeah, well, you wouldn't, would you? You thought I was an idiot. Just like everybody else. Poor Randy, he's a lousy Debunker, he's a fool . . . Whatever. You don't know anything. The Lamaru do, and so do I."

The pride in his voice, even after everything that had happened, made her wince. "Randy . . ."

"No, don't 'Randy' me, don't you fucking 'Randy' me! The Lamaru needed me, they promised me—they promised me everything. And they gave it to me, too. When they take over, I'll be a leader. I'll be in charge." His defiance sent fresh waves of terror pumping through her blood. Nothing in the world was more dangerous than someone who believed they were about to get everything they wanted—someone who believed in the empty promises of madmen.

Without looking away, Chess knelt slowly by her bag and reached for it with her stiff and aching right hand. It took her two tries to close her fingers over the tongue of the zipper.

Randy glared at her. "First you take *my* case, just wave those miniscule tits at Elder Griffin and get handed the case that should have been mine, then you poke around that airport and power up my ghost. We had him, don't you understand? We had him under control, until you did that!"

"I'm sorry," she said, because it seemed to be what he wanted. What was she supposed to say?

Her stiff fingers closed over the cloth-wrapped amulet. When she handed this to him he would kill her. Slit her throat, probably, then be ready to stab Terrible when Terrible leapt for him. And it would look like Ereshdiran did it somehow, or at least that's what Randy would say, and why would anyone doubt him? The regular police didn't have jurisdiction in Church matters at all.

"When the Lamaru are in charge, things will be different. No more laws regulating what magic people are allowed to do and what they're allowed to believe in. No more lies, no more answers to questions that shouldn't have them. Look around you, Chessie. Do you honestly think this is a good world we live in? Do you honestly think it's good for people to obey laws out of fear, and to know exactly what happens when they die, and to believe in nothing but themselves and power? There's no mystery. There's no hope. It's like a little hell, this world." Randy shook his head, his lips curling.

"And the Lamaru want to put the mystery back, the hope. And they needed *me* to help them do it, me and *my* skills. Me, to show them how to get into the City, me to help raise the thief. What the fuck were you doing at that airport, anyway?"

"How did you get involved with them?" She wasn't about to give him an answer, and she didn't think he would notice. Her thinking might have been fuzzy from drugs sometimes, but Randy had left sanity behind a while ago.

For a minute Chess felt sorry for him. He was right. He had been something of a laughingstock at Church, like a mascot nobody took seriously. Then all of the sudden he had a family, and a powerful magic group wanting to learn from him, promising him power and wealth and respect . . . and now he couldn't escape. They would kill him if he tried, and he knew it. Behind his boasts she heard the panic in his voice.

As for his comments about the world they lived in . . . she couldn't even consider that. Such thoughts were heresy, and the Church had given her more hope than she'd ever known could exist. Maybe he had a point about answers, but then, if the answers were there, didn't people have a right to them?

She glanced at Terrible again. This time he moved, flexing the fingers of his right hand. With his arms folded he was pointing to her right, where Randy crouched.

Where he *crouched*. He was only balancing on the balls of his feet. It would be simple to knock him off balance. If she could hit him—he had her right hand crowded, but she couldn't use her right anyway. It was too difficult to bend her fingers. Her left, though, if she could swing around and catch him with a left, she might be able to knock him far enough away that Terrible could get him.

She blinked, hoping he read her agreement in it, and tensed her arms.

"I met one of them at the Sp—just give me my amulet."

"I can help you, Randy." Her mind whirred. So the Lamaru were meeting—or at least recruiting—at the Bankhead? Where did their money come from? She looked up, tried to catch his eyes with hers, but he refused to let her. "I can help you, we can get rid of them together, the Church will understand, they'll—"

"Shut up!" His free hand raised, preparing to strike. Terrible made a sound low in his throat, but she didn't dare look at him, and Randy dropped his hand back to her neck.

"I can help—"

"You don't get it, do you, you stupid bitch? *I don't*

want your help. All this—all this mess, it's your fault, and they're holding me responsible for it, and if you don't give me that amulet they'll kill me, too, not just—" He snapped his mouth shut, like he was about to reveal a secret. Like she didn't already know the Lamaru wanted her dead. "Just give it to me. They need me. I can talk to them, I can tell them it was an accident and you don't know anything."

Yeah. She believed that one. She drew in a shaky breath. "Okay. Here it is."

She twisted her upper body, crowding him with her right side as she pretended she was going to give him the amulet with her right hand. He was holding the knife in his right hand, so had to take his left off her neck to make an awkward attempt to collect the amulet.

She'd never been very good with her fists, much preferring weapons, but she made do with what she had, driving her left across her body. It felt unnatural and strange, but it worked. Her fist connected with his eye, knocking him backward. Chess let the amulet fall from her hand and grabbed her knife, driving it forward, but Randy was too fast. He caught her hand and squeezed.

The butt of the knife slammed into her injured palm. Pain clouded her vision. She screamed and rolled sideways, trying to pull away from him, but he squeezed harder. Through a haze of tears she saw his face, his lips twisted in rage. He raised his right hand. Moonlight hit the edge of the blade.

Terrible grabbed him, lifted him, threw him. Randy hit the wall with a room-shaking thud and fell back to the floor. It would have been comical if he hadn't sprung back up so quickly.

He made a sound somewhere between a howl and a scream and lifted the knife, but Terrible was too fast. He shoved himself forward, one hand grabbing Randy's wrist while his big shoulders pushed Randy back to the wall again. He slammed Randy's hand against it hard enough to crack the plaster. The knife fell to the floor.

Randy's left hand pounded at Terrible's back, stopping only when the tip of Terrible's blade hit his throat.

"What action you want?"

"We'll bring him with us," Chess said. "I think I saw some rope downstairs. We'll tie him up, and he can come along and send the Dreamthief back."

"You can't send him back," Randy said. "Don't you understand? Without the amulet we don't have the control we had. He's getting stronger, you saw what he did to my mom down there. We have him trapped, but he's breaking free, I need the amulet to—"

The lights snapped off. All the lights, leaving them standing alone with the warm darkness breathing around them. Her skin burned and itched along the lines of her tattoos.

Randy's whisper crackled like dead leaves. "He's here."

Chapter Thirty-four

[
"You cannot defeat the dead. Only the Church can do so, and through training, Church employees."
—*The Book of Truth*, Veraxis, Article 5
]

The amulet had fallen to the floor in the struggle. Chess knelt and ran her fingers over the carpet. Her back felt like someone had painted a target on it. Where was Ereshdiran? In front of her, those long stained-ivory teeth exposed? Behind her, about to summon enough power to slip a noose around her neck, to slit her throat?

The darkness was so complete, not a hint of light anywhere. Too dark. Dark like the mouth of a predator.

Randy's sobs echoed in the room. "He's here, he's here, please find the amulet, Chessie hurry . . ."

It was hard to focus on anything, even with adrenaline coursing through her body. Suddenly she was sleepy, so relaxed and sleepy, and it was so dark and the carpet was soft and thick. She could lie down here, curl up into a warm cozy ball and take a nap, she could . . .

"Stay awake!" she yelled, but her voice was drowned out by shattering glass. Behind her? The mirror, the dresser mirror. Ereshdiran must have smashed it. He'd gained so much strength since she saw him before, he could kill Randy, he could kill Terrible—would he kill her now? Did he still need her, with all the power he drew from the sleepers downstairs? The sleepers in the whole neighborhood?

Fear helped her eyes stay open as she fumbled into her bag, her movements clumsy and painful. The speed was in there, the Baggie Lex gave her.

"Chess?"

"Stay awake, Terrible, stay awake, just stay where you were, don't move!"

Randy screamed. Something warm and wet splattered over Chess's face, in her hair. Blood. She didn't dare try to wipe it away, not when she needed both her hands to hunt for the two items that might keep her alive.

"Chess!"

The screaming continued, turning into sobs. She heard them moving, heard the bed creak as they ran into it. Something brushed against her hair but she had no idea if it was human or not. And all the while her eyelids got heavier, the fuzzy comfort of sleep slid into her head.

Ereshdiran appeared in front of her, his luminous face only inches from hers, his mouth open in a crooked, shrieking grin. Chess screamed and lost the Baggie just as her fingers touched it. It disappeared again into the depths of her bag.

Terrible grunted. Randy screamed. Cold wind blew across the back of her neck. The Dreamthief was playing with them, playing with her. Something sliced at the back of her left hand, just a kiss from the blade, a portent of what would come. She gasped and tried to ignore the feel of her own blood dribbling from the wound.

She found the Baggie, yanked it out, slid her fingernail into the seal with shaking hands. She had to stay awake, had to stay awake long enough . . .

The floor shook. The whole house shook. Ereshdiran's power, strong the last time she'd seen him here, now sparked off him. He could bring this place down on them, would do it if she wasn't fast enough—and the bastard would use some of her own power to do it. She could feel him pulling at her.

Terrible roared her name but she didn't answer, focusing on the powder against her hand. No hairpin, no key, there wasn't time. She scooped up as much as she could under her fingernail—not much, she kept her nails fairly short—and brought it to her face, hoping she wouldn't miss.

She did. Something smashed across the room—a lamp crashing, she thought—and she ended up poking herself in the eye with a nailful of speed. A gasp escaped her throat, her eye felt like a bee had stung it, but it woke her up enough to try again while tears streamed down her face. All the while the room got colder and colder, so cold her toes were numb. Had she escaped after all? Was she asleep, in a dream, deep in the bowels of the thief?

Another crash, a thud. Randy screaming her name, sounding very far away. He'd been right beside her, where was he now? She ignored it, falling to her knees, her neck retreating between her shoulders as she tried again.

This time she made it. It wasn't a big bump but it was enough. Her heart rate increased, her eyes snapped open.

"Terrible? Terrible, here." She waved her hand in the air, trying to find him, and finally closed her fingers around one thick calf. It moved. His hand found hers, and she pressed the Baggie into it. "We have to stay awake."

She heard the plastic rustle, heard him inhale once, twice. Then his hand squeezed her arm and he lifted her to her feet, pulling her against him as she lost her balance and they both hit the wall. His shirt was wet, with sweat or blood she didn't know.

"No! Noooo!" Randy's scream turned into a gurgle, a horrible choking sound, then stopped dead. Chess's skin crawled. She found her flashlight, knowing it wouldn't work, and switched it on.

It did work. The beam fell on Randy's face, on his

wide, staring eyes and the blood still trickling from the gaping hole where his throat should have been. She barely had time to take it in when the Dreamthief shoved the piece of mirror he'd used to kill Randy into the flashlight's beam, throwing the light back at her, blinding her.

The light fell from her hand as Terrible grabbed her, his fingers painfully tight around her arm, ripping her out of her stupor and shoving her toward where the door had been. She couldn't see a thing, the white spots in front of her eyes worse than the darkness.

"The amulet, we have to have—"

"I got it, just go!" Still holding her, he flung himself forward. She heard something thunk into the plaster where they'd just been as they fell through the door and onto the landing.

Pictures flew from the walls as Chess and Terrible tore down the stairs, in what could have been a run but was more like a tumble. She twisted her ankle at the bottom but did not let herself stop, feeling the Dreamthief behind them, knowing there was no escape.

They burst out into the shadowy night and started running across the lawn, heading for Terrible's car on the next block. Probably not the safest place to be, but all Chess could think to do was try and get away. Get away, get to the airport, get the ritual done. She had no choice. Even the spells and wards at the Church might not be strong enough to protect her, not with the thief connected to her through blood.

Her chest felt ready to explode by the time they were halfway up the street. She didn't dare look back. There was no point in looking back. He was after them, of course he was after them, they had the amulet. The one thing that might be able to control him, and the one thing that would draw him to her.

"Give me the amulet," she managed to gasp.

He didn't ask questions, but pressed it into her palm and closed her fingers around it.

Ereshdiran darted past them, a black streak in the orange streetlight glow. Chess sucked as much air as she could into her aching lungs and said the generic Banishing words she'd learned five years before, the first words of power any Church employee learned. *"Arcranda beliam dishager!"*

They didn't stop to see if it worked. It probably hadn't, and it certainly hadn't worked permanently. But if it bought them a few minutes, enough time to get in the car and get moving, enough time to keep Banishing him until she could start the ritual, it would be worth it.

They reached the car, finally, yanking the doors open and throwing themselves inside. Terrible had the keys in the ignition and the engine started before she'd managed to sit up straight, and they peeled away in a cloud of heavy exhaust, the rear end of the car fishtailing as it leapt away from the curb.

The Chevelle ate up the highway, sliding in and out of traffic with a low, contented purr. Chess stared out the window, watching other cars disappear behind them, until her hands stopped shaking.

The first thing she did was another bump, a proper one this time. The second was to drink half her water and hand it to Terrible to finish.

"You right, Chess? You get hurt?"

"No, I'm okay. You?"

He shrugged. Light from the dash caught on the shard of mirror protruding from his left arm.

"You're not, you got stabbed—"

"Ain't so bad. I been got worse."

"Oh? Like what?" She just wanted him to talk, about

anything. Just wanted to hear his calm, low voice like gravel poured over the rough ground of her terror.

"Aye. Dame I know bit me once."

She laughed in spite of herself, a surprised laugh like a hiccup. "You mean you let a girl hurt you?"

"Some dames I let do whatany they want."

She had no idea how to reply to that; her face heated. He was joking, had to be. She would never forget the look on his face at Trickster's, how pissed off he'd been, how he'd just given up on her.

Even though she wasn't supposed to remember it at all. So what did he mean? If he thought she didn't remember— Oh, fuck it. Best to ignore the whole thing.

After a minute he cleared his throat and said, "So Randy. He brung the ghost to get money, aye?"

"Yeah." She spoke a little too loudly, a little too grateful for the change of subject. "Well, basically. First he was going to fake a haunting, to get a payout from the Church. But then I got the case instead of him—he was next in the queue, but Elder Griffin gave it to me—so they had to get a real ghost, because I would have caught them faking it. I guess they didn't realize that I'd found the amulet, and my—my blood had touched it. Um, had fed the thief and given him power. But they were already raising him and I guess they figured it would be easy enough to send him to the Mortons' house before they used him against the Church, so . . . Yeah. He did it."

"Not that Goody."

"No." She wished he hadn't mentioned that. It was embarrassing enough having been so stupid and wrong, without being reminded that he knew she'd been stupid and wrong. "Randy and the Mortons went to the Spa, and that's where he met whoever recruited him into the Lamaru. He just . . . gave her the key ring. I mean, I assume."

"Trying to get what he want from her, aye? Figure he play her on the good side, she give him the push-up."

"And she probably would have, if—"

Ereshdiran's face appeared in the center of the windshield, leering at them, his black cloak flying around him like tentacles whipping the air. Chess screamed, cringing against the back of her seat, then hitting the door when Terrible swerved to the left.

Ereshdiran disappeared. Something heavy hit the roof of the car, bowing it down. Terrible sped up, so fast the lines on the road blurred, skipping onto the shoulder and opening the powerful engine all the way. The cars they passed disappeared but the weight stayed on the roof.

"It's not him," she said, as the thing slammed onto the car again. "He doesn't have weight, he's holding something—"

Terrible's right arm shot out and hit her chest, knocking the wind out of her. He slammed on the brakes. The heavy nose of the car angled down, the rear rising. Rubber howled against cement. Ereshdiran flew forward, dropping the stone he'd been beating the car with. It rolled off to the side. Terrible threw the car back into first and slammed the gas so hard the engine shrieked.

"No, you can't—"

They hit Ereshdiran, drove right through him. For a second, ice filled her body, filled her mind, making her scream again. The sensation ended before the sound had a chance to hit the air.

The Dreamthief came back, pouring himself into the car, his chilling fingers slithering over her skin. Terrible gasped; she looked over to see the shard of mirror in his arm twisting, disappearing into his flesh. His fingers convulsed on the wheel but the car did not slow down, did not waver.

She lifted the amulet, shouted the Banishing words. The thief winced but did not disappear. She shouted again, louder, using every bit of breath and power she had in her body. He wavered, the mirror slipping from his fingers as they grew transparent again.

One more time. *"Arcranda beliam dishager!"*

It worked. Ereshdiran disappeared as the Chevelle swooped down the exit ramp, heading for the airport. The airport, and the end of it all. One way or another.

Chapter Thirty-five

> "The Church is ever vigilant on your behalf, and this is fact."
>
> —*The Book of Truth*, Veraxis, Article 2

A crowd waited for them in the muddy parking lot. Bump in full regalia, complete with ragged cape. Some of his men, smoking cigarettes, standing tough in little groups like mine clusters. They all turned, hands automatically dropping to knife holsters at their waists when the headlights hit them, then relaxing again when they recognized the car.

"Ay, lookie be my ladybird." Bump oozed toward the car as Chess got out, his shiny boots gleaming. "Ready do your witchy thing?"

She nodded, figuring if she pretended she was ready she eventually would be. Probably when it was all over.

"Benefit. Slipknot set up on yon fuckin field, yay? Terrible chatter me what you needing, on the earlier. All ready your fuckin thing, get done, we straight."

"Right." She guessed Terrible had called when she was in the Church; she hadn't even thought to ask him if he'd arranged to have everything set up for her. Everything except what was in her bag, and in the trunk of his car. All of her equipment.

"So why the stand here? We fuckin move, yay?"

Again, she nodded. Her throat felt too constricted to push words through.

The walk through the fence, across the scattered chunks of runway, felt like a funeral procession. Which in a way she guessed it was. Slipknot, at least, would be set free—or at least, sent into a more comfortable prison. The rest of them . . .

Her phone buzzed at her hip. Lex again. He'd called a dozen times, left messages she hadn't bothered to listen to. The men were walking ahead of her, their backs swaying gently as they picked their way through the rubble. She answered the phone.

"Tulip! Damn, thought maybe you was dead. Why you didn't wait for me before?"

"I told you why. I couldn't hear you very well, and—"

"Aye, check it. Need to talk to you, like now. Come meet me."

"I can't, I'm—"

"I know where you at, and I know what you up to. Gotta get some words in first. I'm at the far end of the runway, dig? Over the fence. By them houses. Get over here, we gotta get straight ere you do all you might think again on later."

"I can't," she repeated. Terrible glanced back at her, and she lowered her voice. "This isn't about—it's not about what we talked about."

"This about that thief, aye? Gotta talk to you, tulip. Don't care how you fix it. You get here. I got some knowledge you need right."

"Why can't you just tell—" she started, but he'd already hung up. Shit.

Ahead of her, off to the left in the center of the field, Slipknot's corpse made a pale splotch on a platform fashioned from rough wooden crates. Best to have him off the ground, make sure nothing interfered . . . They were almost there.

"I have to go to the bathroom." It wasn't a great excuse, but it was the only one she could think of that would be irrefutably believed and would give her some privacy. Being caught here with Lex would not be healthy at all.

"Ain't it wait?" Bump looked her up and down, as if trying to assess how badly she needed to go. And of course, she realized she kind of did need to go, which worked out wonderfully. Now she'd have to talk to Lex and not go, which meant she would still have to when she got back, unless she wanted to take the time to both talk to Lex *and* go, in which case they would wonder just what exactly she was doing.

"No. It can't wait."

He nodded. "Terrible, go with she ladybird, keep your eyes on right."

Terrible shook his head. "Give her some private, Bump. C'mon. She ain't gonna run, not with that thing after her, aye?"

Guilt worked its way into her bones, so deep it almost hurt. "I'll be right back."

"I gots men all over that fuckin edge, yay? Tell they I say let you be."

She nodded and headed for the far edge, trying to move quickly enough that it looked like she needed to get there but not so quickly that it looked as if she was about to wet her pants. Her face burned.

Pitted metal cut into her hands, especially her wounded right one. An added bonus, rust working into her burn. She grabbed her water bottle when she got over the fence and poured some onto her palm, but it was too dark to know if it really helped. Nothing to do but forget it and get on with the job.

For a minute she stood, looking uncertainly around, aware that in removing herself from the sight of Terrible and Bump she'd also made herself vulnerable. If Lex's plan to keep the airport from reopening included kidnapping her—again—she'd just handed herself to him on a shiny tray of deceit.

No sound but the dry wind hit her ears. The houses were dark, abandoned-looking in the pale washed-out glow of the moon. Their inhabitants were probably asleep. A trickle of sweat ran down her spine. They were asleep, all of them. She could almost feel them sleeping, turning fitfully in their rumpled, damp beds, their dreams being converted to energy for the thing she was about to fight. Alone.

Lex grabbed her hand. She jumped and swung automatically, but he ducked. His soft laugh caressed her skin. "Jumpy, tulip?"

"What do you want, Lex? This isn't really a good time."

"Oh?" His hands settled on her waist, fingers curving to draw her close. In spite of herself she shivered, closing her eyes at the feel of his teeth scraping the base of her throat. "Feels like a good time to me."

With effort she pulled away. "No, it's not. I had to tell them I needed to go to the bathroom, they'll be waiting for me. So talk fast."

"Aye, right. You ain't forget our agreement, I hope."

"No, I didn't forget. This isn't about the ghosts. It's about the thief, and he could show up again any minute, so—"

"Bump gonna be expecting you finish the job. What you gonna tell him, he ask?"

"I thought you didn't care."

"Maybe I do. A little."

"You said you had some information for me."

He watched her for a minute, his expression blank. "Aye, got some right. Been doing some looking on my own, tulip. Keeping my ear down, aye? Had people here today, my people, seen them Lamarus. And they *know*, dig? What's on the happening."

"They've known all along, those guys who broke in and—"

"Nay, nay. Ain't what I mean. They know you, where

you live, aye. But they know what's going down here. They know you charging it off tonight. Gonna be some shit here, so get it done, get out clean. Head for the tunnel, I catch you there."

"Why?"

"Huh?"

"Why? What if I do end up Banishing those ghosts tonight, what then? Will you still be waiting for me, or what? What are you going to do to me?"

Even in the dim moonlight she could see his smile. "Aw, tulip. Seems to me you oughta know by now what I do. Thought you got pretty familiar with it."

"That's not what I meant." Only willpower kept her voice from getting shaky.

He kissed her, still holding her hips close enough that she had to lean back. Her already shaky nerves went into overload, speed and adrenaline and lust combining to make her knees weak, and she clung to him in a way that would have embarrassed her if she hadn't been so desperate to pretend none of this was happening.

"I got belief in you," he said finally. "You ain't stupid. You figure something out."

"That's a big help."

"You forgetting, I ain't a helpful guy."

She snorted and turned back toward the fence. In another minute they would send someone to look for her, if they hadn't already. "I'll keep that in mind."

"Okay." She dropped her bag on the ground next to Slipknot's foul remains and planted her hands on her hips. Her head grew lighter, but she forced herself to ignore it. She could not mess this up. It was her life on the line now, in more ways than one. "It's extremely important that no one goes to sleep. What we're dealing with . . . he feeds on sleep, or he can. He can make you tired. So whatever you need to do to stay awake, do it."

They nodded, good little soldiers one and all, with the exception of Bump and Terrible. Bump stood apart from it all, the diamonds on his fingers throwing off moonlight sparks. And Terrible . . . He just watched, waiting, the tension in his body evident.

"Also, I think the people who did this to start with may be here tonight. Might show up, I mean. Nothing can break my circle. If that circle breaks once I've gotten started we've got a problem, and I mean a real problem. So you guys have to keep everyone away from it, okay? Come over here, please, I want to mark you all first. It might help."

It only took a few minutes to finish scrawling sigils on their foreheads with the new piece of black chalk she'd bought that afternoon. When she was done they looked like members of a bizarre chorus line. She half expected them to start dancing.

"Spread you out, keep watch," Bump said. "Let ladybird do she fuckin work. You sleep, you die, yay? No fuckin sleeping."

Grass rustled under their feet as they moved, but Chess didn't watch. Feeling like a floor show, she checked her compass, knelt and set up her stang holder, put her other odds and ends at its base while she marked off a septagram with her feet and placed a candle at each point. The septagram would provide extra energy, extra protection; she'd only used one once before, but it was part of the established Church curriculum. A few Debunkers used them every time.

Wind lifted her hair from her shoulders as she finished and looked around, half expecting to see Ereshdiran's pink teeth bared at her. Instead she saw only blank ground, only the backs of Bump's men as they kept watch like they'd been told.

And Terrible. She threw him a quick smile, and he nodded back. Working now, no time for such frivolities as being pleasant. Or he was simply nervous. Having faced the Dreamthief, having seen Randy's body and felt the house shake, he knew far better than the others what they were up against. And that didn't even take into account the unknown number of Lamaru who might show up at any moment, ready for battle.

Not her concern. At least not if she was lucky. Only a dozen or so men stood between her and whoever might show up, but they were certainly tough enough.

With the chalk she drew more sigils on her forehead and cheeks, coloring the final lines on some of her tattoos to activate them. She'd never marked up this much before.

Her new skull came out next, then the cauldron and charcoal, which she lit with a wooden match. It would burn, then smoke out so she could add the herbs.

A few more minutes and she was ready, the herbs and various other accoutrements lined up in their pouches next to the cauldron, the amulet in her pocket ready to be pulled out when needed. If not for the extra candles and the iron firedish, it would have looked almost like she was setting up a regular ritual. Thank the Church for training her so thoroughly, and thank magic itself for having rules. Once you knew the rules thoroughly enough you could manipulate them and get whatever results you needed.

One more step. She washed a couple of Cepts down with water and, bending over deep in a semifruitful attempt to block the wind, did two more bumps.

"Terrible? Could you come here?"

He did, silent across the grass. She handed him the speed. "You might want more of this. Just to be safe."

"He ain't shown up yet. Think he off putting people to sleep?"

"Yeah, I think maybe he is."

His eyes flickered over her little altar setup. "Everything ready?"

"Looks like it. I'm going to cast the circle now, light the candles, and then hopefully we'll get this over with."

"Not hopeful, aye? It will get over."

She bit her lip. "If . . . if something goes wrong and I don't make it, you need to go to Doyle. He might be an egotistical shitbag as a human being but he's good at his job. He knows some other guys who've seen the thief, maybe they can get the Church to act, but either way they'll finish it. Only do me a favor. Don't—don't tell him how I got involved. About Bump, I mean."

He didn't try to talk her out of her fears, or discount them. Just gave her his eyes, nodded. "He don't need to have knowledge about you. Ain't his business."

"And my apartment. There's . . . there's some stuff there, the Church would take possession of everything."

"I'll take care of it."

"Thanks."

"Listen, Chess." He shifted on his feet, shoved his hands in his pockets. "I been thinking—"

Shouts from the far corner cut him off, Bump's men. Chess leapt to her feet, craning her neck to see as Terrible spun away from her to take back his place. Guarding her, the last line of defense. If he . . . if he fell, so would she.

The Lamaru had arrived. Time to get started.

Chapter Thirty-six

"Leave soul magic to the Church."
—*You Can Do This! A Guide for Beginners,*
by Molly Brooks-Cahill

Salt poured through her shaking fingers, creating as heavy a line as she could to mark the edge of the circle. She didn't always do a full cast, but this spell required it absolutely. No chances could be taken.

Power crawled from the ground under her feet, oozing over her skin. Her tattoos heated. Her hair stood on end. The ultimate rush, the ultimate high, more power than she'd ever felt before. Certainly more than she'd ever raised on her own, so much she didn't know if she could contain it. Fear joined the party, tingling up from her stomach to pool in her chest. She felt her lips stretch into a shaky grin as she whispered the words she needed, calling the escorts of the dead.

When she'd finished the circle was visible, a deep glowing blue, shimmering in the air so bright her eyes ached.

The wind died. Good. The wall of light was working.

She walked the septagram again, lighting each candle in turn with a fresh match, dropping the used sticks into the firedish. Each candle got another word, another physical expression of energy expended with each spoken syllable. *Eratosh, Astagosh, Bidamosh. Ligorosh, Hapmalosh, Kolabosh,* and *Septazosh.* On *Septazosh* the flames blazed, shooting sparks up to disappear into the glowing roof of the circle.

Shouts and the sound of flesh against flesh filtered through the circle, but far away. They weren't close yet, but that could change any second. She moved faster, forcing herself to use the fear, to give herself to it. A second of decision, a relaxing of the boundaries of her mind, and she slipped through.

Her heart still raced, but it was pure high now, clean and sparkling. She wasn't Cesaria anymore. She was power. She was the gate.

Slipknot's cold, squashy fingers didn't want to close around the lump of silver she placed in his palm, covering the now-unreadable runes carved there. No surprise, nor was the muffled thud of his squashed-looking heart. She felt it, too, that extra power. The connection to the Dreamthief, tugging at her, refusing to let her forget even for a moment that he was there.

She pulled a length of twine from her bag and looped it around his fist, tying it securely but gently. With the black chalk she drew the passport she'd designed for him directly onto one of the few usable spots on his arm.

Into the smoking cauldron went asafetida, pungent and slightly greasy in the still air. Then ajenjible, and finally a handful of the corrideira Edsel ground for her earlier.

Smoke plumed in the air, twisting and curling, forming shapes she couldn't identify but saw with eyes in her soul, whispering words she felt but did not hear. The skull shifted, as though the ground beneath it had trembled, but did not move.

"I call on the escorts of the City of the Dead," she murmured, slipping her ritual knife from its case. "To set this man Slipknot free from his mortal remains. To take him to his rest. To sever him from his worldly prison and the power keeping him here."

The skull moved again, but did not rise. The shouts outside the circle grew louder.

Chess held her left hand low over the top of the skull. "I offer an appeasement to the escorts for their aid."

With the sharp tip she sliced the skin of her left pinky finger, a quick, deep cut. Blood dripped from the wound, purple-black in the bluish light. It spattered on top of the skull, tiny droplets sparkling as it flew into the air.

Something thumped to her left. Inside the circle. Slipknot's heart sped up as energy filled his soul. Her own kicked up in reply. On top of all the speed, she felt like she had a freight train in her chest, barely contained by bone and muscle. Chess twisted back to the cauldron and dripped blood into it, then added a hair plucked from Slipknot's head.

"Escorts, I call you!"

The last ingredient went into the cauldron, powdered crow skull. The smoke turned black, exploded from the wide iron mouth, and rolled to the roof of the circle, blocking the pure deep blue.

Smoke entered her lungs, insinuating itself into her body through her nose and mouth, curling around her arms. Her tattoos tingled and ached as if they were being recut into her skin.

Through the dark haze she saw the skull lift, move. More bones appeared, sketched out behind, built by and black from the thick, acrid smoke.

The shouts outside got closer, louder, as muscle and sinew grew on the bones, weaved itself together. Coarse black hair poured itself over the raw flesh. The dog's eyes burned purple-green, iridescent, feeding on the same power that ran through Chess like a bolt of lightning. A long, low growl left its throat and crawled up her spine. Psychopomps shouldn't growl like that.

With shaking hands she sprinkled the remaining powdered crow bone over the ruined body on the pallet.

Energy blew back at her, dark and feverish, invading her body. Her voice creaked like a rusty hinge. "Set this man free, *cadeskia regontu balaktor*!"

Slipknot's heart beat faster, louder, pounding arrythmically in her ears. Her own heart tried to syncopate but couldn't, her chest ached. This was too much, too much, she couldn't handle it . . .

Thin, high screams filled the air and she realized they were hers, hers and Slipknot's as his soul escaped from the wreckage that used to house it and saw what it had become. He screamed, black eyes wide in his pale face, his mouth a gaping dark tear, screamed in terror and freedom and the horror he'd experienced.

She spilled water down her front as she forced some into her mouth, chasing away the awful smoke-and-speed drymouth.

"Slipknot, go! I call on the escort to take you to the City, I order you to go!"

The dog leapt. Slipknot's screams turned shrill, so high-pitched she could barely hear them. This was wrong, she was losing it, too much energy circled around and her body couldn't control it all, she was falling, she could feel him pulling her, sucking her with him through their connection . . .

Her right hand hit the edge of the firedish. Pain roared up her arm, bringing her back. She focused everything she could on cutting the invisible cord binding them, renouncing him.

It gave, with a sharp pang like a rubber glove snapping back into place. Her eyes filled with tears and dragged back into focus just in time to see the ragged hole, to see Slipknot reaching for her, trying to go back to the world he knew, as the dog gripped his arm in its heavy jaws and dragged him down into the emptiness of silent death.

Her vision flipped to black for a moment, the blackness of sleep. Not her sleep; the sleep of the thief, the sleep of those whose power he was using. Without Slipknot there to filter it, the full weight of the blood connection fell to her. *Oh, fuck . . .*

Flashes of dreams, images of people in their beds, hundreds of them, uneasy on rumpled damp bedsheets, curled into balls on hard streets. She struggled to get it under control, to return to herself. Her hands twisted on each other, her muscles shook. Finally she pressed her left thumb into the palm of her right hand, sending screaming pain up her arm from the wound.

It worked. Her sight returned. She slammed back into herself, into the circle, and realized with both Slipknot and the dog gone, some of the power lessened, enough for her to take a breath. The cauldron burned her uninjured left hand as she lifted it, tipping its contents into the firedish and adding a handful of dried melidia.

Directly in front of her the blue wall wavered. They were close, so close, their shouts drowning out her thoughts. Her entire body shook. This was the dangerous part, and if she didn't do it perfectly, didn't end it now, the circle would be breached and she would lose. Lose and be lost.

The match head scraped across the rim of the firedish. "Ereshdiran," she whispered, speaking his name for the first time. Just saying it hurt her tongue. "Ereshdiran *kalepta barima.*"

Someone shouted her name. Terrible. Terrible shouted her name. She opened her mouth to answer but her voice died in her throat. The thief appeared, his cloak moving in a breeze she could not feel, the hood thrown back to reveal shiny, pale skin stretched tight over the bones of his skull.

Something pulsed beneath that skin. Moving veins, veins that were not veins at all. They were worms, maggots like the ones in her hand. A low moan escaped her throat. He was going to eat her. He would drag her into the infested hell from whence he came and she would stay there, screaming while they overran her. While they ate her again and again, crawling under her skin too or burrowing through it, holes in her skin, holes in her brain . . .

She couldn't stop staring at them, at his glittering hypnotic eyes and those teeth glowing in the dark blue-black air. Couldn't stop seeing her own face reflected in them, miniature images of herself alone against a backdrop of nothing at all.

Hands appeared, long, curving fingers with blood-stained nails. They reached for her. She wanted to move but couldn't, couldn't even breathe. Even stuffed with adrenaline and speed as she was, her eyelids fluttered, her thoughts softened. Somewhere inside she knew what was happening, screamed and beat against her own flesh, but she could not will her body to obey.

Terrible shouted her name again, breaking the spell. She dropped the match. The melidia caught, sending a wall of flame into the air, separating Chess from the cruel infernal promise of those solid shark eyes.

She grabbed the amulet, ignoring the jolt of electric pain. Ignoring, too, the certainty that her cauterized wound would burst open again and worms would swarm. Flames seared her skin as she held the amulet over the firedish and summoned as much of the power circling through her as she could.

"Ereshdiran I command you to return. Return to your place of silence, return to your place of hiding, return to the place where you hold no power. I command this by fire, I command it by smoke. Return!"

She dropped the amulet into the flames.

A body flew into the circle, knocking her over. The blue wall disappeared. The circle had broken.

Her ears rang as the shouts and sounds of fighting,

which had been muffled by the circle, slammed into them. Bodies ducked and danced around her, chaos destroying her stang and her careful arrangement. One of the fighting men stepped on her leg. She jerked it away, ignoring the pain, her eyes focused hard on what had been her altar.

The firedish fell over. The amulet spilled out, barely melted by the inferno that should have destroyed it.

Some instinct told her to yank her sleeve over her hand before she grabbed it. It wouldn't lessen the heat much but it would hopefully keep the amulet's design from imprinting her skin, possibly binding Ereshdiran to her forever instead of just until the amulet was destroyed.

Cold grass prickled her skin as she rolled away from the brawling bodies in what had been a ritual space. The Dreamthief followed. She caught a glimpse of him, pressing one talonlike finger against the head of a fighter, knocking him into sleep. A knife fell from the fighter's hand—he was one of the Lamaru, not Bump's—and Ereshdiran picked it up, flipping it expertly in his hand and stalking toward her.

She had the amulet. She had it, and he was bound to her, which meant supposedly she could control him, but she knew it wouldn't work. Just to be certain, she tried it, shouting the Banishing words with every bit of breath and power she had. He didn't so much as flicker.

Her feet pounded the ground as she turned left, making a wide circle around the brawling bodies. Blood flew through the air, weapons caught the moon like strobe lights. The air was heavy with sweat and blood and hot pain, thick with energy unlike anything she'd ever felt. Above her several birds flew in formation, avian psychopomps collecting souls. Death stalked the runways, death hovered overhead, and Ereshdiran did not halt his steady advance.

He was playing with her, waiting for her to tire out, taking whatever power he needed from the men nearby.

Not as many of them as it had looked originally, but none of the men seemed ready to admit defeat. Bump's men were powered by speed and loyalty, and the Lamaru, she had no idea but she guessed it was rage and greed and any number of illicit magics.

The thief turned, heading in her direction, and she saw her opening. She ducked down, narrowly avoiding being clipped in the head by a fist, and ran as hard as she could back to the remains of her altar. She had some melidia left, some crow's bone and corrideira. They might give her enough strength to Banish him for a few minutes, long enough for her to set the fire back up, cast another circle.

She darted past another fighting couple and grabbed what she could. A heavy body fell on her. One of Bump's men, out cold or dead. She didn't know which. All she knew was the ground swooped up from its rightful place and hit her, the edge of the amulet sliced through her shirt to bite her skin deep, and the thief was closing in on her with a triumphant smile as her blood poured over his amulet again.

Chapter Thirty-seven

Her stomach burned, so hot it felt cold, as something in her gut shifted and moved. He was drawing from her, using her, strengthening their bond. She felt herself being sucked into the raging caverns of his black eyes, sucked in and thrown into the dreams of the city's sleepers.

Voices raised behind her, as if the witches sensed what had happened. A chant, words of power, flying into the air and gathering strength. She couldn't breathe. Her lungs refused to expand, her limbs did not want to move. She tried to crawl forward but fell, unable even to support herself.

Below her in the earth, power still lurked. She'd felt it earlier when she cast the circle, she knew it was there. Her tired mind rebelled, against what she didn't even know anymore and wasn't sure it mattered. This was it, she'd lost. She was bound to him, connected, and he would drain her dry like a fucking battery and turn his attentions to someone else, to everyone else. And her soul, that worthless little thing, would be trapped here in her wasting body. Not in the City but without any of the reasons to stay out of the City. No pills. No smoke. No nothing that made life worth living. Just a soul, stuck perhaps at the bottom of that well forever. Stuck here at the airport.

In her left hand she clasped the ingredients she'd grabbed. Blood still trickled from her pinky and dripped to the dirt. Her blood, feeding the earth. Her blood, feeding the Dreamthief. The earth . . . haunted . . . the City beneath it and the Lamaru's plan to set the spirits free . . .

"Chess! Chess!" Terrible's roar, audible over the interrupted chants. At least someone was looking for her, someone noticed. What had he said they called them, the pilots? Flying aces? At least she'd done something right, at least she'd learned what was really haunting the airport . . . flying aces. Dozens of them. Here. Aces in the hole. Aces up the sleeve. She could certainly use one of those.

Aces who still haunted here, above the ground. Aces who hadn't gone below to the City. The words kept circling in her head, like they should mean something, like she was trying to tell herself something but couldn't get through the thick, black static of the thief's connection.

She forced herself to relax and rest her forehead on the ground. The City. The murderous ghosts, the Lamaru controlling ghosts . . . controlling what they summoned . . .

The smell of dirt, dirt and smoke and green things, filled her nose, cleared her head just enough for her to open up, to focus on her pinky and her blood as it poured into the earth.

Her swirling thoughts snapped into place. The airport was haunted. Real ghosts. Real ghosts who'd been here for just over a hundred years, who'd been created when the place burned, when . . . sleep deprivation caused madness. Madmen who died sometimes splintered apart, became something else, twisted and merged and formed new entities.

Like Dreamthieves.

If this was where he'd come from, if he was made from discarded parts of the airport's ghosts, they would seek to reabsorb him. They would overpower him, dissolve him.

If she was right. If she wasn't . . . if she wasn't she'd just better hope she was strong enough, because an entire battalion of ghosts would take them all out, every living person on the field, in about two minutes.

Fuck it. She didn't have a choice, did she? Story of her life. Either the thief and Lamaru would kill them all or the ghosts would, but at least with the ghosts she had a chance. She forced energy into her blood, into the earth, and opened herself to it as wide as she could, waiting for it to leap back into her, to flood her senses. Waiting for it the way she waited for her pills to dissolve, every muscle in her body tense and expectant—but this would be more than her pills, more than any drug. The ultimate rush. The Summoning words hesitated on her tongue, ready to leap from her mouth into the air the second the power hit her.

Nothing happened. She could feel the thief advancing, knew he would be on top of her any second. This had to work, had to work, she had no idea how she would fix it later or what it might mean to Bump or Lex if she did, but at least she might be alive to do so, relax . . .

Energy surged up from the ground, into her finger, through her. Earth power, solid power. The kind spirits could not draw on, not like humans could. It was their prison, they could not pass through it and they could not use it.

She flipped over. The thief was there, only a few feet away. Not much time at all. Her fingers closed around a match, scraped it on her jeans, touched it to the herbs spilling from her hand.

"*Kadira tam! Kadira tam!* You are compelled! With blood I summon you and with blood I compel you!" Wind tore the last words from her throat. Nothing happened.

Shit. She'd never done it before, was breaking half a dozen Church laws by even attempting to do it now.

The Dreamthief stood directly above her, knife at the ready. She raised her leg, trying to kick him away, but it passed through him. Only the knife and the hand holding it were solid. Good.

She lay back, as though too weak and afraid to do anything else, and waited for him to lunge. The opening would come, be ready . . .

He moved, dropping down, and she shoved herself up as hard as she could. His blade sliced her arm but she barely noticed, too distracted by the freezing pain of passing directly through him.

She didn't bother to break her fall as she came out behind him, but let herself land on her chest with a thud. The rest of the melidia was still there on the ground, it might be enough.

Over the now-quieting shouts of the fighting men came another sound, a low, heavy buzz like a drill. She ignored it. She'd failed, but she was still alive, and she would not go down without a fight. If he was connected to her she could unconnect him.

The melidia *was* there. The black chalk was gone, but she had her knife. Not the best option but an option.

The buzzing drone grew louder, drowning out everything else. Chess grabbed her knife and brought the point to her left arm, gritting her teeth against the pain, glancing up to watch the Dreamthief pick himself up off the ground.

Hands on her, barely closing around her shoulders before an ugly crack rent the air. The witch's body crumpled to the ground, his head twisted sideways. Terrible's feet by her leg. He'd broken the man's neck.

She slid the knife along her arm. Up, over, down . . . a Bind rune, a protective rune, a rune of purity, slashed into her flesh. Agony grabbed hold of her with sharp teeth and made her vision waver as the runes warred with the thief's evil tinge in her blood.

Wind swept over her skin, whipped her hair around her face. She grabbed the melidia and leapt to her feet, stumbling over bodies as the thief lunged for her again. His knife drove into the spot where she was only seconds before.

That was when she realized no one was fighting. They'd stopped. They'd stopped, and they were staring at the sky as planes droned and swooped overhead, so many it seemed the sky was made of them. They were looking up.

It had worked. The ghosts had come.

Ducking her head, she weaved through the men and dumped the last of the melidia out of the Baggie when she reached the edge of the crowd. It lit with a hiss. She squeezed the wound on her pinky, dripping blood on the pile, and dropped the amulet into it.

Flesh smacked against flesh behind her. Her head turned instinctively and she saw Terrible again, his teeth bared in pain and rage, his hands closed around the thief's lone solid hand hovering above her head.

The thief disappeared.

White lights turned the runway into an alien landscape, colorless and bizarre, as the first plane dove in for a landing. Men scattered, resuming their fighting in twos and threes.

"Ereshdiran, I command you to return. Return to your place of silence, return to your place of hiding, return to the place where you hold no power. I command this by fire, I command it by smoke. Return!"

Another plane, and another. Spectral men emerged, climbing from the open holes as the propellers slowed.

Ereshdiran reappeared, at her side. He'd lost the knife when he disappeared, but his teeth looked solid enough, as well as both of his hands.

Chess steeled herself and grabbed them, like dipping

her hands into dry ice. She reached for the power in the ground, reached for the dead pilots, and drew them in.

She screamed. Her stomach twisted and lurched in her belly, her legs went weak. She just had to hold him until the amulet melted, just long enough . . . she drove power into the fire, heating it, forcing it to burn so bright she had to close her eyes.

He disappeared again, leaving her gripping nothing, with energy surging through her body like a speeding car.

The fire. She held her hands over it as close as she could bear, anticipating his next move.

She was wrong. A Lamaru leapt for it, his face twisted toward her so she could see the thief staring at her from his eyes. Possession; a clever move, but a bad one. He'd forgotten humans could be hurt, that they died.

Terrible's knife flashed. Blood spattered over her hair and face. The witch fell, still scrabbling at his throat with clawed hands. The thief emerged from his body like the moon rising over the trees.

The witch's blood hit her fire, building it with more of Ereshdiran's own power. The thief wavered, trying to disappear. His ugly, bulging eyes shifted to the right, watching, as the ghosts advanced on him.

Another plane landed. Another, practically on top of one another, the precision in their movements as breathtaking as it was terrifying. Still the sky was full, still the amulet burned at her feet. It hissed and popped as the copper melted.

"I compel you!" Chess squeezed her finger, shook it and her arm. Blood flew from her wounds into the air, ran down her hand to the ground. She lifted it, pointed her dripping finger at Ereshdiran, and shoved as much energy as she could pull from the ground into her next words, so much her throat burned and her eyes watered. "I summoned you and you are compelled! By blood and power you will obey me! Ereshdiran *tama longram!*"

For one heart-stopping minute the ghosts didn't move, and her stomach flew into her throat. If she'd been wrong about Ereshdiran's origins, or if she'd brought them here but wasn't able to control them, they were all dead. Had she used enough power?

Ghosts brushed past her, through her, stalking Ereshdiran. His mouth opened, a smudgy hole in his face as they crowded around him, closing in, closing ranks.

Terrible's breath caught. Chess dragged her gaze away just long enough to see him, his head thrown back, for once ignoring everything around him. His fingers closed around hers. "Look," he said quietly. "Look at them."

The planes cut patterns through the air. They shot straight up into the sky then dove back down. And every minute it seemed more of them appeared, more and more, different planes, newer-looking ones, older ones.

Movements across the field. Bumps' men, victorious, dragging bodies across the gritty landscape. Where was Bump? She hadn't seen him since the ritual started. He'd probably gone back to his car, waited and watched, let the others do the work. What else could anyone expect?

Her legs weakened suddenly, like someone had smacked her in the backs of the knees. Before she could straighten she felt them, felt people waking in their beds all over the city with their hearts pounding, already forgetting the details of their nightmares but glad to be awake and alive.

The fire went out. Chess looked down and saw only a river of gleaming copper, already cooling into a twisted shape in the grass. She held her hand over it, opened up. Nothing. Clean. The copper was empty . . . and so was she. No more thief lurking inside. Nothing but her own self, and the overwhelming power of the earth and the ghosts. She closed her eyes, held on to it for a minute. Feeling good. Feeling alive, and actually glad to be so. Then, regretfully, letting it go. That power wasn't hers. She released it, let it seep down through her body to ripple out from her feet.

A pale, shriveled hand thrust itself into the air between ghosts, Ereshdiran's hand, closing into a desperate fist before shrinking back on itself and disappearing. Chess shivered, and suddenly she couldn't stop shivering. Balancing on her own was impossible; she leaned against Terrible, clutching at his shirt, and realized he was shaking, too. The ground was shaking, rolling beneath their feet like it was trying to give birth.

Too late, she realized her mistake. She'd taken earth energy and combined it with her own, used it to call and power the ghosts; now she'd returned that ghost-tinged energy to the ground, and it was reacting to the unnatural mix. Violently.

As the world started to spin around her, as she half-ran, half let Terrible drag her toward the fence and the parking lot, she saw the planes were disappearing one by one from the sky, from the runways. It was like a meteor shower overhead, lights zooming through the darkness and popping off. She hadn't Banished them, hadn't had a chance . . . hadn't needed to.

She stumbled. Her ankle screamed but she ignored it, her legs aching and her breath coming in gasps. Bump's men caught up, passed them.

The dilapidated wooden building collapsed. Water surged from the well beside it, a geyser of sewage. Chess ran harder. They weren't far now, the fence was just ahead—

Cracks formed in the mud, snaking in front of her, to the sides. Blackness oozed around the edges of her vision. She couldn't keep up this pace. Rocks flew through the air, chunks of concrete, sharp bits of gravel that stung everywhere they hit.

The fence ripped, poles falling apart. The rusted links bounced and dissolved under her feet as they ran across it and got in the car. Terrible started the engine and threw it into reverse, slamming the gas, sending a shower of gravel out from under the big, broad tires. The last thing Chess saw as they drove away was an enormous slab of concrete from the runway, standing vertical, sinking like a wrecked ship back into the earth.

Chapter Thirty-eight

"So the sun rose on the eighth morning, and the people saw the spirits had gone. They might have thanked God, but they knew the Truth. So instead they thanked the Church."

—*The Book of Truth*, Origins, Article 1000

Terrible lit two cigarettes and handed her one, keeping his eyes on the road. She didn't think she'd ever had one that tasted better.

It was over, the whole thing was over. No more Ereshdiran, no more Mortons, no more danger. She could go home, once she'd bought a new mattress. She could go back to working on her own job and not Bump's.

"So," she said, grabbing the baby wipes out of her bag and scrubbing her exposed skin with it. "So that was fun."

"Ain't a usual kind of night, leastaways."

"What's going to happen to them? The ones Bump caught, I mean."

He glanced at her. Right. She probably didn't want to know the answer to that one. She could probably guess anyway.

"I guess Bump's not going to be able to use the airport after all, huh."

"Look like not." He shrugged. "Bump always got other plans. You ain't need to worry. You did what he asked, aye?"

There was that damn twinge of guilt again. No, it hadn't been her fault that the airport collapsed on itself.

But she'd called the ghosts. She'd done it to save her life, to defeat Ereshdiran, but she'd called them, and she'd done it without caring what happened to the airport.

It wasn't the thought of Bump making her feel guilty. He'd used her, jacked up her debt with some bullshit about interest and used it to force her into an investigation she didn't want to be part of. Hell, if she hadn't been out to Chester and found that amulet, chances were none of this would have happened. She could have asked the Elders for help to Banish the Dreamthief from the Mortons' place. Brain would be alive. Randy might be alive.

Randy had slit his own throat, that was true. Getting involved with the Lamaru, calling or allowing them to call such an entity . . . She shook her head. Foolishness, but foolishness she could almost understand. That need to belong was so strong in people, it seemed. So strong she fought against it every day. So strong that even when she thought she'd beaten it for good it popped back up.

Randy had never been strong like that, and he'd been taken. Even then it might have been okay if it weren't for her blood, for Ereshdiran hooking into her soul like a poisonous barb and using her power combined with Slip-knot's to overcome his captors. So she had been a contributing cause in that one . . . at Bump's order.

Just like Bump's orders had led Brain to her, had allowed Randy to hear from blabbermouth Doyle about Brain showing up at her place, so Randy and the Lamaru could make that connection and know they'd been seen. At least she assumed that was how it happened; it wasn't like anyone was around she could ask except Doyle, and she had a feeling he wouldn't be too eager to talk to her.

No, she didn't feel guilty about Bump not being able to use Chester Airport. She felt guilty because she'd lied. To Terrible. He trusted her, and she'd betrayed that trust. Several times.

It wasn't anything she could apologize for or explain. It just was.

"Hey, how'd you make that happen, anyroad? You bring them ghosts? How'd you make em go after him like that?"

Her spirits lifted a bit. At least somebody cared about what she'd done. "He was part of them. Made from them, after they went crazy and burned down the airport—sleep deprivation, remember? They splintered, or something. So I set them free to take him back, and they did, and since I used his energy and earth energy to call them, once he was gone and I gave the energy back they had to go."

He nodded. "Awful smart, aye."

For a second irritation pricked the back of her neck. Wasn't he going to express some sort of amazement? Was "awful smart" really all she was going to get?

But then she realized, with an odd, blushing sort of warmth, that it had never occurred to him that she wouldn't be able to solve the problem. That while she'd been flailing around in the dirt, scared shitless that she was about to kill them all, he'd had complete faith in her ability to save them. Just as she'd never really doubted he could protect her from the Lamaru.

Wasn't that an uncomfortable thought.

"What you gonna tell them up the Church? About what's-his-name back there, the one got himself dead?"

She thought about it for a second, glad to have something to distract her, even for a moment. "The truth, or as much of it as I can. The Mortons were my case. He was involved in it. I'll have to say I only found out about the connection tonight, and that's why I didn't call them, but . . . they don't really need to know about the rest of it."

"So you all roses with them, aye? Done a good job and all."

"Yeah. Yeah, I guess so." It didn't feel much like it, though. It felt like she'd done something wrong, like there was a brand-new stain on her soul. She turned toward the window and caught her own reflection, her eyes wide and dark under her bangs.

"You cool? Ain't talking much."

"Yeah, I'm just . . . I'm sorry. I know you were looking forward to using the airport again."

He tilted his head, glancing at her with an amused look. "You joke, aye? Saw something way better than some single-engine puddlejumper in that sky this night, Chess. Ain't trade that for nothing. Worth it all the way up. Like I said, there's other places. Bump always got some plans. Like you, aye? Got some plans for now? I mean, now?"

"N—yeah, actually. I do. I'm supposed to meet someone. I mean, I said I would, after I was done. He—they're waiting for me."

Pause. Barely a pause, but she noticed it. "See? Already on to the next move. Chess. Where I drop you?"

The tunnel where Lex waited wasn't far, down the street from a convenience store. She told Terrible to leave her there, and they pulled up outside much more quickly than she'd thought.

What was she supposed to say? She looked over at him, his face filthy, swollen and bruised from the fighting and stained with neon red from the lights outside. It had been . . . good, to work with him. To spend time with him. Like having a real friend for the first time in her life. But how was she supposed to say something like that without sounding like an idiot? What did you say to people, when you actually wanted them around?

"Here." She tugged out a fresh baby wipe. "You're all covered in yuck."

He didn't move a muscle while she ran the damp cloth over his face. She had to use her left hand to do it, while her right braced his chin. His skin warmed her fingers.

"Close your eyes."

He did. She used a new wipe for them, sliding it over his skin until she realized she'd been doing it for too long and stopped.

The wipe crumpled in her fist. "Okay, well, I'll see you, right?"

"Aye, you know, I'm always around."

"No, I mean . . ." Shit! What did people say? "I mean, you could call me, if you want. Just to hang out or something, you know?"

His gaze flicked over her face, searching for something. Whether or not he found it she didn't know, but he nodded. "Aye. Sure, Chess. I give you a ring up."

There had to be more to say, but whatever it was she couldn't think of it. And Lex was waiting. So she held out her hand. He shook it, careful not to touch her burned palm.

She got out of the car, and watched him drive away until the throaty rumble of the Chevelle blended into the sounds of the city.

"So you lived after all, tulip. Getting worried, me. Heard all hell broke loose up there."

"You didn't stay to watch?"

The smile spread across his face, slow and smooth as he took her hand, lifted her bag off her shoulder, and slung it over his own. Damn. She did like him, didn't she. How did that happen? "I watched some."

"Good show?"

"Not bad, not bad at all. You looking like a straight warrior with all them markings and shit on you."

"You watched for a while, if you saw that."

"Some watch TV, aye. Some go for live entertainment."

"So you like to watch, Lex. I never would have guessed."

He laughed. "Just keeping an eye on my investments, me. No more airport, aye?"

"No. But . . . that wasn't why I did it."

He shrugged. "Ain't the intent, it's the outcome that matters. And I'm thinking this outcome ain't a bad one, aye? Even if you looking banged up?"

"Yeah, but—"

"Aw, nay. All done, tulip. Let's not us bother with it anymore. Let's us get back to my place, you show me where it hurts. Sound good?"

Her grin was genuine in spite of herself. "Yeah. Yeah, that sounds pretty good."

She let him take her hand and lead her through the tunnel.

Elder Griffin placed his hand on her arm, watching the other Debunkers file out of the room. To call that morning's meeting "subdued" would be like calling Downside "dirty."

"Cesaria," he said, his blue eyes dark. "I needs must speak to you for a moment."

Shit. Her heart sank. They'd caught her out, she didn't know how, maybe Doyle had said something or—had she slipped up somewhere? She'd studied her notes so hard, she thought she'd kept her story straight, but maybe . . .

"Sit down." He pulled a chair out for her. She sank into it, half expecting steel clasps to come out from beneath the arms and lock her in.

He sat beside her. "Are you certain you feel all right? Watching your friend die like that, even though 'twas his doing . . ." He shook his head. "I am here if you would like to talk about it, my dear."

"Thanks, but I'm okay. Really." Relief flooded through her, almost as sweet as the cozy warmth of her pills. She was safe. They hadn't caught her, she was safe.

"I'm very proud of you. You know, the Grand Elder never considered the Lamaru to be much of a threat. The idea that they actually managed to turn one of our own, to infiltrate us, is quite disturbing."

She didn't really know what to say. Should she agree? Disagree? What? So she simply nodded.

"We have of course sent the Enforcers out to look for them. Searching through some of Randy's effects . . ." He shook his head, touched her arm again lightly.

"I apologize. I know 'tisn't a pleasant subject. But we believe we may have found some things that will help lead us to the Lamaru, perhaps even eradicate them—we've already found their agent at the Bankhead Spa, and she is being questioned. And we'd like you to do a report specifically giving us everything you learned about their organization. I'm sure I don't have to tell you to be on your guard until we've eliminated them. Far more dangerous than we imagined, Cesaria. I would hate to see you endangered."

She shook her head. As if she ever let her guard down.

"Perhaps you would be interested in moving back? There are several available cottages on grounds. You would be safer."

The very thought made her skin crawl. "No, thanks. I'm fine, really. I'm sure the Black Squad will be able to catch them." Actually, she wasn't at all sure, but this was her home they were talking about. "I'd like to stay where I am."

His bright head dipped. "As you wish."

"Thanks."

Silence fell between them. Chess wondered if she should get up, if they were done. But Elder Griffin didn't seem done. He watched her, smiling.

"In truth, I'm not the only one who's proud. The Elders had a discussion this morn, about what you did. We are very pleased."

"Thanks." She was starting to feel like a broken record. The story she'd told them had been a simple one: The Lamaru recruited Randy and in return for his help they'd put Ereshdiran into the Morton home. No mention of the airport, or Slipknot, or the blood connection between herself and the thief. She would have left the Lamaru out of it entirely had she not asked Doyle about them the day before. The Mortons surely wouldn't have mentioned them, if they even knew the full scope of the plot; Chess hadn't heard any of their testimonies yet. She only knew they were alive and awake and somewhere in a detention cell.

Elder Griffin reached into the file on the long, shiny glass table and pulled out an envelope and two sheets of paper, which he handed to her.

The paper was official Church stationery. The first sheet was a letter of commendation. The second . . . She had to read it twice before the words meant something.

"Technically it's not a promotion," Elder Griffin said. "You will still be a Debunker. You'll just occasionally be helping other departments with their investigations. For a bonus each time, of course."

The irony made her want to laugh, in a sick, cynical way. She'd lied to everyone, and she was being rewarded for it. Seemed to be the way her life was working these days, though, what with the free pills in her bag from Lex and the erased debt from Bump. For however long that lasted.

She set the letter on the table and opened the envelope, then looked up. "You gave me my bonus already, remember? Before the meeting?"

"This is in addition to that. We felt something was called for, for defeating the Lamaru plot."

It wasn't much. But it would cover the new bed she'd bought, and a week or two's worth of food. Or a nice long weekend in the pipe room . . .

Her head still spinning, she thanked Elder Griffin again and headed out of the building, into the soft autumn sunshine.

Doyle waited for her by her car. His face was full of colorful bruises, like he'd been painting and made a mess. "Hey, Chessie, you got a minute?"

"Not really."

"Please." He reached for her, caught himself and shoved his hand into his pocket. His left one dangled by his side, the pinky splinted and wrapped. She almost wished she could feel guilty about it. "I just wanted to say sorry. For . . . what I did. I honestly didn't mean to. I just . . . you know, you treated me pretty shitty."

"Uh-huh. Well, thanks for the apology. I have to go now."

"Can't we just talk about it?"

"Nope." She needed new tires. Hell, she needed a new car. Maybe now she'd get one, if she found one she liked. The bonus for Banishing Ereshdiran hadn't been as much as she'd hoped, but it was enough, especially since she could cut down on her purchases from Bump—at least for a little while, until Slobag and Lex decided she'd been paid enough and cut her off.

And really, she should spend the money now, while she had it, before she got too itchy and blew it on beer or the pipes or whatever else she could get her hands on.

"I'm not a bad person, you know," Doyle said.

"Hey there, tulip. Who's your friend?"

Chess turned around and swallowed her surprise. Lex. She hadn't seen him or heard from him in three days, since the morning after the airport showdown, and she wasn't sure if she was relieved or sad about that. A bit of both, really, but it was nice to see him just the same.

Lex stared at Doyle, his eyes narrowing.

Shit. Even she couldn't be that mean, could she? Terrible

had already more than taken care of whatever residual anger she felt toward Doyle.

"Just a guy I work with," she said.

"I have a name, you know." He glared at her. "I'm Doyle."

Lex grinned. "You Doyle, aye? Guessing you just the guy I been lookin for, then."

Chess lit a cigarette and turned her back on them as Doyle started to run. She didn't need to watch, any more than she needed to think of the future. Instead she looked at the Church, rising from the earth like a plume of pure white smoke, gazing at her with benevolent detachment. She thought of the City, of the dead, empty souls milling around, waiting for their week of freedom, separated from her by hundreds of feet of solid earth. Where they belonged.

And for the first time she believed there might be a place where she belonged, too, outside of the Church and her position there. And maybe one day she'd have the strength or the courage to accept it. For now . . .

She ground out her smoke with her toe, and went to find Lex. She had a whole empty afternoon in front of her, and a tattoo that was desperate for some air.

Acknowledgments

So many people to thank. I dedicated it to Cori, for being the first and best reader, but she wasn't the only early reader; my great friends Stacey Jay, Caitlin Kittredge, and Mark Henry were invaluable. I can trace my friendship with Caitlin right back to the early stages of this book, and if nothing else, it would be special to me for that. Great big thanks and love go to my wonderful husband, Stephen, who continues to put up with me; my two daughters who try very hard to be good while Mommy works; and my father and brother. Special mention to my mom, the registered nurse, who thankfully is used to questions like, "So, if I inject motor oil, would that kill me right away?" and doesn't bat an eye. I also have to thank my agent, Chris Lotts, who is awesome and loves shortbread. You wouldn't be holding this book in your hands if not for him and for Liz Scheier, who acquired the series and edited the first two books; working with Liz was an absolute dream. Huge thanks also to my wonderful new editor, Shauna Summers, and to her fantastic assistant, Jessica Sebor, and to everyone at Del Rey; I cannot say enough how great they all are and how welcome and valued they have all made me feel.

All of Team Seattle deserves enormous, drunken, mushy appreciation, especially Jaye Wells, Richelle Mead, and Jackie Kessler (a fellow Satellite member). Kaz Mahoney, Synde Korman, Todd Thomas, Jill Myles, Seeley DeBorn, Kirsten Saell, Bernita Harris, Bernard DeLeo, Jane Smith, Colleen Lindsay, Briana St. James, Justin Coker, Derrick Beasley, Tom Gallier, Fae Sutherland, and Derek Tatum all deserve extra thanks for being my friends and making me laugh; if your name isn't here it's because I'm the terrible friend, not you. All of my fellow Reluctant Adults. Jessica Wade and Jim McCarthy. Paul Goat Allen, Rachel Smith, Lisa Trevethan, Kimberly Swan, and Mrs. Giggles. And of course, thanks to Evil Editor and the Minions, Miss Snark and the Snarklings, and all of my blog readers, Facebook pals, and Twitter followers; seriously, it may not seem like a big deal, but when you spend all your time alone with a computer and your own misery and neuroses, knowing there are other people out there really does make a difference. I continue to be amazed that anyone pays any attention to anything I say.

Huge, special thanks go to all of the bands I mention in this book. My life would be very different and a lot worse without your music.

Last of all, thanks to you, the reader holding this book. You're the reason for all of this. I hope I don't let you down.

Yearning for your next Unholy fix?

Read on for a sneak peek inside the next novel in
Stacia Kane's dark and sexy series:

UNHOLY MAGIC

Published by Del Rey Books

"Hey, Chess," he said. She got the words not just from
his voice, barely a rumbling murmur over "Garageland,"
but from watching his lips move. "Figured you ain't coming after all, getting so late. You right?"

"Yeah. Right up. The job went on longer than I expected."

"Lookin pale."

She shrugged and drank her beer. No point discussing
it, not when they could barely hear each other. "When
are they going on?"

"Few minutes, maybe. Not long. They— Hold on."
From his pocket he produced a small black phone and
flipped it open. The stark white glow of the screen invaded the darkness of the corner and highlighted his furrowed brow. "Fuck."

"What's—"

He cut her off with a look, a quick jerk of the head to
indicate she should follow. This she did, trying to stay in
his wake as he cut through the crowd back to the front
of the room, narrowly avoiding razoring her cheek on
some guy's Liberty spikes, and out the front door.

Desultory clumps of people huddled outside, braving
the cold to get a free listen once the band started playing.

They shuffled out of the way when Terrible headed for the side of the building. Chess followed. For a second the cold soothed her heated skin before it became too much and she shivered. She should have brought a jacket, but they were such pains in the ass to hold on to in a club.

"Got problems." He didn't look at her as he dialed the phone and lifted it to his ear. "You know Red Berta, aye?"

"I know who she is." Red Berta handled most of Bump's girls—which meant she handled all of the Downside prostitutes west of Forty-third.

"Aye, well— Hey. Aye." Whoever he'd called must have answered. "Aye, she— When they find it? Shit. Aye, hang on. I'll be there."

She knew before he snapped the phone shut that he wanted her to go with him. What she didn't know was why.

"What's going on?"

He stood for a moment with his eyes narrowed, sliding the phone back into his pocket without paying attention while he worked out whatever it was he needed to work out. "Feel like riding with me?"

"What's going on?"

"Dead body." His other hand went into his pocket. The movement made his shoulders look even broader, but the threat of his size had never been less evident. "One of Bump's girls. Third one they find."

"Somebody's killing hookers?"

He shrugged. "Looking like a ghost doing the killing. Wouldn't ask otherwise."

"What, just in the streets?"

"Ain't you cold? Whyn't you come on, Chess. Warmer in the car, aye? Just take a look." His head turned back toward the huddled crowd. Right. Probably not a good idea to discuss this in public. So she nodded, and followed him across the street while the music kept playing inside the bar.

Terrible's '69 BT Chevelle straddled the curb two doors down, making the streetlight look like it was set up just to display it. New black paint gleamed in the orangeish glare. Chess was almost afraid to touch it, the way she would be afraid to approach any predator. The car seemed ready to leap forward on its fat black tires at any moment and start swallowing the road.

Sitting on the leather seat was like sitting on a block of ice, but Chess didn't mention it. Terrible didn't seem in the mood for jokes. Instead she waited for him to talk, knowing he'd get to it in his own time.

They'd gone about ten blocks through the abandoned streets west of Downside's red-light district before he did.

"First hooker," he said. "But the third body, dig? Bump ain't paid much attention before, outside getting pissed. Dealer first. Slick Michigan, know him?"

She shook her head. The heater was starting to work; she could have relaxed if it weren't for her nerves. The last thing she wanted to do was get involved with a murderous ghost. Another murderous ghost, that was—she still hadn't fully recovered from the Dreamthief.

Terrible kept talking while she grabbed her pillbox and popped a couple of Cepts, washing them down with the beer she still held. "Found him maybe five weeks ago, down by the docks. Nobody think much of it. You know how them docks get. And Slick weren't exactly the calm type. Figure he gets into a fight, aye? Plays with some boy got a quick knife hand."

"He was knifed?"

"Aye."

"But then—"

He glanced at her. "Second one came a couple weeks ago, guessing. Little Tag. He a runner, aye? Ain't sell, ain't handle much. Just carryin from one place to another. Found him in an alley off Brewster."

"I didn't even know there were alleys off Brewster." She looked out the window. They'd gone south first, down to Mather. Now Terrible swung the big car left against the light. What was a hooker doing this far off the drag, and this close to the end of Bump's territory?

"Aye. Ain't much good in them places, neither. Nobody even sure how long he was there. He body . . . ain't pretty, if you dig. Hardly any left." He took a long pull off his own beer and set it back down between his thighs, then pulled two cigarettes from his pocket and lit them.

Chess took the one he offered her and leaned back in her seat, letting the smoke curl out of her mouth and up toward the roof. "And now a girl."

"Aye."

"You still haven't told me why you think it's a ghost."

"Ain't sure it's a ghost. Not me, not Bump. Got others thinking so, though."

"So you want me to come in and say it isn't?"

"Be a help, aye."

"But what if it is?"

He glanced at her as he pulled the car up by a burned-out building. "You think be a ghost, Bump gonna call the Church ask them take care of it? Or you think he come to you?"

Shit.